Chapter 1

The first match Tony Flynn tossed out the passenger window died before it hit the ground, so he took out his Zippo lighter and lit the rest of the pack. He held it upside down until it almost burned his hand then tossed it out the window. The trail of gasoline they'd laid ignited immediately and quickly burned a serpentine line from the curb, across the sidewalk, and up the lawn to a hastily planted cross.

"Get out of Malbrook!" Tony shouted as the cross exploded in flames. He slapped Corky's thigh with the back of his hand and Corky pressed the gas pedal of his red Dodge pickup to the floor.

"What if the house catches fire?" Corky asked.

"They'll move sooner," Tony said with a short laugh.

"You really think they'll leave?"

"The only question is when," Tony said as a satisfied grin slid across his mouth.

A tall black man in his fifties charged out the front door of the dark gray colonial house in pajama bottoms and boots with a Louisville Slugger in his hand. He was too late to catch even a glimpse of the pickup.

Charles Foster hadn't expected a welcoming committee when they moved to Malbrook, but standoffish neighbors resistant to change was the worst he had anticipated. He'd done his research before moving his family from Queens to Nassau County. According to the census, Malbrook had been ninety-six percent white in 1970, and Charles reasoned that the percentage had probably gone down with 1980 less than four months away. He'd thought the world had come a long way in the past ten years, but now he wasn't so sure.

Charles hit the cross with three mighty swings without budging it before the bat split just above his hands. A car screeched to a halt across the street, and he spun quickly with the jagged handle of the bat. He noted the blue flashing light on the dashboard which indicated the car belonged to a volunteer fireman and his tensed muscles eased slightly.

Devin Ryder jumped from his 1977 Mustang and yelled, "Wait, stop!" as Charles attempted to push the cross over with his foot. Devin was a twenty-six-year-old volunteer firefighter who lived four blocks away. His dark blue sweatshirt, white shorts and sneakers without socks was an ensemble hastily pulled from a pile of clothes in a basket in his bedroom that he hadn't put away.

"How can you ask me to do nothing while a cross burns on my lawn?"

"A fire truck will be here in a few minutes," Devin said as he stamped out the trail of fire between the curb and the cross. "If you knock it down, it will leave an imprint of the cross." Devin put a hand on the larger man's shoulder. "One spot and this little trail will be much easier to fix."

Charles stepped away from the cross as a firetruck turned the far corner. It pulled in front of his house as a police car stopped across the street.

It took only minutes for the volunteer firemen to extinguish the fire. Once they removed the cross, Charles kicked the pile of dirt on the side back into the hole and stamped it down.

It was three-thirty a.m. when Charles went inside and joined his wife to give his statement to police. Neither could provide any useful information since they had been asleep and hadn't even seen the vehicle. Charles confirmed Connie's assessment that while the neighbors hadn't been friendly, they hadn't been hostile either.

The two officers weren't optimistic about making an arrest since there were no leads, but they assured the Fosters they would canvass the area for witnesses.

"Don't bother," Charles said. "I doubt anyone around here will help."

"Don't be so pessimistic," Connie said. "It's like my mama always said; people will live up of down to your expectations."

"I don't know about you, but I wasn't expecting this from people," Charles said.

*   *   *

Nick Hallocek stood at the pay phone in the rear of his bar. He had already dialed the precinct twice but hung up both times without saying a word. Even though the call would be anonymous, he was nervous about saying the wrong thing.

"Here goes nothing," he said softly to himself as he fed the dime into the slot for the third time and dialed.

"Seventeenth precinct, Officer Blake speaking, how may I assist you?"

Nick froze, unable to speak.

"Hello? Speak now or forever hold your peace," Blake said.

"Um, I have information about last night's cross burning," Nick finally managed as he scribbled the officer's name.

"What kind of information?"

"The names of the two men who burned the cross are Tony Flynn and John Corcoran," Nick said, relieved.

"How is it that you have their names?"

"I overheard them talking last night at the White Castle in Lynbrook."

"Did you talk to them?" Blake asked.

"No. I only know them through friends, so we've never socialized. I saw them leave in a pickup with the license plate CORKY 1."

"Do you happen to know the make of the pickup?"

"I think it's a Dodge," he said, and hung up. He had given them all the information he was going to, and he didn't want to be on the phone any longer than he had to.

Nick had done his civic duty, even if it was just to clear his bar of two annoying lowlifes. If the cross burning had been carried out by any other patron, Nick wouldn't have cared; he didn't want blacks in Malbrook just as much as the next person. But this worked out perfectly.

Nick's was a dive bar, but for many in the working-class town it was a place to enjoy a beer every now and then. Tony and Corky were Friday and Saturday night regulars, usually after they got shit-faced at Tony's apartment a few blocks away. Nick often said they were as useful as tits on a bull.

*   *   *

Nick's story was quickly confirmed and detectives from the seventeenth precinct were dispatched to Tony Flynn's apartment in Malbrook and John and Shirley Corcoran's house in Westbury. Tony's apartment was empty, and the owner of the home where Tony had a basement apartment confirmed he had left the house at noon. Detectives in Westbury had more luck since Corky's pickup was parked in the driveway.

Shirley pulled a robe over her light sundress and answered the door as the detectives were preparing to leave.

"May I help you?" she asked.

The taller detective held his badge in front of the screen door for Shirley to examine and said, "I'm Detective Briggs and this is Detective Leighton. We were wondering if we could have a few words with John."

"Who is it Ma?" Corky called from upstairs.

"My husband isn't home right now. He's at work."

"We're actually looking for your son."

"Why are you looking for my son?"

"We believe he may have witnessed a crime," Briggs said.

"I'll go get him," she said, and opened the door to let them in.

She returned a moment later with a short sullen-looking pudgy teen trailing behind her.

"What can I do for you?" Corky asked and hoped he didn't sound as scared as he felt.

"We need you to come with us and answer some questions," Briggs said.

"Can this wait?" Corky asked. "I have to work at six."

"What do you do?" Leighton asked.

"I pump gas at the Shell station on Cherry Lane."

"Your mother should call and tell them you won't be in tonight," Briggs said.

"What? Why?" Corky asked.

"I think you know why," Briggs said, his demeanor so calm it sounded as if he was asking Corky to go for a cup of coffee.

John "Corky" Corcoran broke into tears as Detective Leighton placed the handcuffs on him and led him to the unmarked car. On the way past the pickup, Leighton lifted the tarp on the back and saw a metal gas can and a shovel with fresh dirt. He looked at Corky and shook his head. Briggs helped Corky into the back of car and then radioed for officers to impound the pickup. They waited for the officers and the tow-truck to arrive before they left.

*   *   *

Briggs entered the interrogation room first and leaned against the wall while Leighton sat across from Corky. Briggs was the senior member of the team and a few years older than Leighton.

Leighton shook his head and said, "You're in some serious trouble; your buddy threw you under the bus. He said it was all your idea."

Corky had turned nineteen three weeks earlier, but looked younger thanks to his baby face and a mustache that wouldn't fill in. His brown eyes glistened from the tears that were waiting to fall.

"Tony told us everything," Leighton added. "He said he tried to stop you, and even went with you to try to talk you out of it."

"That's not true," Corky said. His considerable belly shook as he sobbed into his chubby hands and pondered his predicament. "It was Tony's idea."

Corky had never been arrested and hadn't thought to exercise his right to remain silent after being Mirandized. With little coaxing, Corky took the detectives through the entire process, from the lumberyard in Westbury where they had purchased the wood, to his friend's house where they nailed the cross together and finally to the Foster's house. Corky admitted to pouring the gasoline while Tony dug the hole and planted the cross but was adamant that Tony set the fire. To corroborate his story, Corky gave the name of a friend they had discussed the plan with days earlier. He giftwrapped the case for the detectives in less than an hour.

*   *   *

Tony stopped at a payphone in front of the Times Square Store in Lawrence and called Corky to make plans for dinner at a nearby Beefsteak Charlie's. He had purchased one album and shoplifted three others, which was better than joining a record club and being sent shitty albums he had no use for, like some of his friends.

He got a busy signal the first three times and decided to get two slices of Sicilian pizza at Uncle Guido's Pizzeria next door before trying again. He ate two corner slices and talked music with the sixteen-year-old girl behind the counter before he went back out to try Corky's number again.

Corky's mother picked up on the first ring. "John?" she said in a near-panic, hoping it was finally her husband.

"It's me, Tony."

Shirley began to sob.

"What's wrong?" Tony asked. "Is Corky there?"

"He's been arrested," she said through her sobs.

"Arrested? For what?" Tony asked, though he already knew.

"I don't know. I'm sorry, I have to free up the line for my husband to call," she said, and hung up.

Instead of making plans for dinner, Tony drove back to his apartment to collect some belongings. He scrapped the plan when he saw two men parked in a blue four door sedan across the street from the house. *It can't be a coincidence. Fucking Corky!* The fat bastard must have given the police his name. *How did they even find Corky?*

If police were already at his apartment, he didn't think it would be safe to stop anywhere in Nassau County, so he waited until he got to Rosedale before he stopped at a payphone and called information to find the closest Dime Savings Bank branch in Queens. He drove to Flushing and cleaned out his account before he parked in Laguardia Airport's long-term lot. He would surprise his brother and stay with him until everything blew over, which would probably be no more than a week or two. He wasn't sure what Corky had been charged with, but with a shoplifting arrest already under his belt, Tony wasn't sticking around to find out. His plane touched down in Memphis before the police learned he had a brother.

Chapter 2

Alex Moran was glad to be done with the first week of school at Malbrook West High, which everyone in town just referred to as West. It was finally his turn to enjoy the privileges that came with being a senior. His graduation requirements had been fulfilled, he had taken the SATs twice and done well enough that his guidance counsellor assured him he would be accepted to all five colleges to which he planned to apply. He looked at the small stack of envelopes on the table, perused the names of each school and tossed them on the kitchen counter. He wasn't ready to choose a college; he wasn't even ready to choose a major. *How can they expect me to make a decision that could affect the rest of my life when I'm not even old enough to drive?*

Alex pushed open the side door, ran down the three steps and hopped on his bike. It was three days into his senior year at Malbrook West High and he was stressed out.

At the front of the driveway, Alex met up with his cousin, Dave Kane, who was riding a wheelie on the curb in front of the house waiting for him. The two of them rode their BMX bikes through town to Westwood Park and then along the asphalt track that circled the lake at the center with the kind of reckless abandon that only those who believed they were invulnerable could muster. The small lake was the showplace of the modest village and boasted two newly installed fountains in the middle that kept the water circulating throughout the winter to prevent it from freezing.

Two months younger than Alex, on the wrong side of the school cutoff date, Dave had just started his junior year at Malbrook East. The two schools carried on a fierce rivalry that escalated to violence on occasion but had no effect on the cousins.

The cousins were as close as brothers, though they looked nothing alike. Dave had inherited the blond hair and blue eyes of his Irish parents, while Alex sported his Irish father's easy smile, but more closely resembled his Chinese mother. His dark brown hair and slightly elongated brown eyes gave him a distinctly Asian appearance.

The boys took turns performing tricks on their bikes, each one increasing in difficulty as they strove to outdo one another. Alex road a wheelie and twirled his handlebars as Dave spun around on his front tire with his back tire in the air. Dave let his back tire down and pedaled hard toward a pushup bar mounted a foot above the ground. Dave veered away at the last second and did a three-sixty in the air that would have cleared the bar.

"You're such a wuss," mocked Alex.

Alex rode at the bar, pushed down hard on his handlebars and yanked the bike up at the last moment. His front tire cleared the bar easily, but his back tire grazed it and forced him to land awkwardly. He skidded to a stop inches from Dave's front tire.

"One day you're gonna hit that bar hard and I'm gonna laugh my ass off," Dave said.

"If you'd give yourself a chance, you could probably do it with the three-sixty."

"Unlike you, I don't have a death wish."

"It's called balls, and you should grow a pair," Alex joked.

The good-natured ribbing continued. Both cousins were extremely competitive and took riding seriously. Dave was the more skilled rider, but Alex took risks that pushed his abilities to their limits and forced Dave out of his comfort zone.

Dave stopped and maneuvered his Mongoose between the fences while Alex followed with his Tensor Comrade. The boys had customized their bikes to make them stand out. Alex had wanted a Mongoose—which was lighter and more maneuverable than the Tensor—but Dave had gotten his bike a month before him, and as much as he wanted the Mongoose, Alex knew everyone would call him gay for getting the same bike as his cousin. Aside from the frame, there was little about Alex's bike that was from the original Tensor, though his father had him keep the original parts in the garage rather than sell them. Alex had replaced the silver metal rims with yellow plastic rims and taken off the handbrakes when he changed the handlebars. Dave's bike was stock, but the custom metallic green and white paint made it stand out.

Tonight, both boys wore two different versions of their Phi Gamma Alpha shirts. Dave had chosen black with an orange coat of arms and Greek letters while Alex wore the much brighter orange with simple black Greek letters. Alex's orange shirt was partially concealed by his wrestling windbreaker.

"Remind me again why I'm going to this meeting," Alex said as he leaned forward on his handlebars, lifted the rear tire off the ground and spun the bike in a circle beneath him.

"The only meeting our chapter had this summer was last Friday when I couldn't make it," Dave said, and mimicked Alex's trick.

The boys rode between parked cars and stopped at Breuer Boulevard as drivers of a Porsche 944 and a Datsun 280ZX that each looked like they had just rolled off showroom floors revved their engines. Racing was rare on Breuer because there were only two lanes in each direction and the lights in the busier section of town were out of sync and usually allowed cars to advance just one long block before reaching another red light. The two teen drivers were either from a more affluent neighborhood and not aware of the situation, or drunk.

Alex and Dave watched the cars speed past as the traffic light a block ahead turned yellow. Instead of braking, both cars accelerated and sped through it. The Porsche, which was in the right lane, nearly hit a tan station wagon with a couple in their early thirties and their three children in the seatless back. The boys crossed the street and turned in the opposite direction as the taillights disappeared.

"What happened at the meeting?" Alex asked as they pedaled down Burns Street.

"It's not what happened then, it's what's supposed to happen tonight."

"What?"

"Probably just more of Marco's bullshit."

"What kind of bullshit?"

"The usual. You know Marco's always talking shit."

Alex scrunched up his face and said, "There's something about that kid that makes me want to punch him in the face repeatedly."

"You're probably not the only one, but most people wouldn't mess with the little psycho."

"If he ever gave me a reason, I'd kick his ass six ways to Sunday."

Dave gave a sideways glance and smiled. "Just keep in mind he always has a switchblade in his front right pocket."

"He could have a machete and I'd still kick his ass," Alex said as he stood with one foot on the seat and the other on the handlebars.

*   *   *

Marco Scotti's acne-covered face wore a scowl as he searched the first floor of his once beautiful Cape Cod house for his black Phi Gamma Alpha shirt. He was sure he had left it on the arm of the black leather, cat-clawed, couch. He had already rifled through every drawer in the house like a cop on a drug raid. He tossed the sofa pillows across the room, flipped its cushions, and slammed them down in frustration. He pounded his fist into the back of the couch.

"Fuck!" he said in a restrained voice. He had just spent half an hour lying with his little sister, Hannah, to get her to sleep and the last thing he wanted was to wake her.

"Are you looking for this rag?" his stepfather, Frank asked, casually waving the shirt back and forth.

Frank had developed a sour disposition toward Marco over the past few years and would now give wicked stepmothers a run for their money. He would just as soon smack Marco in the face as say hello to him, though to

Marco's three-year old sister—Frank's biological daughter—he was a gentle teddy bear.

Frank was an unemployed auto mechanic and had been for the better part of two years. He had collected unemployment checks until they ran out, but instead of looking for a job, Frank stayed home with the baby and drank beer as he ate his way through the afternoon television schedule.

Marco's dislike for Frank had started years earlier when Frank's only sin was that he had married Marco's mother. Back then, Frank was fifty pounds lighter and a fair athlete, while Marco was a skinny seventh grader with bad skin and no real ambition other than to get through each school day while doing just enough work to keep him out of summer school. Marco's plan failed as he had taken at least two classes in summer school for four consecutive years.

For his part, Frank had done his best to endear himself to Marco when he started dating Maria and thought with some guidance from a proper male role model, Marco could turn out to be a good kid. Once Frank and Maria were married and Frank moved in, it didn't take long for him to realize that all efforts to peacefully coexist with Marco would be thwarted, because Marco thought of Frank as another loser his mother had brought home after his father left, which had been shortly after Marco's seventh birthday. Undeterred by Marco's refusal to attend Yankees, Jets or Knicks games with him, Frank's final attempt was an invitation for Marco to join him fishing on his friend's boat. Fishing was the one thing Maria assured Frank that Marco enjoyed, though she never considered that it might have been because he had only gone with his father. The attempt ended with what Frank considered to be the final straw in their relationship, and the first salvo fired in the ongoing pissing contest that Frank always won.

"Just because you're fucking my mother doesn't mean you're my father!" Marco had yelled. It was the first and last time Marco raised his voice to Frank. The unexpected backhand that caught Marco's face had sent him flying across the living room and into the entertainment center, scraping the needle through the remainder of Led Zeppelin's "Stairway to Heaven," forever ruining the better side of the album, which gave Frank a second reason to hit Marco, despite the album belonging to Marco. Marco had spent days listening to the record backwards, trying to find more phrases like "my sweet Satan" that he had managed to locate after a friend had told him where to listen.

The memory of that first slap was at the forefront of Marco's mind whenever he had a confrontation with Frank, and this moment was no different. "Give me my shirt," Marco said in a measured voice.

"Why don't you come take it from me?" Frank taunted.

It was a dare Marco had to consider carefully. *Will the likely outcome be worth it?* Frank was listing slightly to his left, which indicated he was passed buzzed and full on drunk. Any attempt to grab the shirt would be met by a slap, punch, or even a shove into the wall, and that was more dangerous when Frank was drunk.

For a short time, Frank had been a mellow drunk who watched television and drank himself into oblivion, a point at which he would pull a blanket over himself and fall asleep with the television on. That Frank was long gone and had been since the night he caught Maria comforting a nineteen-year-old male server named Jude in her car. The server's girlfriend had just broken up with him and he was devastated. Frank arrived and saw Maria hugging the young man and stroking his thick brown hair while whispering comforting words in his ear. He knew his wife was a good listener, but alone in a car in an embrace with a server was anything but okay in Frank's book. Frank got out of his car and walked toward his wife, unseen by the two. When Maria finally broke the hug, the young man leaned forward and kissed her. Before she even had time to react, the door behind the boy was ripped open and Frank tossed him on the ground and began to pound him with blow after vicious blow as Maria pleaded with him to stop and tried to pull him away. Frank didn't stay around for an explanation and Maria couldn't chase after him because she had to tend to Jude, who was barely conscious.

Their relationship went sour for months as Frank refused to listen to Maria's explanation or even sleep in the same bed. The job offer he was coming to tell her about was withdrawn when he didn't show up for work the entire first week because he couldn't bear the thought of his wife with someone else and drank himself into a coma-like state for ten consecutive days. He had difficulty finding another job once he and Maria finally sorted things out, so all financial responsibilities fell on Maria.

Marco stepped forward with a plan to grab the shirt and duck quickly before Frank could hit him. He figured with a little luck the fat bastard would lose his balance and topple over into the glass coffee table and maybe sever an artery and bleed out in the living room while Marco went to his meeting and his mother was at work. No help. No call for an ambulance. Marco would close the door behind him and forget Frank ever existed.

The maneuver might have worked to perfection if Frank's grip on the shirt hadn't been so firm. Marco grabbed and ducked, but Frank pulled him back up and punched him in the stomach hard enough to knock all the air from Marco's lungs. Marco fell to his knees and then crumpled to the floor and gasped for breath. Frank tossed the shirt on the floor next to Marco and stepped on it as he walked past.

"Next time I find that shirt on my couch I'm using it to wipe my ass," Frank said as he walked into the kitchen to grab another beer.

Marco waited for his breath to return, then stumbled out the front door and pulled the shirt over his head. "I'm gonna kill you one day, you fuckin' kike."

$$* \qquad * \qquad *$$

There were five members Alex recognized from East's chapter of Phi. Both chapters had roughly the same number of members but there were major differences. Aside from Dave, only two of the other twenty or so members looked remotely athletic. To pledge West's

Kappa Psi chapter, a candidate had to be in at least ninth grade, a member of a junior varsity or varsity sports team, or a member of an academic club with a cumulative average above ninety. Alex suspected that aside from Dave, perhaps four or five members fit the criteria, and that was being generous.

Aside from the Daily News covers from the Yankees' World Series championships in 1977 and 1978 taped to the brown paneled walls above the two couches, Peter's basement hadn't been updated in more than a decade. The floor was the original black and white linoleum that was installed when the house was built in 1903. It was scuffed and cracked in dozens of places. In the far corner was a dark gray oil tank with boxes of old photos stacked on top.

"This meeting is called to order," Peter Ryan said and banged his gavel. He sat behind a folding table near the bottom of the stairs.

At six-foot-two and 260 pounds, Peter was their biggest member. Though he looked uncomfortable when he spoke and hesitated before he gave responses, one angry look was all it took to shut someone up. He wasn't very vocal, but when it came to Phi members or anyone who was being bullied—aside from the razzing Phi's younger members took as a rite of passage, he was protective. Peter was the reason that no one in school messed with any of their members as well as any seventh or eighth graders. Peter was a gentle guy who watched over anyone who was being hassled, whether he knew them or not. Anyone who had the nerve to raise their voice to a girl or even a female teacher was quickly put in their place. He didn't have a great reputation as a student, but he was considered a good guy by everyone who knew him.

As vice president, Marco sat to Peter's right and whispered to him throughout the meeting. Peter was president, but it was obvious to everyone that Marco was the one who really ran the chapter.

The last few minutes of the meeting seemed to happen in slow motion. Marco reached on the floor behind him and picked up what looked like a banner. He handed one side to Peter, and they let it fall in front of them to reveal a red flag with a black swastika in the middle of a white circle.

"It's the real shit. Me and Peter got it in the city last Saturday," Marco boasted. Everyone who grew up on Long Island called Manhattan "the city" while the other four boroughs that made up New York City were referred to by name.

"It was used during World War II," Peter added with the wonderment of a child explaining a prized possession at show and tell.

Alex doubted the flag's authenticity, but it didn't make the scene unfolding before him any less disturbing. Most members were standing and playfully mimicking the Nazi salute.

Dave read the disgust and confusion on Alex's face as he scanned the room and hoped it was all a bad joke. Any hope for a punchline vanished when Peter and Marco draped the flag over the table and simultaneously kicked their combat boots together and gave the Nazi salute.

"I make a motion that this flag be hung before future meetings," Marco said to raucous applause. Everyone at the meeting knew the motion would be coming, and many clamored for a chance to second it, while a few others hoped the enthusiasm would be weak so they would have a chance to object without being singled out.

"Second!" five or six of the members shouted so quickly it was impossible for Steven, who as secretary was taking copious notes on a legal pad, to know who had been first. He credited Kip Daniels since he was closest to

Marco, though it didn't matter since none of it be added to the official secretary's book that had to be submitted to the grand chapter for review at the conclusion of each school year.

"All in favor?" Peter asked, though it was just a formality.

The house shook from the sound of most of the teenage boys shouting, "Aye!"

"All opposed?" Peter asked.

A few boys looked around uncomfortably for others who might object, but none were brave enough to put their well-being on the line. The silence that filled the room made it feel like it had been sucked into a vacuum. Peter nodded his approval, and said, "Zis motion is passed," in a poor attempt at a German accent.

The slow-motion scene gave way to a five-minute frenzy as Alex struggled to make sense of what he had witnessed. The only thing he later remembered was a motion for Peter to buy beer that he nixed because he was grounded.

After the conclusion of the meeting, Alex stood alone under the green and white awning behind the house as Dave talked to several brothers Alex didn't know. Alex watched as everyone left, noting the most animated were the smallest brothers, who he assumed were probably in eighth or ninth grade.

Dave's ashen face told Alex all he needed to know as he joined him on the back patio to collect their bikes.

"What the fuck was that?" Alex whispered.

"I don't know."

"That shit is messed up," Alex said.

Tommy Regan poked his head around the back of the house and startled them. Tommy was Dave's closest friend, and one of the few Alex knew well. Like Dave, Tommy was clean-cut and athletic.

"Are you guys coming?" Tommy asked.

"I don't think so," Dave said.

"Wait," Alex said. "Where are you guys gonna be?"

"The tunnel under Sunset, closer to the woods than the train station."

"I have to call my girlfriend, but I'll meet you guys over there," Alex said.

"I'll take a ride with you," Dave said. "There's a phone by the candy store on Kennedy."

Alex pulled his wallet from his back pocket, but Dave was already handing Tommy a ten-dollar bill. "Can you pick up some Bud for us? Two sixes or two eights should be good. If they don't have Bud get something else. Just don't get quarts, they're piss warm after ten minutes.

"Bud. No quarts. Got it."

"I've got money," Alex said.

"You're with my chapter, so it's my treat," Dave said.

Alex and Dave rode down the driveway and out to the left while most of the others, including Tommy, headed right.

"We won't stay long," Alex said once they turned the corner.

"Why are we even going?"

Alex hopped his bike on the curb and rode up the sidewalk to the payphone in front of Sandy's Candy Store. "I'm curious to see who's really into this Nazi shit."

Alex put a dime in the coin slot and dialed Julie's number while Dave rode a wheelie across the street to give him privacy. By the time Dave turned back, Alex had already hung up.

"Everything okay?"

"Yeah, Julie has a few friends over."

"Everything okay between you two?"

"Same as always."

"Her dad's still a dick?"

"That's never gonna change," Alex said.

"What if you tell him you'll convert?" Dave suggested.

"He knows I'd never do that," Alex said as they passed Malbrook Station.

Chapter 3

Jevonte Jenkins stepped between unopened boxes stacked in the living room and plopped down on the couch. Along with his Uncle Jesse and cousin, Daryl, he had been unloading, moving, and unpacking boxes since his uncle had pulled the U-Haul truck into the driveway around three o'clock that afternoon. They had worked steadily except for a short break when his aunt brought McDonald's for dinner. Jevonte looked out the front window into darkness that was broken only by an upstairs light across the street. He checked his watch; it was nine-fifteen.

Jevonte was a mousy black youth who had celebrated his sixteenth birthday three days earlier and was still awaiting the growth spurt everyone assured him would be coming. Even though his arms ached, he wouldn't mention it and suffer the inevitable teasing from his cousin.

Jesse Jenkins was the proud new owner of the gray colonial house they had been unpacking boxes in. He sat across from Jevonte on a second couch and asked, "Are you ready for me to drive you home?"

"I think I'll walk," Jevonte said.

"Are you sure? It's dark out."

"Don't worry, Pops, there are enough white people around here to show him out of town," Daryl joked. Daryl was two years older than Jevonte and looked like a taller, more muscular version of his cousin.

"Now don't go starting that," Jesse said.

"I'm just kidding," Daryl said, and flashed a thousand-watt smile.

"I know but keep those jokes within the confines of this house."

Daryl feigned being offended until his father shook his head and dismissed the look.

"I'm a psychology major. Do you think I'd be stupid enough to give people around here a reason not to like me?" He immediately added, "Other than the color of my skin."

Jevonte and Daryl burst into fits of laughter, and despite his best effort not to, Jesse joined them.

Jevonte stood, stretched out his arms and legs and rolled his neck twice.

"Are you sure you don't want a ride?" Jesse asked as he stepped between Jevonte and the front door. "You must be tired."

"I'm fine," Jevonte said. When he saw his uncle's doubt, he added, "Honestly."

"Okay, I'm not going to force you."

Jesse shook Jevonte's hand, thanked him, and Daryl walked him out the front door.

"Take care, cuz. Give me a call when you get home."

"Will do."

Jevonte put the Walkman's headphones over his ears and started down the block. Ten minutes into his walk, he regretted not accepting the ride.

*   *   *

Inside the graffiti covered tunnel under Sunset Highway, Marco played air guitar as Jimmy Kessler's boom box blared The Who's "Baba O'Riley" at full volume. Jimmy was a tall, gangly kid with long, wavy brown hair parted in the middle, the pathetic start of a mustache, and the look of someone who is perpetually

stoned. He sat against the wall across from Tommy and
drank a can of Schlitz.

"Did you guys hear something?" Tommy asked.

Jimmy hit PAUSE and the music stopped. The only
sound was cars passing overhead.

"You know what I heard?" Marco asked.

"What'd you hear?" Jimmy asked with a slight slur.

Jimmy missed the first half of the meeting because
he was drinking with his girlfriend and lost track of time.
He also lost track of how much of his brother's beer they
drank until it was gone. His brother would undoubtedly
pummel him tomorrow, and if any of his brother's friends
were over, they would tie him to the tree in the front yard,
which had recently become Larry's favorite method of
torturing Jimmy. Last time they left him in the afternoon
heat of late August until his mother came home and cut him
loose three hours later. Once Jimmy started drinking,
consequences became irrelevant.

"I heard a great song stopped right in the middle,"
Marco said. "Now turn the music back on."

"Dave and his cousin are supposed to meet us here,"
Tommy said.

"So?" Marco said.

"I thought it was them."

Marco spun towards the opening as Jimmy pressed PLAY. "Wait," Marco said, and Jimmy killed the music.

On occasion, cops checked the tunnel for under-age drinking. If they found anyone with beer or liquor, they let them off with a warning and confiscated it for when their shift was over. It was prudent to take the loss and leave quietly, which was what everyone did. Except Stan Barrett.

In July 1972, Stan Barrett and five friends were drinking beer behind the bandshell at the Village Green when two officers showed up before anyone had even finished a beer. Depending on who told the story, there was anywhere from one to six cases of beer in the open trunks of the two cars. The story went further off the rails after that because no one seemed to agree on anything other than Stan being arrested. Some claimed Stan merely suggested the cops let them close the trunks, keep the beer, and leave, before one of the officers shoved him against the car, frisked him and found a knife. Others claimed he pulled a bowie knife, nun chucks or a pellet gun that was tucked in the back his pants and was quickly subdued and then beaten.

Marco almost tossed his switchblade aside but decided to keep it. He looked back and nodded toward Dave and Alex as they entered the far side of the tunnel.

"Let them stay with the beer for a minute while we see what's out there," Marco said.

"We'll be right back," Tommy called. "Stay with the beer."

"And the boombox," Jimmy added.

Marco stepped into the woods and Jimmy and Tommy dutifully followed. They left everything behind for Dave and Alex to look after.

Jevonte Jenkins walked without a care. He felt refreshed after laying in the large open area in the middle of the woods, where he paused Michael Jackson's music and stared up at the stars in stillness and silence. He wasn't sure if he'd been there ten minutes or an hour, but whatever it had been, it was enough to recharge him for the remainder of his walk. He heard music over his Walkman for a few minutes before it stopped. He paid it no mind until it started again—this time much closer—and immediately stopped. Three boys peered into the darkness before they stepped out from beneath the overpass. Jevonte didn't know who, or what, they were looking for, but decided it would be better to stay where he was, partially hidden by a tree since he didn't know anyone in the immediate area. When the last song on Side A of the cassette ended, the button clicked up and he shifted his feet, rustled some leaves, and drew Marco's attention.

"Get him!" Marco yelled.

The words brought Jevonte into razor sharp focus and he ripped off his headphones and ran. His first thought was to turn back to his uncle's house, but he discarded the idea in favor of a footbridge that crossed Overlook Pond at its narrowest point. If he could get across, the chase was over. His heart pounded as he ran, too scared to look back.

It took a moment for Marco's words to register with Jimmy, and by that time his friends had a considerable lead. Even though Jimmy was drunk, he ran hard and picked up ground quickly.

Marco tripped, tumbled forward, and rolled sideways. Jimmy was too close to go around, but when he tried to hurdle him, his left boot caught Marco flush in the ear and Marco cried out in pain.

Alex rode to the edge of the woods and watched four silhouettes he couldn't identify disappear. He didn't hear Marco yell, "Get back here, nigger!" Even if they had, the word wasn't likely to make either think they were chasing a black person since—in Malbrook—the word had been repurposed to mean someone who wasn't liked.

Dave picked up a can of Schlitz, tossed it to Alex, and grabbed another for himself.

"I guess they didn't have Budweiser," Alex said.

"Yeah, right. Marco probably used our money to buy all the beer," Dave said as he started the cassette and let it play until the end of "Bargain" before rewinding it. When it stopped, he played it from the beginning.

"Where'd they go?" Alex asked.

"Someone probably pissed Marco off, and now they're gonna kick his ass."

"Someone from your own fraternity?"

"Maybe. Or someone wearing another frat's colors."

Alex thought it odd that opposite sides of the same town could be so different. On the west side of Malbrook boys fought over girls, disagreements, and general stupidity. Colors were irrelevant. With three fraternities to choose from, some elementary school friends were bound to join another, but it didn't mean friendships had to end; it meant some friends went to different meetings. On the east side of town, that apparently wasn't true.

"Let's check it out," Alex said.

Dave looked at the beer and the boom box. He didn't want to get involved in one of Marco's fights, but he knew Alex would go regardless. He'd take the boom box, but the beer had to stay. If someone took off with their beer, there would be hell to pay later, but they would deal with that when the time came, if necessary.

Fallen branches prevented them from riding with their usual abandon, but neither was in a hurry until they heard a high-pitched cry of, "Help!" in the distance.

Jevonte screamed repeatedly as he neared the bridge. He wouldn't look back, but he felt them gaining.

At the edge of the woods where houses ran up to dead ends, a porch light went on and the front door opened. Directly across the street from the first house, another door opened.

The three boys were familiar with the area around the pond and stayed several feet away where the ground was firm. They closed the gap as Jevonte trudged through the softer ground.

Jevonte reached the bridge and planted his muddy left foot to turn, but it slid out from under him. He slammed into the wooden railing and nearly went over. As he steadied himself to run, Jimmy grabbed him.

"Help! Help!" Jevonte cried again as Jimmy threw him on the ground at Marco's feet and then pounced on him and put a hand over his mouth.

"Where you think you're going, nigger?" Marco asked as he caught his breath.

Jevonte attempted to answer but his response was muffled by Jimmy's hand.

Jimmy clutched the back of Jevonte's jeans and yanked him to his feet, unintentionally giving Jevonte a wedgie.

Marco stepped closer and eyed Jevonte.

Jevonte kicked wildly at Marco and as he stepped back to avoid it, his left foot landed on wet leaves, and he fell into a painful split that made Tommy wince and then laugh quietly to himself.

Jevonte elbowed Jimmy's ribs and pulled free, but when he turned to run, Tommy caught the lower back of his tee shirt. Jevonte spun and hit Tommy just below his left eye with a backhanded fist. The blow dazed Tommy, but he held on as he fell to his knees, and it gave Marco a chance to get to his feet and grab Jevonte from behind.

Jimmy pounded his fist into Jevonte's stomach, and Marco let him fall to the ground.

"Pick him up," Marco said.

"Did you see what that nigger did?" Jimmy asked.

Marco's eyes fixed on Jimmy as he waited for compliance.

"I ought to kill you," Jimmy said as he grabbed one of Jevonte's arms and yanked him to his feet so Tommy could hold the other.

"Check it out, two old guys are looking this way," Tommy said as the weak beam of a flashlight caught his eye.

Ed Healey and Jeff Marks stood at the end of Fairview Street by three railroad ties that separated the street from the woods. Ed banged his hand against the side of his flashlight as the light flickered.

Marco turned, saw the two and pulled out his switchblade. He clicked it open and held it to Jevonte's lips. "Yell and I won't think twice about slitting your throat."

"You hurt him bad enough. Let's go before they call the cops," Tommy said. "If they haven't already."

Marco lifted the switchblade to Jevonte's eyes and then back and forth as Jevonte's eyes followed. "We're not going anywhere until we teach this nigger that he doesn't belong in our town."

"I was just passing through," Jevonte said in a voice that was barely a whisper.

"He's probably looking for a bike to steal from someone's garage," Marco said. "And I bet he stole that Walkman. Didn't you, nigger?"

"Want me to take it?" Jimmy asked.

"Don't be disgusting, I wouldn't even touch it."

"Well, he ain't keeping it," Jimmy said, and ripped the Walkman from Jevonte's belt and hurled it into the pond.

Tommy looked at the sparse traffic on Sunset and back to the two older men by the dead end. He wanted to walk away but worried about the repercussions. He'd experienced it once and didn't want an encore.

"Niggers are not welcome in my town," Marco said as he took a step back. He folded his knife and slipped it in his pocket.

"My cousin just moved here," Jevonte said.

"Tell your cousin to move somewhere else or he'll get the same treatment. If I ever see either of you in my town, I'll kill you. Got it?"

Jevonte started to answer but Marco spun and kicked him in the stomach, and all that escaped was Jevonte's breath. He wanted to fall, but Jimmy and Tommy held him up.

Marco yanked the short hair on Jevonte's head back and punched his jaw. Jevonte's head dropped. As Jevonte regained focus, another punch connected with his chin and a third with his eye. He was defenseless as Marco pounded his face with a steady stream of punches.

When Alex and Dave were finally close enough to see, Alex jumped off his bike and threw it to the ground.

"Alex, don't forget Marco's switchblade," Dave called after him.

Jevonte's face was covered in blood as Marco's fist came forward. His eyes were swollen nearly closed, so he didn't see Marco's fist disappear as Alex drove him into the ground with a blindside tackle.

Tommy and Jimmy were too surprised by Alex's tackle to move. They continued to hold Jevonte even though he was in no condition to escape.

"Get the fuck off of me!" Marco yelled.

Alex pulled Marco up by his left arm and twisted it behind his back. Marco's free hand reached into his pocket and Alex pulled the narrow strip of Marco's mohawk and said, "Take out that knife and it's the last thing you'll ever do." Marco's hand came out empty.

Dave left the boom box by the bikes and stood beside Alex.

"Let him go!" Alex yelled.

Tommy let go immediately and held his hands up with his palms out, in a gesture that said, *"No harm, no foul,"* though it was far too late. Jimmy held firm, and as much as Alex wanted to be done with the situation, he was almost glad. He yanked Marco's arm farther up his back than any arm should have been able to go without breaking, and Marco squealed in pain.

Alex put his mouth beside Marco's ear and said, "Tell him to let go or so help me, I'll break your fuckin' arm!"

Marco was vulnerable but the smug look never left his face. He turned to Dave and said, "Tell your faggoty ass cousin to get his hands off me, or the nigger ain't the only one who's gonna get a beating."

"Are you threatening me?" Alex asked, and spun Marco around to face him. "Don't kid yourself. With or without your knife, that's a fight you won't walk away from with teeth."

Dave moved to Alex's right in case Jimmy had any thoughts of jumping in to help Marco. He knew Jimmy would back Marco, but Tommy would stay put if the fight escalated. Dave didn't relish the thought of making enemies of Marco and Jimmy, but there was no way he'd let Alex fight alone.

"You better watch what you say or—"

Alex slammed Marco to the ground and planted his right knee firmly on his chest.

"That was about to be your second threat. I may be the only one here who knows what a pussy you are, but if you say anything else that even remotely resembles a threat, you'll be sipping your meals through a straw for a month."

Through the hazy vision of his right eye, Jevonte saw "Alex" on the front of his windbreaker, and when Alex turned, he saw an arcing "Malbrook West" across the top of his back and "Wrestling" straight across the lower part.

Alex leaned over and spit a wad of phlegm just to the right of Marco's face, intentionally missing his ear. "I'm gonna let you up, and if you don't get the fuck out of here immediately, I'll consider it a threat."

"I've never considered you my brother," Marco said.

"One phone call about your flag and you won't have to worry about considering *anyone* your brother."

Marco stood and brushed himself off. He turned away and said, "Let's go."

Jimmy shoved Jevonte toward Alex and as he fell, he hit the side of his head on the trunk of a fallen tree. Jimmy threw a shoulder into Dave as he walked past to get his boom box.

"What's your problem?"

"I ain't the one with the problem," Jimmy said and laughed as he hurried to catch up.

The lights from three police cars cut through the darkness at the end of Fairview Street. Tommy looked back at Dave and said, "Are you coming?"

Jimmy grabbed Tommy's neck and squeezed. "Are you fucking kidding me? Leave those nigger lovers with their friend."

"If either of you tell anyone about tonight, I'll kill you both!" Marco yelled.

"He's a lot tougher from a distance," Alex said, as he leaned over Jevonte to see if he was okay.

Jevonte fought with everything he had left to keep his eyes—which were little more than two slits—open. He uttered an unintelligible word that was supposed to be, "Thanks," as he reached up and touched Alex's name on the front of his windbreaker before it fell to the ground.

"What did he say?"

"I don't know," Alex said. He held Jevonte's limp hand in his own. "Police are coming, and an ambulance should be here shortly. You're gonna be okay."

"We should get out of here," Dave said, as three police officers charged toward them.

"We've got to go. Hang in there."

Alex turned his windbreaker inside out. If anyone read it, he would be identified within a day. They grabbed the bikes and rode across the bridge to a grassy area where fallen branches and trees no longer impeded their riding. Neither attempted any tricks; their only goal was getting across Sunset and back to Dave's house.

Alex stopped at a guardrail that separated the sidewalk from an embankment, and every few years kept a car from a deadly trip down the hill into a cluster of trees. He watched a paramedic kneel by Jevonte's side, just as he had done moments earlier.

It would have been impossible to get Jevonte to an ambulance on anything with wheels, and the responding officers were prepared with a stretcher. Two officers placed the stretcher beside Jevonte while the paramedic carefully rolled him enough to slide the stretcher under him. Once he was safely on the stretcher with straps holding him in place, the two officers carried him to the ambulance.

"That little psycho might have killed him if we hadn't shown up," Alex said as they crossed Sunset's first three lanes and rode along the narrow island that separated the south side eastbound lanes from the north side westbound lanes.

Dave jumped his bike on the island as it widened closer to the intersection by Malbrook Station. "As much as I'd like to share credit, you stopped it. Hell, you were the one who suggested we follow them. I was content to sit in the tunnel and drink beer until they came back."

"If you hadn't told me what they were up to, I would have been right beside you."

"Let's go," Dave said as a police car passed, slowed down and made a U-turn.

They crossed the rest of the highway and rode between a half dozen taxis waiting for fares when the next train pulled in. The line of taxis was twice as long during peak hours.

The patrol car sped up and turned ahead of them. The lights and siren were off, but it was stopped by the side of the road.

"Maybe we should split up," Alex suggested.

"Meet back at my house."

"You cut through the Village Green, and I'll go that way," Alex said, indicating the direction of the police car with his chin.

"Are you crazy?"

"They'll follow me, and you can get back to your house."

"Why is it better if they chase you?" Dave asked.

"I don't live around here, so it's less likely they'd think I was involved. Besides, you said I like to live dangerously." Alex awkwardly snapped the top three buttons on his windbreaker to hide his Phi shirt.

"I said you have a death wish."

"Same thing," Alex said.

"Play it safe for once," Dave shouted as Alex rode away.

Alex didn't see the second patrol car until he reached the corner. It was at the light two blocks ahead facing south while the first faced north. His plan to turn right and see if the patrol car turned to follow him was useless. He turned left to go north and the lights and sirens on both cars went on. He peaked over his shoulder as he raced past the post office and through a village parking lot toward his favorite pizza parlor, which was in the business district just beyond the parking lot they shared with a few of the other stores on Kennedy Avenue. "I should have stayed home tonight," he said softly, even as the adrenaline rush pushed him to pedal harder. As he turned left on Kennedy he peeked over his shoulder and saw no pursuit. Slightly disappointed, he continued to Dave's house.

Chapter 4

By mid-morning, Jevonte's second floor hospital room looked like a florist shop. People from all over Nassau County and Queens sent flowers with notes wishing him a speedy recovery. Jevonte's father, Jackson, who was usually referred to as Jack or Jackie, and his mother, Angelie, were having a difficult time agreeing on flower placement. Jack was content to put the flowers that arrived earliest near Jevonte's bed and continue outward as more arrived, but Angelie rearranged them so her favorites were closest to Jevonte.

Detectives Calvin Henderson and Nicky Tallerico stood at the door and watched the process with amusement before they knocked softly and entered. The detectives introduced themselves and got their first look at the victim. They spent a few minutes getting some general background information and a feel for who Jevonte's parents were. Henderson did most of the talking and was able to get a sense that Jack and Angelie were more concerned with Randy's recovery and protecting others like him than getting immediate justice. They wanted justice, but Henderson sensed they wouldn't go off half-cocked on the evening news screaming for an arrest.

The detectives were told that Jevonte had slept through the night, and from the look of his battered face it was probably the best thing for him. Neither detective had much hope that after being the victim of such a violent attack in an unlit area Jevonte would be able to provide much help, but they would exhaust all avenues to apprehend his attackers.

Henderson and Tallerico had been assigned the case not only for their efficiency, but because they were the most experienced partners of different races in the sixteenth precinct, which covered the entire town of Malbrook. They had been working together since Tallerico had been promoted to detective four years earlier.

Henderson was one of three black detectives in the precinct. He had been on the force nearly two decades and it hadn't always been easy, especially when he was promoted to detective after just two years. That move, though well justified by his impeccable record, number of arrests, and outstanding test scores, had been met with outrage. Two white officers who felt they had been unjustly passed over, handed in resignations that were supposed to be a wakeup call for officials but ended up being a wakeup call to all officers when they were accepted, and the officers were dismissed the same day.

When the department refused to let the officers rescind their resignations, they pled their cases unsuccessfully through the union.

Morale wise, the year that followed had been the worst of Henderson's career. Many of his fellow detectives refused to partner with him out of loyalty to their former colleagues. If not for three large drug busts Henderson was forced to make alone—and the commendations that followed—the year would have been a total loss. As the integration of the precinct continued, incidents of racism subsided, and for the most part, at least within the precinct house, eventually stopped. In the community they served, acceptance was still a work-in-progress.

When Angelie finished arranging the bouquets, she sat beside Jack in a hard, tan plastic chair that was inexplicably less comfortable than it appeared. After the second delivery, she asked for any others to be held at the nurse's station until the detectives left.

"I'm sorry about all of this," Angelie said, and slid her seat over for a clear view of both detectives.

"No need to apologize," Henderson said. "If it was one of my sons, my wife would be doing the same thing."

"Is there anyone you can think of who would want to harm your son?" Henderson asked once Jack and Angelie were comfortable.

Angelie took Jack's hand and held it in her lap. She was attractive and light-skinned with shoulder length hair and an athletic body that Jack described as having curves in all the right places on her five-foot-four frame. At six months shy of forty, Jack was eight inches taller, much darker, and a little plump around the midsection due to many twelve-hour days behind his desk and not enough time to exercise.

"No," Jack said. "He's a good kid. He studies hard and does well in school—"

"He's in the National Honor Society," Angelie chimed in. "But I don't think anyone would begrudge him that. Like Jack said, he's a good boy."

"We're not suggesting otherwise, we just need to know if there is anyone in particular, we should talk to," Henderson assured them.

"We need to follow up every lead quickly to have the best chance at catching the perpetrators," Tallerico added. "We're not trying to suggest anything negative about your son; we just need to be thorough."

"All his friends are nice kids. They do well in school and as far as I know they don't get in trouble," Jack said. "As for anyone else, you'll have to wait and ask Jevonte."

"Now, Mrs. Jenkins, you said earlier that Jevonte was walking home from your brother-in-law's house, correct?" Henderson asked.

"Yes."

"Had he walked home that way before? Could anyone have known his routine and targeted him?"

"Jevonte was helping my brother-in-law move in, so it was his first time walking home that way."

Henderson nodded as he noted her response. "And I believe you also said that Jevonte declined a ride home?"

"That's right," she said.

"Is there any chance Jevonte was going to meet someone, and that's why he passed up the ride? A girlfriend, perhaps?"

"Jevonte's a little shy around the ladies," Jack said.

"Unlike his father," Angelie said. "But he couldn't have planned anything because he didn't know when they were going to finish. I spoke to him around six and he said after they finished eating, they were going to unpack the bedrooms and call it a day."

"Okay, I think that's all for now," Henderson said. He took two business cards from his wallet and handed one to each. "If you think of anything else, or if Jevonte wakes up and can help us with any of the details, call us immediately."

"We'll do that," Jack said. "And thank you, detectives, we appreciate it."

"Anytime," Henderson said. "We'll check in with you tomorrow if we don't hear from you first."

* * *

Alex woke on the floor of Dave's bedroom and rubbed the sleep from his eyes. Worrying had kept him awake until exhaustion won out, but the moment his eyes opened, the events of the previous night began to play over in his head.

He sat up and glanced at Dave's bed, surprised to see it empty since Dave almost never woke before eleven on weekends. He went to the bathroom, looked in the mirror and shook his head. His black hair looked like a bad comb-over. He reached into his back pocket and pulled out a comb from behind his tri-fold nylon wallet. He turned on the cold water, splashed some on his face, and slapped each cheek several times. He leaned as close as he could to the faucet, cupped water in his hands and ran it through his hair until it was sufficiently wet, then added some mousse from below the sink and blow dried it. He squeezed Colgate on his finger and ran it back and forth across his front teeth and then took a sip of water and swirled it in his mouth. It wasn't an ideal way to start a day, but it was the best he could do.

Alex went down to the living room and joined Dave on the couch where he was eating a bowl of Lucky Charms on a plastic tray table and watching television.

"What time did you get up?" Alex asked. "And how did you get out of your room without waking me?"

Dave checked the clock above the loveseat: ten-fifteen. "I woke up about an hour ago and couldn't get back to sleep, so I stepped over you and came downstairs. You were snoring pretty loud." Dave swallowed a quick spoonful of cereal and added, "They're going to a live press conference with Reverend Ralph in a minute."

"Why are you watching that?" Alex asked, initially making no connection between the minister and the previous night's attack. "Oh," he said when he realized.

*   *   *

Reverend Ralph Wilson walked slowly to a podium that had been hastily assembled near the front entrance of Malbrook Medical Center. The belt on his gray pinstriped suit was fastened below his robust midsection and his black tie was slightly askew. The salt and pepper hair of the short, heavyset, 51-year-old almost appeared to be an extension of his suit.

The fiery black minister bowed his head and stood silently for a moment before looking up to scan the sea of reporters. He knew the reporters from the major news outlets, but there were a few from smaller papers he didn't recognize.

"I am here today to ask for justice for Jevonte Jenkins, who is in this hospital behind me fighting for his life." The reverend paused and bowed his head momentarily as if speaking the words caused great pain. "Jevonte Jenkins is a good kid. He is an honor student at Rosedale High School. He has no gang affiliation, nor was he wearing colors to identify him as such. Jevonte

Jenkins's only *crime* was being a black child in a white neighborhood."

The reverend paused to let his words sink in. His eyes shifted to his left where his top advisor, Dwight Stedman, watched from just beyond the reporters. Dwight was a tall, solidly built black man with a dark mustache and a full beard in stark contrast to his shaved head. He nodded slightly to indicate Reverend Ralph was hitting his marks.

"Malbrook is supposed to be a nice neighborhood." He pounded his fist on the podium and startled the audience. "Let me tell you something; crimes like this do not happen in nice neighborhoods!" He pounded his fist on the podium a second time with a less jarring effect. "This young man did nothing wrong, and we will not stand idly by and let the animals—and that's what his attackers are—go happily along with their lives while Jevonte lies in a hospital bed trying to recover."

One of the reporters in front raised her hand and quickly asked, "What is Jevonte's condition?"

The reverend looked at Dwight, who was already on his way to the podium.

"Jevonte's parents asked me not to comment on his condition," the reverend said.

"Reverend Ralph will not be taking questions at this time," Dwight said when he reached the microphone. He held up a small banner that read: NO JUSTICE FOR JEVONTE . . . NO PEACE FOR MALBROOK. He stepped to the side to let Reverend Ralph finish.

"Next Saturday, we will march through Malbrook so we can see what these cowards have to say. Let's see them hide in the light of day as we march the route Jevonte Jenkins was taking when he was attacked. And you can be certain that we will not rest until the responsible parties are brought to justice. Thank you."

Reverend Ralph walked to a black Cadillac Deville while reporters yelled questions that would yield no fruit for their articles. The car drove away as reporters exchanged looks of annoyance.

*   *   *

Jevonte's hospital room contained two beds, though his parents were told by administrators that the second bed would remain unoccupied for the duration of his stay unless unforeseen circumstances left them with no other option. Daryl pressed the button on the television remote and the screen went blank. Reverend Ralph had left reporters with nothing but dead air to fill, and most sent it back to the studio without further speculation.

Daryl leaned beside his cousin's swollen face, put his mouth to his ear, which was partially covered by a bandage, and whispered, "Don't you worry, cuz, we'll take care of this."

Jevonte's swollen eyes opened slightly, and his lips parted, but his dry mouth produced no words. He tried to wet the inside of his mouth with his tongue, but his mouth felt like it was filled with cotton balls. He tapped Daryl's hand and pointed to a small can of ginger ale on a tray beside the bed.

"You're awake. That's great," Daryl said.

Jevonte tapped his hand several more times and pointed to the ginger ale. He tried to speak but his mouth was too dry.

"You want the ginger ale?" Daryl asked, then realized the predicament. "Tap my hand once for yes and twice for no."

Daryl waited a moment after the tap to make sure there was no second, then popped the top of the ginger ale, slid in a straw, and held it to Jevonte's mouth. It took three attempts before Jevonte was able to suck long enough to get the soda all the way to his mouth.

"Your mom and dad went to the cafeteria to grab something to eat. I'll get them."

"Wait," Jevonte said. His strained voice was barely a whisper.

"What?" Daryl asked and leaned closer.

Jevonte took shallow breaths as he spit out one word at a time. "Last . . . year's . . . Malbrook . . . West . . . yearbook," Jevonte said. He winced as the struggle to get the words out sent waves of pain through his cracked ribs.

"What about it?" Daryl asked, and quickly added, "Maybe you should just rest for now and tell me when you're feeling better."

Jevonte tapped Daryl's hand twice. *"No."* He was determined to finish. "Library," Jevonte said.

"You want me to go to the library?"

"Yearbook," Jevonte said. He hoped Daryl made the connection because the pain in his ribs was getting worse.

Daryl glanced at the door to make sure no one was coming in. "You want me to get the Malbrook West yearbook from the library?"

Jevonte tapped once. He knew the only way he could communicate more than a word or two at a time was to take deeper breaths, but each would come with great pain. He winced as he took a deep breath and said, "Wrestling team. Alex. Oriental." He immediately took another breath and said, "Knows who did this. Saved me."

"Okay, so I go to the Malbrook Library and check out West High's wrestling photo for an Oriental kid named Alex," Daryl said, and knew the next step before Jevonte spoke. "Then I check the phone book to see where he lives."

Jevonte tapped Daryl's hand once and his tense body relaxed.

"When I find him, I'll get the names of the kids who did this to you. And then—" Daryl took Jevonte's hand. "We'll make them regret being born," Daryl said. He heard footsteps outside and looked up as his aunt and uncle entered.

"How's our patient doing?" Angelie asked.

"He's awake. I helped him drink a little ginger ale. I hope that's okay," Daryl said.

"That's wonderful," Angelie said, and leaned down to kiss Jevonte's forehead just above his left eye, which was one of the few spots not covered by a bandage. "How are you doing, baby boy?" she asked.

"Baby boy," Daryl repeated and snickered.

Jevonte tucked all but his middle finger into his right palm where only Daryl could see, and Daryl laughed.

"Has he said anything?" Jack asked. He kissed two of his fingers and touched them to Jevonte's forehead.

"He tried. It was better when I asked him yes or no questions and had him tap once for yes and twice for no," Daryl said. "That's how I figured out he wanted a drink."

Angelie put Jevonte's hand on top of her own and asked, "Are you okay with that?"

Jevonte tapped once. Through the tiny slits, he saw his mother's swollen eyes.

"Are you in a lot of pain?" she asked.

Jevonte tapped twice and widened his lips attempting to smile. Jack wasn't fooled and winked at Jevonte. *Good job.*

"Two detectives were here earlier," Angelie said. "Do you think you can give them any information that might help?"

"Tomorrow," Jevonte whispered.

Jevonte's strained voice tore through Angelie's soul. She brought the hand Jevonte had been tapping to her mouth, looked at the dull florescent lights above his bed and fought back tears.

A tear dripped from Jevonte's left eye and quickly disappeared in bandages.

"Why don't you go to the nurse's station and get some water? Just take a minute or two to pull yourself together," Jack suggested. "Don't let him see you cry."

Her fierce mother instinct told her not to leave her child. She had sat beside him all night and prayed she would never see him like this again. She kissed his forehead and said, "I need to get some water."

"Okay," Jevonte said.

Jack listened to her footsteps grow faint and then said, "I know you're in a lot of pain, but you told your mother what she needed to hear, and that's brave of you. But be honest with me." He slid his hand beneath his son's. "Do you want me to ask the doctor to increase your pain medication?"

Jevonte tapped twice. An increase in medication might help with the pain, but he worried it might lengthen his stay.

"Are you sure?"

Jevonte tapped once and Jack felt a sense of relief.

"Diagnosis," Jevonte said.

Jack and Angelie had gotten the information from the doctor at four a.m. when they were both exhausted. He tried to remember what they had been told. "You have a concussion, four broken ribs, a bruised sternum, and your left arm was dislocated when they brought you in. From what we were told, you were lucky you were out when they popped it back into place because it's extremely painful." Jack looked at Daryl, who was staring at the parking lot below and the elementary school's playground beyond it. "Aside from that, you have seven stitches above your left eye, and six more under your left ear. And then there's your lip, your eyes and the bruises and scrapes on your arms and legs. They're all probably painful, but none are life threatening."

"Thank you," Jevonte said softly. "Sleepy," he added then closed his eyes and drifted off to sleep.

"That's a relief," Daryl said. "When Reverend Ralph wouldn't take questions, I got worried."

"He didn't take questions because he never bothered to find out. He just wants to get his face on the news." Jack looked out the door before he added, "Don't mention him in front of your aunt."

"Why?"

"She asked him not to march, but he's got his own agenda."

"Why doesn't she want him to march?"

Jack heard footsteps and turned in time to see a nurse passing the door. "He's going to gather as many of his followers as he can right in front of your house. Considering you moved in yesterday, do you think that's going to endear you to your neighbors?"

"Probably not."

"And if he's so concerned about justice for Jevonte, why didn't he bother to come in and check on him? Jevonte will probably be released before they march, and then everyone will think *we* overstated his injuries."

It was apparent that his aunt wasn't the only one with distaste for the reverend.

"I should probably get going," Daryl said as he looked out the window.

"Did Jevonte tell you anything useful?" Jack asked with a half-smile.

Daryl couldn't lie to his uncle. "I asked if he caught any of their names or could describe anything about them."

"What did he say?" Jack asked. Before Daryl could answer, he reconsidered and said, "Forget I asked. Jevonte can tell me if he wants."

"Some kids attacked him, and another kid stopped them." Daryl stopped just shy of telling him Alex's name. "He knows more, but I didn't want to push him."

∗   ∗   ∗

In the living room of Dave's house, Alex ran a hand through his hair. The color in his face vanished when

Reverend Ralph spoke of the victim and had yet to return. He leaned against the back of the couch with dark wooden sides and cushions that had thick plastic covering them. The plastic was probably ideal when Dave was young, but now they were unnecessary.

"The empty beer cans under the highway have our fingerprints on them," Alex said in a semi-panic.

"Even if the police have our fingerprints, they have nothing to compare them to. Neither of us has ever been arrested." Dave, for the moment, was the voice of reason.

"But Reverend Ralph said that kid might die."

"No, he didn't. He said he's recovering," Dave said. "His name is Jevonte Jenkins, so you don't have to call him 'that kid' anymore."

"Thanks, but knowing his name makes me feel worse."

"You may be the reason Jevonte's alive," Dave said as he finished the last of his cereal. "He has to be doing better than when we left him." Dave drank the remainder of the milk in his bowl. "This is funny because I'm usually the one who worries about everything."

Alex grabbed the phone from the coffee table at the end of the couch. The living room phone was a convenience Alex wasn't used to since few people he knew had them. It even had the luxury of pushbuttons instead of a rotary dial.

"Who are you calling?" Dave asked as he searched for something to watch on television.

"I'm gonna call my dad to pick me up."

"What's wrong with your bike?"

"Nothing. But I'm wearing the same clothes as last night," Alex said, as he rolled his windbreaker into a ball.

Alex told his father his front tire was flat, and he needed a ride home. After he hung up, they went outside and let the air out of his tire. Later in the afternoon he would have to waste an hour in the garage or the basement pretending to fix it, which wasn't a big deal since he wasn't in the mood to go out and he was still exhausted.

Alex leaned the bike with the flattened tire against the back of the house and Dave laughed at him for being paranoid. They went to the front stoop and waited for Alex's father.

Doug Moran pulled in front of the house in his Dodge Dart and Alex rolled his bike to the car and put it in the trunk. With all of Doug's tools, the trunk wouldn't close, so Doug lifted it out and took some rope from behind his toolbox and tied the trunk closed. "Do you want to drive?"

There were two months until Alex's seventeenth birthday, but he completed Driver's Education over the summer and passed his road test in Long Beach the following week. Normally, Alex would have jumped at the opportunity.

"No, I have a headache," Alex said.

Doug leaned over and put his hand on Alex's forehead.

"It doesn't feel like you have a fever." Doug's first instinct was always a cursory check for fever.

"I think I slept wrong, because my neck's a little stiff, too."

"When we get home, I'll get the heating pad," Doug said.

"Thanks, Dad, but I'm not five, I can get the heating pad."

Doug patted Alex's left leg. Alex was becoming more independent, but Doug still felt the need to baby him when he was sick. Alex had gotten to the point where Doug felt his parenting was almost unnecessary. He missed doing the little things for Alex. He missed reading him bedtime stories and often falling asleep himself while he waited for Alex to doze off. Doug's role as a father had changed dramatically, and it would change even more once Alex got his driver's license and no longer needed rides. Doug had looked forward to this freedom, but now he found himself longing for the times when he was Alex's hero and Alex thought he knew everything and could do anything.

Doug left the radio off and didn't ask questions. He pulled all the way up the driveway past the side door and Alex's Mustang, which was off to the right side of the garage. The village ordinance of no cars parked on the street between two and five a.m. would make getting out in the morning more difficult once Alex got his Mustang on the road, but they would cross that bridge when they came to it. They still had some cosmetic work to do, but it was mechanically sound and could be registered, inspected, and insured before Alex's birthday.

Alex untied the trunk before Doug shooed him away and told him to go in and lie down. Alex did as he was told and Doug took the bike out, tossed the rope in the trunk, closed it, and started walking the bike to the garage.

"Hey, Dad, if you don't mind, can you put it in the basement?"

"Sure thing," Doug said, and reversed course.

*   *   *

Isaiah Fisher pulled his powder blue 1970 Camaro into the Malbrook Public Library parking lot. The early afternoon sun beat down on a group of boys playing tackle football on the Village Green, and Isaiah found a spot parallel to the entrance facing the football game.

"You guys wait here. I'll be right out," Daryl said.

"Why do we have to wait in the car?" Tyrone Spears asked from the back seat. "You think we're not civilized?" Tyrone was a tall, lanky, nineteen-year-old. His electric smile matched his playful personality, which was in stark contrast to Isaiah, who at six-foot-three was a half inch taller and more powerfully built with a ceaselessly stoic look on his face.

"You look like you've been shot. You've got ketchup all over your shirt," Daryl said.

"I can't help it if Isaiah doesn't know how to drive," Tyrone said. "He speeds up, stops short, speeds up again. It was inevitable."

"You want to walk home?" Isaiah asked.

"No, I'm good," Tyrone said. "You're a good driver; I'm just a messy eater."

"Get going," Isaiah said. "If it's like our library it probably closes in a half hour or so."

"You've been to our library?" Tyrone joked.

Daryl was about to close the door when Isaiah said, "You can leave it open." He looked back and pointedly said, "Tyrone wants to walk home."

"No, really, I'm good," Tyrone said. "I meant to say *I've* never been to our library."

Daryl crossed the newly paved parking lot and stopped by the sidewalk to look at a book return box that looked like a mailbox. He reached the door just ahead of an older man who was leaving and held the door for him. The man smiled and nodded politely.

Inside the library to the right was a thin redheaded woman at the Help Desk. She had probably been dying her hair for the better part of three decades, and the creases around her lips suggested she had been smoking even longer.

Daryl stood quietly at the desk and waited for the woman to notice him.

"Can I help you?" she asked.

"Can you please tell me where I can find the high school yearbooks?" Daryl asked.

Her warm, pleasant smile was replaced by a quizzical look before she pointed to a section just past the card catalogue file that had a REFERENCE sign above it. "Just walk through there and turn to the lower bookcase on the left and the yearbooks are on the nearside on the second and third shelves."

"Thank you," Daryl said, and followed her directions.

Aside from missing the yearbook from 1969, the rest were in order starting with Malbrook West's first graduating class in 1959. Malbrook East's yearbooks were on the shelf below.

Daryl found West's most recent yearbook, which was a pristine copy from earlier in 1980, and thumbed past the senior portraits, faculty, and finally the clubs before he found the sports teams. The wrestling photo was last. There were two Alex's on the team, but only one was Oriental, which was how Jevonte had described him. Daryl checked the photo and corresponding names below before he copied the name on a sheet of paper he had brought. Moran didn't sound Oriental, but the other Alex on the team was Alex Pandrea, and he looked as Italian as his last name suggested. Daryl was about to close the yearbook when he noticed a photo of Alex on the opposite page with large wrestling trophies on a table in front of him. The caption under the photo read, "Alex Moran State Wrestling Champion" and Daryl nodded, impressed.

"Thank you," Daryl said to the woman at the desk as he walked out. She smiled and waved politely.

Daryl took his usual spot in the passenger seat of Isaiah's car. He picked up the phone book he had brought from home and ripped off the shrink wrap and flipped through the pages until he found one with the names Manfred at the top left and Muncy at the top right.

"Any luck?" Tyrone asked.

"Give me a second," Daryl said as he scanned the page. "There's only one Moran, and the first initial is D."

"D as in dum, da, dum, dum," Tyrone said, mimicking the beginning of the Dragnet television show.

"Or Daryl," he said as he copied the address and phone number. Daryl pulled the map of Malbrook from the back of the phone book and spread it out on his lap. He found Monroe Street on the back and the corresponding grid letter and number.

"You want to go by now?" Isaiah asked.

"Nah, I just wanted to see if the listing was in the right section for West High," Daryl said.

"Well, don't keep us in suspense," Tyrone said.

"It's pretty far, but I think so. Now let's find a payphone and call."

"Do you want me to call? I'm good on the phone, and I do a great impression of a white person," Tyrone said.

"Assuming that white person is a redneck," Daryl said.

"Just go," Isaiah said to Daryl as he pulled in front of a candy store.

Daryl put a dime in the same phone Alex had used the previous night.

Doug answered on the second ring and said, "Hello?"

"Is Alex there?"

"He's not feeling well," Doug said. "Would you like to leave a message? I can have him call you back."

"No, thank you. I'll talk to him in school on Monday," Daryl said, and hung up.

"Yes!" Tyrone yelled.

Daryl sat in the front seat and let out a deep breath. "Okay, so now we have his name, address, and phone number."

"What next?" Isaiah asked.

"I'll talk to Jevonte tomorrow, and we'll figure things out from there," Daryl said.

Chapter 5

Annie Moran was a no-nonsense, third-generation Chinese American with a New York accent that surprised people when they met her. She had long black hair that reached almost to her waist, and eyes that were so dark it was nearly impossible to see where her pupils ended. Annie was the second of her parents' three girls, and as the middle child had pushed the boundaries her parents had set for her older sister at every opportunity. Much to her annoyance, her younger sister pushed them twice as far.

Annie arrived home just after four o'clock with two Alexander's bags that she quickly took up to the bedroom and put in the back of the closet. Doug wasn't the type to snoop when his birthday neared—the way she was—but if he didn't see the bags, he couldn't guess what she bought him.

Doug sat on the couch and watched a movie with his feet on the coffee table and a glass of Pepsi on the end table next to them. He had given up on the nacho cheese Doritos earlier while there was still more than half a bag left which was unusual for him.

"Where's Alex?" Annie asked and gave Doug a quick peck on his lips.

"He's in his room sleeping," Doug said as the movie went to a commercial. "He has a headache."

"He probably drank too much. I figured that's why he slept at your sister's house."

"I don't think so," Doug said. He pulled Annie down on his lap and nuzzled her neck. He gently nibbled her earlobe and whispered, "Not everyone is a wild child like my wife was growing up."

"You, sir, are mistaken," she said, and playfully slapped his face. "I wasn't wild, I was fiercely independent."

"How old were you the first time you smoked pot?"

"So, why don't you think drinking caused his headache?" Annie asked, changing the subject, and conceding Doug's point.

"His front tire was flat, and he has a stiff neck. Maybe he had an accident on his bike."

"I always tell him to be careful," Annie said, concerned. "They do crazy things on their bikes. Yesterday I saw him and one of his friends riding their bikes while sitting on their handlebars and pedaling backwards."

"They're kids. It's what they do," Doug said with a hint of admiration.

"If he hits a bump he could fall backwards and slam his head on the ground." She turned quickly to Doug. "Do you think that's what happened? Maybe he has a concussion."

"I don't think his headache was that bad, but if he's not up by six we should check on him."

"I've got a better idea," Annie said. She took the bag of Doritos to the kitchen and tossed them in a basket on top of the refrigerator to eliminate temptation. She dialed her sister-in-law's number.

"Dr. Everett doesn't make house calls anymore," Doug joked. It seemed almost impossible that doctors once had, but Dr. Everett had stopped around the time Alex started kindergarten.

Annie stepped into the dining room and held up her right index finger. *I'll fill you in when I get off the phone.* She stepped back into the kitchen where the television wouldn't be a distraction.

The movie came back on, and Doug began laughing almost immediately as Dick Van Dyke planned a Christmas

Eve heist of Gimbel's. Dick Van Dyke and Jerry Lewis were Doug's two favorite actors. He'd often thought they would have made a great team, though it wasn't likely to happen since Jerry Lewis had long since taken up his tireless effort to raise money for Muscular Dystrophy research, which included hosting a telethon every Labor Day weekend.

Annie looked relieved when she came back in the room.

"Well?"

"Judy said according to Dave there was no accident and Alex didn't know his tire was flat until this morning. She said they weren't out late but didn't know what time they went to bed."

"Who?" Alex asked as he entered the room. He woke a few minutes earlier to discover his fake headache had become real.

"You and Dave. I called Aunt Judy to find out if she knew anything about your headache."

"It wasn't really bothering me until this morning."

"How do you feel now?" Doug asked.

"A little better," Alex lied. "I'm just hungry."

"I was about to make some turkey sandwiches. Grab an apple or a pear while I get them ready."

"Sounds good," Alex said. He grabbed a golden delicious apple from the refrigerator and sat beside his father on the couch.

"You got a phone call this afternoon, but they didn't leave a message."

"Who was it?" Alex asked after he swallowed a bite of his apple.

"I didn't recognize the voice, but he said he'll see you in school on Monday, so I figured it wasn't important."

*   *   *

Alex's headache was gone by the time John called two hours later. His only plans for the night were to stay home and watch television, but John persisted until Alex caved and agreed to go out.

As Alex settled into the passenger seat of John's Maverick, John popped a cassette in and cranked the stereo volume's knob and Van Halen's "Runnin' with the Devil" shook the car.

"What do you think?" John shouted over the music.

"I think I'm going deaf," Alex said, and lowered it to a tolerable level.

"I had it installed today. It's a top-of-the-line Pioneer stereo with a cassette player, and an equalizer." John moved the controls on the equalizer up and down to demonstrate how he could control the bass and treble. "With Blaupunkt speakers in front and back, this is easily the best car stereo in our school."

"The stereo is probably worth more than your car."

"Nah, they're probably worth about the same."

He pulled slowly to the corner and turned right before pressing the gas pedal to the floor. Alex stared blankly out the window at the people they passed. It never occurred to him before that everyone who lived within a mile of his home was white.

Alex had a half dozen friends he could trust with almost anything and John was at the top of the list. They became friends in kindergarten and even though they excelled in different areas, they had been best friends since. They had pledged Phi together and been numbers one and two on hell night, with John getting his shots with the paddles and shaved down wooden baseball bats first, and Alex following.

"What's up with you? It's the first night of rec as seniors and you look like you're facing midterms," John said.

"Before we go to rec, there's something I need to talk to you about. And you've got to swear you won't tell anyone."

"I won't tell anyone," John said and crossed his fingers over his heart.

"Swear."

"On my grandmother's life," John said.

"Your grandmother is dead," Alex said.

"I meant the other one."

"They're both dead," Alex said and laughed.

"That must be why they stopped sending me birthday cards," John said. "I guess I'll have to swear on my own life."

"You know that black kid who got beat up last night?" Alex asked.

"Sure, I had lunch with him this afternoon."

"You're such an asshole sometimes," Alex said and punched John in the arm for good measure.

"Mike says I'm an asshole all the time."

"Sometimes you're actually a decent human being," Alex said.

"Don't let any girls hear that. It'll ruin my reputation as a bad boy."

"The only reputation—" Alex began and stopped. "We're getting off the subject here. You heard about the black kid who got beat up last night, right?"

"Hasn't everyone? They won't stop talking about it."

"I was there," Alex said.

"*You* beat up the black kid?" John asked in a shocked voice as he pulled to the curb. "You're the last person I'd suspect."

"I didn't beat him up, it was some of those asshole brothers from Dave's chapter," Alex said. "I stopped them."

"Holy shit," John said, and blew out a breath. "You scared me. But I don't get it. Who? Why?"

"I went to their meeting with Dave last night."

"Why?" John asked. "Aside from Dave and maybe one or two others, they're a bunch of pothead derelicts."

"Actually, it's worse than that."

"What's worse than pothead derelicts?"

"They hung a Nazi flag at their meeting. Dave brought me along so I could help him figure out what to do."

Nine freshmen walked toward them on the sidewalk. The group was spread out in an unusual way, which made it difficult to tell the pecking order that had probably been established by the end of seventh grade. With groups of more than five, the leaders were typically easy to spot because everyone circled around them and tried to engage them in conversation. This group seemed to be comprised of alphas confident enough not to be concerned about leadership.

"What did you tell him?" John asked as he pulled back into traffic.

"We never got a chance to talk about it. A few guys were going to the tunnel under Sunset to drink, so we tagged along to see how serious they were about the Nazi thing."

"What did you . . . hold that thought," John said and sped up to catch a car with three girls in it. The car had a Golden Tornado bumper sticker from Lawrence High School, which meant the girls were probably from Cedarhurst, Lawrence, Woodmere, or Inwood. It was something he learned from the lone girl he had dated from the school. He had met her at his job at Beefsteak Charlie's in Lawrence where he was recently promoted to waiter. He honked and waved for the girl in the passenger seat to roll her window down.

"Where are you ladies off to?" John asked.

The girl smiled and said, "We're going to see Innocence at Hammerhead's."

"They're really good," John said. "Probably because they're from Malbrook."

"You're from Malbrook?" she asked.

"That we are," John said. "But I work in Lawrence."

"Where?" a cute girl in the backseat yelled.

"I never tell a girl until after the second date," he joked. It was all part of the game.

John began to assess their looks and found nothing wrong from the shoulders up, though moving cars and poor lighting hid many flaws. The laws of physics worked against him.

"Isn't it a little early?" John asked. "What time do they go on?"

The cute blond in the backseat leaned forward and poked her head out the window. "They go on at ten, but ladies drink free until then, so we're gonna catch a buzz."

"Will your boyfriends be there?" John asked.

"No boyfriends," the blond said. "We're single and ready to mingle."

John hadn't noticed at first, but she was slurring some of her words, which didn't bode well for a girl heading to a bar this early. Her cuteness factor had gone down while his opportunity to get laid went up.

"Why don't you ladies go and enjoy some free drinks, and maybe we'll meet up with you later."

The girl in the passenger seat threw her hands up and out the window and yelled, 'Woo, hoo, see you later!" The driver sped up and lost them.

John's expression was a cross between a smile and a smirk.

"You're not actually thinking about meeting them, are you?" Alex asked.

"No way! If they were sober, two of the three are in the six to eight range, but keep in mind that's an observation made from the driver of a moving vehicle at night, so I could be way off. Assuming they're in that range, there's other factors at play, and the most important is what happens when girls drink. One group gets cuter and slutty looking, the second group gets loud and annoying, and the third group gets uglier."

"Where do they fall?" Alex asked. John's "insights" were amusing, but the ones about girls were often his best.

"The driver was a six. She's the mascot."

"Mascot?"

"You know, the ugly friend who takes all the messages from guys. Think of it like cheerleaders, and how the ugly one who can do all the moves dresses as the mascot, so no one looks at her face. She's still technically a cheerleader, but not really. Every group has one. The mascot is always out. She'd be your best chance to get laid, but not tonight. The girl in the front passenger seat might be an eight, but she drops to a four when she drinks because she loves the way it makes her feel. The problem with her is that she'll never shut up, even when you're banging her."

"Which leaves the girl in the backseat as the best option," Alex said.

"Not a chance. She's already slurring her words, so by ten o'clock she'll probably be shit-faced and sloppy, and I'm going to guess down to a three in attractiveness. She's the type of girl who would go out to your car, take off her pants, and throw up in the backseat. If you ever meet one of those, go to her car."

"So those three are definitely out?" Alex asked.

"If I was desperate to get laid, I'd bang the driver. But the only way that would work was if she switched with the girl in the backseat. The girl in the front passenger seat is out in any scenario because you'd need a pry bar to get away from her."

"Pry bar?" Alex asked.

John put his hands up and said, "Woo, hoo," to mock her. "Dating her would be like dating a leper because you'd never be able to get rid of her."

"You can't get rid of lepers?" Alex asked.

"Picture this. You have goodbye sex, leave your house, and then break the bad news to her. The minute she gets home she calls and tells you she thinks one of her fingers fell off in your house, and she needs to find it." John nodded. "That's the way it is with lepers and girls like woo hoo."

"Why would a leper need a finger that fell off? It's not like they can reattach it."

"I don't know. Maybe they save them like my parents saved my baby teeth."

"Do you actually believe all your bullshit?" Alex asked.

"They're stone-cold facts."

"Are you avoiding the other conversation I'm trying to have with you?"

"No, I want to hear what happened. It's just that when I see a car full of girls it reminds me that while I currently don't have a girlfriend, I do still have a cock." John waited a few seconds and then added, "It also reminds me of the song we heard on the radio over the summer. I think it was 'While You See a Chance' by Steve Winwood, though I haven't been able to find it on an album, or single, despite six trips to Sam Goody in Green Acres."

"Okay, forget about all that and focus on what I'm telling you. The other chapter hung a Nazi flag at their meeting, and the members were doing the Nazi salute. Then three of them beat the crap out of a helpless black kid, and if I hadn't stopped them, they might have killed him."

"Killed him? Don't you think you might be overreacting?" John asked.

"You didn't see them. Two of them were holding the kid up and the third kid was punching and kicking him."

"What do you want to do?" John asked as he pulled into an empty lot that once belonged to Pier One Imports.

"I don't know," Alex said. He knew John would back him no matter what he decided, but he needed help making the decision. "If I give police the names, it's betraying brothers, but if I don't, things could get worse."

"In case you turn up dead, who are these three losers?" John asked, joking.

Alex laughed. "Dave's friend Tommy, I don't know his last name, and the other two were that kid Jimmy who looks like he's always stoned, and—"

"Do you know why he always looks stoned?"

"Why?"

"Because he's always stoned."

"I never would have guessed," Alex said. "Thank you."

"Let me guess who the last one was. The little pizza face with the Napoleon complex. What's his name? Marco?"

"Bingo."

"Bingo? Now I get why he always looks pissed. If my parents named me Bingo, I probably would have run away and changed it." John's humor wasn't always appropriate, but it usually helped calm Alex when he was uptight.

"We should find Bingo and his buddies and beat the shit out of them," John suggested.

"We can't. They're brothers."

"Not if we tell the national chapter they hang a Nazi flag at their meetings. Or that they have a member named Bingo. I think that alone should be reason enough to dismember their chapter."

"Dismember their chapter?"

"Yeah, get rid of it," John said.

"Dismember means to cut their bodies into pieces," Alex said.

"Good idea, right?"

Alex tried not to laugh as he considered John's real suggestion. The trouble was proving it. "Maybe Dave can suggest a picture of the four officers that sit at the table at the head of the room because the flag hangs off the table in front of them. He can make two copies and give one to the secretary to include with the minutes of the meeting. And the second copy would go anonymously to the National Chapter."

"They're stupid, but not that stupid," John said, shooting down Alex's plan. "Tell me what happened last night, and we'll figure it out."

Alex had gone over the events of the evening so many times in his mind that he could share even small details with John. John listened intently without interrupting, which was no small accomplishment for him.

"There are two things wrong with that story," John said once Alex finished.

"That's exactly what happened," Alex said.

"I mean there were two things you should have done differently."

"What?" Alex asked.

"You should have broken Bingo's arm and spit in his face."

John was right, he should have broken Marco's arm after Marco threatened him. And spitting in Marco's face would have been infinitely more satisfying.

"Let's forget about it for now and go to rec and wreak havoc in European handball!" John said. He cut the wheel sharply and made an illegal U-turn in front of the group of stores that included a Chinese restaurant, a pizza parlor, and a bar.

The idea sounded great to Alex. He needed the adrenaline rush of intense competition to take his mind off the past twenty-four hours.

*   *   *

West High's version of European handball was a hybrid of basketball and soccer combined with the physicality of hockey. Alex, John and four friends played as "shirts" against four juniors and two other friends who had transferred to catholic high schools in ninth grade as "skins." The fast-paced game, played with a volleyball, went back and forth across the basketball court on the boys' side of the gym. The goalies roamed back and forth protecting nets that were six feet high and twelve feet wide, ready for shots that could come at any time. Alex used the maximum five dribbles before he passed the ball to John just inside the top of the key where a tan masking tape line extended across the gym and marked where players had to use two hands to shoot. John caught the pass, dribbled twice, and jumped as if he was going for a layup, but then flipped the ball between his legs and past the goalie for the game winner. It was their second consecutive win and except for the goalie, the entire team was sweating through their t-shirts.

"Don't think this game will be that easy," Mike Thatcher said as he walked to the center of the court followed by five friends from the football team. They shook hands all around and Alex tossed the ball to the opposing goalie, Declan, who was the football team's center and nose tackle.

Declan had been dubbed "red-headed stepchild" by Mike because of his bright red hair and the lack of recognition he received as an offensive lineman, despite his penchant for destroying the defenders he blocked. Only his closest friends used his nickname since he was six-foot-five and weighed two-hundred-forty pounds.

The game had gone back and forth and was tied at eight when Mike caught a pass just outside the tan line and was picked up by Alex on defense. Mike turned his back to Alex and used his twenty-pound weight advantage to back Alex towards the goal. Alex planted a forearm in Mike's back, dug in and held him in place.

"Are you ready, Alex?" Mike asked.

"Ready to watch you dribble in place until rec is over?"

"Ready for me to make you my nigger?" Mike pivoted on his left foot and spun quickly to his right.

Alex anticipated the move since he had seen it dozens of times during gym class when they were usually on the same team. He slapped the ball back towards half court with his left hand, scooped it up with his right, dribbled twice and fired a shot at the bottom left side of the goal that skipped past Declan.

"Point game," John said as they retreated.

Declan threw an outlet pass over Alex's head to Mike. Mike reached back to fire a shot, but Alex hit his arm as it came forward and deflected the ball into the corner and sent Mike crashing into the wall.

"If you want full contact, play football," Mike said and shoved Alex.

"If you want no contact, go on the girl's side and play badminton," Alex said as he pushed back while the game continued around them. The few people who didn't know them were probably waiting for punches to be thrown, but the incident was just good-natured fun between friends.

"Game!" John yelled.

Mike and Alex turned in time to see Declan grab the ball from the back of the net and fire it across the gym. They laughed as Declan stormed out of the gym.

"You're kind of cute when you get angry," Mike joked.

On occasion, Mike's personality mimicked John's, though Mike knew when he had to buckle down and get serious. He was one of a handful of students at West who came from an upper middle-class family. His family was borderline wealthy. It showed in the brand new black and white Camaro Rally Sport he had gotten for his seventeenth birthday and his seemingly endless supply of Jordache and Sergio Valente jeans and Lacoste and Ralph Lauren Polo shirts.

"And you're kind of a dick when you know you're going to lose," Alex said.

"Good thing I don't lose too often," Mike said, offering no denial. "We're going to Kwan's house to have a few beers and play poker if you want to come," Mike offered.

Kwan's real name was John Darvick, but aside from teachers and his parents no one had called him John in nearly four years. The moniker had come during a night of drinking beneath the bleachers during the summer between seventh and eighth grade when some football players were debating the hotness of the junior high cheerleaders. No one remembered exactly how it happened other than it had come from Mike just before he deposited a large portion of his dinner in the middle of the group. John liked the nickname since it distinguished him from the other six Johns in the grade.

"I think I'll to pass, I'm pretty much tapped out," Alex said and pulled his Adidas tee shirt over his head and walked to the locker room to get a fresh one.

"If you change your mind, you know where to find us," Mike said.

Chapter 6

By the time Detectives Henderson and Tallerico stopped by the hospital late Sunday afternoon, Jevonte was able to sit semi-comfortably and speak in a hoarse whisper. The detectives shook hands with Angelie, Jack, and finally Jevonte.

"It's good to see you awake," Henderson said.

"Thank you."

Based on Jevonte's appearance the previous day, Henderson hadn't expected to speak to him before Monday, and even then, he doubted Jevonte would provide any useful information. Seeing him awake and alert was cause for optimism.

"I'm sorry we have to meet under these circumstances, and while your wounds are still fresh, but the sooner we can get information out, the better our chances of catching the perpetrators," Henderson said in a reassuring tone that put everyone at ease.

Henderson was tall, muscular, and even though he was on their side, he was still intimidating. Seeing him the second time was comforting.

Henderson had grown up in a melting pot neighborhood in Queens where his friends spanned many ethnicities. Things he learned about their cultures and traditions helped him identify with people he dealt with on the job.

Tallerico was a few inches shorter, but the intensity that shone through his brown eyes made him equally imposing. He had grown up several miles away in Rockville Centre, a town still nearly devoid of minorities. He learned from observing the subtle differences in Henderson's interactions with minorities and white people, which changed from case to case depending on his initial impression. Tallerico often called Henderson a master manipulator, but Henderson insisted he was simply good with people.

"Do you think you'd be up to answering some questions?" Henderson asked.

The swelling around Jevonte's eyes had gone down considerably and he was able to look to his father for guidance. "Sure," Jevonte said after getting a slight nod.

Daryl entered the room and after greeting his aunt and uncle was introduced to the detectives. "Do you want me to wait outside?"

"I was with Daryl all day Friday, and he was the last person I talked to before I started walking home." Jevonte wanted Daryl in the room to get an opinion on the detectives. His parents had been impressed, but Daryl was a better judge.

"Every bit of information helps," Henderson said.

Daryl sat between two bouquets on the windowsill.

Henderson sat on the edge of the bed, making sure to be gentle so he wouldn't cause Jevonte discomfort. Tallerico pulled a chair over from the opposite side of the room and took out a pad and a pen.

"This might be a bit tedious, but I'm going to start from the beginning. How were you feeling when you left your uncle's house?" Henderson asked.

"I was a little tired and my uncle thought it would be better to drive me home, but it was a clear night and I figured I could see the stars from one of the clearings in the woods. There's less light pollution there."

"Light pollution?" Henderson asked.

"When there are a lot of lights close together it makes it difficult to view the stars."

"I had no idea," Henderson said.

"Being in the National Honor Society is no fluke," Tallerico added.

"You got that right," Daryl said.

"Jevonte loves astronomy," Angelie added.

Henderson flipped back through his notes. "Your uncle moved in on Friday, but it sounds like you had been through the woods before."

"No, that was my first time."

"How did you know about the bridge and clearings?"

Angelie saw Jevonte shift and helped adjust his pillows.

"We've driven past the pond and the woods plenty of times, and during the winter when there are no leaves on the trees, you can see straight through to the houses on the far side. It looked like you can see pretty much everything from the bridge they added a few years ago, or from the big clearing in the middle where they play football in the snow."

"Your observation skills are impressive," Tallerico said.

Beneath his bandages, Jevonte could feel himself blush.

"Did you notice anyone else before you were attacked. Is there any chance they spotted you earlier and followed you?" Henderson asked.

Jevonte almost shook his head, which would have been painful, but stopped himself. "I was wearing headphones and listening to a Michael Jackson cassette on my Walkman, and I heard loud music coming from the overpass." He hesitated a moment and then said, "One of them talk my Walkman and threw it in the pond."

"The one you just got for your birthday?" his mother asked. She looked to Henderson. "He just got it last month."

"I'm sorry," Henderson said. "Hopefully, we'll catch them, and they'll have to make restitution."

"Did you recognize the other music?" Tallerico asked, to get the interview back on track because he knew the likelihood of getting the money back was unlikely.

"Not really. It was definitely rock, though."

"Do you think you were targeted, or was it a case of being in the wrong place at the wrong time?" Henderson asked, to confirm his theory.

"Wrong place, wrong time, wrong skin color," Jevonte said and took a sip of his 7-Up and cleared his throat.

"Wrong skin color?"

"They said, 'Niggers don't belong in Malbrook,' or something like that."

Rather than having the detectives ask questions, Jevonte described his attack for them in vivid, though slightly altered details, and intentionally changed the descriptions of his attackers. He answered questions when they needed clarification and told them about the Malbrook West windbreaker he had seen and let them believe it was worn by one of his attackers. He knew they wanted justice for him, and the idealism within them probably believed they could get it, but Jevonte believed equal justice was a myth. He had already heard two people on television say that if the situation was reversed, black teens would be facing time in a juvenile detention center while their white counterparts in his case would likely get nothing more than slaps on their wrists from a judge, and pats on their backs from their friends.

Jevonte felt a pang of guilt when the detectives thanked him before they left, and probably believed they had a better chance to apprehend his attackers. In a perfect world Jevonte would have trusted the justice system. But he had seen first-hand that the world was far from perfect.

*   *   *

After he finished breakfast on Monday morning, Alex felt rejuvenated. Thoughts of Friday night still swam laps in the back of his mind, but at the forefront were the school year ahead and the conditioning program he had completed twenty minutes ahead of his six-thirty goal. The sit ups, pushups, pull-ups, and three mile run were finished with enough time to take a hot shower and eat a bowl of Cheerios at a pace that was more suited to a human than his usual pace, which was the equivalent of shoveling dirt in a hole. He had just finished brushing his teeth in the downstairs bathroom when he heard several gentle taps on the side door. He grabbed his books and met John at his car.

When John turned off the stereo as soon as he sat, Alex knew something was wrong. Usually, John cranked up the volume for a few seconds to clear any lingering cobwebs from Alex's head before the ride to school.

"What gives?"

"I'm guessing you didn't see the paper yet," John said.

Alex shook his head. For a moment he thought the police might have arrested Marco, Jimmy, and Tommy, but knew John would have been smiling if that had happened. John handed him an article he'd taken from the Daily News after he told his father it was extra credit for a current events project. His father's laugh made John doubt he believed him.

Alex read the smaller column on the left first. He smiled as he read Jevonte's condition, which was better than he anticipated, and suggested he might be released from the hospital by the end of the day, but his smile turned to a look of panic as he read the descriptions of Jevonte's attackers in the second article.

"Aside from—" Alex stopped as he read the last paragraph. "One of his attackers was wearing a Malbrook West windbreaker?"

"Messed up, right?"

Alex ran his hand through his hair. *How could Jevonte have gotten everything so wrong?* He wondered if a concussion could distort a person's memory.

"What should I do?" Alex asked. "The descriptions are all wrong."

"He did say his attackers were all white, and as much as I hate to break it to you, nine out of ten people would say you're oriental."

"And the tenth?" Alex asked.

"Probably mongoloid, but definitely not white."

Alex wished he could find humor the way John always did, but his entire future seemed to hinge on one stupid year of high school. At least John was right about him not being white. But that was from John's perspective as a white person. People of different races might see others differently. He had heard many white people say all black and Spanish people looked alike, so why couldn't a black person say the same about other races? *Could Jevonte think all light-skinned people look alike?* It still wouldn't explain getting the heights wrong.

Alex took off his windbreaker and shoved it under the passenger seat.

"What are you doing?"

"I can't wear it," Alex said.

"Oh, I get that, but why would hiding it in *my* car be a good idea? If the police take a stroll through the parking lot and catch a glimpse of that jammed under my seat, *I'll* look guilty. And most people think *I'm* white." John managed to sound serious but laughed when Alex pulled his windbreaker out.

"What?"

"Chill out, I'm kidding. There's no way anyone could see your jacket balled up and jammed under the seat."

"Don't mess with me," Alex said.

John sped up and hit the bump at the entrance to the school parking and Alex slammed his head into the roof.

"What did I just say?"

"I'm helping take your mind off it," John said.

"By giving me a concussion? Thanks a lot."

John intentionally made a sharp left turn into one of the closest parking spaces and slammed on his brakes to stop just shy of the curb. Alex crashed into the door and braced himself so he wouldn't hit the dashboard.

"You're welcome," John said.

John grabbed his bottle of RC Cola and checked under the cap to see if he won any money. Nope. He waited for Alex to grab his books from the floor before he locked the door and reminded Alex to do the same. Now that he had a new stereo, he checked twice to make sure his door was locked and made Alex do the same.

"Where are your books?" Alex asked.

John had only a brown lunch bag, and at the rate he was eating, it would be in the garbage before he entered the building.

"Nobody takes books home the first weekend."

"I guess no one told them," Alex said and nodded toward the group entering the school in front of them where each person had at least two or three books.

"We're seniors," John said, as if it explained everything.

Alex pulled the door open and put an arm across John's chest to stop him as he was about to walk through.

"Ladies first," Alex said, and held the door for two pretty junior girls.

"Thank you, Alex," Lisa Mills said, and Stacy Haber smiled politely.

"You're welcome," Alex said, and then shoved John through and followed him into the hallway outside the gym.

"Try not to look guilty," John said just before the brim of his backward facing Yankees cap was slapped and sent flying in front of him. John knew who it was without turning. "Thanks a lot, dick."

Mike picked up the cap, brushed off imaginary dirt and placed it on John's head the proper way. "There. All better?"

"No," John said as he turned the cap around. "How many times do I have to tell you to respect all things Yankee? Twenty-two World Series Championships and counting."

"My team's only been in existence eighteen years," Mike said, referring to the Mets. "But I'll give it to you, the Yankees may have the best team money can buy, even if they don't have the best record."

"Finally, you admit it," John said.

Alex hoped Mike hadn't heard John's comment before he knocked off his hat.

"That wasn't a compliment," Mike said. "They bought their last two championships."

"Face it, everyone wants to play for the Yankees."

"Because they pay them more than anyone else will. If they don't win it all this year, I bet they'll pay someone two or three million dollars a year to play for them," Mike said a little louder than he intended and two eighth grade boys turned to look at him. "What are you two homos looking at?" he asked, which was all it took to ensure they wouldn't look his way again. "They're ruining baseball."

"You're just jealous because the best players want to play for the Yankees," John said.

"Because they pay them more than any other team will!"

"Exactly!" John said.

"Do you even understand that we're arguing?" Mike asked incredulously.

The first bell rang, and seventh graders facing their first Monday of the school year scrambled as if their lives depended on making it to the appropriate classroom before the next bell. Even the eighth graders who had done the same thing the previous year laughed at the mad scramble.

"I'll catch you guys at lunch," John said.

"You don't have the same lunch period as us," Mike said.

"I have study hall fifth, so it's the same thing."

"I thought you have study hall third," Alex said as he grabbed a book from his locker and closed it.

"So?" John said.

"How many classes are you taking?" Mike asked.

"I have gym or physics first period depending on the day, then physics second period, you know my third, fourth, and fifth, then I have English sixth, calculus seventh, and I finish up with a class on historical fiction."

"He's taking three classes and an elective?" Mike asked when John walked away.

"You realize it's John you're talking about?"

John was loyal almost to a fault, but took nothing seriously, especially school. He had never been a note taker, yet he excelled at taking tests with little effort. He finished his graduation requirements by the end of eleventh grade and while most students in his situation would have taken advanced placement classes that counted towards college, John decided senior year would be about having fun. He reasoned that once he began studying aviation at Farmingdale University, he would have to work his ass off.

John's original plan was to join the Air Force. That lasted until his father informed him of the strict discipline involved, and the likelihood he would never get to fly jets. He gave up on the Air Force idea after putting together five model airplanes, three of which he later learned were Navy fighters. He had wanted to be a pilot since he was five and travelled with his parents to his aunt's wedding in Texas. "Love at first flight," his mother had called it, and it never abated.

*   *   *

Before anyone even settled in, the first announcement of the day extended homeroom by ten minutes. Alex didn't mind since his first class was home economics, and the only reason he had taken it was to spend time with Julie, who was taking the class as a junior. It hadn't worked out though since Julie had home economics sixth period, and neither could switch because of schedule conflicts.

Alex's homeroom teacher was Mr. Mullen, a short, portly social studies teacher who decided over the summer that his brown toupee wasn't fooling anyone and discarded it to embrace his baldness. Alex thought the natural look worked better for him.

As Mr. Mullen took attendance, Alex couldn't shake the feeling that his eyes seemed to linger on him longer than usual. He wanted to dismiss the thought as ridiculous, but the morning news was still eating at him.

The ten minutes that followed attendance were spent recapping the events from the previous Friday night, followed by the standard, "Anyone with information should speak to the police, their guidance counselor, a teacher, or a responsible adult they trust."

*   *   *

The discussion at the lunch table was dominated by who everyone was going to suggest for bids at the Phi meeting that night. There was a consensus on a few who would receive bids, while other suggestions garnered skepticism. Alex was happy to talk about something other than Friday night.

"How many bids do you think we'll give out this year?" Andrew Clarkson asked. Andrew was a skinny sophomore who ran cross country and was a member of the student council and the drama club. He was a solid student, but in a chapter dominated by jocks who played football, basketball and baseball, his smaller size and lack of elite athletic skills had led to a spirited debate about giving him a bid the prior year. He aced his interview, acted as a model "dog," as high school fraternities called their pledges, and was an all-around good brother.

"We have eleven seniors, so I think Kyle said he wanted to give out at least eighteen bids."

"Why eighteen?" Andrew asked.

"Kyle wants to make sure that each senior is replaced," Alex said.

"Why eighteen if there are only eleven seniors?" Andrew asked.

"One or two will blow their interviews, because that happens every year. Another one, maybe two, will quit while pledging because they're used to having things done for them and can't hack it when it's the other way around," Mike said. "And for some reason beyond comprehension, a couple will choose not to join."

"Kyle knows what he's doing," Alex said. "He wants to leave the chapter in better shape than when we joined."

Kyle was the chapter president and one of the top students in West's senior class. Tall, lean, and handsome, the blond haired, blue-eyed chapter president came from one of the wealthiest families in Malbrook. Despite being able to afford a home in one of Long Island's more exclusive neighborhoods, both of his parents, who had grown up in Malbrook, wanted to raise their children in more modest circumstances so they wouldn't grow up feeling entitled. They didn't want their children to be in constant competition over who had the nicest clothes or cars. With an upbringing that kept him grounded, Kyle was one of the nicest kids in the school.

"Is it true that Kyle wants to give bids to niggers?" Andrew asked, and immediately dropped several notches in the eyes of some brothers at the table.

"If I ever hear you use that word again, I'll hit you so hard that when you wake up your clothes will be out of style," Mike said. Despite the message, his voice never rose above his normal speaking volume.

Alex wasn't sure which amused him more, Andrew's fear or Mike's anger. Mike probably used the word more than anyone Alex knew.

"But . . . I've heard you use it before," Andrew said.

"When you look in the mirror who do you see?" Mike asked.

Andrew took a moment to process the question before he said, "Me."

"That's right. When you look in the mirror and see my face staring back at you, you can say it! Until then you refer to them as colored, black or negroes. Understand?"

"Yes," Andrew said though his expression suggested otherwise.

"Isn't it against the rules to let *niggers* in?" Richie asked.

Richie Dillon was no longer the athlete he'd been as a freshman two years earlier, and his muscular frame had been overrun by fat. His current friends were considerably different than when he joined Phi. He had blown a promising athletic career with self-indulgence and a swelled head and blamed everyone but himself when he was sent from the varsity to the junior varsity football team before being cut for having a bad attitude. Since then, he had distanced himself from his friends on the football team, which included many of his Phi brothers.

"First of all—and this goes for everyone—lose the word nigger from your vocabularies right now. I hear you say it and you'll answer to me," Mike said.

"Ooh, I'm scared," Richie said, and shook his hands in mock fear.

"You're too stupid to be scared," Mike said. "But you should be."

"If you've got a problem, we can take it outside," Richie said.

"Unfortunately, you're in Phi, and being an asshole doesn't give me the right to kick your ass. But everyone knows you care more about your pothead friends than you do about Phi, so if you stand up right now and say, 'I quit

Phi,' I'd be happy to go outside and kick the shit out of you."

"What if I don't want to say it?"

"Everyone will know you're a pussy," Mike said.

"Why don't *you* stand up and quit?" Richie asked.

"I'm not the asshole, Rich, you are," Mike said, and everyone at the table laughed.

"He has a really good point," Alex said. "You are an asshole."

Richie glared at Mike and stood up and said, "I quit Phi!" He turned to Mike and said, "Now let's go outside so I can fuck up your face."

Mike picked up his tray, dumped the contents in the garbage, and sat.

"Let's go!" Richie said.

"No one tells a Phi brother what to do!" Mike said.

"We'll see what everyone says about you being a chicken shit at tonight's meeting," Richie said.

"You can't come to the meeting, you just quit," Mike said.

"Everyone at this table heard you," Alex said as he stood next to Mike.

"I was joking," Richie said.

"That's not something you joke about, dick," Mike said.

"You're out," Alex said.

"You two better hope I don't catch you alone."

Mike and Alex shook their hands in mock fear as Richie had earlier. "I think he might be threatening us," Mike said.

"He can't be *that* stupid, can he?" Alex asked.

"Well, he is an asshole, so it's possible," Mike said.

"Fuck yous both," Richie said. He dumped his tray in the garbage and stormed out.

"I can't believe you got him to quit," Alex said.

"That asshole never belonged in Phi in the first place," Mike said.

Alex looked at Andrew, who was still trying to grasp what had just happened and said, "Just so you know, we have chapters on Long Island and in New Jersey where our black membership outnumbers whites."

The bell rang and Alex and Mike headed out of the cafeteria. They were halfway down the hall when John caught up with them. Mike turned just in time to avoid getting a slap on the back of his neck.

"What happened to meeting us for lunch?" Mike asked. "If I'd known you weren't going to show I would have moved my car out of the lot before third period so I could have driven."

"Yeah, thanks a lot," Alex added. "I love cafeteria pizza."

"Mr. Frasier wouldn't let me leave study hall," John said.

"That might have been more convincing if you came from his classroom," Mike said.

"Not to mention we saw you come in," Alex added.

John looked back down the hall and said, "There's no way you could've seen."

"We didn't until you just admitted it, asshole," Mike said. "Now, what's with the goofy grin?"

"I just got a blowjob from the hottest girl in eleventh grade," John said.

"I'm almost afraid to ask who that might be," Mike said.

"Katy Becker."

"You ditched us for Katy Becker?" Mike asked. "Do you know how many guys she's gone down on?"

"Add one more to the list," John said.

"Please tell me you at least checked her mouth before you let her blow you," Mike said.

"Why would I check her mouth?"

"She has herpes. If she had an open sore, she could give you herpes two," Mike said. "That's two as in the number, not as in also. She could've given you genital herpes." Mike cringed for effect.

"Is that true, Alex?" John asked.

"If someone with herpes gives you a blowjob while they have an open sore, yes, it's true," Alex confirmed.

"Fuck me," John said.

"That's what you should have told her," Mike said.

"What difference would that make?" John asked.

"Everyone knows you can't have herpes one and two, so if her mouth has it, her pussy can't," Mike said.

"Is that true, Alex?"

"What am I, the herpes expert?" Alex said. "He's messing with you. She doesn't have herpes. But it serves you right for being an asshole."

"We could have kept this going for days," Mike said, and shook his head in disappointment.

∗   ∗   ∗

Since Kyle's induction in ninth grade, nearly every Phi meeting of the West High chapter had been held in his house. The spacious family room in the rear with pocket doors that sealed the sound out of the front of the house and sliding glass doors that led to the spacious backyard made it an ideal meeting room. The property was nearly twice the size of the standard lot in Malbrook, which meant induction parties that doubled as fundraising keg parties, were also held there.

Kyle's father, Albert, had been a member of Phi in the Canarsie section of Brooklyn from 1951 until he graduated in 1955, and considered it the best part of his high school experience. He shared his high school fraternity stories with Kyle and was thrilled when he joined West High's chapter. Albert considered it his chance to give back to the fraternity that added so much to his youth, and to his son, and a new generation of Phi brothers. Kyle was a legacy but had earned brotherhood and the presidency on his own merit.

With gavel to block, Kyle called the meeting to order at seven-thirty. The secretary noted the time in the book before reading the minutes from the previous meeting, which was one of four held during the summer and had taken place three weeks earlier. As always, the first meeting of each school year was spent suggesting candidates for bids and debating their qualifications. A second set of bids would go out in the early spring to students who had transferred to West High prior to or during ninth grade.

Kyle sat at the center of the officer's table, which also accommodated the vice president, treasurer, secretary, and at times, the sergeant-at-arms. As the minutes were read by Lucas Price, Kyle watched the expressions of members who hadn't attended the previous meeting when they had discussed giving bids to black students. It was no secret, and the reactions were what he expected. The house shook for a full minute after the treasurer, Carl Keppler, announced that after hosting four parties during the summer, they had $468.50 in their treasury. The applause was just as loud when he announced that with half the profits from each party being set aside for charity, they had so far raised $401.00 that would be used to buy toys to donate to Toy for Tots. They needed another $109.00 to surpass the March donation they had made to the Easter Seals Telethon.

With the formalities out of the way, Kyle stood to address the room. "I have spoken to many brothers about an issue I feel is quite important for the future success of this chapter. I have spoken to some who are here now, as well as others who have graduated in the past five to ten years and I've gotten views from more brothers than I initially thought possible," Kyle started. "I am happy to report that the views were remarkably one-sided. I'm sure everyone in this room knows what I'm talking about, so I officially make a motion that for the first time in our chapter's history we give bids to black students who fit the criteria of our brotherhood." Kyle didn't have to wait to gauge the reaction as half the brothers in the room shouted, "Second."

"Hold on a second before we take a vote on this," Angelo Martello said. "What possible benefit would they bring to our fraternity? It's bad enough they're moving into our town and taking spots on our sports teams. Some people are saying that two of the starting five on our basketball team are gonna be niggers."

Kyle had anticipated opposition when he saw Angelo sitting beside Barry Shannon. Neither had attended summer meetings or parties. Angelo had beaten Barry to the objection by a fraction of a second. If Richie hadn't quit earlier in the day, he would have rounded out the group. Along with Richie, Angelo and Barry typically used their free time away from sports to dabble in marijuana and when Angelo could get it from his mother's medicine cabinet, Valium. The three of them would almost certainly move on to harder drugs.

"That is actually a great point," Kyle said. "It does seem likely that two of the five starters on our basketball team will be black, and one of them will be taking my starting guard position."

"We can't hold that against them," Alex said.

"Alex is right," John agreed. "And since Alex is graduating this year, we're losing the one half-minority brother we have. I don't think any of us want to pass down a chapter with no minorities." John's words broke the slight tension in the room, and even got a smile from Kyle.

"I want to be clear that I wasn't suggesting we keep them out because they take positions from white athletes. Rather, I think we should recognize their achievements by giving them bids. If someone is better at my position than me, they deserve to start. Phi is synonymous with superior athletes and students. I was reminded many times while talking to brothers that skin color should never be a factor."

The cheers Kyle received came as a surprise. The stony-faced looks from Barry and Angelo did not.

"Before you all start celebrating, there's something you should consider," Barry said. "If you let niggers in this fraternity, I don't want to be a part of it."

"That goes for me, too," Angelo said.

"I hereby accept your resignations from this fraternity," Kyle said.

"What do you mean resignations?" Angelo asked.

"You just stated you don't want to be a part of this fraternity as we move forward. That is a resignation," Kyle said. "Will the sergeant-at-arms please escort our two former brothers out?"

"Gladly," Declan said, as he lifted the officer's table forward so he could step out from behind it.

"I'm not quitting," Barry said.

"Too late, you already did," Declan said. "Now, you can both leave, or I can make you both leave."

Any thought of protest ended when every brother in the room stood to back Declan. Declan opened the door and waited for the two to leave before he closed and locked it.

"Good riddance," John said.

"I believe that's the first time in our chapter's history we had three brothers quit in one day. It's a good thing though because it opens up the opportunity to let new brothers in. If we hadn't gotten rid of the worst, they could have, and most likely would have, blocked any chance we had to integrate our chapter."

"How do you want me to enter this in the minutes?" Lucas asked. He was a junior who had been elected secretary at the previous meeting.

"Write it any way you can understand and explain it. Change the derogatory term they used to N, dash, dash, dash," Kyle said. A motion never to use the word again at meetings or fraternity run events was passed without opposition.

"Are we going to do this on a trial basis and limit the number of black pledges?" Alex asked after being recognized by Kyle.

"Why should we do that?" Kyle asked.

"We really don't know any of them that well. They might be smart kids and great athletes, but how can we be sure they belong in Phi?"

Earlier in the day, Kyle asked Alex to bring up the subject because Alex was a brother that everyone respected.

"That's a great point," Kyle said. "Based on the standards of our chapter, I've had some help identifying eleven eligible black students. If we only give out a few bids it might look like we're trying to divide and conquer. We need to be all in or forget it completely."

"I say all in," Mike said. "I make a motion that we give bids to all those who Kyle suggests."

His enthusiasm and motion were met with some skeptical looks.

"Second," John and Alex said simultaneously.

"All in favor?" Kyle said.

Nearly every hand in the room went up.

"All opposed?" Kyle said and all hands remained down. "Let the record reflect that nineteen brothers were in favor, none were opposed, and one abstained."

"Wait. Who didn't vote?" Mike asked.

"Me," said a brother named Justin who just started his sophomore year.

"Why?"

"You remember my brother, right? He's a dick about things like this and thinks we should keep blacks out. He's going to ask if I voted to include them, and while I agree with our decision, when he asks, I can honestly say that I didn't vote for it and maybe he won't kick my ass."

"Just so you all know, I approved his decision not to vote earlier today. His brother Seth was one of the few people I spoke to who opposed letting blacks in," Kyle said.

"I think today was a pretty great day," John said.

"Partly because you're an asshole," Alex said.

"What's that supposed to mean?" John asked.

"If you hadn't ditched us at lunch, Mike wouldn't have gotten Richie to quit."

"Okay, let's have a show of hands for who would ditch two brothers at lunch to get a blow job," John asked.

Everyone in the room raised a hand, including Mike and Alex.

"Thank you!" John said, and raised his arms in a triumphant V.

"Okay, that's fair," Mike said. "Now let's have a show of hands for who would have ditched two brothers at lunch if the girl who was blowing you *behind the A&P* was Katy Becker?"

"Katy Becker? I wouldn't let her suck my thumb," Declan said, and shook his head in disappointment.

John quietly pulled his Yankee cap down over his face.

Chapter 7

When the final bell rang Tuesday afternoon, Marco finished his swastika doodle before gathering his books to leave. He stayed in on Saturday and Sunday, and on Monday everyone he spoke to told him the nigger was blaming West High students for the attack. Marco had also sent friends to find Alex's girlfriend's house on Monday, and they hadn't disappointed with their information. If Alex showed up today, Marco and his friends would make him regret Friday night.

At his desk in the back of the last row, Marco closed his notebook and stood. When he reached the front of the classroom, Mr. Schwartz blocked his exit. With his desk to Marco's left, and a row of student desks to Marco's right there was no room for Marco to step around him.

"Do you mind? School's over; I'd like to leave."

"I'd like to talk to you about your first test score," Mr. Schwartz said.

"What kind of teacher gives a test on the fourth day of school?"

"I went over every question on the test during Friday's class," Mr. Schwartz said. "My intention was to have everyone begin with a high grade to start the year."

"How'd that work out for ya?"

"Aside from your forty-eight, it worked out very well. The other students in the class averaged a ninety-three."

"Great for them."

"I'm offering you a chance to make up the test tomorrow after school, and I'll use the higher of the two grades. Does that sound fair?"

"Can I go now?" Marco asked. His eyes never rose to meet Mr. Schwartz's.

"I'm trying to help you," Mr. Schwartz said as he stepped aside.

At twenty-seven, Ben Schwartz was still an idealist. He knew Marco would likely ignore his offer and stick with his failing grade, but he refused to give up on any of his students, even if they had given up on themselves. He had seen several of his past students make great strides to begin the new school year, and that made him even more determined to help Marco.

*　　　　*　　　　*

The couch in Julie's living room—or sofa in the parlor as her parents called it—was beautiful, but uncomfortable. It was low and narrow with a back that was six inches shorter than most other couches. It seemed to have been designed to keep visitors from overstaying their welcome.

Alex sat with the requisite six-inch gap between Julie and himself. Her hand rested on his between them. Across the room, Leonard Fishman poured cognac from a bottle of Louis XIII Napoleon Brandy into an over-sized snifter. The bottle hadn't contained the original cognac in years because each time he emptied it, he refilled it with Remy Martin VSOP. He told only his wife, who would never have allowed him to buy an eight-hundred-dollar bottle of cognac every two months, despite a salary which rendered the cost a non-issue. His friends, however, thought him generous to share it, most complimenting the exceptional smoothness and taste they could have gotten at their local liquor store for less than forty dollars.

Leonard Fishman was a short, rotund man who struggled through the late 1960s and the early 1970s to get his delivery service in Manhattan to profitability, and then acquiring his competition or driving them out of business. He had worked hard for his wealth and when he furnished his newest office on the forty-third floor of the Larsen Building on Fifth Avenue it bespoke his accomplishments. When he closed his office door each morning to begin work, his tie was loosened, and his jacket was hung in the corner on a two-thousand-dollar gold coat rack before he sat behind his impressive antique mahogany desk.

"You don't seem like yourself today," Julie whispered, tilting her head slightly in front of Alex so her curly chestnut hair blocked his view of the television.

He smiled, but as usual when her father was in the room, it looked forced. Leonard Fishman had made it clear that Alex wasn't good enough for his daughter. Alex wasn't Jewish, which was the first and only necessary strike against him, though Alex was certain from other equally prejudicial and often offensive remarks, that if religion hadn't been a factor, his mixed ethnicity would have been equally damning to their relationship. And though Mr. Fishman had never said it, Alex was certain his family wasn't wealthy enough to meet Mr. Fishman's standards.

Alex was just standing to leave when a news anchor appeared on television and said, "Coming up at five, go behind the scenes of Reverend Ralph's march—"

Alex quickly reached behind Julie, grabbed the remote and clicked off the television before the anchor finished the sentence. The television's wireless remote was the only thing in the house besides Julie that Alex liked. It was a luxury that made sense.

"Thank you," Leonard said, assuming it was Julie who had turned it off since only family members were permitted to use the remote. "I've heard as much on that subject as I can take."

"They're marching on Saturday," Julie said.

Lawrence put his Daily News crossword puzzle in his lap and sipped his cognac. "They can march until doomsday, and it won't make one bit of difference."

"Why is that, Mr. Fishman?" Alex asked.

"Because Malbrook is a predominantly white town, and no one cares about his march," Lawrence said. He rarely gave Alex the courtesy of looking at him as he spoke, and this was no exception.

"What do you think about what happened last Friday?" Alex asked, hoping Lawrence wouldn't hold anything back.

"It doesn't matter what I think. He's using that kid for his own political gain."

"I thought he was trying to promote racial equality and harmony," Julie said.

"If he wanted to promote racial harmony, why is he only present for crimes against his people? Racial harmony goes both ways, doesn't it? How come he was nowhere to be found when that white kid was jumped by two black teens in Freeport last month?" Lawrence asked.

"I don't remember hearing about a white kid getting jumped in Freeport," Alex said.

"That's my point. Black crimes against white people rarely get news coverage because they're so prevalent," Lawrence said.

"If they don't get news coverage, how do you know they're prevalent?" Alex challenged.

"This march is a supposed to be a really big deal," Julie said, unintentionally helping her father dodge the question.

"Important to who? No one in Malbrook cares about his march," Lawrence said. Frustrated with his inability to concentrate, he tossed the paper in the magazine rack beside the couch.

"Isn't it important to the black community? It's a free country. Don't black people have the right to be in Malbrook?" Alex asked.

"That kid shouldn't have had a reason to be in Malbrook!"

"I'm not sure I'm following you," Alex lied.

"This all started last year when those two morons burned a cross on that black family's lawn," Lawrence said.

"How does that relate to this?" Alex asked.

"That cross burning brought all kinds of unwanted attention to Malbrook. And once that happened, people started to panic. And when people panic, they sell."

"So, how did that change anything?" Alex asked, forcing the conversation to continue. The aggravation in Lawrence's voice gave Alex satisfaction.

"Once news of the cross burning broke, white people didn't want to buy houses in Malbrook, because they know there are black people living here," Lawrence said. He swirled the cognac in his glass then took a sip.

"But why would black people want to move here after a cross burning?" Alex asked.

Lawrence was obviously annoyed with the conversation but apparently felt compelled to put Julie's boyfriend in his place. "Because the people who panicked sold their homes for below market value, and gave more black families a chance to move in."

"So, the white people who sold were stupid, and black people who bought were smart," Alex said.

"They were so smart that at least fourteen black families moved to Malbrook in the past year," Lawrence said, fuming, as he took the bait.

"Fourteen? Are you keeping a tally?" Alex asked. For more than a year Alex had held his tongue as Lawrence spouted rude, racist, and elitist comments, and he was too tired to stay quiet any longer.

Lawrence turned to Alex and anger flushed his face. Alex had been looking out the window!

"I have an interest since I own a home in Malbrook," Lawrence said, and waited for Alex to face him. When Alex failed to do so, Lawrence said, "Show some respect and look at me when I'm talking to you."

"I was taught to show respect to those who show me respect, which you don't!" Alex said. "And here's a news flash: black people have the right to live in nice neighborhoods. And believe it or not, they're allowed to drink from any water fountain they want, they don't have to give up their seats on buses for white people, and they can go in the front door of any restaurant they choose. Welcome to 1980!"

Julie squeezed Alex's hand to quiet him. The tension between her father and Alex worried her.

"Leave my house!" Lawrence demanded with his eyes riveted to his snifter.

"Show some respect and look at me," Alex said, throwing Lawrence's words back in his face. "Unless you were talking to your fake expensive cognac, in which case I'd understand why you'd want it out of your house."

"Alex!" Julie cried. "You promised not to say anything! I'm not even supposed to know."

"I promised not to tell anyone *else*. *He* already knows it's not the real stuff," Alex said, as Lawrence's eyes finally met his smirk.

"You are no longer welcome in my house," Leonard said.

"No longer? I was never welcome in your house."

Julie followed Alex to the door and had to catch it before he closed it. "That's it? Not even a kiss goodbye?"

"I didn't think he'd let you follow me."

Julie had seen Alex lose his temper on one other occasion, but his face never turned its present shade of crimson. "You shouldn't let him get to you."

"Every time I come to your house I have to deal with his asinine comments, and you just sit there and pretend not to notice."

"I've pretended no such thing."

Alex contemplated the ramifications of his next sentence. It was a formality, since any chance of remaining a couple had been obliterated. He knew from the beginning they would break up, but always assumed he would be on the receiving end after Julie's father made her life miserable enough. Even as he walked across their living room—*not the fucking parlor as they called it*—he thought she'd stop him and yell that they were through. That would have been preferable.

"Aren't you going to say anything?" Julie asked.

"I've got to go," Alex said.

She grabbed the back of his shirt as he walked down the steps of her wraparound porch, but Alex pulled free. He collected his bike from behind the white privacy fence in the driveway and considered spitting on the windshield or Mr. Fishman's Jaguar but didn't. He walked his bike out and slammed the gate behind him.

"Bye," he said, and turned toward the street.

"You seriously have nothing else to say to me?"

"Like what?"

"Like, you're sorry for your behavior," she said with an annoying twang. The inflection wasn't common, and usually only happened when she was spoke of disagreements with her friends.

"*I'm* sorry? Sorry for what? Sorry your father's an asshole?" He looked through the open front door, raised his voice and said, "Okay, you win. I'm sorry your father's an asshole!" He had no doubt Mr. Fishman heard him. *Fuck him!*

"You can't talk about my father that way!" she yelled.

"That's right, you're the only one who can say anything bad about him." Alex made sure he could be heard in the house. "When he treats you like shit you say he's an asshole. Fuck that; he's an asshole all of the time!"

"Get out of here!" Julie yelled as her tears began to flow in earnest.

"Gladly. And when your father pisses you off, don't come looking for me, because it's over."

The words were so sudden and so final that Alex almost surprised himself.

If Alex had turned back, he would have seen Julie sit on the bottom step and sob into her crossed arms. A bit farther down the road he would have seen Jimmy's car pull from the curb. Seconds later, he would have seen Marco say something to Julie and Julie flip him off without ever looking up. But Alex never looked back.

*   *   *

"That bitch gave me the finger," Marco said, amused.

"Want me to stop?" Jimmy asked.

"Nah, we'll deal with her soon enough," Marco said. "Just hang back and keep Alex in sight."

The late afternoon sun was shining low in the west as Alex turned down a side street. He focused on riding; he would deal with the breakup later, along with his anger, pain, and relief. He alternated jumping his bike on the curb, riding a short distance, and hopping back down before the next driveway. As he turned on Kennedy Avenue, he caught a glimpse of Marco leaning out the passenger window of Jimmy's 1971 Cougar.

"Where ya goin', Alex?" Marco taunted. He took an aluminum bat from his lap and pointed it at Alex as if it were a rifle.

Alex looked back at the two and laughed. He now had a legitimate reason to beat the shit out of Marco. And Jimmy, too. He knew he would have to wait since it was highly likely that Jimmy also had a bat. He stayed on the sidewalk in front of the local businesses that lined the entirety of Kennedy. He would deal with Marco soon enough, and it would be on his own terms.

*   *   *

Jevonte settled in on the couch as his mother went upstairs to collect pillows from his bed. The doctors had urged his parents to keep him home from school for the week, which was only three days thanks to observation of Rosh Hashanah on Thursday and Friday. It would be the first time since second grade he was absent more than twice.

Though Angelie wanted Jevonte to rest, he convinced her to let Daryl pick up his school assignments. He looked like a different person since he left the hospital. The moment his wheelchair arrived at his father's waiting car, per hospital protocol, he felt the tension within him subside and his strength return.

Angelie returned and helped Jevonte move forward so she could slide two pillows behind him. He had a plastic tray table beside him with textbooks stacked on top.

"Comfortable?" she asked.

"More comfortable than I've been in days. Thanks, Mom."

Angelie leaned over and kissed his forehead. "If you need anything, let me know and I'll get it. Doctor Ross said you need to rest as much as possible." She left the room only after he agreed to call her if he needed anything.

Jevonte had no intention of keeping his promise. His parents had been through enough in the past few days and needed a break from the constant worrying and trips to the hospital. They needed the rest as much as he did.

The side door opened and closed, and Daryl walked in and dropped a folder on Jevonte's books. "How you feelin', cuz?"

"Not too bad," Jevonte said.

Daryl usually plopped down in one of the chairs immediately, but instead he leaned against the radiator cover.

"I'd ask how long you get to stay home from school, but in your case, I guess I should ask when you get to go back."

"Monday," Jevonte groused.

Daryl shifted his weight, then reached up and touched the ceiling.

"You seem kind of antsy. What's up?"

Daryl looked over both shoulders to be sure they were alone before he leaned closer to Jevonte and said, "We're going to pay Alex a visit."

"Who is *we?*"

"Isaiah, Tyrone and me. They're outside. Tyrone knows where Alex lives, and I figure I should get to know my new town a little better."

"Do you think it's a good idea? It's not too late for me to give the police Alex's name."

"We're just gonna catch up with him and see what he'll tell us, if anything. From the way you described him, I'm not sure he'd even give us his friends' names."

"They weren't his friends. I got the impression he didn't even like them," Jevonte said. "What if he won't give you names?"

"We'll thank him and be on our way."

"Why do I get the feeling there's more to it than that?" Jevonte asked.

"There's not. All we're going to do is talk. You have my word."

"Thanks, Daryl. For everything," Jevonte said, and held up the work Daryl had dropped off.

"No problem." Daryl stopped at the candy dish on the dining room table and took some Skittles. "When I was in high school, I wouldn't have thanked someone for dropping off schoolwork."

Jevonte nodded and smiled.

*   *   *

Aside from the occasional straggler, the sidewalks of Kennedy were empty as Alex rode through town. Jimmy followed at a safe distance, which Alex assumed was in case he changed direction. Alex knew he could lose them easily, even if he just stopped on a block with no parking on the right where Jimmy would be swept helplessly along with the flow of traffic. Alex had no intention of stopping or turning down one of the numerous alleys until he reached Hawthorne Street, which was the last block before Sunset. The warm breeze on his face and the chase, however slow, kept his mind off Julie.

The second to last block of Kennedy had an empty bus stop and Jimmy caught up and pulled closer to the curb. Marco leaned out the window and was nearly decapitated by a sign as he turned to grab his bat. Alex doubted Marco was stupid enough to throw the bat with the storefront windows behind him but couldn't rule it out completely. Alex was halfway across Hawthorne when he made a right turn. Jimmy cut the wheel sharply and nearly hit a parked car. A block later, just shy of the post office, an older woman with bluish gray hair pulled her ancient Chevy out of a parking lot in front of Alex. Alex stopped, spun his bike around and was past Jimmy before he could react.

"Turn around!" Marco yelled.

"It's a one way street," Jimmy said.

"Then back the fuck up!"

"I'll go around the block and catch up with him by the school. That's where we want him anyway," Jimmy said.

"We're not going to catch him at all with you driving two miles an hour."

Jimmy motioned to the Chevy and said, "I can't drive through her."

"Then go around her," Marco said.

Jimmy swerved left, went around her, and then cut her off as he made a right turn. The startled woman stopped inches shy of hitting them.

"Did you see that old bag's face?" Marco asked, laughing. "I thought she was gonna have a heart attack."

If Marco had been looking at Jimmy, he would have seen the same expression.

*   *   *

"Pull over so I can take a look at the map," Daryl said. Isaiah pulled to the curb in front of Wetzel Avenue Elementary School, just past the parking lot entrance. Daryl turned to Tyrone and said, "I thought you said you know where his house is."

"No, Isaiah said his house was by the school, and I said I know where the school is." Tyrone pointed. "Ta da!"

Daryl flipped the map over.

In the rearview mirror, Isaiah caught a glimpse of two young women pushing strollers. "Maybe they can help."

Daryl rolled down his window and leaned out. The moment the young mothers spotted him, they stopped and turned hastily in the opposite direction.

"I'm pretty sure I know where they'd tell us to go, because that did not look planned," Tyrone said.

"If you're not gonna help, keep your mouth shut," Daryl said.

Tyrone made a zipping motion across his mouth and tossed away the imaginary key.

"Where is the baseball field," Daryl said, looking up from the map.

"Am I allowed to speak?" Tyrone asked.

"Do you ever take anything seriously?" Isaiah asked.

"Absolutely," Tyrone said. "My second amendment rights, my fifth amendment rights, six of the Ten Commandments, and anything my mom says when she uses my middle name." The answer came so quickly it almost seemed rehearsed.

"You don't own a gun and you've never been asked to be a witness against yourself," Daryl said. "I get the mother part, but which four Commandments do you have a problem with?"

"I don't like the two about coveting. I mean, how can I control if my neighbor's wife is hot and makes me want to fuck her and drive off in her husband's Ferrari?"

"He's got a point," Isaiah said, and Daryl nodded in agreement.

"And the other two?" Daryl asked.

"I don't agree with the one about stealing, because some people are poor and have no other choice. And I definitely don't agree with the one about adultery."

"I'll give you stealing out of necessity, but you think you should be able to cheat on your wife?" Daryl asked.

"I'm not talking about cheating; I'm talking about sex when you're not married. Remember what Sister Kathleen told us in fourth grade?"

"You're an idiot," Daryl said. "If everything the nuns taught us was true, you would have gone blind from masturbating by the time you were fourteen."

"Hold up a sec. You're telling me I've limited my masturbating to preserve my eyesight, and it doesn't cause blindness?"

"Limited it to what? Three times a day?" Isaiah asked.

"Why, is three times a day a lot?" Tyrone asked.

"Shit," Isaiah said. He pulled to the corner and turned right.

"Where are you going?" Daryl asked.

"I think I saw the kid we're looking for cut through the schoolyard," Isaiah said. He drove to the next corner and made another right. He didn't want to draw any attention, so he drove at a more reasonable speed.

"What makes you think it was him?" Daryl asked, as Tyrone hummed the "Mission Impossible" theme song.

"He looked oriental, and he was riding a BMX bike."

"Good enough for me," Daryl said.

A block before they reached the opposite side of the school, they came to a stop sign at Surrey Lane. Isaiah recognized the name as Alex's block. "Check out the street sign. Should I go to the school, or his house?"

"Go to his house," Daryl said.

Isaiah drove slowly so Tyrone could check house numbers on the left while Daryl checked the numbers on the right. "That's it," Tyrone said.

Isaiah made a U-turn at the corner and parked in front of Alex's neighbor's house. "He was riding pretty fast, so he should be here any second."

*   *   *

Alex hopped his bike over the first speed bump in the school parking lot and heard Jimmy's car fishtail in behind him. They had done some homework, Alex thought.

Jimmy hit the first speed bump and momentarily lost control of his car before he slammed on the brakes and skidded to a stop.

"Why are you stopping?"

"I'm not gonna fuck up my car because of this asshole."

Alex rode to the concrete stairs on the right, but the gate at the top was closed and padlocked. With that option off the table, he continued straight and peeked back as Jimmy flashed his lights twice. He looked ahead and saw a car by the far exit pull towards him. There were still two options, and he decided to turn left toward the school's baseball field, which had so many rocks on the infield it was used only when spring was exceptionally rainy, and games had to be made up before the playoffs. He rode through the outfield grass, across the infield, and skidded to a stop on home plate, shooting rocks into the backstop and the eight-foot fence beyond it that backed up to a row of houses. The only way out was the way he had come.

Jimmy pulled up to a thick metal chain that stretched across the blacktop and was removed only when busses needed access before and after school. They exited the car, and just as Alex expected, each had a bat. They stepped over the chain and walked through the outfield.

"It's hell night, Alex," Marco called.

A Chevy Nova pulled beside Jimmy's car and the driver revved its engine several times before shutting it off. Peter stepped out of the driver's side, and Steven Price, the secretary of their chapter, stepped out of the passenger side.

Alex breathed a sigh of relief when he realized they were the only two in the car. It had occurred to him only after he reached the baseball field that if there were more than four, he would have had to swallow his pride and call to the houses beyond the fence for help. He recognized Peter from his size but couldn't identify Steven.

Steven was slightly taller than Marco, but thinner and less intimidating despite a similar haircut. He was liked by his brothers for his willingness to help without asking questions. Steven was the logical choice for president when Peter graduated.

Instead of following, Peter and Steven stayed with the cars, content to watch from a distance. If police stopped by, which was unlikely, Steven would drive Jimmy's car and Marco and Jimmy would climb the fence behind the backstop. Steven leaned in Jimmy's car to confirm the keys were in the ignition, then leaned against the top of the open door, just as Peter was doing on his car.

"This should be fun," Peter said.

"What did he do?" Steven asked. He had heard one version from Tommy and wondered if Marco's version matched.

"Let's just say he pissed off Marco and leave it at that," Peter said.

The subject was closed. He could only assume Tommy's version was accurate.

*   *   *

As they sat in front of Alex's house, Daryl began to feel uncomfortable. He folded the map and put it away.

"You sure the kid was oriental?" Daryl asked.

"Pretty sure. Want me to drive back to the school?"

"Might as well," Daryl said. "I don't want his neighbors calling the cops."

"I was thinking the same thing," Isaiah said.

"I wonder how fast police respond to calls around here," Tyrone said.

"Let's not find out," Daryl said.

*   *   *

Alex rode back and forth across home plate, keeping an eye on Marco and Jimmy as they walked through the outfield, and beyond them to the cars.

"You won't be walking away from this with teeth," Marco said.

Alex stopped his bike with his front tire on home plate and his back tire in the air and held it as he smirked at Marco.

"I'm gonna knock that stupid smile off your face in a minute!" Marco said. "As for your bike, I haven't decided whether I'll keep it, or bust it into pieces."

"Funny, but I don't see either option working out for you," Alex said, and let his back tire down.

"You won't think it's funny in a few minutes," Marco said as they reached the dirt infield between first and second base.

With Marco and Jimmy walking side by side, Alex knew he could easily ride along the first base line and leave them behind. As far as Alex could tell, the boys by the cars didn't have bats, so once he passed Jimmy and Marco, he was home free. As much as avoiding them made more sense, he refused to give Marco the satisfaction. He took a deep breath and rode straight at Marco, who was standing on Jimmy's left. If either of them threw their bat and hit him, he was in trouble, but he didn't think they would risk losing their weapon with an errant throw.

"He's gonna make it easy for us," Marco said, and readied himself in an awkward batter's stance.

Alex closed in, turned his handlebars sharply to the left and hit the brakes. Dirt and rocks shot up at Marco and Jimmy's faces, temporarily blinding them as Alex rode past.

Marco fumed as he wiped his eyes and gave chase, losing ground quickly as Alex rode straight for Peter's car. Marco pounded his bat into the ground in frustration.

Peter ran to one side of the chain, which allowed walkers and bike riders to pass, while Steven hurried to the other side. Alex rode full speed at Peter's car and jumped his bike over the chain and onto the Nova's hood, leaving a dent where he landed. He rode over the top of the car, jumped off the back and landed in stride. He held his right hand up with his middle finger extended.

"You're fucking dead!" Peter yelled when he saw the dents. He jumped in and barely waited for Steven to close the door before he put it in reverse and sped backward to the larger opening.

Marco jumped in Jimmy's car and pulled the door closed. Jimmy walked slowly to his car wiping blood from a gash over his left eye where a rock cut him. Marco rolled down the window and yelled, "Move your fuckin' ass!"

Jimmy didn't rush; Marco would have to wait. He settled in and turned his car around. Between the dirt and blood, his eyes refused to stay focused, and clarity came and went with each blink and swipe of his left hand.

"Why are you driving so slow? We're never gonna catch him like this!"

"I can't fuckin' see!"

Marco clicked open his switchblade, looked at the blade and said, "I'm gonna stick this in his fuckin' chest and twist it 'til his eyes roll back in his head."

*   *   *

Isaiah pulled to the curb near the back entrance of the school. The only bike they saw was three blocks away and was being ridden by a young boy.

"Before Tyrone says something stupid, that's not the kid I saw," Isaiah said.

"Are you sure?" Tyrone asked as he looked down the block.

"He's joking," Daryl said. "Now how 'bout Tyrone and me go check out the schoolyard."

"You want me to come?" Isaiah asked.

"Nah, we're good. Wait here," Daryl said.

Tyrone and Daryl walked to the corner of the school lot, which was hidden behind a tall row of hedges that ran the length of the backyards in the neighboring apartment building. Tyrone turned the blind corner just ahead of Daryl, and Alex hit him at full speed. Alex flipped awkwardly over the handlebars and his shoulder hit Tyrone's chest and sent him tumbling backwards on the sidewalk while Alex fell sideways into a low fence on the school's side of the hedges.

Peter saw the crash and skidded to a stop. Jimmy still couldn't see clearly and stopped too late to avoid hitting Peter's rear bumper. Peter looked back, pissed, and was about to open the door when he saw Daryl standing over Alex, and a few feet away, Tyrone sitting up and getting his bearings. Peter quickly decided two niggers on foot meant carloads were probably close by. He leaned on the horn and Steven waved for Jimmy to back up.

It took Jimmy a moment to understand before he pushed the shifter forward into reverse and pushed the pedal to the floor. Jimmy's car jerked to the left and the raised white GOODYEAR lettering on the tires and the Crager rims they were wrapped around scraped along the curb.

Alex held his head as he sat up and felt blood as it trickled from his scalp down to his left ear. He watched someone pick up his bike and roll it towards him.

"Are you okay?" Daryl asked as he offered Alex his hand. "You want to get up, or just sit a while?"

Alex clasped Daryl's hand and said, "I think I'm okay," and Daryl pulled him to his feet.

"Don't worry about me, I'm good," Tyrone said.

"That's what I figured," Daryl said, and winked at Alex.

"I'm sorry, I usually don't ride on this sidewalk, but the guys in those two cars were chasing me." Alex watched Tyrone get up slowly. "Are you okay?"

"He's fine," Isaiah answered as he joined them by the entrance. "He's pretty much indestructible as far as we can tell."

"I'm lucky you guys came along when you did," Alex said.

"It's karma," Daryl said. "You came along for Jevonte and now we're here for you."

"I'm not sure what you mean," Alex said, but couldn't hide the *Oh fuck!* look on his face.

"You're a good guy, but a bad liar," Tyrone said. He checked his elbow and saw blood coming through his shirt. "Girlfriends make you a better liar."

"Try to ignore most of what he says," Daryl said.

"If not all," Isaiah added.

"Seriously, I don't know what you're talking about," Alex said. This time he sounded more believable.

"I feel bad, then, because Jevonte is *really* good with details, but I don't have that gift," Daryl said.

"Jevonte is pretty much a genius. He don't miss a thing," Tyrone said.

"Like your Malbrook West wrestling jacket with Alex on the front. You were wearing it Friday night," Daryl said.

"And your fraternity shirt," Tyrone added.

"When Jevonte saw your name, it set a bunch of things in motion. We went to the library and checked out the wrestling team photo from your yearbook. Guess who was the only oriental kid on the team named Alex?"

"That would be you, Alex Moran," Tyrone said and smiled.

Alex wiped blood from his scalp with the bottom of his shirt and sat against the fence. He was mentally and physically exhausted.

"From there we checked the Malbrook phonebook, and luckily there was only one Moran, and when I called and asked for you, it turned out it was the right Moran, though you weren't available to talk," Daryl said. "We figured we'd give you some time to sort through your feelings, and here we are."

"Ta da!" Tyrone added, as he stepped toward Alex and spread his arms in a goofy dramatic gesture.

Alex couldn't deny it, and he wasn't sure if there was any sense anyway. They had seen his yearbook photo, so they knew they had the right guy.

"You sure you're okay?" Daryl asked. "You took a pretty good spill."

"It's been a long couple of days. When Jevonte said one of his attackers had a West windbreaker, I thought maybe his memory was jumbled and he thought I did it." Alex took a deep breath and said, "I can't believe you found me."

"According to Jevonte, once you got there the beating stopped, and he was able to focus better."

"They did a job on him before I got there, so I'm amazed he remembered anything."

"Jevonte said you made them look like the pussies they are." Daryl paused a moment and then added, "He also said you stayed with him until police got there, and that's when he saw your name."

"Yeah," Tyrone added, "Jevonte said the minute you got there the only beating was you pulling some crazy karate shit on a little guy with a big attitude." Tyrone did a spinning jump kick that almost caught Isaiah before he pretended to flip an invisible enemy. "He said you were a cross between Bruce Lee and Batman."

"Jevonte exaggerated," Alex said as he stretched his legs and leaned forward to touch his toes. "I twisted that little dipshit's arm behind his back and threw him on the ground, but that was it. Two basic wrestling moves."

Daryl sat on the ground beside Alex. "I guess you've probably figured out why we're here."

"I wasn't sure at first, but I'm guessing you want their names."

"What did you think we wanted at first?" Isaiah asked.

"I thought maybe Jevonte was confused and sent you guys to beat the shit out of me as payback."

"That would have sucked," Tyrone said. "You save someone, and then instead of a thank you, you get your ass kicked."

"Would you shut up and let him talk," Isaiah said.

"We promised Jevonte we would just leave if you didn't give us the names, so you have choices." Daryl rubbed his hands together and then put them on the knees of his Levis. "We know the kids who beat up Jevonte are your brothers from another chapter, so you might not be able to give us their names, and we respect that."

"You weren't kidding when you said Jevonte doesn't miss a thing." Alex marveled at the things Jevonte remembered and put together. "There's one thing I don't get though; why did he tell the police that one of the kids who beat him was from West High?"

"Jevonte knew you were the only one from West because you mentioned something about the other kid's chapter, which meant a different school," Daryl said. "He told the detectives he saw a Malbrook West jacket, but never said one of the attackers was wearing it. He didn't lie, he just let them draw the wrong conclusion." Daryl watched the *holy shit* look reappear on Alex's face again. "He figured if the police were concentrating on the west side of town, it would leave the other side free for us to find the kids responsible and take care of things. Once we realized how far you live from the school, we figured it wouldn't be a problem."

"After the shit they just pulled, I can give you their names with a clear conscience," Alex said, and ran a hand through his hair and found where the blood had come from. The bleeding had stopped, and the small cut had already started to clot.

The timing of both Marco and Jevonte's cousin and his friends couldn't have been better. If they had come a day earlier, Alex would have had to think hard before giving up the names, but after being chased by cars and threatened with bats, his only regret was that he wouldn't be there to see it happen.

"Were the guys in the cars the same ones who beat up Jevonte?" Daryl asked.

"No, the two assholes in the first car weren't part of it, but the two in the second car were. The third kid wasn't there. He's not like the other two." Alex reconsidered his statement and said, "Well, as far as I know he's not."

"Why did they come after you? You didn't talk to the police, and as far as they know, they're in the clear," Isaiah said.

"When I called that little asshole out, he walked away like a pussy, which isn't good for the reputation of a kid everyone thinks is crazy. He probably told the other guys I pulled a knife on him so they'd help him."

"If they came after you, how's your cousin?" Daryl asked.

"I haven't spoken to him. I guess I should call him."

"Do it soon," Isaiah said.

"Thanks, I will. And just out of curiosity, what would you have done if I didn't give you their names?"

"Jevonte would have called the detectives and given them all the details he left out, including your name, and the police would either show up at your school or your house and you'd have to tell them what you know," Daryl said.

"That's it?"

"The problem with that is their names probably wouldn't make it into the papers because they're probably minors, but your name would since you're the hero. For your good deed, you would probably be known as the kid from Malbrook who saved a black kid and turned in his white brothers." Daryl stretched his lips in opposite directions to accentuate the dilemma. "I'm new to Malbrook, so I'm not sure what it would do to your popularity, but in Rosedale you'd be watching your back until you moved far enough away that you had no chance of running into anyone you grew up with. We don't have fraternities, but no one—and I mean no one—fucks with the Knights."

Being chased made the decision easy for Alex. *Fuck them!* He wasn't giving the names to save himself from being ostracized, he was doing it because they deserved what they were going to get, and maybe the assholes from the other side of town would back off. The irony was they would probably have been better off getting arrested.

"I do have one other question," Alex said.

"Shoot," Daryl said.

"Did you purposely not tell me your names?"

"Sorry, that was unintentional. I'm Jevonte's cousin, Daryl." He gestured to the other two and said, "The mean looking one is Isaiah, and the goofy one you ran over is Tyrone."

"Mean looking?" Isaiah asked.

"Just a little," Daryl said, as he held two fingers a smidge apart.

Alex gave Daryl the names, as well as one or two others to be wary of since their chapter travelled in packs. He mentioned Tommy was a good kid who probably didn't deserve the same treatment, but assured Daryl he trusted Jevonte's memory more than his own judgment. He wasn't sure it would help Tommy, but at least when he spoke to Dave, he could say he tried.

Daryl wrote down his phone number for Alex and told him to call if there were any more problems.

Chapter 8

Isaiah's car disappeared around the corner as Alex checked his bike. Every emotion Alex had suppressed stormed to the forefront as he sat on his bike and rested his head on the crossbar. One Friday night on the other side of town had left him emotionally and physically drained twice. He had three new friends, yet never felt so alone. He wanted to go to his room and cry for everything that was wrong in his life. And his town. *His fucked up racist town!*

He considered the consequences from his interactions since school had ended. His relationship with Julie was over. Marco and Jimmy would get what they had coming to them, but aside from avenging one wrong with another, it wouldn't make things better and would probably just be another dark day in Malbrook's history. Had giving them the names been the best thing to do? He still had time to call Daryl and then the police to stop the potential escalation of racial tension that had permeated the air since Friday night. *Would their arrests even matter? Racial tension wouldn't go away.* And when it died down, he'd probably have to deal with Marco and his band of derelicts again.

He rode slowly to be sure his bike was okay. He wished he could say the same for himself, but his left shoulder and ankle were throbbing from his fall. Instead of leaving his bike behind the house under the awning like usual, he carried it down to the basement so he could check it thoroughly after dinner.

Alex limped up the stairs and stopped in the bathroom just off the kitchen. Like most homes in Malbrook with a second bathroom on the main floor, it contained a toilet, a small sink with a mirror above it and a trash can below. Alex cleaned off the dried blood he had forgotten about, tucked his shirt into his pants to hide the bloodstain, and kissed his mother on the cheek as he passed through the kitchen.

He sat on the couch in the living room and closed his eyes. He lifted his foot to untie his Nikes. He pushed off his right sneaker with his left foot, and then hooked the left sneaker under the couch to remove it.

Thankfully, the interviews, which in past years had been the night after bids had been given out, were scheduled for Thursday to give potential black pledges extra time to speak with Phi brothers to see if it was right for them. Alex considered it a lucky break since he wasn't sure he had the right mindset to judge anyone. Eighteen bids had been issued. Usually, the majority went to freshmen since it was the minimum grade requirement for induction in their chapter, but this year there had been more sophomore and junior bids than any year since the chapter's inception.

Alex heard his father's car pull in the driveway and listened for the side door. It didn't open immediately, which meant his father was talking with one of their neighbors. He was glad for the few extra minutes of rest. He hoped his father would go upstairs to change before dinner as he occasionally did so Alex could set the table without worrying about favoring his sore ankle.

The side door opened and closed, and Doug's entrance was nearly identical to Alex's. He washed up in the small bathroom, stopped in the kitchen to kiss Annie, and went to the living room.

"How was school?"

"No tests and not much homework, so no complaints here."

"That's good to hear," Doug said as he thumbed through the mail on the coffee table. He glanced at each envelope, tossed them back on the table, and disappeared upstairs.

Tuesday dinners were the latest in the Moran home because Doug had a series of meetings that started at two o'clock and sometimes finished after eight. If his meetings were running late, Doug called by five o'clock to let Annie know not to hold dinner.

Alex set the table while Annie plated the food in the kitchen. He set down napkins with knives and forks, and two bottles of Stammer soda, one orange and one cola that his father bought at Poppi's Beverage Mart. He put out glasses with ice last because none of them liked their soda watered down. The pain in his left ankle was already subsiding.

Dinner began quietly as they enjoyed a tender pot roast with potatoes and carrots that Annie had cooked in the crock pot while she was at work. Once they started eating, the usual conversation began.

Annie recapped her day at the bank, which as usual had one occurrence that made them wonder how people could be so careless with their money. The previous night, someone slid a deposit envelope with checks *and* cash under the tiny space below the bank's door to make a deposit as soon as the bank opened. The person was fortunate the bank's manager saw it and was honest enough to deposit the seven hundred dollars and the checks.

Nothing of consequence happened during Doug's meetings, which meant clients were happy. It also meant there were no schedule or budget adjustments to deal with, and Doug could relax, unlike some Tuesday nights when he would be in his basement office until after midnight.

Alex was hesitant to volunteer any information beyond what he had already told his father. He tried to skip through his day, but Annie insisted on details. Sharing stories at dinner was a family tradition that Annie would not give up.

"Nothing exciting happened *in* school today, but we gave out our bids for Phi yesterday, and the few guys I talked to today said they were all coming down for interviews tomorrow, so hopefully we'll have a good turnout. Oh, and after school, I broke up with Julie."

"What?" Annie and Doug asked simultaneously, neither hiding their surprise.

"I thought things were going well," Annie said.

"Things were fine with her for the most part, but her father was a different story."

"If her father doesn't like you, that poor girl has no chance," Annie said.

"She said she didn't see that her father was always rude to me."

"Then you're better off without her," Annie said.

Doug nodded in agreement. He and Annie had discussed it when Alex first mentioned Julie's father. They agreed not to discourage him from seeing her even though it would probably be a painful lesson.

"Have either of you seen any strange cars in the neighborhood recently?" Doug asked, changing the subject so Alex wouldn't have to go to in depth on his breakup.

"No more than usual," Annie said.

"I don't pay much attention unless it's a Corvette," Alex said. It wasn't a lie, but it was low on the truth scale.

"Marv said he saw a car he didn't recognize stop in front of our house a little while ago. There were at least two black guys," Doug said.

"Did he say when?" Alex asked.

"About a half hour ago. They came down the block, turned around, and stopped for a few minutes. He said he thought the one in the passenger seat was looking at a map, so they might've just been lost."

"That was a couple of our prospective pledges. I gave them our address and phone number in case they had questions about Phi. I ran into them by the school."

"I'll let Marv know," Doug said. "And it's nice that you took initiative like that." He sipped his soda and looked pointedly at Alex. "My concern was that it might have been some guys looking for someone with a West shirt to take their frustrations out on."

"You don't think they'd attack a random person, do you?" Annie asked.

"I would hope not, but for the time being, I think Alex should refrain from wearing anything identifying him as a West student."

"I won't. But if it's random, I think they'd look closer to school."

"Just be careful," Annie said. "Sometimes when you're on your bike you don't notice what's going on around you."

Had she made the comment hours earlier, Alex would have laughed and called her overprotective. After what happened with Marco, though, he had to admit she was right. When he rode, he blocked out almost everything else.

"I'll be careful, Mom." Alex took his plate and glass to the kitchen and rinsed them off. He cleared the table except for the bottle of orange soda and Doug's glass.

"Don't forget, we have a meeting with your guidance counselor in the morning," Doug said.

"Thanks for reminding me. I have to call John and tell him not to pick me up."

* * *

The phone rang as Alex finished his homework. Annie answered, spoke briefly, and laughed before she called up to Alex.

"I'll be right there," Alex said. He knew from her laugh that it wasn't Julie, which was good because the little bit of homework had taken twice as long as it should have when he realized he was angrier with Julie than her father.

"What are you doing right now?" John asked.

The question was always dangerous when John asked because it could lead to almost anywhere and anything. Alex had to be adamant about staying home.

"I'm getting ready to watch Happy Days, and then Angie, and if I get really crazy, I might finish with Three's Company."

"Good. I'll swing by in ten minutes, and we'll go shoot some pool at the new place by the mall?"

"Not tonight."

"Give me one good reason and I'll hang up and you won't see me until tomorrow."

John was persistent, often illogical, and unusually persuasive, so Alex had to be careful when giving his reason. John's reasoning was often so out of sync with reality that Alex felt compelled to join him. To John's credit, Alex was rarely disappointed.

"I'll give you the quick version because I don't want to talk about it on the phone."

"Go for it."

"First, I broke up with Julie. Then, on my way home from her house, Marco and three of his buddies came after me with bats, and that was the normal part of my afternoon."

"Are you okay?"

"I'm fine. I'll tell you about it tomorrow."

"If you need to talk, I can be at your house in five minutes."

"I'm beat. I don't even want to think about it 'til tomorrow. Which reminds me, my dad is taking me to school tomorrow."

"Seriously? You hit me with this and then you're going to make me wait even longer?"

"It's the only day my dad could make it in to see Mr. Reynolds this month."

"He's going in to talk to your guidance counsellor?" John asked, as if the very idea was ludicrous.

"Unlike you, I haven't figured out what I want to do with my life."

"Is that an invitation to come by and help figure it out."

"I'll see you tomorrow at lunch." Alex laughed and hung up.

*   *   *

It was fifth period before John caught up with Alex and stopped him before he reached his locker and rushed him out the door. They had to walk a few blocks to his car, which he had "Ralphed" during second period. Ralphing was a term juniors and seniors used for moving their cars to Ralph Road prior to third period so they could take them out for lunch.

"You look better than I expected," John said, and threw an arm around Alex's neck. "I was worried I was gonna have to gather up some brothers, get in a few cars and settle things like in the old days."

"No need for a rumble."

Rumbles had been more prevalent in the sixties and early seventies when small fights turned into fraternity wars that always ended with an all-out brawl that usually only ended when the police showed up. Alex hadn't heard of a single rumble on Long Island since he'd been inducted. The most common cause of a rumble was when a brother from one fraternity was jumped by members of a rival fraternity—usually from another town—and had their colors stolen. Most fraternities tried to recover stolen colors, but Phi was so relentless that the practice of stealing Phi colors had all but stopped because the number of rival fraternity officers they had put in the hospital. When a Phi brother from any chapter was jumped, phone calls went out to chapter presidents and within hours Phi had one hundred brothers strong, all in colors, standing outside the house of the other fraternity's president. If the offending chapter was unlucky, Phi brothers would swarm a meeting, pummel the officers, take everyone's colors, and leave. By 1973 everyone knew not to fuck with Phi.

Alex explained everything that had happened after school, from his fight with Julie's father, to the breakup, and the chase by Marco and friends that followed, right through giving Daryl the names. The only thing he left out were names. He felt better getting some things off his chest after having spent most of the morning altering his routes to avoid Julie.

"It appears things will be taken care of, so what else is troubling you, grasshopper?" John said in a poor imitation of a character from the television series "Kung Fu."

Alex didn't relax until they finished the conversation and walked back to the school.

"Did I do the right thing?"

John clapped a hand on Alex's back and said, "Yes. And besides, does it really matter? It's out of your hands."

During the first few weeks of school, the first bell of the day and the bell that followed each of the three lunch periods caused a panic in most seventh graders and the handful of ninth graders who were attending public school for the first time after eight or nine years in a parochial school. The stress on their faces was comical to students who had been in the school more than a year.

"Were we that small?" Alex asked after watching two seventh grade boys hustle through the door.

John took a close look and said, "We were probably smaller. Remember, you wrestled at ninety-two pounds in seventh grade?"

Alex didn't crack the five-foot mark until midway through eighth grade, and the hundred-pound mark until a few months later. His attempt to put on weight was unsuccessful until his parents allowed him to work out in the weight room. He began lifting three days each week after school and on Saturday. On days he didn't work out, he jogged three miles.

"Would you be worried if everyone involved was white?" John asked, redirecting the conversation.

"I don't think it would have happened if Jevonte had been white."

"Right, but what if they jumped a white kid from another frat and you broke it up. Would you worry?"

"Probably not, but since it's not the case I hope it doesn't make things worse."

"Make what worse? What are you guys talking about?" Mike asked as he caught up with them at the entrance outside the gym. He was wearing his football jersey from the previous year, which he claimed was an aphrodisiac to sophomore and junior girls.

"My teen angst," John said. "We were talking about how cool I am on the outside while inside I'm filled with angst, and Alex said he hopes it doesn't get worse."

"I'd be shocked if you even know what angst means."

"Just because you don't know the definition of something doesn't mean you can't be full of it," John said, and pulled the door open.

"Do you know the definition of shit? Because you're definitely full of that," Mike said.

"Amen to that," Alex said as he broke off towards his locker. "I'll catch you guys later."

"I'll see you at Kyle's house tonight," Mike said.

"Meet me by my car after school," John said.

"Excelente dente," Alex said, and felt a twinge of embarrassment. The phrase had been so prevalent a year earlier but now sounded stupid. And that was exactly how he felt.

*   *   *

Jevonte sat on the couch with two freshly fluffed pillows behind him and a pile of completed work on the tray beside him. His mother wouldn't leave him alone for long, because despite their agreement, he insisted on doing things for himself.

Daryl sat on the recliner and marveled at Jevonte's methodical attack on his work. Every sheet of work he brought had been completed and organized.

"Don't you ever just kick back and relax for a day and forget about school?" Daryl pressed the button on the cable box and tuned to channel eleven for a "Gilligan's Island" rerun.

"Kids who relax don't go to Ivy League schools," Jevonte said.

"Kids with our skin color only go to Ivy League schools when they have an outstanding jump shot, can throw a baseball ninety miles an hour, or can play one of twenty-two positions on a football team. Ivory League might be a better name for it."

Daryl's belief of discrimination was solidified when the valedictorian of his class two years earlier failed to get into any of the three Ivy League schools to which he applied. He had been rejected despite a grade point average over 104—which Daryl hadn't even known was possible—and a 1560 on the SATs, while being class president, school newspaper editor, and captain of the debate team.

"Not every black person at Princeton or Yale is an athlete," Jevonte said with unwavering optimism.

"You're right. But the ones who aren't are called janitors."

"Maybe I'll learn to golf," Jevonte said.

"A black golfer? That'll be the day. Tennis maybe. At least I can name one black tennis pro."

"Moving on," Jevonte said. "Have you given any more thought to what I said about giving the names to the police?"

Daryl leaned against the back of the chair and his feet automatically flew up. Jevonte and his mother had given his father the chair as a birthday present two months earlier, and Daryl still couldn't decide whether he liked it better than the soft chair with the ottoman that it had replaced.

"I don't think you'd get justice. Isaiah pointed something out to me. If you look at the papers from Sunday and Monday; there's page after page of articles saying the police have so many officers on the case and they won't stop until they make an arrest. Then look at today's paper and there's nothing but Reverend Ralph's march." Daryl clasped his hands behind his head. "So, I'm thinking justice is a crock of shit, and we should handle it ourselves."

"I know you must have already planned something, so what is it, and when is it happening?"

"I'd go tonight, or even this weekend, but Isaiah wants to wait until the week after the march when things calm down."

Jevonte walked to the kitchen, poured himself a glass of water, and tossed in a few ice cubes from the freezer. "I never hear Isaiah say much, but when I do, I'm impressed."

"He's what they call a scholar athlete," Daryl said as he watched Jevonte walk gingerly back to the couch. "I think that's the first time I've seen you walk since you left my house last Friday."

"There's only so much sitting I can take, but every time I even shift my weight, my mom comes running to help."

"Baby boy," Daryl teased.

"Oh, shut up," Jevonte said, and laughed. His mother's term of affection was rarely used when others were around, and usually only when Jevonte was upset.

"Well, what do you think?" Daryl asked.

"I think it's really strange that Gilligan and the Skipper wear the same clothes every day and Ginger has an endless supply of dresses and costumes. The Howells supposedly own private yachts, but they took a three-hour tour on the S.S. Minnow and brought along a trunk full of money. The professor can fix just about anything except the boat. Mar—"

"I'm serious."

"I'm serious, too, doesn't all that seem strange to you? It's like everyone knew they weren't coming back except the Skipper and Gilligan," Jevonte said. "But then again, I believe the CIA helped Lee Harvey Oswald kill John F. Kennedy."

"It does seem strange, and you may be right about the CIA, but I was wondering what you thought about the plan for us to go a week from Saturday?"

Jevonte put his chemistry textbook on the stack of papers. "When you say—"

"Not a chance!" Daryl said.

"I didn't even finish my question."

"You were going to ask if you could come, and the answer is no. You need to be as far away from this as possible with a solid alibi. It would be great if you were at a party."

"I'm pretty sure if I was going to be invited to a party next weekend, I would have gotten an invitation by now."

"Actually, Tyrone's brother is having a party at their house and told me to invite you."

"What kind of party is it?"

"I guess you'd call it an alibi party. No money or presents necessary," Daryl said and laughed.

"You know my mom isn't going to let me go out for like a month, but I wish I could be there when you get back."

"I can always make an excuse to stay here that night."

"Doesn't it seem strange that you and your friends are doing this for me?" Jevonte asked. "It was fine when I was ten and you guys set some older kids straight. But I'm sixteen now; when does it end?"

"Set kids straight? I like that. But this time it's like the march. It's not just for you, it's for every black kid in Malbrook."

"Like the march?" Jevonte asked with a puzzled look.

"*Like* the march. Only this has a *real* purpose. We're doing this so those assholes—or anyone else for that matter—never think about trying it again with anyone."

"But won't it make them more likely to retaliate?"

"If that kid's as big a pussy as Alex says he is, none of his friends will do shit. Malbrook is *my* town now, and we're gonna clean it up one racist piece of shit at a time."

A car sped by and Jevonte pulled the curtain back and looked out the window. He caught a glimpse of a yellow Chevelle he recognized and released the curtain. Since he was comfortable enough to lean forward without pain, he checked every car that sounded like it might be speeding. The newspapers had respected his privacy, but Reverend Ralph mentioned their addresses numerous times. It was unlikely anyone would mess with his house, but it wouldn't stop him from watching.

"You should go into politics," Jevonte said. "You have an answer for everything, and you're younger, smarter, and better looking than Reverend Ralph."

"I appreciate the smarter part, but younger is out of my control and saying I'm better looking is like saying I see better than Stevie Wonder," Daryl said. "Oh, before I forget, I wanted to show you something." He pulled a small brown envelope from his pocket, slid out a blue card and tossed it to Jevonte.

"What's this?"

"Thanks to you, and my new driver's license, I am the proud owner of a Malbrook Veterans Memorial Library card."

Jevonte looked at the card with the shiny metal strip and flipped it back to Daryl. "What made you get a library card? Your Rosedale card must have expired years ago."

"I wouldn't have bothered, but when I went back to check yearbook photos of the three kids we're looking for, there was a nasty older lady at the desk, and every time I looked over, no matter where I was, she was watching me like I was gonna steal something. I thought maybe she'd never seen a black person before, and I had my new license in my wallet, so I went to the desk to show her I wasn't lost. Before I said anything, she asked what I wanted. And she was a bitch. So I said, 'How kin I git me one of them thar liberry cards y'all white folks have?'"

"No, you didn't."

"Yes, I did. She was so snotty and told me I had to be a resident of Malbrook, so I pulled out my license and plopped it on the counter. She about fainted. Ten minutes later I was checking out my first album."

"Album?"

"Who knew? I wandered around while she got my card ready, and they had this whole aisle filled with records. They had an Earth, Wind and Fire album I wanted, so I checked it out, took it home, and copied it to a brand-new Mem-or-ex tape." Daryl sounded out Memorex, because months earlier Daryl had bought a dozen Memrex tapes at a Uniondale flea market without realizing they were cheap knockoffs.

"They have records you can check out?"

"I'm not getting too excited because most of what I saw was Frank Sinatra, Doris Day, and Bing Crosby," Daryl said. "I was surprised they had an album I like. Probably got it by mistake."

"You didn't look to see what else they had?"

"I didn't bother because you can only check out one album at a time. And get this; there's a sign that says albums are not to be copied. They might as well tell you where not to buy cassettes, too."

Daryl pushed his feet down and the recliner collapsed beneath the chair and catapulted him forward. "Cuz, I'd love to hang out all night, but I've got to get my ass moving." Jevonte started to get up, but Daryl stopped him. "Relax I can let myself out."

*   *   *

Word of Phi's emergency meeting spread shortly after school ended on Wednesday. Notice was given late so Marco could control which brothers would, and would not, hear about it. Since Dave worked as a busboy and left school directly from his last class, he wouldn't hear. Even if Dave heard, Marco knew he was too responsible to call in sick on short notice. He was predictable and dependable, which were okay, but his moral compass opposed Marco's, and that was a punishable offense.

Marco helped Peter drape the Nazi flag over the front of the table which was all that was necessary to set up for the meeting. No more than fifteen brothers were expected, and that was all they needed to push their limited agenda through, and Dave would be expelled from the fraternity. A few minutes later, brothers began to file in through the side door and directly to the basement. Tommy arrived last, slightly out of breath.

"This meeting is called to order," Peter said, and banged his gavel on the table. "We are going to skip the reading of last week's minutes and get down to business."

"I only heard about the meeting ten minutes ago, so can you fill me in on the emergency," Tommy said.

"Brother Marco will explain," Peter said. He looked to his right and turned the floor over to Marco.

"I've heard people outside our fraternity saying we were responsible for beating that nigger last Friday." Marco stepped in front of the table.

"Now, *we* know it's true, but other people shouldn't. If the wrong person finds out and calls the police, we're fucked." Marco paced between brothers, making eye contact with each. "The part that pisses me off is that when I ask them where they heard it, the answer I keep getting is Dave. Dave—"

"That's bullshit!" Tommy yelled as he jumped to his feet.

"Brother Marco has the floor! No speaking out of turn!" Peter yelled and banged his gavel.

"When he's done, I want a chance to speak," Tommy said.

"Duly noted. Now sit the fuck down."

Marco's eyes met Tommy's and he smirked. "That's right, sit doggy."

Tommy narrowed his eyes and stared at Marco until the smirk was gone.

"Where is Dave? Why isn't he at this meeting?" Marco asked, trying to elicit a feeling that Dave hadn't come because he was hiding something.

"He's working," Tommy said. "He works every Wednesday night."

"And he can't call in sick one time to make it to an emergency meeting?"

"Dave probably doesn't know about this meeting. I just found out myself."

"Says you!"

"Who else *could* say it but me?"

Peter banged his gavel. "This is your last warning. No more speaking out of turn!"

"He asked questions and I answered them! How is that speaking out of turn?"

"Just shut the fuck up and let Brother Marco finish," Peter said.

Tommy swallowed his words for the moment.

"I make a motion that we expel Dave Kane from this fraternity," Marco said, and set up what was just a formality.

"On what grounds?" Tommy yelled before anyone could second the motion.

"Conduct detrimental to the fraternity," Marco said.

"Dave has never done anything detrimental to this fraternity. Dave attends every *scheduled* meeting, pays his dues on time, and helps with everything that's related to this fraternity."

"Fuck that!" Marco yelled louder than he intended, and Peter leaned forward and smacked his left arm. Marco gave Peter an apologetic look and turned back to Tommy. "I'll tell you why Dave should be out. First, he brings his gook cousin from that fuckin' pansy chapter on the other side of town. Then Dave and his cousin turn against us when we're beating up the nigger. I know we all agree that niggers don't belong in our town. And then last night, we pay a visit to that slanty-eyed scumbag to clear the air and we're attacked by niggers."

"You're so full of shit," Tommy said.

"No, he's not," Peter said. "If you don't believe me, look at what those fucking animals did to my car."

"Ask Jimmy and Steven, they were there, too," Marco said.

Jimmy nodded as Steven continued to take notes and didn't look up.

"I heard a rumor that they're letting niggers in that chapter. First gooks, and now niggers? We don't need niggers in Malbrook, much less in our fraternity!"

"Why do you have a problem with anyone who's not white?" Tommy asked.

"I have no problem with anyone as long as they know their place. And if they're not white, their place is not in Malbrook. If they don't understand, we need to teach them." Marco stepped back and leaned against the officer's table. "After their nigger march on Saturday, they'll really push for arrests."

Peter stood and towered over Marco. His eyes shifted to Tommy. "Since you're one of the guys involved, I'd think you'd be on board with Marco's motion."

"Marco's motion is bullshit! Everyone knows Dave would never talk about fraternity business, but Marco says whatever he wants whenever he wants. The reason Marco wants Dave out is because Alex called him out, and Marco wussed out."

"You're full of shit! We had to go because the cops showed up."

"That's enough, if anyone seconds the motion, we can put it to a vote," Peter said.

Three boys simultaneously shouted, "Second."

"This is fuckin' ridiculous. If you're gonna vote on Dave, vote on me at the same time, because if Dave's out, I'm out."

"Fine," Peter said. "Wait outside, and make sure you close the door behind you."

Tommy shook his head, gave Marco a *fuck you* look and walked up the stairs and out the side door. He pulled the door closed behind him with enough force to shake the side of the house.

Tommy had barely closed the door when he heard someone coming up the steps. Marco opened the door, laughed, and said, "You're both out."

Tommy mistook Marco's laugh and pulled the door before Marco yanked it closed. "You heard me. Get the fuck out of here while you have a chance."

Tommy collected his bike and walked it down the driveway. He didn't understand how it could happen. He and Dave had too many friends to be voted out. As he started to pedal, he realized none of their friends were there. The meeting was a bunch of Marco's followers called together to kick Dave out. It was a fluke that Tommy had overheard two brothers in the deli talking about the meeting. If he hadn't been buying milk for his mother, he wouldn't have known about the meeting. He finally understood why Marco looked surprised to see him.

Tommy rode towards his house and then the steak house, but knew Dave would be too busy to talk, and giving him bad news while he was working was a bad idea. He rode aimlessly until he found himself at Westwood Park. He circled the track, riding as hard as he could. He figured he would continue until he collapsed from exhaustion, the police made him leave, or nine-forty, which would give him enough time to be at the steak house when Dave finished.

His head began to clear on the third lap. He felt a strange calmness settle in as he rode down the sloping grass to the empty basketball and tennis courts, stopped by the fence and looked past them to the pond he skated on when he was younger. Like most teens in Malbrook, he learned to skate on a frozen pond. *Fuck school! Fuck Marco! Fuck Phi!* He took the first and third ones back, and then pushed off the fence and pedaled back up to the path. He pedaled until his muscles screamed for him to stop, and then pedaled more.

*　　　*　　　*

The interior of the two-car garage at the back corner of Kyle's property line was usually well lit, but during interviews the lights were turned off as soon as all brothers were seated. No officer's table was necessary. Once they were all seated, each brother was handed one black and one white marble for voting purposes.

Each candidate was blindfolded upon arrival and seated against the side fence far enough away to make eavesdropping impossible. When they were brought in, each brother was allowed, but not obligated, to ask one question. After the candidate answered, the brother would drop a white or black marble in the bowl that was passed around to indicate it was their turn to ask. If a candidate was particularly impressive, some of the latter brothers just dropped their white marble in and passed the bowl along instead of prolonging the inevitable outcome. They could do the same with the black marble. If there were three black marbles in the bowl at the end of an interview, the candidate was dismissed, though that was rare since prospective pledges were screened thoroughly.

Quentin Blake, a sophomore honor student, and the school's probable starting point guard for the upcoming basketball season, was the first candidate to enter the dark garage to be interviewed. He would have the distinction of being the first black candidate ever interviewed by their chapter. He was a lean six-two with light brown skin and a close-cropped haircut. He was led into the garage by Declan and positioned to face Kyle. Kyle shined his flashlight on Quentin's face and told him to remove the blindfold.

Kyle started with a basic question that would be asked of every candidate at some point. "If you had to start a fire and had only one match, a Phi jacket, and an American flag, which would you use the match to light?"

"I would light the Phi jacket, sir," Quentin said with confidence.

Kyle dropped a white marble in the bowl, covered it with a black cloth and passed it, along with the flashlight, to Mike, who was seated to his left.

"Why would you light the Phi jacket?" Mike asked.

"I mean no disrespect, sir, but I'd have no other choice. I would never do anything to disrespect my country, as I'm sure no one in this room would, sir."

Mike dropped a white marble in and passed the bowl and flashlight to the next brother. The process went on until it reached John, who was last and sat to Kyle's right, on the opposite side of the garage's side entrance. John hadn't planned to ask a question, but no one had asked what he thought was most obvious. They had asked the usual, "Why do you think you would be a good candidate?" and "What would you bring to the fraternity?" and other similar questions, but not something he thought was essential to the candidate.

"Why would you want to join a fraternity chapter that has never allowed blacks to join?" John asked.

Across the garage, Alex smiled. It had taken until senior year, but John finally asked a serious question during an interview.

Quentin answered with the same confidence he had displayed throughout. "I have met many Phi brothers and know them all to be outstanding individuals. When I see someone wearing Phi colors, I know they are a leader, and though I understand it will take time, I want people to look at me that way. As far as having no blacks, it's understandable since there haven't been many in the student body. And lastly, sir, because I admire all that Jackie Robinson accomplished, and want to follow his example."

John dropped the last marble into the bowl and passed it to Kyle. Declan led Quentin outside. Quentin looked at the blindfolded candidates sitting silently along the fence and was glad his interview was over.

Kyle held the bowl in his lap. Based solely on Quentin's answers, every marble in the bowl should have been white, but anonymity was a wildcard. If the bowl contained three black marbles, there was no point in interviewing other black candidates.

The lights were turned on as Kyle pulled several white marbles at a time and transferred them to a second bowl so brothers could collect their marbles. When the final marble was placed in the second bowl, Kyle felt a sense of disappointment. Along with twenty-six white marbles was a lone black marble. As much as Kyle wanted to know who was holding a white marble, a system based on honor left him no recourse, despite dishonorable intent.

"If I see another black marble after an interview like that, I am going to make it my mission to find out who put it in and kick the living-shit out of you!" Mike said in a loud whisper to be sure those outside could not hear.

"As much as I agree with Brother Mike's sentiment, I have to remind everyone that these procedures are in place to keep everything anonymous," Kyle said.

Alex stood and said, "Maybe it's time to change the anonymous bullshit. There's no secrecy when we vote on motions, so why should this be different? I make a motion that voting take place at the end of each interview and no longer be anonymous."

Alex had barely finished speaking when John stood and said, "Second."

Kyle looked to Guy, who had been the secretary before relinquishing his role to become the treasurer, and the only one aside from himself familiar with Phi's bylaws. "Is there anything that requires us to keep the vote anonymous?"

Guy was a senior who had grown five inches over the last few months of eleventh grade and summer. For most of high school, he had been overweight and slightly less coordinated than most of the others, but he cut his weight by twenty pounds through exercise and limiting his soda intake over the ten weeks of summer vacation and had gone from what had generously been called stocky to lean and muscular. A few cheerleaders had even taken notice, but after years of rejection he wasn't ready for one girlfriend.

"There's nothing in the bylaws that says it has to be anonymous," Guy said. "It was adopted in the mid '60s."

"Okay then, after Quentin is given his information, we'll vote on the motion."

It was slightly disappointing to Quentin that without the darkness and flashlights it was just an ordinary garage. All brothers were seated in what was supposed to be a circle, but more closely resembled a rectangle. A purposely awkward moment passed before everyone turned to Kyle.

"Quentin Blake, you have been chosen to join the brotherhood of Phi Gamma Alpha. A pledge period of two weeks, excluding Sundays, is outlined in the materials that our secretary, Lucas Price, will give you in a moment." Kyle looked to Lucas and Lucas nodded to let him know he had the materials ready. "Do you wish to proceed with the pledging process set to begin on Monday, September 15th and culminate with hell night on Friday, September 26th?"

"Yes, sir!" Quentin said.

Lucas handed Quentin a folder with several papers inside and said, "A suit jacket or sports coat with a dress shirt and tie must be worn each day of pledging. If you do not have one, a brother will provide one for you. It will be your responsibility to have it cleaned before you return it. Do you have a suit jacket or a sports coat?"

"Yes, sir!" Quentin said enthusiastically.

Before Lucas opened the door for Quentin, he said, "Make sure you call me if you have any questions. My number is in the packet."

"Mine is in there, too," Kyle added. "Don't hesitate to call with questions or concerns."

"Thank you, sirs!"

The moment Declan closed the garage door behind Quentin, Kyle called the room to order. "Brother Alex has made a motion to eliminate the secrecy of the voting process, and it has been seconded by Brother John. All in favor?"

Every brother shouted, "Aye," in unison. "All opposed?" The garage was silent.

"Can we make the vote retroactive?" Alex asked. He was joking, but John took it seriously.

"That would be great. Everyone holds up their remaining marble and we beat the shit out of the one with the white marble."

"As much as that might be fun for all but one of us, we can't do that," Guy said. "Bylaws are to be observed from the point at which they are adopted."

The fraternity's bylaws contained more than two hundred pages of rules. Many were obvious, but they had to be written for legal purposes, while others were for rare occurrences and special circumstances. The original ten handwritten pages of bylaws by the four founding brothers had expanded with each new chapter and their unique circumstances. The last of the four founders had been the only one to live long enough to see the fraternity flourish to over seventy chapters in New York, New Jersey, and Pennsylvania. When the organization reached more than two thousand members, the ruling Alpha Beta Chapter, or ABC as it was commonly called, decided it was necessary to incorporate. Before incorporating, every bylaw from every chapter was scrutinized and either added or discarded. The fraternity's bylaws were reviewed every five years, and each chapter submitted potential changes, though they could keep their own chapter bylaws in addition if they were not contrary to the fraternity's.

Lucas was still getting up to speed on being secretary and hadn't had a chance to finish reading the bylaws, so aside from Guy, who had been required to know them, Kyle was the only brother who had read the most recent version. Kyle was also the only brother who knew Guy was lying.

Until mid-August, Guy liked everyone. Guy had always been just one of the brothers. He was athletic, but not elite, smart, but not in honors classes, and when he showed up for football camp in the best shape of his life, the coaches "rewarded" him by moving him from tight end where he had played since seventh grade, to wide receiver. As a tight end he only caught three or four passes a year but was in to block on every offensive play. Moving to wide receiver meant the potential to score touchdowns, but there were already black flankers and split ends who were faster and had better hands. It all added up to less playing time for Guy. After being a varsity starter in his sophomore and junior years, he would be relegated to coming off the bench as a senior when the season started the following week. It was a bitter pill to swallow, and with no recourse on the football field, he wanted to keep his two teammates, who were waiting outside, out of Phi.

"Okay, get your marbles and let's move on," Kyle said.

Of the fifteen candidates interviewed, only two—both of whom were white—weren't invited to pledge. Their interviews had gone so poorly that they had been eliminated less than halfway through the process.

By far, the final interview was the worst, and as a legacy, the most surprising. Jimmy Palma was undone by his first answer. When Kyle asked how he felt about potentially having black brothers, the soon-to-be ex-candidate replied, "Phi is too smart to let niggers drag it down, so I don't see it as a problem."

An answer so definitively wrong had consequences, though no physical harm could be inflicted during the interview process. Mike asked for "the bag" and had Declan affix the candidate's blindfold. Jimmy laughed. He knew he was about to be subjected to the gag reflex challenge and was overly confident because his older brother, who had graduated in 1975 told him as a legacy, he was guaranteed membership, which was generally true but not automatic. Once his blindfold was on, he was ordered to his knees in front of Mike. Kwan held a piece of fresh dog shit on a stick just below Jimmy's nose. Mike asked, "Do you want to join Phi badly enough to eat dog shit?"

Every "extreme" act within the fraternity had an accompanying legend passed down, and the gag reflex challenge was no exception. Allegedly, a candidate in Brooklyn during the 1950s had performed so poorly on the first few questions that brothers fed him dog shit instead of the over-ripe banana and he vomited so much on his way home that he became dehydrated and passed out on the side of the road. By the time he was discovered the following morning, he had suffered severe brain damage.

Jimmy confidently barked, "Yes, sir."

While Kwan held the shit beneath Jimmy's nose, Mike ordered Jimmy to open his mouth. Jimmy had to be told to open wider twice before Mike was able to slide a half inch piece of over-ripe, way-too-soft, banana in his mouth.

"Swallow it," Mike ordered.

The soft banana rested on Jimmy's tongue momentarily as he tried to maneuver it to the back of his mouth and let it slide down his throat. He stayed with it for a few seconds, then gagged, spit it out, and vomited. He tore the blindfold off, and tried to focus, but the garage was too dark. John pushed the door open, and Kyle calmly said, "Get out."

Jimmy's stomach was still churning as he left the garage.

Thirteen candidates agreed to start the pledging process. Seven were white and six were black.

Chapter 9

The employee exit at Morgan's Steak House was in the rear. The twenty-by-twenty area had a six-foot privacy fence with green and white slats running diagonally through it, which enclosed the building's air conditioning unit, a small rack where busboys locked their bikes and two dumpsters that constantly smelled like rancid beef. The gate to the area was twenty feet from the railroad trestle where trains passed frequently throughout the early dinner hours and more sporadically later.

Dave took a deep breath and held it as he pushed the back door open. He walked quickly to his bike and removed the lock. He had two locks but used the simpler one for work since it only had four sets of numbers from zero to nine. For everywhere else, he used a Master Lock like the ones he used at school. He could remove the work lock in less than ten seconds and that gave him enough time to get through the gate before he had to inhale again.

He closed the gate behind him and breathed in a gulp of fresh air. He was surprised to see Tommy standing against the wall of the train trestle. No one stood under the trestle because pigeons constantly dropped shit from their perches beneath it.

"What are you doing here?"

"I missed you at the meeting tonight," Tommy said.

"What meeting?"

"I asked the same thing. I found out at the last minute, which gave me enough time to make it to the meeting and get kicked out along with you."

"Why would we get kicked out?"

"For you it was conduct detrimental to the fraternity. Marco said you told people outside the fraternity about last Friday night, and—"

"That's bullshit!"

"That's what I said. I said Marco wanted you out because Alex made him look like a pussy. That didn't change anything, so I told them if they voted you out, vote me out, too."

"You got kicked out because of me?" Dave asked.

"You would have done the same for me."

Tommy was right, but it didn't make Dave feel any better. He was still digesting the news.

"How did Marco get enough votes?"

"I didn't realize at the time, but the only ones there were the officers and the ninth graders."

"Marco's minions," Dave said.

"Exactly."

The lights in the large two-family houses by the creek cast long shadows that made Dave feel smaller. A silence hung in the air as they walked their bikes down the road, kicking the occasional pebbles that had made their way out of the grassy area in the grooves of someone's sneakers.

Five blocks from the steakhouse, Dave finally threw his bike down and yelled in frustration. He sat on the curb, stretched his legs in front of him and stared at the ground. Dave had never been close friends with Marco, but Tommy had, and that should have counted for something.

"One day I'm going to pummel that little shit," Dave said.

Tommy laid his bike on the grass next to Dave's and scooted down the cement to the water. Dave followed.

"I was thinking about kicking Marco's ass myself but being out means we can't touch him."

"Have you talked to Alex?"

"I missed his call last night, so I haven't talked to him since Saturday. Why?"

"Marco said they went to talk to him yesterday and ended up being chased by niggers. Peter said they messed up his car, but I never looked."

"I was wondering what happened to it."

"It's messed up?"

"There's a dent in the front on top of his hood and in back on his trunk."

"I still think they're full of shit." Tommy checked his watch. It was almost eleven. "Can you call tomorrow and find out what really happened?"

"I'll call him when I get up."

*   *   *

Alex started his morning workout at nine o'clock, which was later than usual, even during a day off. Alex woke at five-thirty on school days and usually around seven-forty-five on weekends and holidays. On school days, it meant jogging before sunrise, but he enjoyed the early morning quiet and how running beneath the stars made him feel like the only person in the world.

Alex never set his alarm clock on days off, but when he woke an hour later than usual, he knew it was mental fatigue. He planned to ride to Dave's house at some point during the day but decided to test his ankle on the streets and sidewalks of Malbrook while adding two miles of uneven concrete surface to his workout.

He made it to the house early enough to know Dave would still be sleeping. With neither car in the driveway Alex went in the garage and took the spare key to the side door from the bottom of an old Maxwell House can that was home to various sized screwdrivers.

Alex let himself in, padded up the steps to the kitchen, and took a quick drink from the faucet. He slipped off his sneakers and left them at the bottom of the stairs. He walked carefully up to the second floor, stepping on the sides, and skipping the creaky third step. He pushed Dave's door open and saw him sleeping with his back to him. Alex tiptoed to the side of the bed.

"Wake up!" he shouted in Dave's ear.

Dave nearly jumped out of his skin as he flipped away and slammed his back into the wall. He balled his hands into fists before he realized it was Alex.

"Are you trying to give me a heart attack?"

Dave had done the same thing to Alex numerous times and Alex was glad to exact a small measure of revenge. "Payback's a bitch," Alex said through laughter.

Any other time Dave would have laughed along with Alex once his heart rate returned to normal. Instead, he turned to the wall and pulled his pillow over his head.

"Come on, wake up. I've got a great story to tell you," Alex said as he sat at Dave's desk.

Dave lifted the pillow and said, "I heard Marco's version from Tommy."

"This should be good. What did he say?"

"Marco said he went with Peter, Jimmy and Steven to see you and clear the air." Before Alex could interrupt, Dave added, "I knew *that* was bullshit. He also said when they found you niggers chased them and messed up Peter's car. And just so we're clear, nigger is Marco's word, not mine."

"Please tell me Tommy didn't believe him."

"Oh, please. He knows Marco's full of shit."

"The part about Marco and those other three assholes coming to see me was true, but unless coming after me with bats is their way of clearing the air, that's all that was true."

Alex recounted everything that happened once again. The part about the breakup with Julie was already getting easier.

"You're the one who dented Peter's car?" Dave asked. His spirits lifted slightly at the thought of Peter watching Alex ride over his car.

"Man, was he pissed."

"I guess jumping the bar at the park was a good thing after all," Dave conceded.

"The last thing I thought of before I pulled up was you saying that one day I was gonna miss and you'd laugh your ass off."

"If it's any consolation, in that situation, I wouldn't have laughed," Dave said. "Do you want to know what else Marco said at the meeting last night?"

"There's more?" Alex was exasperated by the thought of Marco's lies.

"He said I told people about what happened Friday night, and I should be kicked out of Phi." Dave managed to keep his voice even.

"Please tell me someone put him in his place."

"Tommy did. Tommy even told them if they were going to vote me out, to vote him out, too."

"They actually voted on it?"

"Yup. And they voted us both out." Dave's voice cracked as the emotion hit him.

"What? That asshole had you and Tommy thrown out of Phi? There's no fucking way I'm letting that happen!" Alex said. "I'll have their entire chapter expelled before I'd let that happen!"

Alex thought about calling every brother from his chapter and going to Marco's to clear the air. The thought gave him a better idea.

"I have to make a phone call," Alex said, and hurried to the kitchen.

When Kyle picked up, Alex didn't go through a long lead in because anything he told Kyle would be kept in confidence. He brought Kyle up to speed, and Kyle knew the plan before Alex tried to explain. Alex hung up the phone confident Kyle would talk circles around Peter, and within ten minutes Marco would be stewing in bad news. Then it was open season on Marco.

Alex yelled up to Dave, who still didn't want to get out of bed, and told him to call Tommy. When Dave didn't answer, Alex went up and said, "I need you to call Tommy and tell him not to talk to anyone about what happened last night. It's taken care of and neither of you are out."

"How?"

"Call Tommy and I'll explain it to both of you at the same time," Alex said. "But call him now while I go down to the kitchen."

Dave called from his parents' bedroom while Alex went to the kitchen. Tommy answered as Dave was about to hang up.

"Hello," Tommy said in a voice groggy from sleep.

"Hey, Tommy, it's Alex. I'm at Dave's house, and he's on the other extension."

"I guess he told you what happened."

"Don't worry, neither one of you are out."

"What? How?" Tommy asked.

"Yeah, how is that possible?"

"This conversation cannot go beyond the three of us and our chapter president, Kyle. Okay?"

"Yes," they agreed.

"I just got off the phone with Kyle, and as far as anyone is concerned, when they brought out the Nazi flag, Dave asked me for a transfer to our chapter, which is why I was at the meeting in the first place. Our records will show that to be the case. After Dave told you, you transferred, too, and since neither of you were members of their chapter, a motion to have you kicked out isn't valid."

"That's genius," Tommy said.

"There's more, but some of it is just in case. As of this past Sunday, you are both officially transferred to our chapter. If they ask why Tommy was at the meeting, Kyle is telling Peter he advised Tommy to officially let them know."

"But if I already transferred, why would I worry about a vote?"

"You got caught up in the moment defending Dave."

"That is great! I can't thank you enough," Tommy said.

"Pissing Marco off without even having to see him is thanks enough," Alex said. "But there's something else I have to tell you."

Alex knew it would ruin the mood, but Tommy needed to know he had a target on his back from more than just Marco. He explained how everything had transpired with Jevonte and his cousin and how they had tracked him down.

"You said one of them gave you their phone number, right?" Tommy asked.

"Yes, but please don't ask for it. I can tell them anything you want, but I can't give you the number," Alex said.

"I wouldn't put you in that position. I deserve whatever is coming to me. If I could go back and change that night, I would. I hate that I was part of it."

"I told them you were a good guy," Alex said. "I just don't understand how you went along with it."

"It's not an excuse, but last summer Marco and I were walking home from Green Acres and guys from Omega drove past and Marco yelled something stupid. The car stopped, backed up, and four guys jumped out. I think Marco purposely tripped me and then took off when he saw them coming after us, so I ran in a different direction, hopped a fence, and got away. I honestly don't know if they even came after me or if they knew Marco had been the one who said something and chased him instead. They beat the living shit out of him—"

"I like these Omega guys," Alex joked.

"Two days later, I'm walking home from Westwood Park at night, and I get jumped by a pack of guys who were in all black hiding behind trees. They knew I would be there."

"How'd they find you?"

"They didn't. Marco promised bids to eight kids if they jumped me, so of course they did. I found out a month or so after they were inducted that it was to teach me never to abandon a brother, which was bullshit considering Marco ran first. It's no excuse, but that's why I did it."

"Why did you want the phone number?"

"I don't. I wanted to know if you can call and tell them they don't have to look for me." Tommy swallowed hard. "I'll meet them whenever and wherever they want, and if it's possible, I'd like a chance to apologize to Jevonte."

"That's pretty brave of you."

"No, the brave thing would have been to stop Marco."

Alex wanted to say something to the contrary, but Tommy was right. After an awkward silence, he said, "I have to free up the phone for Kyle to call, but Dave will call you back in a little while."

"Thanks again, Alex."

A day that had started in the shitter for Dave had taken a turn. He was still in Phi, and for a bonus, Marco was headed for a beating of epic proportions. The only negative was on Tommy's end but facing up to his mistake was best.

Dave and Alex sat in the living room while they waited for the call from Kyle. It took a while for Kyle to explain the conversation because he started laughing whenever he brought up Peter's objections and how frustrated and confused Peter had been.

"I hate to be mean, but that kid sounds about as smart as a box of rocks," Kyle said.

"He's pretty big though," Alex said.

"I got that impression. I kept expecting him to say, 'We're gonna live off the fat of the land, George. The fat of the land,' or whatever Lenny always said in <u>Of Mice and Men</u>."

"That's him," Alex said.

"Who?" Dave mouthed.

"I'll tell you after," Alex said as he held his hand over the mouthpiece. Before they hung up, Alex handed the phone to Dave.

"Thank you for sticking your neck out for Tommy and me."

"Anything to help a brother. Let Alex know if anyone from your old chapter gives you or Tommy any crap. I warned Peter that if you or Tommy are touched by anyone, whether it's their chapter, another fraternity, or basically just anyone, I am holding him and Marco responsible and they will get a beating the likes of which they have never seen."

The receiver had been in its cradle only seconds when the phone rang. Dave picked up and said, "Hello."

"This isn't over!" Marco yelled.

"You would shit yourself if you knew just how right you are," Dave said, and laughed.

"What's that supposed to mean?"

"You fucked with the wrong family. Don't bother to call back." Dave disconnected the call. He placed the handset on the table but changed his mind and hung it up.

"Marco?"

"Must have just gotten the news," Dave said, with a smile.

"We're a tough family now, are we?" Alex asked.

"Who said I was talking about our family?"

Alex smiled as he realized the implication, and how Marco would assume the same thing. Dave followed him outside where Alex stretched his legs for the jog home. His ankle had held up so well on the jog to Dave's that he almost forgot he had been worried about it.

"I've got to go, and you should give Tommy a call and tell him it's all set. If Marco calls again, let me know."

"Thanks. And I mean for everything," Dave said as they shook hands.

"I got you into this mess in the first place."

Dave followed him to the garage to return the key to the Maxwell House can.

"You wouldn't have been there if I hadn't insisted you come to our meeting."

Alex pushed against the side of the garage and continued to stretch. He forgot how difficult it could be to stop in the middle of a jog.

"Do you realize you never accept credit for anything?" Alex asked. He let the thought sink in as he jogged off.

Chapter 10

Shortly after nine-thirty on Saturday morning, four yellow school buses turned onto Ewell Road. The lead bus pulled in front of Jesse Jenkins's house and stopped. Reverend Ralph was the first to exit, followed by advisers and then protesters. He wore a black Adidas sweat suit with red and white trim and black and white Adidas sneakers that matched almost too well.

Extra buses had been arranged for two days earlier after a rumor circulated that any car on nearby streets that residents didn't recognize would be keyed. Later rumors claimed the cars would also have nails driven through the tires.

Jesse ate an apple while he watched from his front stoop as the black protesters exited the buses. Even after the buses had emptied, the crowd continued to grow as protesters who couldn't get seats on the buses were dropped off. Daryl pushed the front door open and sat beside his father.

Daryl was too embarrassed to admit his initial reaction had been to march. The idea lasted only until he spoke to his uncle, and if it hadn't ended there it would have ended when he spoke to his father.

"Why are you out here all by yourself?" Daryl asked.

Jesse was lost in thought as he watched Reverend Ralph direct people to different areas. It was apparent from Jesse's expression that this wasn't how he envisioned his first month in Malbrook.

"I want any neighbors who happen to be home to see that I'm not marching."

Reverend Ralph waddled up to the freshly painted silver fence that stretched around the length of the property at a height just above his plump belly. Jesse had finished painting the fence two hours earlier to discourage anyone from entering his yard. Reverend Ralph stopped just shy of touching it and Jesse silently wished he had. It would have made his day to see Reverend Ralph with a bright silver stripe across his pristine sweat suit.

"Why don't you gentlemen come march with us?" Reverend Ralph asked.

"Jevonte's parents, who happen to be my brother and my sister-in-law, asked you not to march, so why would you ignore their wishes?"

Daryl perked up as he listened to his father chastise the reverend. His father was so laid back that Daryl had never heard him use a curse stronger than crap.

"This march is bigger than one victim," the reverend said in a pompous voice. "This is about the rights of our people to be in, and live in, nice neighborhoods. You above anyone else here should understand that."

"I understand your march completely, and it never had anything to do with Jevonte," Jesse said. He raised his voice and added, "Why don't you give everyone an update on Jevonte's health? You've been to his house, right? No, that's right, today will be the first time."

The sarcasm was biting, and Reverend Ralph silently seethed. With no defense for his lack of action, he pasted on a smile and turned back to his followers.

A reporter from the South Shore Press, a weekly paper that published different editions for the towns on Long Island's south shore, was standing on the sidewalk a few feet away and caught the exchange. He hoped his tape recorder had as well. Pulling double duty as a staff photographer, he managed to get three photos of the reverend's face in rapid succession before he composed himself and retreated to the street. He hoped at least one photo captured the essence of Reverend Ralph's displeasure.

Reverend Ralph scanned the crowd and motioned for two women to join him in front. Both were in their early thirties, and at the higher end of the group's beauty spectrum. He had each take a side of a long pole that held a white cloth banner with black letters that read: "NO JUSTICE FOR JEVONTE . . . NO PEACE FOR MALBROOK!" He raised the bullhorn over his head and swung it forward to start the march.

"No justice for Jevonte," Reverend Ralph shouted into the bullhorn, but the volume was too high, and it came out distorted.

One of his advisors adjusted the bullhorn's volume to an appropriate level and Reverend Ralph repeated his mantra. The crowd behind responded with, "No peace for Malbrook!"

It was no surprise that aside from Jesse, Daryl, and some reporters, the block had no spectators. Houses appeared to have been abandoned for the day. Shades were down and curtains were drawn, and cars were either pulled to the backs of driveways or into garages.

As they marched up Kennedy, a man opened the window of a second-floor apartment. "This isn't the route Jevonte took! You're a liar!"

It took every ounce of restraint Reverend Ralph had to ignore the heckler. It was true that he initially said they would march the route Jevonte had taken, but he amended it days later to include Kennedy Avenue up to Malbrook Boulevard and back down Franklin Avenue and across Sunset Highway where they would resume Jevonte's route a quarter of a mile from where he was attacked.

The reporters who followed along the beginning of the route scribbled notes as they kept to the sidewalk. Only one of New York's three large networks sent a field reporter, Marcy Hemlock, and she had done nothing to endear herself to Reverend Ralph during the week. She interviewed Malbrook residents of different races and asked about the incident before getting their views on the march. Every interview that aired claimed that while the incident was appalling, it was not indicative of the feelings and behavior of the majority of Malbrook residents, and while Reverend Ralph and the protesters were within their rights to march, they would have preferred they respect the wishes of the victim's family.

Once the protesters had made their way down Franklin Avenue and crossed over Sunset Highway, they were back on Jevonte's route. Reverend Ralph handed the megaphone to one of the men walking behind him to give his voice a rest and strategize with advisers.

*   *   *

Alex and John sat on the front stoop of the Thatcher's two-story cape. The house had been dormered several years earlier and extensive brickwork had been added to the facade over the past summer. It included a new brick stoop that curved outward on each side. Mike pushed the screen door open, handed each of his friends a can of Budweiser, and popped the top on his own can before sitting.

"How is it that you use the word nigger so freely, and yet you support black people every chance you get?" Alex asked.

"Yeah," John agreed.

"It's kind of funny," Mike said, and took a sip of beer. "I've never called anyone I don't like a nigger because I've never meant it as a negative."

"There's a positive way to call someone a nigger?" Alex asked.

"You guys know my brother Jason is in the Malbrook Volunteer Fire Department, right?" They both nodded, and Mike said, "Well, three of his closest friends in the department are black, and two aren't even from Malbrook! They're friends of Jason's from Adelphi, but they hung out at the firehouse so much and live close enough that the chief let them join. Since I'm a junior firefighter until I turn eighteen in January, I hang out at the firehouse with them. There's a basketball hoop on the side of the firehouse and sometimes they let me play."

"Oh, now I get it," John said.

"You do?" Alex asked.

"No. I have no freakin' clue." John popped the top on his first beer and shot the empty can at the garbage can by the side fence and missed by several feet.

"We can see why *you* never played basketball," Mike said.

"The can is empty, and I didn't compensate for the wind."

"Or your shitty aim," Mike said. "Anyway, when we play basketball and I'm guarding one of the black guys with the ball they always say, 'Are you ready, Mikey, I'm gonna make you my nigger.' They say it to each other, too, so I got used to hearing it. And not just on the basketball court. Sometimes when they say, 'my nigger' it means 'my friend,' and other times it's like saying, 'my bitch.' I figured since they're using the word, it's okay for me to use it."

"They call you Mikey?" John asked and burst into laughter.

"That's what you got out of it?"

"Well, you've got to admit, Mikey, it is kind of funny," John said, and he and Alex laughed.

"You call them niggers?" Alex asked.

"Nigger," Mike corrected. "But only because they know me. I wouldn't call someone I don't know nigger."

"Mikey the nigger," John said. "If we join the mafia, that could be your name."

"Does it hurt?" Mike asked.

"What?"

"Being that stupid! None of us are Italian, moron."

"What does that have to do with anything?" John asked. He shaded his eyes from the sun and looked down the block. In the distance he saw the protesters.

"This is exhausting. Can you take this one, Alex?"

"Being Italian is a requirement for joining the mafia."

John eyed them suspiciously, but let it go. He would check on it later.

When they finally heard the first chants, Alex, Mike, and John walked to the curb for a better view. It reminded Alex of the Memorial Day parades he had marched in with his Little League team.

For no reason, John began to clap. The spontaneous act surprised his friends, but they joined in. In the moments it took the protesters to pass, Alex understood what they were fighting for, and in the eyes of many protesters, the small gesture was a ray of hope.

*　　　　　*　　　　　*

The press conference lasted twenty minutes. Reverend Ralph read a prepared statement in which he spoke of the attack and the extent of Jevonte's injuries in more detail, and informed reporters that Jevonte had been released from the hospital—which everyone on Long Island already knew—and was resting at home and eager to get back to school on Monday. When he finished the prepared speech, he spoke of his lack of a response to a heckler, explaining that while *he* had been attacked unjustly, it was only verbal and hardly worth mentioning when compared to the brutal physical attack that Jevonte Jenkins endured. When he finished speaking, he took questions.

"Were you surprised by any reactions, or lack of reactions, along the way?" Charlie Steiner asked. Charlie was a reporter for an upstart local newspaper that didn't have much of a circulation but had ambitions of overtaking Newsday as the best source of news for Long Islanders.

"As you all know, Malbrook is a beautiful town, and for the most part it was a quiet leisurely walk. But there was a moment when three young white men cheered us as we passed. I think everyone who was marching felt it was a truly spiritual moment."

"What about jeers along the way?" Charlie asked, steering him toward the negative, which was what sold newspapers. His journalism professor taught that readers wanted to hear the negative to feel better about their own lives.

"That was expected," Reverend Ralph began. "Freedom of speech is one of the greatest gifts our founding fathers gave us. And while I don't agree with what they said, I appreciate that they had a right to say it." He hesitated a moment. "Just as it was our right to march. We live in a wonderful country, but as I told our supporters, our fight doesn't end here. It will end with the arrest and conviction of the individuals responsible for this cowardly act. Today I stand before you to say that we have a much longer road to walk before we can say that true equality, acceptance, and respect are a reality. But I believe we will get there. Thank you."

*   *   *

Six hours after the conclusion of the press conference, East's Phi chapter held their second meeting in four days. Rumors spread that a motion would be made to remove all officers and hold a new vote after brothers questioned why they hadn't been informed about the emergency meeting. Steven personally called every brother to inform them of the meeting, and except for three with prior commitments, every active brother showed up at Peter's house.

The meeting was moved from the basement to the main floor living room and dining room combined. The move annoyed Peter's mother, but she vacated the living room to watch the thirteen-inch television in her bedroom. If not for his father's bowling night, they would have been relegated to the basement with everyone standing.

Twenty-nine brothers attended, and even with the additional room, they sat shoulder to shoulder on the couches, chairs, and the floor. The usual setup was impossible, so Peter and Marco sat on folding chairs in front of the living room window at the bottom of the stairs and Steven recorded the minutes at the dining room table.

Before the meeting began, Vince Wyatt stood. He was a senior who had attended nearly every meeting since his induction in ninth grade and had been vice president before Marco. He swept his long dirty blond hair from his brown eyes and eyed Marco.

"Before this meeting starts, I want to know why only certain brothers were told about the emergency meeting," Vince said.

"Wait until the minutes are read before you ask questions," Peter said.

"I'm not staying for the meeting."

"If you leave, you're out," Peter said.

"It's a meeting for *this* chapter."

"What's that supposed to mean?" Marco asked.

"It means that some of us aren't happy about the way this chapter is being run, so we've transferred," Vince said. Five more brothers stood.

"You're quitting?" Peter asked.

Steven abbreviated everything as he tried to keep up. He couldn't see Peter's reaction, but imagined his face was red.

"Transferring," Connor Furlong corrected. "We're going to meetings on the other side of town, unless all of the officers step down."

"What's your problem?" Peter asked.

"*Our* problem is that you had a meeting where you tried to kick out one of our most loyal brothers," Vince said. "And you didn't tell anyone who would defend him, which is bullshit!"

"It's not my fault you didn't get the message," Peter said.

"Why don't you read the list of brothers who attended that meeting?" Connor suggested.

"Why should we?" Marco asked. "You're not in our chapter. Go to your meetings on the other side of town because none of the officers are stepping down."

"Now get the fuck out, so we can start our meeting," Peter said.

"Anyone else want to leave?" Marco asked as the six transfers walked out the front door. No one flinched as the front door closed. "Good. Now that all the pussies are gone, we can start the meeting."

Steven continued to catch up with his notes. Since they were from prior to the meeting, he used some extra sheets he had stuffed in the back of the book.

"It might not feel like it, but tonight was a big step forward," Marco said as he stood before the group. "Now that we are rid of the traitors, we have removed the weakness from our chapter, and if that nigger-loving chapter on the other side of town wants them, they can fuckin' have them!"

With the exception of Steven, who was still catching up with his note taking, everyone clapped. Marco raised and then lowered his hands in a gesture for the brothers to quiet down even as he fed off their enthusiasm. He waited for the last of the cheers to die down.

"Tonight, we saw that even people we think are friends may stab us in the back. That's what pussies do. As much as it would feel good to punch these traitors in the face, we must show restraint. Do not look at them. Do not talk to them. I don't care if they were your best friend, you ignore them! They're dead to us!"

"Shouldn't we put it to a vote?" Steven asked.

"Why? You think it's a bad idea?" Marco asked as he stepped forward so he could see Steven.

"No," Steven said. "But the meeting hasn't started, so we can't make decisions on fraternity matters."

"Then this meeting is called to order," Peter said, and pounded his gavel on the wall behind him.

The meeting went as scheduled, with motions passed for every brother not to speak to the transfers. More

than any prior meeting, for Marco it felt like a turning
point. It started as a mutiny and ended as a rally.

Marco stood one last time before the meeting
ended, and the rooms grew silent.

"The officers have been working on a plan for our
chapter, and next Saturday night we will reveal it to
everyone. We are going to make this a chapter no one will
dare fuck with! We'll make it the most feared chapter of
any fraternity on Long Island."

The room erupted as the members stomped their
feet and chanted, "Phi," until Peter's mother yelled down to
keep quiet.

Chapter 11

On Monday morning, the thirteen members of Phi's pledge glass gathered outside the entrance to the gym. All were fifteen to twenty minutes early and ready to begin pledging—or dogging as it was more commonly known—which would lead up to their hell night. Each pledge wore a suit jacket or sport coat with a dress shirt and tie, two white string necklaces, one which held a toothbrush, and the other a small notepad with a pen pushed through the metal spiral that held it together. In their pockets were several packs of Wrigley's Gum in different flavors to give to brothers upon request.

The toothbrushes were used far less than in earlier years since most members wore sneakers to school as opposed to the shoes worn by their earlier counterparts, which apparently needed constant cleaning. If a pledge earned too many demerits, they were sometimes asked to clean a brother's gym locker with their toothbrush, or if a brother had new leather Puma, Nike, or Adidas sneakers, they might request a shine from one of the pledges. Those instances were rare.

The notepads were to remind brothers of the pledge's activities for each day, and to which brother they were to report after the final bell. The notepads were also used to give demerits for a poorly done task or failure to adhere to all given standards, as well as checks or plusses for jobs completed or well done.

The first two days were the most intense because brothers wanted to ensure each pledge was thoroughly committed to joining the fraternity and wasn't wasting their time. Most of the harshest hazing was done by the newest brothers since the experience of being in the pledge's shoes was fresh in their memories and they welcomed the chance to dish out what they had received. Younger brothers had to wait for the older brothers to choose before they got their chance.

If a brother's hazing was deemed too extreme, dangerous, or brutal, they were reprimanded and banned from hazing and hell night. That was usually enough to keep it semi-civilized, though as recently as 1976 a brother was suspended from the hazing activities when he had his pledge dress in black and run back and forth across Sunset Highway ten times after dark in a section of the highway with poor visibility. The pledge didn't complain, but the following day when asked about the previous night's hazing, he described the rush from nearly being hit by two cars.

The only other incident in their chapter's history had involved a former member named Gavin Larsen in 1964. No one with access to chapter records confirmed it, but since he appeared in Phi's yearbook photos from 1961 through 1963, and not his senior year in 1964, it was widely believed.

Gavin was a mild-mannered kid until he stepped on the football field. Teammates joked that he checked his mind at the door and gave every ounce of his strength to punish the opposing team for stepping on *his* football field. During football camp prior to his senior year, he was introduced to steroids and packed twenty extra pounds of muscle onto his already impressive six-foot-two frame. He was a fullback on offense and linebacker on defense being recruited by five Division I football programs until he was dismissed from the team for punching head coach Eric Mastrota during the first game of 1963. The incident happened when Gavin was removed from the game following an unsportsmanlike conduct penalty for hitting a player on the other team well after the whistle had blown. Gavin went to the sideline, threw his helmet down and flipped over the table holding the team's water. When Coach Mastrota put a hand on Gavin's shoulder to calm him, Gavin turned and swung. The punch caught the coach on the chin, and he was out before he hit the ground. Gavin charged at a second coach who ordered him back to the team bus, and it took four of Gavin's teammates to subdue him. Gavin was removed from the team, and the two-way star's football career was over. He received a two-week suspension from school and was barred from playing on any athletic teams for the rest of his senior year.

According to Phi lore, Gavin took his pledge to a desolate part of the train tracks that ran behind houses just before Malbrook's second, much smaller train station known as Booker Station. The station was named after the man who had designed and built many of the houses in the western part of Malbrook. Gavin ordered the young man to stand on the third rail until a train came within fifty feet, and then jump in front it and roll off the tracks. The pledge refused because he had been told touching the third rail could kill a person and told Gavin he would only do it if Gavin demonstrated it was safe. Gavin became so enraged that a mere pledge would suggest such a thing that he beat him so severely his face needed more than twenty stitches. Gavin was expelled from Phi the following day. Rather than repeat his senior year after another two-week suspension made passing his necessary classes impossible, Gavin dropped out of school and enlisted in the army.

The Gavin Larsen story was infinitely more believable than the story of the unnamed pledge from another chapter whose father was a dentist and supposedly gave him several shots of Novocain in each of his ass cheeks prior to hell night. According to the story that was passed down, the pledge was five-foot-three and weighed one hundred pounds. Depending on who told the story, he took anywhere from two to three hundred shots on his ass with paddles and shaved down baseball bats from brothers who were as much as a foot taller and more than twice his weight. When the Novocain wore off, the kid went into shock, and his father discovered him dead the following morning. Ridiculous as it was, the story spread to each new pledge class.

Mike was the first brother to arrive at school. He parked diagonally through the closest two spaces and went to inspect each pledge. Each met Mike's dress and behavior code, so he wrote a check in each notebook. Once he was done, other brothers began the process of degrading them and ordering them to do stupid things for everyone's amusement.

Mike and John claimed Quentin as their pledge for the day, which meant Quentin had to report to John's locker immediately after collecting his books following the final bell. Quentin had no idea what to expect but had prepared himself mentally. To the black pledges, being treated like a pledge was mostly business as usual.

Guy was about to claim a black pledge when Kyle pulled him aside. Kyle led Guy around the side of the school and past the library where no one could hear them.

"Listen Guy, I don't want you claiming any black pledges," Kyle said so matter-of-factly Guy thought it was a joke.

When Guy realized he was serious, he asked, "What's your problem?"

"My problem is one black marble."

"There were what, twenty-five other brothers in the room? What would make you think it was my marble?" Guy asked, agitated. "And don't think I won't bring this up at our next meeting."

"If you feel that strongly, I think you should, but—"

"You bet your ass I will!" Guy said loud enough for the brothers and pledges by the entrance to hear.

"I went over every bylaw before and after the interviews, and you lied," Kyle said.

"Maybe I made a mistake."

"A mistake about what? How would you know what I'm talking about?"

"You've accused me of something you can't prove that calls my character into question," Guy said. He peeked around the corner. Except for Mike, they were too busy to notice.

"You're right, I can't prove you put the black marble in, but how will it look if they find out you lied about being able to show our remaining marble, which everyone was willing to do?"

"You're blackmailing me?"

"No, I'm telling you what will happen if you claim a black pledge or bring up this conversation. It's in your best interest to listen. You don't need to haze any black pledges. You'll barely have time anyway."

"You know what? Fuck you! I'll do what I want," Guy said. He walked to the far entrance by the soccer field.

"Suit yourself," Kyle said.

"Is everything okay?" Alex asked. "Guy sounded pretty pissed off."

"My dad always says it's better to be pissed off than pissed on."

"That's true, but that didn't answer my question," Alex said with a sly smile.

"Nope. And that should be your answer," Kyle said and smiled.

Whatever they had talked about was confidential. Alex had never heard Kyle talk behind anyone's back, and that trait made him an ideal president.

"Who did you pick as your pledge for the day?" Alex asked.

"I didn't pick one. I'll let everyone else put them through the first few days. I just want to be available if anyone needs me. What about you?"

Alex and Kyle walked along the side of the school by the soccer field and entered the doors Guy had gone through.

"Lucas McHugh."

"The short white kid?" Kyle asked.

"That's the one. And isn't it funny that you have to specify he's white?"

"You know what that means?" Kyle asked.

"What?"

"We're making progress."

"That we are," Alex agreed.

*   *   *

After the final bell, Alex went to his locker to find Lucas waiting. Alex took Lucas's notepad and checked to see who would haze Lucas with him.

"Did you get your books from your locker?"

"Yes, sir," Lucas barked.

"Good," Alex said. He flipped to the first page of the notebook. Above Alex's name were three checks and two plusses, and below was Kyle's name. "Did Kyle say we're supposed to meet him somewhere?"

"No, sir," Lucas said, even louder than his earlier reply.

"Let's go. We need to find Kyle." Alex grabbed the few books he needed and closed his locker.

"Yes sir," Lucas yelled, and everyone left in the hall turned to look at him.

Alex led him to Kyle's locker on the first floor.

"Aren't you supposed—"

Kyle put a finger over his closed lips and Alex stopped. Kyle turned to Lucas and said, "Walk to the far end of the hall, put a finger in each ear and hum the national anthem. If anyone comes near you, growl and bark at them."

"Yes sir!"

Lucas walked slowly down the hall and sat against the wall. He started to hum and a girl who appeared to be in seventh grade stopped to watch. He growled, barked, and chased her halfway down the stairs.

"I know what you're going to ask me. There are a few people in our fraternity that I trust implicitly, and you're one of them," Kyle said.

"I didn't get a 1400 on the SATs like some people, so what exactly does implicitly mean?" Alex asked.

"I can trust you with anything. You'll do the right thing, and I don't have to worry that you're going to tell anyone."

They were the same age, but to Alex, Kyle somehow seemed like an older brother. Kyle had always been one of Alex's best friends, though since ninth grade, when Kyle became class president along with part of the school newspaper staff, his activities kept him too busy to hang out with on a regular basis. Alex's mother referred to Kyle as "an old soul" which Alex thought summed him up well. While Alex still hadn't chosen a college major, Kyle had decided to study computer science in seventh grade and had already sold several computer programs he had written. At times it seemed like Kyle was just killing time in high school.

"I can always count on you. You, John, and Mike are three people I know I can trust with anything and that's why I signed Lucas's book and had Mike and John choose their pledge last night and sign first thing this morning." Kyle saw Lucas walking back and said, "Two more times!"

"Yes, sir!" Lucas yelled. His voice could be heard on the first floor.

"Why?" Alex asked.

"Mike has football after school and can't haze anyone but the two guys on the team, but John is free. John won't put a pledge in danger. I had Mike sign with John, and I signed with you. It gives you both the opportunity to have your own pledge each day, and it's two pledges I don't have to worry about."

"But I thought every pledge has to be supervised by two brothers."

"It's what everyone thinks, but it was just for one year. That was also how we limited hazing after dark. It's so we don't have pledges being hazed for ridiculously long hours."

Down the hall, Lucas crouched on the floor while a cute blond girl scratched behind his ears. She ran her hand through his hair and then along his cheek.

"I don't remember getting that kind of treatment when I was a pledge," Alex said.

"Me neither. Is that his girlfriend?"

"I don't know. I've never talked to him except during wrestling. He's a quiet kid."

"Before we graduate, I want to sit down with you and a few others and get rid of outdated chapter bylaws and create new ones."

"Why?" Alex asked.

Kyle watched Lucas, shook his head, and laughed.

"You know how some people aren't the same when they get to eleventh and twelfth grade?"

"Everyone changes."

"I mean drastic changes, like the three assholes who recently quit. The ones who get into drugs, drop academically or quit playing sports." Kyle paused, then added, "Some end up looking like the dregs of humanity, and it's embarrassing that they're brothers. I think we should have bylaws to set standards for academics or athletics, or both."

"Maybe some moral standards, too," Alex said.

"Can you imagine if the brothers we got rid of this week had a black pledge?"

"I don't think it would have been a problem," Alex said.

"No?"

"They wouldn't have gotten past their interviews," Alex said.

"Good point. I want you to look at everything we do, see what needs to be done better, and how to do it."

"Count me in," Alex said. It sounded so lame Alex wished he hadn't said anything. "I have a question though."

"Shoot," Kyle said.

"Is the story about the pledge and the third rail true?"

"Unfortunately, yes," Kyle said.

Alex looked down the hall at Lucas, who for the next ten school days, along with the entire pledge class, would be known only as "pledge" or "dog". The girl who had been scratching him was gone, his fingers were back in his ears, and he was humming too slowly to identify the tune. He must have assumed he finished too quickly and would not make the same mistake. Pledges learned quickly.

"Pledge, front and center!" Kyle yelled.

"Yes, sir!" Lucas left his books and ran down the hall faster than either thought him capable.

Lucas stood at attention and waited for the next command.

"Why did you leave your books back there?" Alex asked.

"When summoned by a brother, a pledge must proceed to that brother posthaste, sir!" Lucas yelled, as if the sentence had been one long word.

Kyle pulled Lucas's notepad forward and slid the pen from the coil. In the book he wrote a plus sign. Next to it he added, QUOTED FROM PLEDGE RULES WHILE EXPLAINING ACTIONS. Lucas wasn't allowed to see what was written in his notebook until hazing finished for the day, and Kyle's expression told him nothing.

*   *   *

Alex could see that Lucas had prepared himself for almost anything. He appeared to be ready to do menial tasks and chores, or silly things for Alex's amusement but Alex thought he might be expecting worse since Lucas was on the wrestling team and Alex was the captain. He was sure by now that Lucas had heard stories about how brothers sometimes bought Long Island Railroad tickets and sent pledges to the city with no additional money and had them bring back specific items to prove they had gone. There was always another brother on the train with the pledge, though they were never told. Alex had never bothered to do any of those things, although he had gone along as an extra brother on the train to tail a dog being sent on a task. As a personal rule, Alex kept his treatment of the pledges respectful.

Alex marched Lucas halfway around the track that circled the football field where the football team was practicing, and up the visiting team's bleachers which were about half the size of the home team's bleachers. He took several minutes to demonstrate his exercise regimen. Rather than watch as Lucas began, Alex joined him. Together, they spent forty minutes on the bleachers going through leg strengthening exercises.

By the time they finished the workout on the smaller bleachers, their shirts were soaked through with sweat. Alex saw the exhaustion in Lucas's eyes and said, "If you need a break let me know."

"No thank you, sir! My mission is to bring success to Phi Gamma Alpha, sir!" He followed behind Alex and marched in silence. "May I ask a question, sir?"

"That's why I'm here," Alex said. He stopped to allow Lucas to catch up and walk beside him, which was something pledges rarely did. Brothers led and pledges followed.

"I'm not complaining, sir, but if you're hazing me, why are you doing the workout?"

Alex knelt to tie his sneaker. Lucas looked away so he was not looking down at him, which would have been cause for a demerit.

"Some brothers haze to be sure a pledge is committed, but I figure if you're here you're committed. I don't want you to quit. There is a good reason why you and every other pledge were asked to join our brotherhood. I want to prepare you to be the best possible brother. I figured you might get something out of my off-season workout, and if you do, that will be good for you. You can take what you like, change what you don't, and make it your own."

"Thank you, sir," Lucas said. "I won't let you down."

"If I thought you would let me down, I wouldn't have bothered. My hope is that when you see wrestlers pledging, you'll do the same for them." Alex said and patted him on the back.

"I will, sir."

Alex marched Lucas to the larger bleachers on the home side and led him through an even more intense workout. Alex knew Lucas wouldn't slack off during the off-season and wasn't surprised when he finished without stopping.

"Great job today, pledge. Now go home, study, and do your homework. Tomorrow's another day, and it might be more difficult. But remember, each day brings you closer to brotherhood."

"Thank you, sir!" Lucas yelled loud enough to turn the heads of football players who weren't participating in special team drills.

*   *   *

After the final bell on Tuesday, Quentin Blake waited by Alex's locker. Alex hadn't planned much for Quentin, since he rarely chose pledges he didn't know personally. They met John and his pledge, Clay Norton, at John's car and drove to Alex's house.

Alex went to the garage and grabbed a blue bucket and two large sponges. He squirted Palmolive in the bucket and filled it with warm water. The thought of having the pledges do menial tasks never appealed to Alex, but there was no harm in having them wash John's car.

The two pledges were extremely thorough in their cleaning detail. By the time they had finished with the Crager rims, they shined like the day John had bought them. When they had almost finished washing the outside of John's car, Alex brought out the vacuum and gave it to Clay to use while Quentin dried the outside. For the finishing touches, Quentin used Armor All on the tires while Clay did the same on the dashboard.

The pledges seemed to enjoy the work, but neither each time the Aerosmith album that was blaring from the car's speakers changed songs, they looked at each other, smiled and shook their heads. Quentin finished the last tire a few minutes after Clay was done. Together, they stood at attention before John and Alex.

"The car is clean, sirs," they said simultaneously.

John inspected the car closely for show, and when he was done, he took each of the pledge's notebooks and wrote a plus sign and, JOB WELL DONE beside it.

"We should get going," John said. "I'll catch you later, Alex."

John nodded his appreciation to Quentin. Clay opened John's door, waited for him to get in, closed it, ran to the passenger side, and jumped in. John sped off.

"Do you want to come in and watch television?" Alex asked, as usual, skipping the practice of calling the pledges pledge or dog when no one else was around. "If you'd rather do homework, that's fine, too. I don't have anything else for you to do, but I'll catch hell if I let you go home too early."

"Are you sure it's okay, sir?" Quentin asked.

"Am I sure what's okay?"

"Are you sure it's okay for me to come in your house, sir? I wouldn't want you to get in trouble, sir."

Alex took three sheets of paper from the back pocket of his Levis and skimmed them. "There's nothing in the rules that says a pledge can't enter a brother's house."

"Forgive me for speaking frankly, sir, but it has been my experience in Malbrook that white people do not welcome black people into their homes."

"When it comes to Phi, forget everything you know about Malbrook. You are a solid student, a great athlete, and from everything I—or any of the brothers I have talked to heard—you are a good person. Skin color is irrelevant."

Quentin had lived in Malbrook nearly three years and all but three of his friends were black. He had gone to catholic school in Queens until the previous year when his parents finally agreed to let him go to West High for ninth grade. Prior to that he hadn't had much of a chance to make friends near his house, and only made friends because he played basketball in the park. He made three white friends who called him now and then to play basketball or football. Not once had he been invited into their homes, and when he invited them, they made excuses. It was so ingrained in him that the simple invitation into Alex's house nearly brought him to tears.

"Thank you, sir. I would be happy to come in and watch television with you," Quentin said.

Quentin sat on the living room couch and watched reruns of "The Brady Bunch" and the experience was almost surreal. When Alex brought him a glass of black cherry soda, he was reminded of times at the park when his white friends shared their drinks with each other, but never offered him a sip. He never gave it a second thought at the time because he was happy to have friends. In retrospect he realized they had never been his friends. They were guys who needed someone to make the sides even. He ignored the things he overheard, like a warning to his friends by an older kid he didn't know not to let his lips touch their soda cans or bottles because niggers carry diseases. Other times, he purposely tuned them out. *Sometimes you need selective hearing to get along in this world,* his father had told him.

Quentin was surprised that Alex's living room was identical to his own, including the furniture configuration. He thought he could probably walk through the house blindfolded and identify each room.

When Alex held out a tin of Charles Chips barbecue flavored potato chips for Quentin to take, Quentin said, "May I have some, sir?"

"That's why I'm holding them in front of you," Alex said, and laughed. "When someone offers you something, you don't have to ask permission."

"Thank you, sir, I'm just not used to this kind of treatment."

"It takes everyone a few days to get used to pledging," Alex said.

"Actually, it's being treated like a person that I'm not used to, sir."

"I hope that doesn't mean I'm going too easy on you," Alex said. He meant it as a joke but felt bad for having said it. "Once you put on your Phi colors, everyone will treat you with respect. It won't fix ignorance, but it's a start."

"Thank you, sir," Quentin said, and reached into the tin and took a handful of the light brown potato chips. "Did you offer me barbecue chips and black cherry soda because of my skin color, sir?"

Alex turned red until Quentin's serious look broke with laughter.

"You had me there," Alex said.

"Sorry, sir, I couldn't resist."

"No, that's good, I want you to be yourself. You may be called pledge for the next two weeks, but you have more than thirty brothers who have your back in any situation," Alex said. "That's a promise."

*   *   *

In the basement of Peter's house, Marco's eyes were fixed on the swastika at the center of the Nazi flag. The flag was spread across one of the couches. The table was covered with paper listing every member of their chapter, a phone book, envelopes and slips of paper.

"Here's one," Marco said. "Silverman, comma, S. Forty-eight Spiegel Street."

Peter printed the name and address on a slip of paper, put it in an envelope and sealed it. "Who should we give that to?"

The list of brothers had dwindled after the recent transfers. Freshmen and sophomores outnumbered juniors and seniors seventeen to eight. In October they would give out thirty bids to eighth and ninth graders and the disparity would be even greater. A chapter with that many young members would be like a small, easily controlled army.

"Spiegel is about seven or eight blocks from here," Marco said. He found two freshmen on the list. "These two can walk there."

Peter printed the names on the outside of the envelope, and asked, "Did you find out Alex's girlfriend's last name?"

"Fishman," Marco said. "I don't know her father's first name, but she lives on Casey Lane. It's on the other side of town so we need a brother who can drive to pair up with one of the younger ones. But not Jimmy, because he's with me."

Peter found the listing, printed the name and address on a slip of paper, and sealed it in an envelope. He chose two names and wrote them on the outside.

Marco flipped through the book. He stopped and ran his finger down the left side of the page. "Holy shit! I hit the mother lode."

"What?"

"There are . . ." Marco stopped to count, "six Golds, two Goldbergs, one Goldman, and three Goldsteins." Marco counted them together and said, "That makes twelve Jewish families on one page. I didn't think we had that many Jewish families living in Malbrook."

"Why else would there be a temple?"

"To piss off good people."

"How do you know all of them are Jewish?" Peter asked.

"Any name that starts with silver or gold is Jewish. It's the same with names that end with man, berg, or stein."

Peter considered it for a moment and then started printing the names and addresses on the slips of papers. "What if they're not Jewish?"

"It's their own fault for having a Jewish name, so fuck 'em if they can't take a joke."

Peter slid paper in front of Marco and said, "Here, write some so we get done faster."

"My handwriting sucks. If I write them, they'll end up at the wrong houses," Marco said and pushed the paper back to Peter.

Chapter 12

After two days of hazing, Phi's pledges had adapted to the routine. It was the same every year. The most difficult day of hazing was the Thursday immediately before hell night because it was a day of complete silence for the pledges. They were permitted to speak only if they were called on in class by a teacher. They couldn't even speak to order lunch. Brothers tried anything they could think of to make the pledges talk. Punishment for failure was a train ride to Penn Station dressed in a miniskirt and a halter top. Any time someone boarded the train, the pledge, was required to show off his sexiest dance moves. It had been six years since anyone made that mistake.

John was late picking up Alex. On the way to school, John ignored the speed limit and most stop signs and pulled into the student lot as the bell beckoning students to homeroom rang. Everyone scattered like roaches under a light.

"Shit," John said as the mad scramble began.

"Worried you'll be late for homeroom?"

"I didn't get a pledge for the day."

"What's the big deal?" Alex asked.

John bit into an apple his mother had packed for him. She worried that John would eat garbage if left to his own devices, so she packed healthy lunches each day. She had been doing it since seventh grade, and with few exceptions the result had been the same. John ate the apple, pear, or orange before he entered school, and the sandwich during homeroom. To buy lunch in seventh and eighth grade he had used money from his Daily News paper route, in ninth grade he used money from his summer landscaping job, and since then he had used the money from his job at Beefsteak Charlie's.

"Kyle wants us each to sign out a black pledge, so no one does anything stupid to make them quit," John said. He took another bite of his apple and tossed what little remained in a trash can outside the gym entrance.

"Look who wants to be a good brother," Alex said, and ruffled John's hair.

"I'm not so good today."

"Mike signed your name and Kyle signed mine. Just ask who you have," Alex whispered as they passed the attendance office.

"How would they know to sign for us?"

"I told Kyle and Mike on Monday because I figured you'd be late picking me up at least once or twice during the two weeks."

"Why didn't you tell me?"

They walked to their homerooms, which were two doors apart on the second floor. "I figured if you thought we had to be early we might get here on time."

"Pretty smart."

"I have my moments," Alex said.

"Do you realize this is reverse racism?"

"There's no such thing as reverse racism," Alex said.

"What would you call it when we're only watching out for the black pledges?"

"Keeping the playing field even," Alex said.

Alex stepped into room 223 just prior to the late bell. John strolled leisurely down to 219, stopping at the water fountain before walking in late. Regardless of what time John walked in, or if he missed homeroom completely, Mrs. Nastase never marked him late. She adored his carefree attitude and found his excuses—which had grown more creative over the years—amusing. She taught English and encouraged him to take a creative writing course in college, but with little interest in reading, he told her writing was out of the question.

*   *   *

The first fire drill of the year came during second period and gave Alex a chance to catch up with a friend he hadn't seen since the end of the previous school year. He was listening to a raunchy vacation story that sounded a little too much like "Grease" to be true when he felt a gentle tug on the back of his shirt.

Alex had avoided Julie since their breakup by altering his routes to each class. He even stayed away from the hall where she and her friends had lockers. Now a fire drill had ruined everything.

"How are you doing?" Julie asked.

There was nothing Alex wanted to say to her. He was angry at the situation and even angrier she had asked. According to John, who was by no means an authority but had moments, proper protocol in failed high school relationships that lasted more than six months was avoidance for a marking period unless cheating was involved, in which case all bets were off. She should have walked past him without a word. What was she expecting him to say? *I miss you.* That was never going to happen. He had kept busy enough to fool everyone, including himself, into thinking life after Julie was nearly perfect.

"I'm okay," he said. "You?"

"Not so great. I've had some time to think about it, and you were right; my father wasn't nice to you." Her eyes filled with tears. "I'm sorry, Alex. I really miss you."

"I—" Alex began and stopped. *Miss you, too* were the first words that came to mind before he held them back. Saying them would change nothing. Her father was an insurmountable obstacle.

"What?"

"Nothing. I want to be friends. I just can't do it right now," Alex said

"So, we're over? You don't even want to try?" Tears streamed down her cheeks. She made no effort to wipe them and despite wanting to, neither did Alex.

"I tried. I really tried. I just can't deal with your father anymore," Alex said, and turned away.

"That's it?" Julie asked.

Haven't I already answered that?

Alex walked toward the bleachers, unnoticed by the teachers who had taken the opportunity to go to the far side of the parking lot to smoke while they waited for the announcement to escort the students back into the school.

*　　　*　　　*

On the opposite side of the school by the two tennis courts, John and Mike discussed how well the pledges had been performing. Alex caught John's eye and he gestured for Mike to turn. They could both see something was wrong by the way Alex walked with his head down and his hands in his pockets.

"We should check on him," John said.

Alex disappeared behind the far side of the bleachers, and Mike's eyes drifted back to the school where a friend was comforting Julie.

"Wait and see if he comes back when the bell rings. He might just need a few minutes alone."

"What if he doesn't come back?" John asked.

"Then we'll go see what's up."

"I have to make up a lab experiment next period," John said.

"In an actual class with a teacher and everything?"

"Oh, shut up," John said.

The bell rang three times in succession and the students lined up to reenter the school.

"You go make up your lab and I'll check on Alex," Mike said.

"Yeah, right," John said. "What's Mr. Roberts gonna do, fail me?"

*   *   *

Alex didn't wipe his tears until he reached the top of the bleachers by the press box and turned back to the football field. He put his feet on the seat in front of him, folded his arms across his spread knees, rested his head on his arms and sobbed.

He knew their relationship was doomed the moment he met Julie's father. The arrogant prick refused to stand when he shook Alex's hand. Alex had almost ended things that night, and as he sat with his back to the school, he wished he had. Alex dated Julie for a month after meeting her father almost out of spite. If he had just accepted the inevitable, the quiet sophomore from the previous year might never have stolen his heart.

Alex was so lost in his thoughts he never heard John and Mike climb the back of the bleachers. It was the first time either had climbed them since freshman year when they played bleacher tag during lunch period at least three times each week and could climb up and down the back in seconds.

Bleacher tag had a blatant disregard for safety that seemed to appeal to the carefree invulnerability of teenagers who imagined they would live forever and never age. During lunch periods, there were often eight or more kids climbing different sections of the bleachers in every way imaginable. They ran across the rows of seats, sometimes ascending or descending as they ran, seldom using the two rows between the three sections that were designed for walking up and down. Most days everyone who played either forgot to eat or ate as they played.

Mike pulled himself through the top of the bleachers first. He was about to say something when he saw Alex's face and decided to keep quiet. John poked his head through a moment later and pulled himself up.

"Hey, Al, you okay?" John asked, ignoring the obvious.

Alex rubbed the tears from his eyes on the sleeves of his blue and white Adidas tee shirt and took a deep breath before he looked up. John and Mike took seats two rows in front facing him.

"I just talked to Julie," Alex said.

"If you think a blowjob would help take your mind off things, I know someone who has the same lunch period as you," John said.

"Come on, John, they just broke up. Alex isn't that hard up that he wants you to give him a blowjob," Mike said.

Alex chuckled.

"You're such a dick," John said.

"If I was a dick I'd be in your mouth," Mike said, and he and Alex laughed.

"And if I was a dick I'd be in your mom, like I was last night," John said.

"My mom isn't a dirty tube sock."

"I know," John said.

"Good comeback," Mike said and laughed again.

John was losing badly, so he put an arm across Mike's chest and pushed him backward. Mike hooked his feet under the seat in front of Alex and caught himself.

"Good try," Mike said.

"Not good enough."

Alex felt his spirit lift as he watched the banter between two of his best friends as dark gray rain clouds rolled in. Getting over the breakup would not be easy, but as the rain suddenly began to drop in sheets, he knew his friends could be counted on to help him through anything life sent his way.

John led the way to the entrance by the teachers' parking lot despite Mike insisting the only unlocked doors would be by the boy's side of the gym. John and Mike pulled at each of six doors, and as Mike predicted, they were all locked.

"What now, genius?" Mike asked.

"Follow me," John said.

Alex and Mike watched from beneath the covered area outside the school entrance as John ran along the side of the building to the second classroom. John pushed up each of the windows of the woodshop until he found one that was unlocked. The woodshop was empty, and the lights were off as John climbed through the window.

John poked his head out and said "Come on. What are you guys waiting for?"

"Just come around and let us in," Alex said.

*   *   *

The heavy rain continued throughout the afternoon, at times accompanied by thunder and lightning. By the end of the school day, the rain had slowed to a steady drizzle, but the football field was unusable, and all outdoor activities were canceled.

The football coaches held a brief meeting before letting the team go. Losing a day of practice three days before their first game could not be considered a tragedy, but it meant cutting back on special teams' preparation on Thursday. Even studying film from the previous year was out since their projector was broken and a new one was not in the budget.

Mike was happy to have a free day and quickly shifted gears to Phi. He and John signed up to haze Xavier Coleman, a sophomore who had moved to Malbrook the previous fall and quickly made his presence felt on the basketball court. He was tall, thin and had a world of confidence.

John was shooting baskets in the gym when Mike came in through the entrance by the boy's locker room. Outside the gym, Xavier stood at attention watching students exit the building into a drizzle that was turning to rain.

Mike dropped his books on the floor and grabbed the basketball after a shot by John bounced off the rim to the left. Mike dribbled twice and shot. "Nothing but net," Mike said as he shot, but the ball hit the far side of the rim, bounced up, hit the near side of the rim, and fell through the net. "Where's our pledge?" Mike asked as he looked around. "And please don't tell me you lost him."

"He's in the hall. His name is Xavier, but everyone calls him X. I mean except for us."

"X? I like that," Mike said. He picked up his books and gave the basketball a soft kick toward the athletic director's office at the far end of the gym.

"I don't get it though; why not call him Z?" John asked.

"You do realize Xavier begins with an X, right?"

"No, but now it makes sense," John said.

"What have you got planned for him?"

"I didn't know it was gonna rain, so I planned to have him cut my lawn and clean out my garage," John said.

"It's always the same boring crap. Don't you have any new ideas?"

"I was thinking of something, but it'll take a few minutes to explain," John said.

"Don't tell me you want to set up an obstacle course, because I'm not standing in the rain again."

"It's not what I was thinking of, but you have to admit it was pretty damn funny when we did it last year."

"It was at that," Mike said and chuckled at the memory. "So, what's your idea this time?"

"We need two more brothers and a second pledge to help," John said.

Mike pushed the gym doors open and found Xavier by the school's trophy case. There were two dozen trophies in the case and Mike was hoping to add a second for football after they had collected their first trophy the previous year. The baseball team had won their conference in his junior year after finishing fifth the year before when he was a sophomore third baseman playing varsity. The football team won six of eight the previous year and as the number three seed upset the second seed in the semifinals before losing the county championship 27-23 on a late touchdown. Only six starters had graduated, which meant they were primed to finish their quest.

"Okay, dog, I want you to go outside and speed walk in slow motion from one set of doors to the other while we work something out," Mike said.

"Yes, sir," Xavier said. He hurried outside and began his odd trek between the gym and lobby entrances. Everyone who passed stopped to watch for a minute or two.

John followed Mike to his brand new black and white Camaro Rally Sport. It was parked, as usual, diagonally through the first two spots.

"Okay, explain," Mike said.

John filled Mike in on what had happened between Alex and Marco. He went over the entire beating in detail, and when he told about the chase by Marco and his friends, he left out Jevonte's cousin. It wasn't until he finished that he realized he had broken his promise to Alex.

"So, what's your plan?" Mike asked.

"We get Marco, tie him up, and bring him to our meeting tonight and let him fight Alex without his friends around."

"It wouldn't be much of a fight," Mike said, amused.

"That's what makes it such a great idea."

By the entrance, Xavier's slow-motion speed walk had garnered a handful of spectators. He even made facial expressions in slow motion.

"Okay, let's do it," Mike said. He called Xavier over to his car and told him to get in. "We'll follow John to his house and drop off his car, and then we have an errand to run."

"Yes, sir!" Xavier shouted and opened the door. "Should I sit in the back seat, sir?"

"Do I look like a chauffeur?"

"No, sir! I just didn't think you'd want a dog in the front seat of your beautiful car, sir!"

"When we pick up John you can move to the back," Mike said. They both slid into the leather bucket seats in the front.

* * *

John silently regretted having told Mike about Marco as they drove across Malbrook followed closely behind by Declan in a second car. Mark, who was also a lineman on the football team, sat in Declan's passenger seat, with their pledge in the back. Mike told Declan they were looking to bring Marco to the meeting as a joke, which was at least partially true, so no one except John and Mike knew the real reason for the hunt. The two cars drove up and down the blocks between Marco's house and East High.

"Do you have any idea where Marco might be?" Mike asked.

John rubbed his hand against the passenger window to clear it. "If it wasn't for this damn rain, we probably would have seen him by now. Maybe we should check the school and send Declan to Marco's house to wait for us there."

Mike shook his head. He heard that Marco rarely went anywhere alone, and though *he* didn't worry Mike, the pack he hung out with did.

"Why not?" John asked.

"There's safety in numbers," Mike said.

"Marco's a pussy," John said. "Any of us could kick his ass."

"I'm aware of that. But what if he has a bunch of his loser buddies with him? That kid Peter is like a gorilla from "Planet of the Apes", so I'd rather fight six on ten than three on ten." Mike checked his rearview mirror and caught Xavier's eye. "What do you think, dog?"

"I am confident that we will be victorious regardless, sir!"

"See, even X thinks we can take them," John said.

"Would fighting three against six or more put the pledge in danger?" Mike asked after he shot John a nasty look for using the dog's nickname.

"Maybe," John conceded.

"Do our hazing instructions say not to put a pledge in danger?"

"Yes," John muttered.

"Then what should we do?" Mike asked.

"Stick together."

They continued around the blocks by the school and then to the pizza parlor and McDonald's where East High students went for lunch. They waited in the lot ten minutes before giving up and parking on opposite ends of Marco's block. After fifteen more minutes without seeing a person, Mike got out of his car and waved Declan down.

Declan and Mike spoke briefly and agreed to abandon the search. As badly as Declan wanted to grab Marco and toss him in the trunk of his car, he was okay with going home to relax. Trying to find Marco wasted an opportunity to have the pledges move his weight bench and nearly four hundred pounds of free weights stacked beside it from the basement to the garage, but there was no rush since he used the weights at school during football season.

After Declan left, Mike pulled in front of Marco's house and gave it one last look. As he drove up the block, Jimmy's car turned the corner. Mike paid no attention, but

Jimmy's eyes fixed on the flashy Camaro he had seen a lot lately.

*   *   *

Everyone who visited Marco's house more than once knew knocking on the door was a bad decision. Jimmy knew better than anyone to avoid Frank. He peeked through the front door at the living room on the left and made sure no one was there before he let himself in and went quickly to the right and down to Marco's room in the basement.

The smell of dirty laundry permeated the entire basement. At any given time, there were up to six loads of dirty laundry waiting to be washed just ten feet from Marco's bed. Marco didn't have a wall, door or even partition to separate his "room" from the rest of the basement, but he had grown immune to the constant stench his guests noticed immediately. His mother collected clothes regularly and dropped them down the chute, but rarely came down to do them until she either had time to wash them all or ran low on clean clothes for her daughter. Some days the mountain of clothes reached halfway to the ceiling.

Marco washed his own clothes, though sometimes it was to the detriment of everyone else's laundry. If the clothes in the washer were mostly dry, Marco tossed them in one of the baskets and replaced them with his own. When his load was finished, he tossed whatever had been in the dryer on top of the clothes in the basket, which gave both loads a damp smell that filled the basement with an unpalatable funk.

Marco was lying on his bed with his eyes closed and headphones on, listening to The Doors. Jimmy pulled one of the earphones off and Marco jumped, half expecting to see Frank standing over him.

"What the fuck? You scared the crap out of me."

"Well, you told me not to just say something, so I tried that."

"Every time something other than my alarm clock wakes me, I expect that dickhead to be standing over me," Marco said. "It fucks with your head. I swear, sometimes I just wanna slit his throat while he's sleeping."

"He probably wants to do the same thing to you."

"Thanks, asshole. And fuck you, too."

"I call it like I see it," Jimmy said.

Jimmy sat on two overturned laundry baskets that doubled as a seat for Marco's company. The baskets alone didn't support Jimmy's weight, so he leaned against the wall behind him to sit semi-comfortably.

"Did Dave's cousin stop by?" Jimmy asked.

"The chink?"

"Yeah."

"Why would that asshole come here?"

"I just saw his friend with the Camaro drive down your block," Jimmy said.

"The RS?" Marco asked. He walked over and looked out the basement window.

"Yup."

"Why would he come here?"

"There is the obvious," Jimmy said. "There were two other guys in the car."

"If he wants to get involved, we'll fuck him and his car up."

"Let's leave cars out of this." Jimmy said. "That would be expensive to repair if we got caught."

"You think I give a fuck? I ain't paying for shit. Let those rich fucks pay."

"And if they fuck up my car? Whose gonna pay for that?" Jimmy asked.

"You're worried about them fucking up that piece of shit you call a car?"

"Fuck you. Mechanically, my car is perfect. In a race I could beat just about any car on the road, including that Camaro. After I putty and sand the passenger side, I'm gonna have it painted metallic black."

"It'll be like greased lightning," Marco said and laughed.

"It's fine when you need a ride."

"I'm just messing with you. You've got a car. I don't even have a bike!"

"Cars are off limits," Jimmy said.

"Fine," Marco said.

Marco usually intended to keep his promises, but when opportunities presented themselves, he felt an obligation to act. He wouldn't look for the car, but if he saw it parked somewhere, he wouldn't hesitate to run his knife along the side.

To put the subject in the past, Marco pulled a joint from his sock drawer. Jimmy's only thought after seeing it was getting high.

"Let's go to the bridge by Westwood," Marco said.

Jimmy started for the stairs.

"Don't go that way, Frank's home," Marco said. He unlatched the basement window, stood on a pipe that ran along the wall and pulled himself out. Jimmy followed.

*   *   *

With the addition of the eight transfers from East's chapter, the den in Kyle's house was packed with teenage boys. Kyle and his father had already worked out how the expansive living room would be set up once the pledge class was inducted, and the den could no longer accommodate all the members. For the next two weeks the pledges attended meetings only to be called in one by one to have their strengths and weaknesses assessed by the brothers.

Prior to attending the meeting, the eight transfers met at Dave's house. There was a slight sense of trepidation among the six newest transfers, because aside from playing Little League and Pee Wee football with some of their West brothers, they had no connection. Dave assured them any worries were unwarranted, because unlike their former chapter which allowed little room for input, West's chapter was run by the brothers as a group. Dave suggested they all attend a meeting, and if any weren't comfortable afterward, they could become an inactive member and the new chapter would pay the fee. It would allow them to wear colors and be immune from retaliation by anyone in their former chapter.

"Alex is sorry he couldn't make it tonight but wanted me to express his gratitude to the new transfers," Kyle said. "He's meeting with Hofstra's wrestling coach."

During the meeting, Kyle invited each transfer to speak about what they hoped to contribute and gain. By the end of the meeting, they all had a sense of the chapter's goals and chose to be active members.

Eight transfers from one chapter to another within the same town without a school closing or being rezoned was unprecedented and would take a thorough explanation to the grand chapter. With help from his father and Alex,

Kyle was working on a presentation without making accusations that could not be proven.

∗   ∗   ∗

The rain stopped just before dawn. Alex jogged around West's track in blue sweats, unaware that four brothers and two pledges had gone looking for Marco the previous afternoon.

On the opposite side of town, despite having no recollection of sleeping, Marco woke for the third time and got out of bed. He turned off his lamp at midnight, checked his clock at three, and then again at four-thirty. He was still having trouble believing Alex's friends had the balls to come looking for him. He realized why it bothered him so much as he was finishing his second bowl of Trix. *They don't fear me yet, but that will change soon enough! After Saturday night, no one will ever cross me again.*

Marco almost fell asleep at the breakfast table. He considered telling his mother he was sick so he could get some sleep but discarded the thought. If Jimmy told anyone about the previous day, they might think he was hiding. Or scared! He sat on the edge of his bed, knowing if he allowed himself to fall backwards and close his eyes, he could sleep for hours. Even as the thought swam through his scrambled brain, he convinced himself that closing his eyes for ten minutes would be enough to get him through the day. He changed the time on his alarm clock and closed his eyes. He was out within minutes and never realized he had forgotten to move the alarm's switch back to its ON position.

*   *   *

Three hours passed before Frank shook Marco awake.

"What's wrong?" Marco asked, so disoriented he couldn't remember what day it was.

"Why are you still in bed? The attendance office called."

"My alarm didn't go off," Marco said.

"It helps if you turn the alarm on."

Marco took a fresh shirt from his dresser and sniffed it before he put it on.

"Don't bother. Your mother already told them you were sick, so do what you want, but stay out of my way."

Marco pulled the shirt off and tossed it on top of a pair of jeans he had worn the previous day. Frank seemed to be in a rare, good mood. Marco knew that could change in a second, so he quietly slid beneath his covers, closed his eyes, and waited for Frank to leave. Once he heard the basement door close, he opened his eyes and stared at the ceiling. He set his alarm for two o'clock and made sure he turned it on. When he woke, he would head over to school. That would quell any rumors.

*   *   *

Marco stood by Peter's car as students filed out of school. His friends didn't waste time at extra help, and sports and other extra-curricular activities didn't appeal to them either. Jimmy was the first one out and waited by the door near the guidance office for Peter and Steven. As they neared Marco, Jimmy said something, and they all laughed.

"What's so fuckin' funny?" Marco asked.

"We were talking about chemistry," Peter said.

"Chemistry's fuckin' hilarious," Marco said.

"What's your problem?" Jimmy asked.

"You three see me and laugh? What's up with that?"

"Why would we laugh at you?" Peter asked.

"You tell me."

Jimmy sat on the back of Peter's car, took out a Marlboro and lit it. He offered one to Marco and Peter, but each declined. Steven didn't smoke cigarettes, though he did occasionally smoke pot.

"We weren't laughing at you," Jimmy said.

"So, it's just a coincidence?"

"Chill, Marco," Steven said. "We were laughing because Heather Greenleaf was reading a paragraph for our class and instead of saying microorganism, she said, micro orgasm. Even Mr. Crowley laughed, and I don't think I'd ever even seen him smile before."

"Besides, why would we laugh at you?" Peter asked.

"Yeah, you should have heard all the rumors that were going around about you," Steven said.

"What rumors?" Marco asked sharply.

Jimmy was the one who answered after slowly exhaling smoke from his nose. "I told these guys how pissed you were about the Camaro by your house yesterday, and by fourth period there were rumors that you went looking for the gook."

The day had taken a sudden surprising upswing. Marco's reputation might not have spread everywhere, but at least it was secure within his own chapter.

"I wouldn't waste my time. Those pussies wouldn't leave school grounds during the day," Marco said.

"So, what'd you do?" Peter asked.

"I worked out a few details before our meeting Saturday night and checked things out by the park."

"Nice," Peter said.

"What's by the park?" Steven asked.

"Don't worry about it," Marco said. "We'll let you know soon enough."

*   *   *

Alex returned from his morning jog and found a note on the table that said John was sick. He didn't care about not having a ride to school, but he had to let Kyle and Mike know not to sign John's name for a pledge.

He waited until seven before calling and began apologizing immediately. Kyle assured him it was fine since both his parents had left to catch the seven-ten train into Penn Station.

John's illness left Kyle no choice but to sign his name along with Mike's and let someone else sign with Alex. He offered Alex a ride to school but Alex declined in favor of walking.

The walk was good because every bit of exercise helped him stay five to seven pounds below his wrestling weight. Friends had suggested bulking up and jumping to a higher weight class, but Alex had already assured the three college coaches he met with he would be wrestling at 162 throughout college.

Alex arrived at school a few minutes earlier than usual, even after stopping at Roscoe's Deli to pick up a bologna and cheese sandwich for lunch. Sandwiches from Roscoe's were somehow tastier and more filling than anything he made at home.

Alex chose his pledge for the day and headed to the bridge. One odd consistency at all three of Malbrook's high schools was a bridge that led to the back of the school. At West High, it was across from the teacher's parking lot and down a path. West's bridge, like the one at Darcy High School, was isolated from houses, but Malbrook East's was used regularly by people who lived in the area because of its proximity to Westwood Park.

It was no secret to students what went on at West High's bridge on Friday mornings, though its year of origin was constantly debated. The first mention of the Friday Morning Drinking Club, or FMDC as it was more commonly known, was graffiti on the inside wall of the bridge that read: FMDC II 1977, which most assumed meant the second year. Others, with older siblings, claimed it was the second incarnation of the club which had been established in the late 1960s, but was inactive for several years for reasons no one knew. The only thing everyone agreed on was that drinking on the bridge on Friday mornings was a tradition and an unofficial club. The members of the previous graduating class had shirts made at the mall with FMDC in white on a black tee shirt, though they were never worn during school hours.

Mike sat with his feet dangling over the side of the bridge six feet above the water holding a Coke bottle half-filled with Bacardi 151. Most FMDC members drank vodka because it was the most difficult liquor for teachers to detect, but Mike stuck to beer or rum because his brother told him that people who drank alcohol they didn't like were more likely to become alcoholics. Mike didn't know if it was true but trusted his brother.

"Holy shit, it's Alex Moran!" Declan said.

Declan swept his hair away from his eyes, reached down and grabbed a Miller bottle from a brown paper bag and tossed it to Alex. "You've got some catching up to do."

Alex caught the bottle with his free hand and put it back in the eight-pack holder. Five of the other seven bottles were empty. "Thanks, but I'll catch up tonight."

Mike spun his legs around to face Alex and almost fell over and into the water.

"One beer won't kill you. We know you need to relax after what happened with Marco," Mike said, slurring several words.

"What do you know about what happened with Marco?" Alex asked.

"How you stopped him—"

"Okay," Alex said, cutting Mike off, which was easy since Mike was speaking slowly anyway. Alex was satisfied that Mike knew, and added, "Let's talk about it later."

"You're a hero, man," Mike said as Alex helped him down.

Alex relieved Mike of the Coke bottle and poured the remainder over the side and into the water.

"Hey, why'd ya go an' do that?" Mike complained.

The answer was obvious, but aside from Declan, few people could dump Mike's drink without paying consequences, and Declan was enjoying the morning too much to worry about keeping an eye on Mike.

"I think you've had enough," Alex said. "Hey, Declan, give me a hand getting Mike to his car so he can sleep it off."

"I still have three bottles of beer," Declan said.

"I'll help you finish them if you help me with Mike."

Alex wasn't prissy, but everyone watched to see if he was serious. He had been to the bridge on Friday mornings a few times but had never taken a sip of alcohol.

"Fine, but you can't pour them out," Declan said, closing a loophole he thought Alex might use.

"I'll drink them," Alex said, and drew an X over his heart.

"Deal," Declan said, and handed Alex one of the bottles. Alex reached down and grabbed a second bottle.

Alex twisted off both caps while everyone watched as if he was attempting a parlor trick. He held the first cap between his right thumb and middle finger and snapped it toward the garbage can. The cap hit halfway up and dropped to the ground. His second shot was closer but still not high enough. Alex held the bottle out and slightly above his head and said, "To the Friday Morning Drinking Club."

Mike sat on the bridge with his head between his legs as if a switch had been flipped and he had gone from sober to drunk instantly. The others raised their bottles and drank. Alex downed the first beer in seconds and followed almost as quickly with the second.

"I don't believe it!" Heather Miller said.

Heather was a cheerleader captain and a member of FMDC since ninth grade. She was the first and only exception to the sophomore to senior rule. She was granted the exception because her body had developed early, and her older sister was a cheerleader at the time.

"Congratulations, Alex, you're officially a member," Heather said.

"Thanks, but this is a one-time deal."

Alex and Declan went over Mike's schedule as they walked him back to his car. They agreed Mike could sleep through the first four periods and Alex would come out before fifth period to get him. That gave Mike more than three hours to sleep off the effects of the rum.

Alex took Mike's keys, opened the passenger door, and pulled the seat forward. He and Declan helped Mike into the back and watched him curl into a fetal position. Alex might have laughed if he hadn't heard that Jimi Hendrix choked to death on his own vomit.

Alex rolled the driver's window down a few inches while Declan did the same on the passenger side. Alex made sure Mike's feet were clear and closed the door.

"I'll have John leave a message with the attendance office that you'll be late," Alex said. "They don't start answering the phones until 7:45, so don't worry. I'll come get you after fourth period for lunch."

Mike grunted, which was more of a reply than either Alex or Declan expected.

*   *   *

The lone payphone on school grounds was in the lobby outside the girl's locker room behind the senior candy stand. The candy stand stayed open from seven-fifteen until the first bell. The candy stand itself didn't present a problem, but its proximity in relation to the girls' locker room and the gym meant noise was unpredictable.

Four sophomore girls stood between the entrances of the boys' and girls' gym alternately talking and laughing. Alex glanced at them before he pulled the bi-fold door closed. He spoke to John briefly impressing on him that his imitation of Mike's father had to be exceptional when he called the attendance office.

Alex's initial thought that John was faking an illness to have another extended weekend was dismissed when he heard John heave, followed by the sound of vomit hitting the bottom of a bucket and twenty seconds of spitting. Alex considered calling the office himself, but a poorly timed call with student noise in the background could get them both in trouble. John wasn't always the most reliable person, but he was at his best when it counted most.

When the bell ending fourth period rang, Alex rushed out to Mike's car. He sidestepped a puddle of vomit by the driver's door to open it and was momentarily relieved that Mike had the sense and coordination to open the door when he refunded his breakfast along with the rum. When he leaned in, the smell of vomit assaulted his nose as it became clear that Mike had failed to get the door open at least once, if not more. He might have laughed at Mike's green face if the putrid smell wasn't threatening to make him contribute to the puddle on the rear mat. He quickly pulled his head out and turned away.

"I need you to drive me home. I don't feel good," Mike said.

"I can't do that, buddy. If you're not in school at least four periods, you won't be eligible to play tomorrow."

Mike made one failed attempt to sit up and Alex stopped him before he tried again. Alex opened the trunk and grabbed a clean shirt from Mike's gym bag and tied the shirt around his face to shield his nose. He carefully tilted the rear floor mat away from himself and folded it over before he lifted it out and dropped it face down beside the driver's door. If it hadn't been a limited-edition set, he would have considered tossing it in the trash. He dragged the mat back and forth along the ground with his foot to remove as much vomit as possible before he folded it over on itself. He retrieved Mike's gym bag from the trunk and threw the mat in its place.

Alex handed Mike one of the packs of Hubba Bubba bubble gum he had picked up at the candy stand after he called John. He used the watermelon flavor to conceal any trace of beer on his own breath, and saved the strawberry to mask Mike's breath, though he hadn't planned for the vomit and doubted anything weaker than Listerine would hide the smell.

Alex opened the passenger door, took Mike's hand, and pulled him to a sitting position. Even without the mat, Alex had to hold his breath as he pulled Mike from the car.

Mike stood against the side of his car and pulled the front of his jersey away from his body. He was relieved to see it was vomit-free.

Alex helped Mike to the nurse's office, where Mike spent the remainder of the school day. With John out with a stomach virus, Mike's "illness" was easier to sell, but Alex had to plead with the nurse not to call his parents and let him remain in school to keep his eligibility for his first football game of the season.

Chapter 13

West's varsity football players boarded the bus to Davidson High School as the town's fire alarm signaled it was noon. On good days the alarms at all four fire houses sounded just twice: once at noon and again at six o'clock. Most Malbrook residents couldn't say why that was, it had just always been that way. For most kids, if they heard the evening alarm and were not in their house, they were in trouble.

In the front row, four coaches discussed the game plan. They had seen which plays the offense executed best, and head coach Jack Parisi, who was starting his eleventh season at the helm, and his offensive coordinator, Kelly Clavin, looked over notes from their practices. It was Kelly's third season as offensive coordinator, and he knew Parisi's preferences. Together they determined which plays they would run in which situations. From there, aside from the occasional gut feeling calls by Parisi, the rest was up to Clavin.

The equipment manager, Casey Lester, took attendance by shouting each player's name based on uniform numbers. Responses were prompt and loud because everyone knew Coach Parisi was listening.

Parisi had made it clear from his first game as coach that pride and intensity were necessary if you wanted to play on game day. During his first year, he benched his starting quarterback for the first half of their game at Malbrook East because of his lethargic response when attendance was taken. At a time when Malbrook had two of the newest football programs in Conference 2AA on Long Island, and it was rare that either won more than two games in a season, the only game that mattered for either school was East versus West. Darcy High was older and larger and played in Conference 1A against schools with student bodies that were two and three times larger than East and West.

Parisi knew benching his quarterback would make him very unpopular if they lost, but he needed to send a message that would resonate with the team. He needed something that would be passed on to each new player. No intensity prior to the game meant no playing time during the game.

Once everyone had been accounted for, the bus driver pulled away from the school. A second bus, which held the cheerleaders, the team doctor, and other staff, followed. Behind the two buses was a procession of cars, most over-filled and driven by high school seniors, some of whom had been celebrating the new season with coolers of beer.

Rhythmic clapping and banging on thigh pads commenced once the bus crossed over the speed bump and out of the lot. Tradition dictated they stop once they reached Sunset Highway, and one of the captains would address the team. For the seniors' final opening road game of the season, they gave the honor to Mike.

Mike had watched the previous day's practice from the sidelines. The "stomach bug" that forced him to miss the first half of the school day and spend the second half on a cot in the nurse's office, kept him from participating, but his dedication in making it to school, and suiting up for practice was praised by his coaches. Only Declan and a few other seniors knew the truth, but none would risk speaking out and getting Mike benched. The mortified look on Mike's face as he was commended by Coach Parisi made keeping the secret worth it.

Mike walked down the center aisle. The vomiting from the previous day left him feeling weak, though he would never admit it. He had learned a valuable lesson and would not let it affect his performance. He drank three vanilla shakes for breakfast because the thought of solid food made his stomach turn.

"Who we gonna beat?" Mike shouted.

"Davidson!" the team yelled in unison.

He repeated it three more times as he continued his trek up and down the aisle. He told his teammates what was expected of them. He laid out their goals for the game and the season and spontaneously told how nervous he was on his first bus ride as a varsity player two years earlier, because he didn't want to let his teammates down.

"Don't worry about letting anyone down," Mike said. "Football is a team sport played by individuals. A great coach who is seated in the front row of this bus once told me, 'If you can look in the mirror after the game and truthfully say you gave it everything you had on every play you were in, you are a winner.' And if everyone on this bus can say that after today's game, the scoreboard will show we are the better team. Today is our first step in bringing the conference championship home to West."

When Mike finished speaking, everyone chanted "Dominate!" until the bus pulled into the Davidson High parking lot. Once the bus stopped, it fell silent as every player put their helmet on.

*　　　　*　　　　*

In the cozy dining room, Jevonte spread out three sheets of blank paper and stacked the "T" volume of the World Book Encyclopedia on top of the Encyclopedia Britannica, along with two Mark Twain biographies he had checked out of the library the previous day. He wrote the word childhood on the first sheet of paper.

Most students dreaded term papers, but Jevonte saw them as an opportunity to become an expert on a subject or person. Mr. Barnes didn't require them to choose their topics for another week, but when the list was posted on the blackboard, Jevonte immediately decided on Mark Twain.

Students who chose their topics on the first day usually roused suspicion in English teachers because in recent years some had tried passing off their older sibling's work as their own if they didn't have the same teacher. Some students quickly found out that teachers kept folders on high scoring papers, and plagiarism meant an automatic zero. Since term papers counted for half of their grade for the marking period, it was impossible to pass even if everything else was perfect. Students learned from those mistakes and began trading with friends from across town or purchasing papers from someone they knew from another town. It seemed that for every safeguard a teacher implemented, students found a way around it.

In Jevonte's case, the thought of plagiarism never crossed Mr. Barnes's mind since Jevonte had a reputation as a highly motivated student and a voracious reader. When Mr. Barnes questioned his motivation for choosing the subject, Jevonte discussed it with him at length.

Jevonte glanced at the clock on the kitchen wall. He had approximately two hours before his parents returned from Roosevelt Field, a large shopping mall about twenty minutes away. He could get a good chunk of reading and note-taking done in that time. He was methodical in his approach but needed a quiet environment since even small distractions could sometimes derail him. His mother called him singularly focused because he never multitasked, and his mind seldom wandered. Whatever he was working on had his full attention. If he had to stop, he put his work aside until he had ample time to continue.

Jevonte didn't take off his sneakers and sit on the couch to read in comfort the way most students might have with the house to themselves. He treated his schoolwork like a job.

Jevonte hadn't been interested in Twain's early life when he took the assignment, but as he read the first biography, he found it fascinating. He turned page after page, trying to understand where Twain—or Samuel

Clemens as he was known prior to adopting his pseudonym—had developed his social conscience.

When Jevonte was in fifth grade, he learned that some libraries had banned <u>Adventures of Huckleberry Finn</u> because of Twain's liberal use of the word "nigger" and "injun" and convinced his mother to take him to the mall to buy the book. She agreed only after Jevonte promised to write a report on it when he finished reading. Jevonte agreed and turned in a report to his mother that surprised her.

Jevonte understood the author's assertion that the writing was predicated on the use of such words being appropriate for the time. People who had never read Twain's books—and that included both of his parents—thought he was a racist who hated anyone who wasn't white, but Jevonte thought Twain used the words to raise social awareness, and therefore wasn't a racist. He read the book one weekend, wrote the report for his mother, and hadn't given it much thought again until he had been called "nigger". Seeing Mark Twain's name among the choices so soon after the attack confirmed in his mind it was a subject he was meant to study.

Each time Jevonte came across the word nigger he thought of Marco, and despite attempts to push the thoughts aside, they found their way back. When he had to read a paragraph for the third time, he decided he was too distracted. Normally, that would have been enough for Jevonte to give up on the project for the day, but he still had plenty of time even if he stopped for a while.

Jevonte took the tri-fold black nylon wallet from his back pocket and pulled the Velcro strips apart. He reached behind the seven singles and found a folded piece of paper with Alex's name, address, and phone number. He stared at the number while working up the nerve to call. He set the phone down twice before he was sure he dialed the number correctly, and even as the phone rang, he wasn't sure he would, or could, speak.

On the third ring, a man picked up and said, "Hello."

Jevonte felt a sense of panic and his voice caught in his throat. Finally, he squeaked out, "May I please speak to Alex?" Even then he wasn't sure what he would say.

"I'm sorry, Alex left for the football game about an hour ago," Doug said.

"Okay, I guess I'll see him there."

"Do you want me to give him a message in case you don't?"

"No, thank you. I'm sure I will."

The front door opened and closed as Jevonte walked to the living room. He turned on the television and sat on the couch as Daryl strolled in from the porch. Daryl sat on the recliner and slid the seat back in one fluid motion.

"Are you ready to celebrate tonight?"

"You know I can't go to the party," Jevonte said.

"You do remember I'm sleeping over tonight, right?" Daryl asked as he pushed up the sleeves of his black Bob Marley t-shirt. "We're going to the party for a while, and once everyone sees us, we'll take care of business and go back to partying like we never left. Everyone will think we'd been there the whole night, and when the party is over, I'll come here, and we'll celebrate."

"Sounds like you've got it all figured out," Jevonte said.

"To really enjoy this kind of chair I think you have to be shorter than six feet," Daryl said and slid to the back of the chair to keep his feet from dangling over the edge. He slid forward and closed his eyes.

Daryl looked calmer than he felt. Going after Marco in Malbrook wouldn't have bothered him if he still lived in Queens, but now that he lived in Malbrook it would reflect poorly on his parents as new residents if he was arrested. Even if *he* had doubts about their new neighborhood, his parents were optimistic about the prospect of making new friends. He assumed Malbrook had its share of arrests each year, but his case would be different because Marco was a small white kid and Daryl was a much bigger, black—and they would only use that word because newspapers didn't print "nigger"—teen who attacked him. The only solution was not to get caught.

As far as anyone could tell from the lack of information in local newspapers during the week following Reverend Ralph's march, no progress had been made in the investigation, and Reverend Ralph didn't seem concerned once he got the coverage for his march. Even after Jesse Jenkins's criticism, the reverend never checked on Jevonte.

The appearance Malbrook residents projected was that life had returned to normal, even as many of the residents met with realtors to put their houses on the market before their neighbors got the same idea. The town had become a realtor's dream, and since Malbrook had an ordinance that banned lawn signs, the state of flux was undetectable. Three houses on the same block were listed within days of one another, and none of the residents were aware of the others. With so many families worried about getting out of Malbrook, every realtor in town had their phones ringing constantly. Through their desire to "escape," they were accelerating Malbrook's changing demographics. If there was an unwritten rule about not selling to minorities, every resident intent on leaving Malbrook was willing to ignore it to get out.

*   *   *

Marco's only concern on Saturday was getting every active brother to their meeting. They would be given an assignment where failure and cowardice would be punished harshly, and when the night was over, no one in Malbrook would ever forget it.

"Macko," Hannah said as she dove on the pile of dirty laundry in the basement. "You not playin' with me."

Marco scooped her up and swung her in a circle. "I'm playing with you, I'm just a little distracted." He kissed her cheek. "Who is my favorite person in the world?"

"Hannah," she squealed.

"That's right. And what is Hannah's favorite thing to eat?"

"Pizza!" she yelled, as if the very word would make it appear.

"No. I'll give you a hint though. It's vanilla and comes in a cone or a bowl."

"Ice keam!" she howled, and her smile turned into a laugh.

"That's right."

Marco lifted Hannah as high as he could and let her fall toward his bed before he caught her and laid her gently on his pillow.

"Maw, maw," she said through her laughter.

"You want more of that? I thought you wanted ice cream," Marco said, and tickled her belly.

"Ice keam," she said.

"Ice cream it is then," Marco said. He held out his arms and Hannah gleefully jumped into them. He carried her upstairs and sat her at a small table in the kitchen. He took a container of vanilla ice cream from the freezer and filled a small bowl. He stuck a spoon in it and placed it on the table in front of Hannah. As he stood, she grabbed his neck and he lifted her up. She kissed his cheek. He kissed the top of her head and placed her back in her seat at the table beside dolls that occupied the other two chairs.

When the phone rang, and Steven told him the football team had beaten the defending county champion Bethpage Memorial Hawks 26 – 21, Marco showed no enthusiasm. School pride was a crock of shit. No one cared about him, so why should he care about the school's football team? As far as Marco was concerned, the football team could have lost by fifty and it would have been fine with him.

"What time you goin' to Peter's?" Marco asked.

"Did you hear me? We beat Bethpage Memorial!"

Marco turned away so Hannah wouldn't hear and said, "Ask me if I give a shit."

"It was the first time in school history."

"Big whoop. It's not like you're on the team."

"But it's our school!" Steven said. "Bethpage Memorial had a nineteen-game winning streak!"

"Really? I still don't give a shit. I can't wait to get the fuck out of that school, and this town for that matter!" Marco said. "What time are you going to Peter's?"

"Around seven," Steven said.

"See you then," Marco said, and hung up.

*   *   *

An impromptu party broke out at Mike's house after their 38 – 0 rout of Davidson. What was supposed to be a close game had turned into a blowout midway through the first quarter. The offense went eighty yards in three plays on their opening drive, and then their defense forced two turnovers which were converted into fourteen more points and a 21 - 0 lead.

News of Malbrook East's victory over Bethpage Memorial, which was their following week's opponent, was relayed to the team as they got off the bus. After Bethpage Memorial was the Homecoming Game against East in week three. If they won those two, they could cruise to the top seed in the conference playoffs. East and West had never made the playoffs in the same year, and it was only the third time the schools had each won their opening game.

Alex filled a clear plastic cup from the first of two kegs of Pabst Blue Ribbon that Mike's father had picked up at Poppi's Beverage Mart. John stood beside him with a large bottle of ginger ale his mother had brought home for him the previous night.

Mike had already forgotten about the previous day and finished four cups of beer before anyone else arrived. He had slowed to a pace that brought him, or whichever one of his friends offered, back to the keg for refills every fifteen to twenty minutes.

As much as Alex loved the thrill of competing one on one in wrestling, seeing how girls flocked to football players made him envy his friends on the team. No other high school sport had the same effect on girls. Even terrible teams had plenty of girls around them.

John followed Alex to the back corner of Mike's patio opposite the garage and sat on a red concrete retaining wall that was three feet high. John opened the bottle of soda and it sprayed everywhere.

"What the hell were you thinking telling those guys about what happened with Marco?" Alex asked in a loud whisper.

"Mike is the only one I told," John said.

"What happened to not telling anyone?"

"We didn't have anything for our pledge to do so I figured if I told Mike, we'd just take a ride over and drag Marco to our meeting so you could beat the crap out of him and give everyone a good laugh."

"And how was I supposed to do that when I wasn't going to the meeting?"

"I kind of forgot about that," John said, and shrugged.

Alex shook his head. It was impossible to tell whether he was amused or annoyed.

"I guess it's a good thing we didn't find him," John said with an apologetic smile. He took a large gulp from the ginger ale bottle and the smile disappeared as he struggled to swallow.

"You look like shit. Why don't you go home and get some rest?" Alex said. "We can talk about it some other time."

"Look around," John said referring to the girls. "There's no way I'm leaving this party," He whispered, "Any word from the other side of town?"

It took Alex a moment to realize John was talking about Daryl and Marco and not the East's football game. He shook his head and said, "I'm sure I'll hear something by tomorrow night."

"Did they say when they were gonna do it?"

"Do you think I'd tell you if they had?"

"Yes. You know I never screw up the same thing twice," John said, and took a more reasonable sip.

"They said the less I know the better," Alex admitted.

"That's probably good. You worry too much anyway." John spotted two sophomore girls. "Why don't we go talk to Debbie and Alyssa. You're single now, so there's no excuse."

"I'm not ready," Alex said.

"Just look at Alyssa. She's mint. Black hair, dark brown eyes, cheerleader, volleyball captain. She's smart, not a slut, and best of all, not Jewish, so if her father hates you, it'll be your fault." John took her in again, practically panting. "I'm telling you, if Alyssa was a church, I'd declare sanctuary and live inside her forever." He put a hand on Alex's shoulder to guide him.

"Why don't you ask her out then?" Alex asked.

"She's not my type."

"Yeah, you did mention she's not a slut," Alex said, and glanced at Alyssa. He couldn't disagree with John's assessment. He caught her eye and she smiled and waved. Alex waved back and noticed the gold cross against her blue blouse. Sanctuary, Alex thought. He turned to John and said, "I can't right now."

"Your loss," John said and walked over to join the girls at the table.

*   *   *

Peter's basement was filled to an uncomfortable capacity thirty minutes prior to the start of the meeting. As instructed, every member wore a black shirt. They had been told that only brothers with black shirts would be admitted. It was a lie.

They were packed in like sardines, but they couldn't move upstairs, outside, or anywhere else. The subject was too sensitive to be overheard, even by Peter's family.

With no room for a table, Peter banged his gavel on the wall twice to call the meeting to order. Marco had purposely left the secretary's book he had borrowed from Steven at home, so there would be no reading of minutes and rehashing the recent exodus of members. Steven was given an old notebook to record the minutes, and Marco would burn them later so there would be no record of the meeting.

"Brother Marco has some things he wants to talk about," Peter said, and turned the floor over to Marco. Along with their new flag, Peter turning the floor over to Marco was a constant at recent meetings.

Marco stood against the wall. When he imagined the moment, he pictured himself walking between brothers and whipping them into a frenzy, but the basement was too crowded to walk anywhere.

"Brothers, tonight is the night we take over not only Malbrook, but all of Long Island—" Marco began.

"Fuckin' A right it is!" a freshman yelled.

Normally, interrupting Marco would have been cause for a backhand to the forehead, but Marco was pleased with the enthusiasm.

"Tonight, you will each be given an assignment to show your loyalty and prove your worthiness. We have been lied to and betrayed, and if you're not as pissed as I am, you don't belong here. For now, we will leave those traitorous pieces of shit alone and focus on others who shouldn't be living in our town." Marco wanted to lay out his plan for the year but decided to hold back on it until everyone returned later in the evening.

When Marco finished, Peter said, "All tasks must be completed by eleven o'clock. You are to be back here no later than midnight. If anyone has a problem with that, get your pussy ass out now because we don't need you. But let me make this clear, if you leave, I will personally make you regret it."

Marco searched every face in the room for signs of fear or hesitation but saw nothing but eager young followers. Whether it was Peter's threat or his own didn't matter.

"Earlier today, Brother Peter talked to those pussies across town," Marco said. "He told them if they accept any more transfers, our deal not to punish traitors is off."

Only Peter and Marco knew it was a lie.

Marco passed Steven a sheet of paper. Steven silently read the sheet and put it on top of the notebook.

"Brother Steven will pass around a sheet to sign. If you sign it and don't complete your assignment you are out. I can't make this more fucking clear! And along with Brother Peter, we will make you regret it."

"Does everyone understand?" Peter asked.

The room went silent as the paper was passed around. After the last brother finished signing, the paper was returned to Steven to confirm everyone had signed.

*   *   *

By the time Daryl slipped out, the party was in full swing. The partygoers dipped and swelled between thirty and fifty people who were in and out of the house, from the basement to the second floor to the backyard and out into the street.

Ten minutes earlier, Isaiah had gone to his car, which he had parked halfway down the block. Gerald and Tyrone followed a few minutes later, and when Daryl saw them all by the car from the upstairs window, he went out to join them.

Gerald was six-foot-four, two-hundred-forty pounds, and in his second year at Eastern Queens Community College where he played linebacker for the school's football team, which was ranked sixteenth in the country among junior colleges. He was offered two scholarships to play Division III football after high school but had opted to stay close to home to help his mother with his three younger siblings, the youngest of whom had Down syndrome. His father was a pilot for Delta and travelled four days at a time, which paid well, but put a strain on Gerald's mother. Having a son and daughter in high school with vastly different issues was difficult enough for any parent but adding a developmentally challenged twelve-year-old daughter made the task even harder, and Gerald refused to let his mother shoulder the load alone despite his parents' insistence that he take the scholarship from either of the Georgia colleges. His decision to stay home had been a good one since he now had scholarship offers from six Division I schools.

Daryl walked out the side door and met up with his friends at Isaiah's car. Gerald and Tyrone climbed into the cramped back seat while Isaiah drove and Daryl rode shotgun.

Daryl would have preferred a car that was less flashy than Isaiah's, but the only other option was Gerald's 1975 Ford Thunderbird, which was roughly the size of a small yacht and too easy to identify. Gerald's car was in mint condition, and easier to get in and out of, but with custom gold pinstriping and wide wheels with gold rims it was a car few who saw forgot.

"Everyone ready to do this?" Isaiah asked.

"Let's go!" Tyrone said.

Isaiah pulled away from the curb slowly. When he got to the corner and turned right, he turned on the headlights. The likelihood that anyone at the party had seen them leave was nil. Even if anyone had, they would never tell.

*　　　　*　　　　*

When the meeting ended, Peter went to the top of the stairs, called the members up in pairs and handed them an envelope and a can of spray paint. The contents of the envelopes were to be discussed with only their partners.

Chapter 14

Marco and Jimmy sat in Peter's backyard smoking cigarettes, trying to relax while waiting for the inevitable sound that meant the evening was underway. The first police siren sounded after twenty minutes. The second, slightly farther away came minutes later.

"Let's go," Marco said.

Peter offered them a drink from a celebratory bottle of tequila he had just opened, but both declined before they each exchanged Phi's secret grip with him and started their walk to the park. Neither spoke. Jimmy was too scared, and Marco was enjoying the sirens.

"There's no turning back now," Marco said as he and Jimmy climbed the twelve-foot fence that separated Westwood Park from the rear lot of Temple Israel. By that time, police sirens were wailing constantly.

*　　　*　　　*

Saturday was the busiest night of the week for police, but officers from Nassau County's Sixteenth Precinct were spread so thin they needed help from the neighboring Seventeenth Precinct to handle the deluge of calls, which numbered eight in a thirty-minute span. Aside from one car accident, the other seven had come from families who'd had a red or black swastika painted on their front door. Five of the seven cases also reported having one or more windows smashed. In the other two cases, the homeowners interrupted the perpetrators and chased them off. It was later noted that two of the swastikas had been painted incorrectly with the lines bent counterclockwise. One of the responding officers claimed that it was a Buddhist symbol, though it was clearly unintentional.

*   *   *

Marco kept his back to the fence on the north side of the lot, which was almost completely dark. The area had been well-lit until two days earlier when Marco and Peter promised bids to five eighth graders with ambitions of joining Phi if they broke three large lights in the rear of the lot. The broken lights had been discovered, but it would be a week before the lights and their covers could be replaced.

The original plan was to make the fire look like an accident, but ideas on how were limited. The initial idea to leave a lit cigarette behind was scratched with the assumption that smoking was not permitted inside the building. The second idea was to create an electrical fire, but neither of the boys knew how. Peter had suggested

Molotov cocktails, but Marco nixed the idea because he wanted to ensure maximum damage, and the only way to do that was from the inside.

Marco smashed a light above the rear door with a crowbar, so that even if they were spotted, they would be difficult to identify. He handed the bar to Jimmy to pry the door open. It was easier than Jimmy expected, which he assumed was because religious leaders didn't expect theft, vandalism, or arson.

Neither boy had ever been inside a temple, and it wasn't what they expected. There were three tables in the outer lobby, and Marco stopped at the first and took out his blue Bic lighter. He picked up a handful of pamphlets that described services available to members, clicked the lighter and held the flame beneath the pamphlets.

"What are you doing?" Jimmy asked.

"What does it look like?" Marco asked. "I'm starting a fire. That's why we're here."

"We agreed to start on the inside and work our way out, so we don't get trapped," Jimmy said, already feeling his stomach knot.

"Fuck that. Let's just get on with it." Marco pulled the meeting minutes he collected from Steven out of his pocket as he moved to the next table. He set the minutes on fire and let them burn halfway through before he picked up a kippah. He held the kippah up to show Jimmy and said, "Hey, look, it's one of those hats kikes use to cover their bald spots." He set it on fire and tossed it on top of the others on the table.

"It's a yarmulke, and if you burn everything by the exit, how the fuck are we supposed to get out?"

"You sound like a pussy, and it's getting on my nerves." When Marco saw how quickly the kippahs burned, he tossed the minutes on top and said, "Oh shit, look at those things. Sucks for them if they have to wear 'em in hell."

"That's why we were supposed to start from the inside," Jimmy said.

The fire was spreading up the wall when Jimmy opened the door to look inside. "It's kinda like a church."

"When's the last time you were in a church?"

Jimmy never told Marco he went to Sunday mass once or twice a month. Going to mass had been something he had done with his parents since he was old enough to remember. It was never faith that made him attend, it was the opportunity to sit and eat pancakes with his parents at the diner afterward and listen to stories about their childhoods. Now he only went when he woke early enough and was in the mood for pancakes. His brother had gone with them until he turned sixteen and decided he'd rather have the house to himself for two hours than go to the diner.

Jimmy removed the lighter from his pocket as he walked past the pews on each side of the sanctuary and stepped up on the bimah stage. He pulled the tasseled ropes on each side of the east-facing Ark and revealed the Torah. He marveled at the elaborate designs as he ran his hands over the covering. He shoved the lighter back in his pocket. Hate had brought him to destroy the house of worship. *But why? It wasn't even his hate.* The idea that Jews had killed their savior, Jesus Christ, had been Marco's way to get everyone on board. Then, he pointed out their cheapness and anything else he could come up with to inspire hate and get them to embrace Hitler's ideology. Now, as Jimmy stared at the Torah, he felt duped.

Before he met Marco, Jimmy was similar in many ways, but different in some. He was unfocused in school but got by with a C average. He had friends, but more often kept to himself. He discovered marijuana in sixth grade when he found a joint in his brother's sock drawer while searching for a few dollars to buy soda and a bag of Doritos. After smoking the joint, he found the relaxed feeling almost euphoric and tore apart his brother's room looking for money, because he didn't just *want* Doritos anymore, he *needed* them. He had no interest in joining Phi other than to gain respect from his brother, who was a senior and president of Phi at the time. That hadn't worked either and rather than take it easy on Jimmy, they showed no mercy. While pledging, Jimmy became friends with Marco, who had a focused rage and a steady supply of marijuana.

Smoke filled the entire room to Jimmy's left, and he saw something moving he assumed must have been Marco. He called Marco's name three times before he ran for the exit, which by now had turned into a wall of fire. Jimmy pulled his shirt up to cover his face as he ran through the doorway to the lobby and then crashed through the outer door into the parking lot. He reached back for the door, but quickly pulled his hand away since there was nothing he could do to help Marco with the fire raging inside.

*　　　　*　　　　*

A police car sped past Isaiah's Camaro as he turned on Kennedy. The siren grew faint as it sped through the empty business district, and an uneasy feeling crept over the car's occupants.

Gerald pulled himself forward so his head was between the front seats and said, "I thought Malbrook is supposed to be a quiet town. That's the third cop car we've seen, and we haven't been here, what, ten minutes?"

"What do you want to do, Dee?" Isaiah asked.

Tyrone grinned and smacked Gerald on the arm and said, "He said, *doody*."

"Would you shut up," Daryl said. "I'm trying to think,"

Gerald slid back in his seat, looked at Tyrone's fake angry face and laughed.

A loud siren blared in the distance. It was followed immediately by a sequence of three separate blasts totaling six, three, and four. After a thirty second break, the sequence sounded again.

"What the hell is that?" Tyrone asked.

"Must be a fire," Daryl said. "My pops told me it's a code to let volunteer firefighters know where to go if they can't get to the firehouse in time."

"Who in their right mind would volunteer when you can work in the city and get paid?" Gerald asked.

"Not me, that's for sure," Tyrone said.

"Tell us something we don't know," Isaiah said.

"Okay. The show 'M*A*S*H' has already lasted more than twice as long as the actual Korean War."

Daryl glanced at Tyrone with an incredulous frown. "Where do you come up with this shit?" he asked. To Gerald he said, "Do me a favor and smack him for me."

Isaiah pulled to a stop sign and said, "Valley Street." He looked to Daryl. "What's his house number?"

"Fifty-one," Daryl said.

To their left was a block with four houses on each side that was separated from a park by another street. Daryl and Isaiah gave a quick glance before Isaiah turned right.

"Odd numbers are on my side," Daryl said.

"What are the next two?" Isaiah asked and slowed until they were barely moving.

"Twenty-seven," Daryl said as they passed the second house on the right. He had to squint to see the number of the next house because the light above the house number by the mailbox was off. "Stop a sec." He moved closer to the glass and held a hand on each side of his face to block the glare from streetlamps. "Thirty-one."

Isaiah counted five houses forward and said, "His house is the one with the silver Buick in the driveway."

Isaiah spotted a Trans Am in a driveway a few houses from the one they determined to be Marco's and parked in front of it. From their four vantage points they could see each corner of the block. There was no movement in Marco's house.

*　　　　*　　　　*

The thick smoke inside the sanctuary made it impossible for Marco to see the exit. He dropped to his knees and crawled down the center aisle. He didn't see Jimmy and didn't care. If Jimmy didn't have the sense to get out, that was his problem. He looked for markings to let him know he was going in the right direction but couldn't find any. He silently cursed who ever thought putting exit signs above doors was a good idea when everyone was supposed to get low during a fire.

By the time Marco crashed through the rear door, flames had engulfed the building. He fell to his knees and coughed for a solid minute.

"We've got to get out of here," Jimmy said. He extended his hand to help Marco up and Marco slapped it away.

"Get the fuck away from me," Marco said between coughing fits.

"Fine," Jimmy said. He tossed aside the crowbar he had wiped clean of fingerprints with his shirt. "I'm outta here, and if you don't get your ass moving pretty quick, you're gonna have to explain why you're here to a bunch of firemen."

"You're just gonna leave me?" Marco asked as he caught his breath.

Jimmy reached the fence—which wasn't so dark with the fire burning out of control—and waited for Marco to catch up. The sirens grew louder as the trucks neared.

"I thought you were a goner," Jimmy said.

"Me too. But I managed to get out, no thanks to you."

Jimmy almost reminded Marco that it was his own fault for starting the fire in the lobby first but decided to keep it to himself for now. He climbed the fence easily as Marco labored behind, still trying to clear his lungs of the smoke he inhaled. Jimmy flipped over the fence and climbed down quickly in case the police showed up from the park side. He moved away from the temple's fence and stood in the darkness behind the wooden fence of a neighboring home.

"Hurry," Jimmy said.

When Marco reached the top, he slipped backwards as he tried to swing his right leg over. The top of his black combat boot caught on the top of the fence and kept his leg from dropping down which would almost certainly have caused him to fall back into the lot. He pulled himself back up, yanked his boot free and was halfway down when a firetruck's headlights caught him. He froze as the firetruck turned back to the burning building, and then he scurried down.

"We fucked that place up," Marco said.

"Yeah," Jimmy agreed, and felt fortunate Marco had been too busy to realize he hadn't helped.

Jimmy glanced in each direction. The plan to be gone by the time anyone arrived was no longer a consideration. Soon the entire area would be swarming with police and firefighters.

Jimmy almost wished he hadn't abstained from smoking pot and drinking alcohol for the past two days. Drugs and alcohol made him fearless and ambivalent, but now he felt a lucidity and fear like he had never experienced before.

He considered the bridge to their left and the street to the right that cut the park in half and played out each scenario in his head. If they crossed the bridge, there was a good chance they would see police from the local precinct. If they managed to avoid them, they would have to get past the park police's small office by the exit. In addition to those officers, there would be auxiliary police since they patrolled the park on weekends. Normally, he wouldn't have worried about auxiliary police because like every other teenager in Malbrook, he considered them a joke, but anyone who spotted them near the fire was dangerous. If they went to the right they would be in the open on the sidewalk, but likely ignored by people who were too preoccupied with fire trucks and police cars roaring past to notice two teens passing on a Saturday night.

"Let's get out of here," Marco said, and started toward the bridge.

"Not that way."

"Why not?" Marco asked. "You wanna stroll down the sidewalk like nothing happened?"

"Yes," Jimmy said, and explained.

Marco didn't want to be in the open. He started toward the bridge and Jimmy walked in the opposite direction.

"Where the fuck you goin', dickhead?" Marco asked.

"I'll take my chances on the sidewalk."

Marco ran and caught up with Jimmy.

"If we get caught, I'm gonna kill you," Marco said. It was a threat Jimmy heard weekly for one reason or another.

"Then go the other way, I'm not forcing you to come with me."

"Just shut the fuck up and keep walking."

*   *   *

Twenty minutes of staring out into darkness in the cramped backseat of Isaiah's car had taken a toll on Gerald. Even being stuck in a small, dingy elevator at the mall for nearly an hour hadn't made him feel claustrophobic, but with each passing moment he felt the car closing in on him.

"I've got to get out and stretch my legs," Gerald said.

"*Now?*" Daryl asked.

One look in the backseat and Daryl understood. Gerald and Tyrone were sitting at forty-five-degree angles, and even then, their knees touched.

"Why don't you guys get out and walk to the corner and back?" Daryl suggested.

"Hold up a sec. Check out what just turned the corner up there," Isaiah said.

All four sets of eyes fixed on Jimmy and Marco as they crossed the street. None of them had seen the two before, but from a distance their heights matched Jevonte's description.

"Please tell me that's them," Tyrone said.

"It could be," Daryl said as he squinted against the darkness and distance.

"What now?" Isaiah asked.

"Wait until they're halfway down the block and then slowly pull up past that kid's house."

"What should I do if it's them and they take off?"

"We'll chase them on foot, and you follow as close as you can, so we get out of here quick." Daryl looked back and said, "I'll take the little guy, and you two take the taller one."

Isaiah waited for Marco and Jimmy to get close enough before he pulled toward them.

Marco sat on the curb to tie his boots. Neither he nor Jimmy noticed Isaiah's Camaro.

Isaiah pulled to the curb just past Marco's house and put the car in park. Daryl opened the passenger door slowly and kept his head down, trying to keep his face hidden as he turned and tilted his seat forward to let Tyrone and Gerald out. Gerald was halfway out when Marco spotted them.

Marco smacked Jimmy's arm and nodded toward Daryl. Before Jimmy had time to assess what was going on, Marco took off in the opposite direction and Daryl, Tyrone and Gerald cut the distance between them in half.

Jimmy jumped up and ran. He passed Marco before the corner and left him behind.

"Wait up."

Fuck you! Jimmy turned left into the park entrance away from the fire recalling a joke about two hunters being chased by a bear. Marco fell further behind as Jimmy crossed a concrete bridge and took the right fork where the path split just beyond it. Jimmy regretted his choice immediately since the left fork had nature trails that branched off in multiple directions, but he had no choice but to stay his course.

Gerald didn't slow down when he caught Marco just past the bridge. He shoved Marco face first into bushes that separated the path and kept going to the right. "I'll get the other one," Gerald said, and continued after Jimmy without breaking stride.

Marco's first instinct was to play possum. Daryl grabbed the back of his neck, squeezed, and yanked him from the bushes.

"Check it out. He pissed himself," Tyrone said, and pointed to Marco's crotch.

"I didn't do nothing," Marco said.

Tyrone did his best Richard Dawson "Family Feud" impersonation and said, "Survey says," and gestured to Daryl.

"Aaant!" Daryl said, mimicking the show's buzzer. "Now shut the fuck up!"

When the chase started, Daryl was reasonably sure they had the right guys, though not positive since running was probably a normal reaction for two white kids who saw them getting out of a car. When he saw the face, all doubt vanished.

"We know who you are," Tyrone said.

"And where you live," Daryl added.

"And who you hang out with." Tyrone tried not to laugh as Marco's eyes shifted back and forth as they spoke.

"I guess we're not the dumb niggers you thought we were," Daryl said. "Huh, Marco?"

The blood drained from Marco's face at the mention of his name, and he turned a ghostly pale.

"I don't know any Marco."

"Damn! We must have the wrong kid," Daryl said.

"You're probably right. Remember, the kid we're looking for is supposed to be tough. He wouldn't piss his pants like this little bitch."

"Maybe we should let him go," Daryl said. "But wait; if he is Marco, he'd probably have a switchblade."

"Do you think he'd mind emptying his pockets?"

"I don't believe he has a choice." Daryl spun Marco around and pressed his face into the fine gravel of a bocce ball court.

Tyrone bent over and looked at the side of Marco's face. "I don't think anyone wants to reach into his piss-soaked front pockets, but he does appear to have a wallet in his back pocket." Tyrone pulled it out and opened it.

"Well, don't keep me in suspense."

"According to his learner's permit, his name is . . . drumroll please." Tyrone paused and then said, "Marco. Congratulations on your learner's permit, Marco, but I'm sorry to tell you that your shitty decisions come with harsh consequences."

Daryl yanked Marco to his feet.

"If you let me go, I won't tell anyone."

"*You* won't tell anyone?" Daryl laughed. "I don't give a shit if you tell *everyone*. If you say a word about this, you'll get your picture in the paper, and Jevonte will go to the police and identify you. After that, no one will give a shit because you had it coming."

"I think he just pissed himself again," Tyrone said as the wet spot on Marco's pants spread. "I bet he wets his bed, too."

Daryl floored Marco with a vicious left hook that split his lip. Marco landed face down on the bocce ball court. He was barely conscious and made no effort to move.

"I think you might have killed him," Tyrone said, and winked at Daryl. "We should get out of here."

"Wait, grab that broken Pepsi bottle over there," Daryl said. "If I carve a Greek letter in his stomach the cops will think it was a rival fraternity."

"No, how 'bout we jam the top up his ass and make it look like it was some kind of queer sex that went wrong," Tyrone suggested.

They watched Marco try to pull himself forward.

"Shit, he's still alive," Tyrone said.

"We better fix that. We don't want him telling anyone."

When Marco's left hand reached the wooden edge of the court, Tyrone stomped a foot down on it and Marco cried out in pain.

"Oh, did I get you?" Tyrone laughed.

Daryl pulled Marco up by the back of his shirt and held him. He slapped Tyrone's hand like a tag team partner.

Tyrone unleashed a powerful right to Marco's jaw, and Marco went limp in Daryl's arms. Daryl let him go and watched his head crash down into the gravel. He was out.

At the park entrance Isaiah whistled three times in succession to let them know they had to leave. Tyrone mimicked the whistle in Gerald's direction. Gerald's return whistle let them know he was on the way.

Daryl knelt beside Marco. "Wake up. I have one more thing to tell you." Daryl slapped Marco's cheeks until his eyes opened. "If anyone asks you or your friend what happened, you say some white kids from another fraternity jumped you. If you mention skin color other than white, your parents will be burying you in a closed casket by Christmas." Daryl stomped on Marco's left leg for good measure.

"You didn't kill him, did you?" Gerald asked when he saw Marco face down on the bocce ball court.

"He'll live," Tyrone said, and then laughed before he added, "But he pissed his pants twice."

They ran from the park and piled in Isaiah's car as two more fire trucks roared past. Their eyes followed the trucks as a thick cloud of smoke billowed over the trees to their left. The sound of sirens cut through the otherwise quiet night. Isaiah checked his mirror, let up on the clutch and pressed the gas pedal to the floor. The tires chirped as he left the curb, again as he slammed the shifter into second, and one final time when he shifted to third before he reached the corner. He turned right and headed for the parkway entrance. A siren and flashing lights made his heart skip a beat when he saw a police car in his rearview mirror.

"What should I do?" Isaiah asked. "I could lose him on the parkway in about two seconds."

"Just pull over, and don't anyone do any stupid shit," Daryl said.

Isaiah pulled to the side of the road a hundred yards shy of the parkway entrance.

"What should I do about these?" Gerald asked as he held up his bloody fists.

"Put them down! I just said *not* to do anything stupid!"

"There's a rag under the seat in front of you, wipe 'em quick," Isaiah said.

The patrol car's door opened. The officer's foot hit the pavement and stayed there as he leaned in and grabbed the radio.

"Why is he taking so long?" Tyrone asked.

"I don't know, but I don't like it," Isaiah said. He looked to Daryl for guidance. "I got a bad feeling about this, Dee. Should I take off?"

"Give it another minute."

The officer pulled his foot back in and yanked the door closed. He backed up, hit the siren, and made a quick U-turn before speeding off in the opposite direction.

"What the fuck just happened?" Isaiah asked.

Tyrone slid forward. "He was probably just fucking with us. I told you not to get the windows tinted too dark, 'cause cops love to pull over cars when they can't see inside."

"Do you really think he would have been less likely to pull us over if he saw the four of us?" Isaiah asked.

"We'll never know now, will we?"

"You're so stupid," Isaiah said. "Someone please slap that dumbass."

Gerald held the back of his right hand up to slap him.

"Don't even think about touching me with that bloody hand," Tyrone said. "You know white people blood carries all kinds of diseases." Tyrone laughed hysterically.

*   *   *

The first two fire trucks to arrive went to the rear lot. Captain Roberts called out orders and the men worked in teams as quickly as possible. The first four firemen entered and went to work on the outer lobby as the next group moved along the wall to the right. Three firefighters made it through the door into the sanctuary before a thundering crack sounded above.

Brad Roberts led the way. He had been a volunteer fireman for 23 years and captain for seven. He'd heard the noise two other times, but never this close. His eyes followed the sound to a large wooden beam directly above them that broke in two. There was little he could do but push the two younger firefighters out of the way.

"Look out!" Brad yelled as the beam and the roof above it crashed down.

In the moment prior to losing consciousness, Brad realized his last words to his wife and two preteen daughters hadn't been, "I love you," as they were every other time he left the house. They were, "We'll finish when I get back, so no cheating." His little yellow car with the blue man driving his pink wife through "The Game of Life" would never reach the "Day of Reckoning" even as he was. His final spin had been a four that would have added twin boys to his little plastic family if he'd had time to move it.

Thanks to Brad, Jason Thatcher and Patrick Phillips were spared from the falling beam, but neither could escape the collapsing roof that sealed them inside the sanctuary. Patrick was knocked unconscious by the same patch of burning roof that killed his captain. The remnants of the roof, which were still burning, covered him from the top of his neck to his ankles.

Jason had been hit on his left shoulder and fell to the right, away from the wall, which saved his life. He struggled to pull himself to Patrick, who at twenty-one was close to his age and one of his best friends. He reached Brad first, saw his eyes, and knew without checking he was dead. Patrick was more difficult to get to, and almost certainly dead, too, but Jason refused to give up. With an effort that drained every ounce of his strength, he pulled himself forward until he found Patrick. He pulled the burning rubble off Patrick's legs, but the weight of the larger pieces on his upper body and the intense heat coupled with his own exhaustion were obstacles Jason couldn't overcome.

"Come on, Pat, we've got to get out of here," Jason said as he patted his friend's cheek.

There was no response from Patrick, so Jason climbed to his knees and lifted a heavy piece of wood from Patrick's body and moved it as far as he could down his back. He removed his glove and slid his hand under Patrick and checked his neck for a pulse. Jason knew he checked properly but refused to believe Patrick was dead until he checked his pulse three additional times. Jason was exhausted as he turned on his back and looked up through a gap in the fallen roof where he could see a patch of night sky. He stared at the one star he could see and silently prayed before he asked for a quick death. He slipped into unconsciousness just before his right leg began to burn.

It took ten minutes for the responding firefighters to break through the wall four feet to the right of the door. They couldn't risk going through the door because Dan McVeigh, who had been sealed out when the roof collapsed, had seen where the trapped firefighters were. Two firefighters extinguished the fire that had burned more than half of Jason's body and carried him outside to an ambulance where paramedics began CPR.

The attempt to recover the bodies of Brad and Patrick proved too difficult. They remained buried beneath the heavier rubble until several hours after sunrise.

Chapter 15

Jimmy wasn't sure how long he'd been unconscious, or how long it had taken him to hobble back to where he could see the streetlight outside the park's entrance. He wasn't sure of anything as he looked at the shattered face of his Timex and saw it was no longer ticking. It wasn't unexpected since it had taken way more than a licking. He didn't know the extent of his own injuries but didn't feel any better than his watch looked. His left eye was swollen shut, and he had lost at least one tooth, and possibly more, though he wasn't willing to put his muddy fingers in his mouth to check. Knowing wouldn't change anything.

The wooden railing across the bridge was a welcome sight, but he had to stop twice to catch his breath before he could hobble the final ten feet. He didn't have to question why it had happened; the guy who beat him made it clear that Jimmy had earned every single punch. He wanted to blame Marco, but the choice had been his own.

Marco sat against a post beyond the bocce ball courts with his knees up and his hands partially covering his eyes. He had poured the last of what was left in a can of Schlitz on his crotch to cover the piss smell so he could blame the wetness on niggers pouring a beer on him. The choice had been questionable since most cheap beer cans and bottles in the park were left by teens, and they rarely left even a drop of beer in them. More likely, what he poured on himself was likely either dirty water from the stream that emptied into Westwood Lake, or piss from teens who decided to "refill" their cans for bums who scavenged for their unfinished beer. Marco's decision masked the urine smell but made the wetness more visible.

Marco spotted a shadow cast from the light on the far side of the bridge. It was Jimmy hobbling toward the park exit.

"Hey, over here," Marco called.

Jimmy looked at Marco, shook his head slowly, and sat on the lower of the two wooden beams that served as the bridge's railing. He leaned over, took three shallow breaths, and decided not to answer.

"What are you waiting for, faggot? I need help," Marco said.

Jimmy raised his right hand to his waist, turned it up and extended his middle finger.

"What's your fuckin' problem? Can't you see I'm hurt?" Marco asked.

Jimmy didn't look Marco's way again. Pain and exhaustion wore on him as he pushed himself forward, each step more difficult than the last. The sirens from five fire trucks rang in his head as he used the upper railing to help him hobble toward the exit.

Marco limped after him, hunched over to hide the wet spot. "Hold up," Marco said as Jimmy reached the park's exit and leaned on the fence for support.

Jimmy turned slightly so Marco could see his battered face.

"What happened to you?"

"Payback," Jimmy said and turned left out of the park, still using the fence to support him.

"You can't go that way, that's where all the cops are," Marco said.

"I need an ambulance."

"You're gonna get us caught, you stupid fuck!" Marco said in a stern whisper.

"Just go. Look out for yourself. It's what you do best."

"What crawled up your ass and died?"

"Reality," Jimmy said, and limped toward the flashing lights as Marco watched.

"Wait," Marco said.

Jimmy stopped as he passed the park's fence to the first house. He tried to turn, but even that simple act was too painful. He shifted his weight to his left leg and almost fell in the bushes that lined the front yard of the house beside the park.

"Are you okay?" Marco asked.

"No."

"You wait here, and I'll go get someone to call an ambulance," Marco said. "Don't say anything. Let me do the talking."

"Fine," Jimmy said. He sat on the curb and put his head back on the grass. Marco limped away while Jimmy looked up at the same star a wounded firefighter had seen a short time earlier.

*　　　　　*　　　　　*

Daryl walked up the driveway to the backyard and blended effortlessly into the party. Tyrone and Gerald walked up moments later and met Daryl. They sat at a table with a few girls they knew. Isaiah sat in his car and tried to calm himself before joining them. He took deep breaths and contemplated whether to drive home and get one of his mother's Valium from the medicine cabinet. She had given it to him once when he was suffering from insomnia after he had tried every over-the-counter sleep aid he could find without success, and the one Valium had provided immediate results and reset his sleep cycle.

Isaiah would have given it more serious consideration if not for a discussion in health class several years earlier. He couldn't remember what drug, or drugs, she had taken, he remembered Karen Ann Quinlan had mixed drugs and alcohol and slipped into a coma and then a vegetative state. He hadn't heard anything about her since, but as far as he knew she was still alive.

During the drive back to Rosedale, Daryl assured Isaiah he had nothing to worry about since he hadn't thrown a punch and neither one could identify him. He also pointed out that it was unlikely the officer who pulled them over had noted Isaiah's license plate before he drove off. And since he did have tinted windows, the officer wouldn't know how many people were in the car or if they were black or white. In the unlikely event they tracked Isaiah down, Daryl told him to explain he was in the area after a miscommunication led him to believe he was supposed to pick Daryl up and bring him to the party. They had to maintain that Daryl was at the party all night since it was his alibi.

As impossible as it seemed, the party was more crowded than when they had left. Two empty Schaefer kegs were left by the side door, which Daryl thought was a bad sign since they had only bought two, but when he got to the backyard, he saw they had been replaced with two Heineken kegs. One was tapped and the second was nearby in a large plastic bucket filled with ice ready to go when the first Heineken keg was finished.

Daryl contemplated calling Jevonte but decided to apprise him of the situation after the party. If police pulled the phone records, the timing would look suspicious. Daryl had a solid alibi, and he was keeping it that way.

Ten minutes after Isaiah returned to the party, the four friends met in the backyard. Daryl handed each a plastic cup before he broke out a bottle of Johnnie Walker Black he had picked up earlier in the day. He poured them each what amounted to a triple shot.

"Thank you, guys," Daryl said, and they clicked their cups together.

As they brought the cups to their mouths, Tyrone said, "Hold up. That's it? That's your toast?"

"I have to agree with Tyrone, that was pretty weak," Isaiah agreed.

They lowered their cups and Daryl reconsidered. There was far too much to say in one toast, but it came to him. He raised his cup and held it between them and waited for the other three to do the same. "If you guys don't know how much I love you by now, and how much I appreciate you always being there for me, then fuck yous all."

"That I can drink to," Tyrone said as he made a pretend glass clinking sound and drank the shot in one gulp.

*   *   *

By the time the ambulance arrived, Jimmy had slipped in and out of consciousness several times. He struggled to keep his right eye open as pain from every part of his body competed for his attention. The grass felt cool against skin that had once been covered by his torn shirt. A bright light shined down on his face and for a second, he thought he was dead. Then he saw the faces of two paramedics standing over him.

"Can you tell us your name?" Kip Reynolds asked as he knelt beside Jimmy.

Kip's partner, Wade Carter, took one look at Jimmy's face and retreated to the rear doors of the newest ambulance in the South Shore Ambulance Company's fleet. The field stretcher Wade slid out resembled a hand truck that had been fitted with soft, red nylon to accommodate an injured person. Wade positioned it on the ground beside Jimmy with the wheels in the street.

"What's your name?" Kip asked again.

"Jimmy."

"Okay, Jimmy. I'm Kip, and this is Wade. We're going to put you in the ambulance and take you to the hospital."

"Where's . . . Marco?" Jimmy asked as Wade lifted his legs slightly and slid them on the field stretcher just above the wheels. Kip gently slid Jimmy's upper body onto the stretcher.

"Marco?" Wade asked.

"My friend who got you," Jimmy managed.

Wade and Kip exchanged a quizzical look as Kip backed into the ambulance. They slid the stretcher in, and Wade pulled the doors closed while Kip secured the stretcher. Once seated, Wade knocked on the partition to let the driver know it was safe to go. The siren wasn't needed since the hospital was less than a mile away.

"Marco," Jimmy said weakly.

"Who is Marco?" Kip asked while securing the blood pressure monitor to Jimmy's upper arm with a Velcro strap.

"My friend," Jimmy said, as if that would explain everything. When neither seemed to understand him, he added, "He called you."

"I'm not sure what you mean," Kip said. "The man in the house you were in front of called us. He said you told him someone beat you up."

Jimmy had a vague recollection of speaking to a man who had appeared in front of the star he was watching before it was completely obscured by smoke. He hadn't known where Marco was either.

The new ambulance van with the higher ceiling and state-of-the-art equipment gave them multiple options on how to treat patients on their way to the hospital. Wade considered the nitrous oxide behind him to better communicate with Jimmy but decided on a clear vial of morphine to numb the pain.

"Where does it hurt?" Wade asked as he slid a drawer to his right open and pulled out a needle.

"Everywhere," Jimmy said.

"I'm going to give you something for the pain," Wade said. "You're going to feel a little pinch." He found a vein on the inside of Jimmy's arm and inserted the needle.

Jimmy's head swam with a feeling that was better than any high he had ever experienced. His body went numb, and the pain faded away. If not for a feeling that bugs were crawling beneath his skin, it would have been perfect.

*　　　　*　　　　*

With fifteen minutes left before midnight, four brothers from the meeting had not returned. Aside from Peter, no one knew where any of them had gone, though

Steven had figured out Marco and Jimmy's assignment after Peter's reaction to the first firetrucks.

Chase Baines was a popular kid who had graduated two years earlier but kept in touch with the fraternity through his younger brother Ben. Some of the younger brothers didn't know who Chase was, but everyone who did know him was surprised to see him walking up the driveway flanked by Ben and Ben's closest friend, and fraternity brother, Kevin Seary.

Chase thought his graduating class was leaving Phi in the capable hands of his younger brother and his friends. Midway through his junior year, Ben started working at Anything Bagel before and after school and had been an inactive member since then. Chase had heard some recent complaints from Kevin, who was also inactive but attended meetings on the rare weeknights when he wasn't working at the tee shirt stand in a mall kiosk. Although Ben kept up with most of Phi's activities and attended parties when he could, tonight's mandatory meeting was the first he had attended since January.

"Chase," Steven said, holding out his hand and waiting for the grip. "How's it going?"

Chase ignored Steven's gesture and passed by him without a word. When Steven looked at Ben and Kevin for an explanation, Ben just shook his head.

There was a quiet tension in the backyard. Marco and Jimmy hadn't returned, and Peter had spent the past two hours at a table by the rear of the garage drinking from a bottle of tequila. He invited everyone to drink from it, but there had been no takers and the bottle was half empty.

Chase made his way through the group to Peter.

"Here for the celebration?" Peter asked and held the bottle out for Chase.

Chase slapped the bottle out of Peter's hand.

"Where's Marco?" Chase asked.

"What's your fucking problem?" Peter asked angrily. He stood and tossed the metal table over in one motion. He had two inches and forty pounds on Chase.

"My problem is that you and your little boyfriend are destroying this fraternity!" Chase said. "Now, where is that little piece of shit?"

"Destroying? We are the strongest, most farred fraternity in the world!" Peter yelled.

"Farred?" Chase mocked Peter's drunken retort.

"You know what I meant," Peter said, slowly and more deliberately.

"I don't care what you meant. Where the fuck is Marco?"

"He hasn't come back yet," Steven said, still processing Chase's snub.

"Back from where?"

"That's none of your fucking business," Peter said.

"You're right, and I'm glad," Chase said, and looked at some of the younger brothers nearby. "Because when this shit goes bad—and trust me it will—everyone who completed their assignment tonight is fucked. And if Marco's not back from wherever he was because he got caught, you can bet he'll do whatever he has to do to save his own ass, even if it means fucking every last one of you over to do it."

"Yeah, right," Peter said. "We're all brothers here. Unlike you, Marco would never turn against a brother!"

"Tell that to Dave Kane!" Chase said pointedly.

"Fuck Dave Kane!" Peter yelled and moved closer to Chase.

"You and Marco tried, remember? Never turn against a brother, because in this fraternity there's always someone who has your back. At least that's the way it used to be before you and Marco fucked it up." Chase looked at the confused faces of the younger brothers and back at Peter. "Do they actually believe the things you tell them? Do they know you guys wanted Dave out because his cousin made Marco look like the pussy he really is?"

"You don't know what you're talking about," Peter said and threw a punch that partially caught Chase's jaw as he tried to avoid it. "If you don't shut your mouth and get out of here, you're gonna be in for a world of hurt."

Chase rubbed his jaw. Peter might be drunk, and didn't hit him flush, but it hurt like hell. Ben and Kevin started towards Peter.

"No!" Chase demanded and the two boys stopped.

"That's right, you better stop," Peter said, towering over the two. "Look around, boys. Not that I'd need help, but you're completely outnumbered."

"I thought we were all brothers," Chase said, getting to his feet. "Or does that not apply to anyone who doesn't agree with you or Marco?"

"Why don't you shut your mouth before I shut it for you," Peter threatened.

Kevin handed Steven an envelope. Steven took out a sheet of loose-leaf paper and read the few sentences quickly.

"What the fuck does it say?" Peter asked, still eyeing Chase.

"It says Kevin is inactive as of the end of tonight's earlier meeting," Steven said. "And Ben was already inactive, so he wasn't bound by your orders."

"Is that true?" Peter yelled. "Can he do that?"

"He just did, asshole," Chase said. He turned to Ben and Kevin and said, "Let's go before the cops show up."

Peter started towards Chase, but Steven and five other brothers stepped in front of him and held him back.

"Let it go," Steven said.

"You think you know something?" Peter yelled after them as they walked down the driveway. "You don't know shit! We're on our way to the top, and you're out!"

Chase stopped and looked at Peter and the rest of the group. They didn't look like a group to be feared. Aside from Peter, they looked like a bunch of scared kids.

*   *   *

Marco crawled the final twenty feet to the basement window on the side of his house that he always left unlocked when he was out. He wasn't sure if Frank was awake, and even though he didn't see him when he peeked through the front window, he wasn't taking any chances. He pushed the window in and up and tried to get the hook through the eye hole in the ceiling to make it easier, but his right hand was throbbing, and he wasn't nearly as coordinated with his left, so he couldn't manage. He turned so he was lying on his stomach facing away from the house and gently pushed the window open with his feet. He slid backwards and let the window slide up his leg as he bent and then gently let his right footrest on a heating pipe before stepping down.

Once in the house, Marco pulled the clothes from the dryer and threw them in a basket. He tossed everything from the washer in the dryer but forgot to turn it on. He removed his clothes and tossed them in the washer. There wasn't much All Temperature Cheer in the large box, but he dumped what was left on his clothes.

The singed sleeves and smoky smell on his shirt kept Marco from getting the ambulance for Jimmy. His only option had been to get home as quickly as possible, and it had taken more than two hours since he couldn't put any weight on his left leg. He would go to sleep and forget the night ever happened. Jimmy had left him in the temple, and he had left Jimmy on the curb, so as far as Marco was concerned, they were even. He considered going up to shower and then calling Peter, but it was too early to be sure Frank had gone to bed, and too late to call Peter's house.

*   *   *

It was almost one a.m. by the time the Parklynn Hospital staff obtained enough information to call Jimmy's parents. They informed his mother that Jimmy's injuries were substantial but not life-threatening. She and her husband arrived ten minutes later and were able to see him briefly before he was taken up to surgery to have his spleen removed.

In the early morning hours after surgery, Jimmy was brought to a recovery room. One of the nurses on duty, Claire Fender, stopped to check on him after hearing him say something while she was walking past his room to check on another patient.

Jimmy was still feeling the effects of the morphine as he rambled on about being beaten near the temple. She pulled a blank piece of paper from the back of his chart on the end of his bed and took notes to preserve details he might later forget. She intended to share the information with the police when they came back in the morning, but the first call she made was to her nephew. He was producing an overnight talk show on a local radio station, and she usually listened while she sat at the desk at the nurses' station. Tonight's show had been mostly about the chaos in Malbrook, and people had been calling in with theory after theory on why everything had happened. She gave him the information she had gathered from Jimmy without going on the air, and he shared it with the deejay as a tip from an anonymous source close to a beating victim. By noon, every news outlet on Long Island was running the story.

When Jimmy's parents were finally allowed in to see him, he complained he was dizzy and couldn't see clearly. When he couldn't remember his name, his mother rushed out to get a doctor.

Chapter 16

John stopped by Alex's house early Sunday afternoon. He didn't call because there was a good chance Alex's father would be back from an early round of golf and napping on the couch. Four Sundays each month, Mr. Moran played nine holes at either Woodmere or Bay Park with three friends he had been golfing with since he had taken up the sport ten years earlier. If there was a fifth Sunday in the month, they played eighteen holes at Eisenhauer Park. Regardless of where they played, they arrived early enough to be one of the first groups to tee off.

Only Mr. Moran's car was in the driveway, and that meant there was a chance Alex wasn't home. The rule for Sundays was Alex either went to church or he didn't leave the house, and no friends were allowed over. That had been an issue when Alex was younger, but now, except for some long-winded, uninteresting homilies, he enjoyed the peace mass brought him. The rule about skipping mass was specific to Alex since Annie never missed it, and Doug wasn't catholic. Out of respect for his wife's faith, Doug never told Alex his belief that while going to mass was good, God probably rewarded those who followed His teachings.

John knocked softly on the side door. There was a fine line between knocking too softly for Alex to hear and hard enough to wake his father. Alex appeared, saw John, and unlocked the door to let him in.

"What are you doing here?" Alex asked, surprised.

"Have you seen the newspaper?"

"I'm pretty sure you know the answer," Alex said as John followed him to his bedroom. "What happened?"

"Payback," John said.

"Why aren't you smiling?"

John tossed the newspaper to Alex and sat in the chair by his desk. He watched Alex's face as he read the headline on the front page.

"Rampage in Malbrook?" Alex asked, perplexed.

"Keep going."

Alex read the article on the second page silently. Confusion gripped him as he read an account that was attributed to a young white male in the hospital. He thought it was Marco until a description of the "unnamed youth who had been badly beaten" was tall and thin.

"Wait a second. They're blaming *everything* on black men in their early twenties?" Alex asked. "Aside from beating the shit out of Jimmy—"

"That's if it was Jimmy. The description fits, but you said they'd never actually seen him before, so they might have gotten the wrong guy," John said. "In any case, they said it was a blue sports car and there were three or four black men."

"His friend has a blue Camaro," Alex said, still not comfortable enough to use Isaiah's name.

"Did you check out the name of the injured fireman?"

Alex read a little more of the article. "Mike's brother Jason?"

"I tried calling Mike this morning, but there's no answer. Everyone's probably at the hospital."

Few things in the article made sense to Alex. The only thing that would ease his mind was to speak with Daryl or Jevonte and find out what really happened.

"Everything about this is wrong," Alex said.

"How long did it take you to figure that out?" John asked.

"You know?"

"Think about everything you've told me about Marco, Jimmy and their chapter," John said. "I mean . . . who is more likely to burn down a temple, four black guys out for revenge against white kids, or kids who hang a Nazi flag at their meetings?"

Alex placed a hand on each side of his head and pushed in as if he was trying not to let his head explode, then slowly slid them to the back of his head and clasped his hands.

"This is my fault," Alex said, pulling a slip of paper from his wallet.

"None of this is your fault," John said, following Alex to the kitchen where the phone was. "And after you do whatever it is you have to do; do you want to take a ride to the hospital and see if we can talk to Mike?"

"Sure," Alex said, listening to the phone ring on the other end.

For twenty minutes, Alex alternated between dialing Daryl's number, which rang endlessly, and Jevonte's number, which had a steady busy signal.

"Before we go to the hospital, let's take a ride to Rosedale and see if we can talk to Jevonte," Alex said. "I need to know what really happened."

"Isn't his cousin's house closer?"

"I'd rather get out of Malbrook for a while." He wrote a quick note and left it on the kitchen counter.

"Sounds like a plan," John said.

Alex tried Jevonte's number one last time before they walked out. Busy signal.

*   *   *

A crowd of black youths gathered in front of Jevonte's house early Sunday morning. None had been asked to come, but as word of what happened in Malbrook spread through Rosedale, a chain of phone calls began. The first five youths to arrive sat silently on Jevonte's stoop as watchmen, not bothering to knock and wake anyone. As more arrived, the crowd grew to fifteen and then twenty by nine a.m., and the chatter grew lively enough to rouse Daryl, who had been sleeping on the living room couch.

Daryl went out the side door and down the driveway where he met some friends. "What's going on?"

"Don't worry about it, Dee," Calvin Rogers answered. "We got your back."

Calvin had been the fat kid in their group since second grade. He had been the butt of many jokes over the years but was good natured enough to let them roll off his back. He was as loyal and dependable as any of Daryl's friends. He had missed the party the previous night because he worked overnights as a security guard near JFK Airport. As he was driving home, he had heard the news about Malbrook on the radio and swung by the house of a friend he knew was probably still up partying. Between them, they alerted everyone they could find. He wasn't aware that Daryl was spending the night at Jevonte's but figured both homes should have protection from people who would assume they were responsible. He called in a favor from a friend who was associated with the Knights and soon ten guys were standing watch on Daryl's stoop.

"What did I miss?" Jevonte asked when he joined them, still rubbing sleep from his eyes.

"Nice pajamas, bro," Calvin said with a laugh.

"What's with all these people?" Jevonte asked, too embarrassed to acknowledge the pajama comment.

"Just a precaution. Same at Daryl's house."

"Why?" Daryl asked.

"Police are looking for three or four black men who fucked with some houses, burned down a temple and beat the shit out of a white kid in Malbrook last night."

"Fucked with houses and burned down a temple?" Jevonte asked narrowing his eyes.

"Don't look at me," Daryl said.

"So, the white kid *was* you," Calvin said, and laughed easily.

"Depends on which white kid you're talking about," Daryl said. He had no issue with Calvin knowing.

"The news said there was only one," Calvin said. "They're looking for a blue sports car."

"Shit," Daryl said. "Let's go inside."

Daryl made three quick phone calls. Twenty minutes later he and Jevonte were sitting in the living room with Gerald, Calvin, and Tyrone while the crowd outside Jevonte's house continued to grow.

"They're blaming us for everything?" Tyrone asked. "Most of that shit happened before we even got to Malbrook."

"First of all, they're blaming three or four black men in their twenties, so stop with the us shit," Daryl said.

"He's right though," Gerald agreed. "Remember Isaiah asked you what you wanted to do because there were cop cars and fire engines everywhere?"

Daryl nodded.

"I read the Daily News article three times, and there's no mention of a police source," Jevonte said. He pulled the living room curtain back and looked out the window. He spotted people at the end of his driveway he didn't recognize.

"Why should that matter?" Tyrone asked.

"It's just strange. The only person mentioned is an unnamed source, which could be anyone."

Daryl took the paper from Jevonte and read it. He was having trouble concentrating enough to grasp the content because he kept thinking, *we should have gone to the police.*

"It doesn't even give the kid's name," Daryl said. "When Jevonte was attacked they gave his name and both of our addresses."

"You do realize you're not white, right?" Tyrone said.

"Didn't you say there were two kids?" Calvin asked.

"I knew we should have kicked that little weasel's ass some more," Tyrone said.

"We did more than enough to send him to the hospital," Daryl said.

"Then why doesn't it mention him?" Tyrone asked.

"How the fuck am I supposed to know?"

"Where is Isaiah?" Jevonte asked. "I thought he was coming over."

"Isaiah's on his way to Earl Scheib to get his car painted," Tyrone said.

"What?" Jevonte asked.

"Don't listen to that fool," Daryl said.

Daryl had spoken to Isaiah earlier, and he was busy helping his mother and then had a paper to write. He didn't seem particularly worried. They agreed it would probably be prudent not to hang out as a group for the time being. Daryl reminded Isaiah to get the bloody rag from beneath the driver's seat in his car and throw it in a neighbor's trash. Considering how stressed Isaiah had been the previous night, Daryl was pleasantly surprised at his calmness, which helped alleviate some of his own stress.

*　　　　*　　　　*

As John drove across the border from Nassau to Queens, he noticed some subtle differences, though he kept them to himself since Alex seemed to be lost in his own thoughts. Blocks were longer and the houses were closer together, and there were delis every few blocks in contrast to the five in Malbrook. John made a left turn off Sunset at a traffic light before it split into a parkway with a service road on each side. He stared at the people of the community as if he suddenly entered a foreign country.

"It just occurred to me that I've never actually been to Rosedale," John said.

"How? You've been to Brooklyn and Staten Island? Not to mention New Jersey?"

"No, I've passed *through* Rosedale, but I don't think I've ever stopped anywhere except a traffic light," John said. "I don't know anyone who lives here." He pulled up to a stop sign and waited for directions.

"Come to think of it, I haven't either," Alex said while looking at the page in his father's Long Island Atlas, which included Queens and Brooklyn. They were closer than he realized. "Make a right at the corner and then the first left."

Once they turned off the main road, Rosedale looked more like Malbrook. People sat on their stoops, children rode bikes while their parents talked with neighbors, and most looked like they had come from a religious service. The major difference seemed to be in their diversity.

"Rosedale is a lot nicer than people give it credit for," Alex said. "The way people talk we should've seen three murders by now."

"It *is* Sunday, so they might be taking the day off. You know, on Sunday God and all the murderers rested."

"You know why people talk so much shit about Rosedale?" Alex asked.

"Why?" John asked.

"Because they think all minorities are criminals."

"Wait, are you trying to tell me that all minorities *aren't* criminals?" John asked in mock surprise. He turned onto Jevonte's street and pulled to the curb.

"Jevonte's house is one-eighteen dash forty-four," Alex said.

"Um, Al, are you seeing what I'm seeing?"

A large crowd congregated in front of a house two blocks ahead. John had no doubt the house number would match the one Alex had just given.

"Just drive, it'll be fine," Alex said.

"The streets around here are all one way," John said, as he pulled away from the curb and continued down the block at a pace that barely registered on the car's speedometer. "If you're wrong, we're dead."

"Trust me."

"Al, think about it," John said. "Why would there be a crowd in front of Jevonte's house?" He pulled to the last stop sign before Jevonte's block. "It's not a party. They're at his house in case there's trouble, and two white kids pulling up is going to look like trouble."

"Pull a little closer and I'll call them. They know me."

There was no traffic behind him as John pulled through the intersection and turned off the radio. His eyes continuously shifted between the group ahead and his rearview mirror. They were halfway down the block when John pulled over.

"I'm gonna stop here," he said.

Alex rolled down his window and slid part of the way out so his feet were on the passenger seat and his ass was on the passenger door. "Daryl! Jevonte! Are you over there?"

"That's a bad way to call to them," John said.

"Shh, I think they heard me."

Three black teens spotted Alex and started towards them. John took one look at the three, slammed the shifter on the steering column into reverse and backed up.

"What are you doing?" Alex asked.

"I'm getting us the fuck out of here! The guy in the middle has a crowbar, and the one on the left has a hammer. I'm not sure about the guy on the right but I doubt it's flowers."

John backed out of the block as the three men gave chase. Alex slid back in his seat. John was worried about cars turning the corner behind them, but he was even more worried about the men chasing them. He accelerated then skidded to a stop at the intersection.

"Why are you stopping now?"

"Any cars coming on your side?" John asked.

"You're clear," Alex said.

John backed through the intersection and skidded to a stop again, gave a quick glance to his right to make sure he was still clear, then turned left and pushed the gas pedal to the floor. The foot pursuit was left behind, but there was no guarantee that others weren't getting in cars to chase them. He wanted to pull over, take a breath and steady his shaking hands, but wouldn't allow himself to until they were safely back in Alex's driveway. John blew out a calming breath and relaxed back into his seat.

"I've suggested some dumb things," John said. "But that was easily the dumbest thing I have ever been a part of, and there's no close second! You freaken called them like you wanted Daryl and Jevonte to come out and fight!"

"I just wanted to talk to them."

"*I* knew that, and *you* knew that, but wouldn't it have been smarter to yell something like, 'Hey, Daryl and Jevonte, it's me Alex; I'm here to help,' or something like that. Maybe then my pathetically short life wouldn't have passed before my eyes."

"I'm sorry," Alex said.

"No, no, it's good, at least I got to see all the sex I had."

"Both times?" Alex asked.

"It's not both *times*, it's both *girls*. *And* the recent blow job."

*   *   *

There were three water stains on the ceiling above Marco's bed. He had never noticed before, but one looked like a bird with its wings spread, the second looked like a kangaroo if he squinted just right and the was just a large brown blob.

Marco wasn't sure if he'd been staring at them for minutes, hours or days. He didn't know, and he didn't want to know. He had unplugged his alarm clock when it started blaring at seven-fifteen, which couldn't have been too long after he had fallen asleep. He didn't remember setting the alarm, but then he barely remembered anything.

Marco heard the phone ring three separate times, but with everyone else out of the house he let it ring until they gave up. *Go fuck yourself if you think I'm getting up to answer your call!* Knocks on the door had likewise gone unanswered.

Marco was still trying to piece together what happened between the time he left Jimmy by the curb and when he woke. He vaguely remembered climbing through the basement window, but not much after that. He was fairly sure at some point during the night he had hobbled upstairs and tripped over one of the cats in the living room though that might have been a dream. If it hadn't been a dream, he was sure Frank had laughed at him, helped him up, said something about him being drunk and given him two Tylenol. Had Frank also helped him back down to his room where he had fallen asleep? He dismissed the entire episode as a pain-induced delusion because the throbbing in his head, leg and hand made him believe he couldn't have taken anything for the pain.

He wanted to believe there had been far too much going on in the area for Jimmy not to have been discovered and taken to the hospital. But with everything else going on, would anyone have bothered to check on a kid lying on the curb staring up at the sky? Marco stopped himself from considering answers. Marco had not made it back to Peter's to find out how the rest of the night went, but given his present level of pain, he didn't particularly care either.

The rumbling in his stomach reminded him the last time he had eaten was the previous night's dinner, and without a working clock in his room there was no way of knowing how long ago that had been. He forced himself up and slowly and deliberately climbed the stairs to the kitchen as he conceived a story about why he hadn't sent help for Jimmy.

Marco grabbed two packs of cherry Pop-Tarts from the pantry and the last of the milk in the refrigerator. He turned on the television, grabbed the cable box, and sat on the couch. He was about to change the channel when an image on the screen stopped him.

A female reporter from NBC stood before the ruins of what had been a Jewish temple the previous day, then they cut to footage of firefighters battling the burning structure as she described the scene.

"Yes!" Marco raised his hands in victory.

The footage stopped and the news cut to Curt Desmond in the studio. Desmond was a weekend anchor trying to break in as a regular and making no headway. With thick brown hair, a mustache and a square jaw, Desmond looked the part and should have been a shoo-in. But despite being visually appealing, test audiences did not like his perceived smugness and personal detachment from his reporting.

"Police are looking for three, or possibly four, black men who were seen in the area at the time of the fire," Desmond began. "Sources tell us that the men are also wanted for questioning in the beating of a white male high school student from Malbrook."

"Fuckin' A!" Marco yelled at the television. "Fuck you, you stupid niggers!"

Marco tore open the Pop-Tarts, folded the first pastry in half and shoved it in his mouth. He squeezed in a few drops of milk directly from the carton to make the pastry soft enough to swallow. He took smaller bites of the next three pastries which afforded his taste buds the opportunity to enjoy them.

When he finished eating, he went to the bathroom and popped six Tylenol caplets into his mouth and washed them down with the remaining milk. He hobbled back down to his room and changed into semi-clean clothes. He sat on the edge of his bed and rested for a few minutes before beginning the painful trek back up to the kitchen to call Peter. The sun was out, the sky was cloudless and blue, and it was shaping up to be a beautiful day.

A knock on the door startled Marco. He opened it and Peter broke into a relieved laugh. Marco waved him in and hobbled into the living room with him and sat on the couch.

"What happened to you last night?" Peter asked.

"It was insane. Jimmy and me go in the temple and start lighting things, and the place goes up like we're using flame throwers. It was fuckin' beautiful."

"But after that. What happened with you and Jimmy?"

"Can you get me a glass of water? I'd get it myself, but my leg is killin' me. Fuckin' nigger just about broke it."

"Sure."

Peter stepped over a wooden train set in the center of the room and walked past a litter box that had so much shit in it the two cats had stopped using it. He held his breath until he got to the kitchen and filled a glass with water. He leaned over the sink to the open kitchen window and took a breath of fresh air before going back to the living room. As bad as Marco's room sometimes smelled, the first floor was now worse.

Peter handed Marco the glass and sat on the steps across from him, as far away from the litter box as he could get. "So, what happened?"

Marco took a sip of water and rubbed his jaw. "We're walking back to my house and a bunch of niggers jump out of a car and chase us. We ran into the park, and I went to the left figuring Jimmy would follow me, but he took off to the right. I'm like, *what the fuck?* I'm thinking we'd be better off together if we have to fight. I don't know what the fuck happened to Jimmy, but next thing I know these two big niggers are wailing on me! I don't know how many punches I even took because at some point one of them connected with a shot to my jaw and I was out cold. When I came to, they were gone and there were police, fire trucks and ambulances everywhere, and I was in so much pain I think I hallucinated. Everything after that punch is a blur. This morning I woke up on the floor next to my bed. I'm not sure how I got home, how I got in my room or anything."

"Holy shit!" Peter said. "When neither of you showed up last night everyone thought you got caught. Everyone was freaking out. We listened to Steve's father's police scanner, but all we heard was something about people being trapped inside the temple and—"

"Trapped inside? Someone was inside?"

"Three firemen. They got one out, but the other two died," Peter said.

"Died?"

"Yeah. Two died and the third one was burned pretty bad," Peter said.

"Died," Marco repeated, stunned.

"Police are looking for niggers," Peter said. "Man, we pulled off the greatest night of terror in the history of

Malbrook, and you guys have the police looking for niggers!"

Peter moved over to the couch, picked up a pillow and sat in its place. He leaned back and suddenly looked exhausted.

"Has anyone talked to Jimmy?" Marco asked.

"Steven went up to see him in the hospital this morning. Their moms are close, so Jimmy's mom called to make sure Steven was okay."

"Jimmy's in the hospital?" Marco asked.

"Yeah. They must have caught him, too. Fucked him up pretty bad."

"Is he okay? Did he say anything?"

"Steven said Jimmy was drifting in and out. They operated on him right after they brought him in."

"Operated?"

"Yeah, they had to remove something. Steven said he was on painkillers and wasn't making sense most of the time. He even said you left him behind."

"Jimmy said *I* left *him* behind?" Marco asked incredulously. "When I woke up, *he* was gone."

"Steven said Jimmy wasn't making sense," Peter said. "I'm just glad you're okay, because when Jimmy turned up in the hospital and we couldn't get in touch with you, we thought they killed you. A few of us searched the park this morning after Steven got back from the hospital."

"Really?" Marco asked, surprised by their concern. He quickly switched gears to the news he had just watched. "Did Jimmy talk to the police?"

"He talked to someone last night, but no one knows who. He'll have to talk to the police today for sure."

"Shit. That is not good," Marco said, remembering times he had seen Jimmy spill secrets after smoking pot.

"Why not?" Peter asked. "He already has them looking for niggers."

"True," Marco said. *But he will have to keep his story straight.* Marco wasn't worried since no one had seen him near the fire, so if anyone was going to take the fall, it was Jimmy. Marco made a mental note to throw out the singed shirt he had worn as soon as Peter left.

Chapter 17

The Dunkin' Donuts container of coffee sitting on Henderson's desk was cold. By eleven a.m., that cup would normally have been finished and in the trash beside his desk, and his "World's Best Father" mug would had been filled and then refilled with coffee from the precinct coffee machine. On most days he would have been on his fourth large cup by now. Henderson did all his coffee drinking before noon.

The notes he and Tallerico had taken while interviewing Jimmy Kessler were strewn all over his desk but still made little sense. According to Kessler's account, he and a kid named Marco Scotti had been walking through Westwood Park when they spotted three black men climbing the fence that separated the temple from the park. He didn't know why, but he said as soon as the men spotted them, the black men chased them to the opposite side of the park and beat them up before they fled in a blue Camaro. He put the Camaro's model year somewhere between 1970 and 1973 because the body style of the earlier models were different, and later body styles had more pronounced front bumpers. The car he described had a hood scoop in the front and a rear spoiler that was "more modern than the original ones," which meant little to Henderson, since he favored Ford's Mustang to Chevy's Camaro.

He compared those notes to the ones he had taken while speaking to the nurse who had been on duty when Jimmy was brought back from surgery. According to the nurse, Jimmy said "niggers" jumped *out of* a blue sports car and chased them, but mentioned nothing about the temple, though where he was found was consistent since it was relatively close. The nurse might have gotten some things wrong, or the Kessler kid might have been talking gibberish since he was on a morphine drip and wasn't answering questions as much as mumbling information. Considering the extent of the kid's injuries, it would have been unlikely he would have gotten a good look at the car after he was beaten, which is why Henderson was inclined to believe the earlier babbling was more truthful. *Why the change?* Questions without answers were piling up quickly.

"Hey, Jess," Henderson called to his partner who was one desk over. "Did you find anything on the kid our beating victim was with?"

Tallerico had just picked up the phone to call someone but returned it to its cradle. "I just got off the phone with the assistant principal, and I was about to call the Scotti kid's house."

"What did the assistant principal have to say?"

Tallerico picked up the notes he had taken while talking to Ted Holmes of East High so he could quote Holmes's personal opinions verbatim. "Let's see; where do I begin?" he said. "Marco is a junior, and he's been in the school since seventh grade. Ted Holmes said it would be generous to call him a D plus student, and he's been to summer school for at least two classes each of the past four years. His absences per year are usually in the high teens and he's not involved in any school sponsored extra-curricular activities, though he is a member of a fraternity, but couldn't recall which."

"This has got to be the only place in the country with high school fraternities."

"Actually, I believe some have chapters as far away as Delaware."

"Where I grew up no one bothered with Greek letters, and they were called gangs."

"Were you in one?" Tallerico asked.

"I had more sense than that. Were you in a *fraternity*?" Henderson did nothing to hide his disdain for the concept of high school fraternities.

"They didn't have any in my high school, but my cousin in West Hempstead wanted me to start a chapter of Omega. I just had too much going on at the time."

"Omega?" Henderson asked.

"Omega Gamma Delta. If I'm not mistaken, it's the biggest high school fraternity on the east coast, if not the country. Alpha Omega Theta and Phi Gamma Alpha were the other two I was familiar enough with to know had certain qualifications that had to be met before they would consider giving out bids."

"Bids?" Henderson took a sip of his cold coffee and nearly spit it out.

"Each fraternity—"

"Hold that thought," Henderson said as he stood and picked up both cups on his desk.

Tallerico stood and followed him to the coffee pot on the opposite side of the room. The squad room was empty except for two officers and a shoplifter they had arrested at the mall. Henderson dropped his Dunkin' Donuts cup in the trash and poured Tallerico a fresh cup before filling his own.

"Okay, you were saying something about bids."

"Each fraternity gives out bids and interviews the candidates. If they're accepted, they have to pledge for however long the fraternity requires. I think it's usually two or three weeks."

Henderson held the glass sugar dispenser upside down over his cup until the coffee neared the top. He grabbed some plastic stirrers from a box next to the coffee maker and stirred as they walked back to their desks.

"And boys do this willingly?" Henderson asked, with an amused look.

"Why are you busting my chops?"

"I find it funny that people talk about high school fraternities like they're a normal thing."

"In the tri-state area they are," Tallerico said.

Henderson took another sip and placed the cup within the ring stain on the corner of his desk. "Anything else about the Scotti kid?"

Tallerico read a note he had circled at the bottom of the paper. "Scotti and Kessler are in the same fraternity and spend a lot of time together on school grounds with a kid named Peter Ryan."

"Does anything about this case strike you as strange?" Henderson asked.

"Where do I start?" Tallerico said and chortled softly. "Why would black men target a temple? Or Jews period. Eight calls on Saturday night, and most had their windows broken and swastikas drawn on their doors."

Henderson opened his desk drawer to check his snack options. Stuffed inside were bags of M&Ms, Skittles, and barbecue potato chips, a banana, and hidden beneath some papers was a bag of homemade chocolate chip cookies. He opened the bag of cookies his wife Mary baked two nights earlier, took two and put the rest back.

"Malbrook is what, ten percent Jewish," Tallerico estimated.

"If that," Henderson said, and looked at the first two pages of the yellow legal pad which were filled with questions. He crossed out two questions Tallerico had gotten answers to that made sense.

"You know what bothers me most about this case?" Henderson mused.

"Everything?" Tallerico suggested, though he knew the question was rhetorical.

"Well, yeah, but the Kessler kid said his friend—"
he looked for the name on his pad.

"Marco Scotti," Tallerico filled in.

"Right. He said Scotti took a pretty good beating
himself, so why didn't he go to the hospital? Or at least the
police station."

"*I* would have."

"Me, too," Henderson agreed. "I think we need to
pay a visit to this Scotti kid."

"I'm with you on that," Tallerico agreed. "We need
to go to his house though, because according to Holmes,
he's not in school today." Tallerico tore the top sheet from
the pad on his desk, folded it and put it in his pocket.

*   *   *

The second week of pledging started less
enthusiastically than the first after word spread that Mike's
brother was the injured firefighter. Everyone was more
concerned with Mike and his family than with hazing.
There had been a constant yet unsuccessful effort to contact
Mike, who had spent Sunday at the hospital and then fallen
asleep in the waiting area on the third floor, just below the

burn unit where his brother was being treated. Except for the five minutes his parents had been permitted to visit with Jason, no one had been allowed on the fourth floor. Burn victims were highly susceptible to infections that could become life threatening, so even they had to view their sleeping son through a window.

John signed for one of the black pledges. He was tempted to sign Mike's name along with his but felt uneasy. No one would question it, and if anyone did, John would say he was meeting Mike at his house so the pledge could clean it before his parents got home. He signed Alex's name in another black pledge's book while Alex went to speak with the athletic director.

The lobby outside the gym was filled with students exchanging theories on who was responsible for the temple fire. Alex heard three people blame it on Jevonte Jenkins and his friends, while others said it was probably one of the black families who already lived in Malbrook and wanted to clear room for their friends to move in and turn it into a "spook town." Each theory sounded dumber than the previous one.

"We should burn down some of those nigger houses," the sophomore boy with the spook town theory said, trying to impress the girls with whom he was standing.

Alex grabbed the front of the kid's Puma shirt and shoved him into the wall between the glass trophy case and the double doors of the gym. "You're everything that's wrong with this town, you little dipshit," Alex said through clenched teeth. "You don't know what you're talking about."

Alex felt himself yanked backwards, and his first thought was that a teacher had seen him shove the kid. When his ass hit the floor, he saw Richie.

The sophomore boy looked down at Alex, enjoying the moment.

"Why are you picking on a little seventh grader, Alex?" Richie sneered. "Why don't you pick on someone your own size? Or is that a problem because you don't have your boyfriends here to protect you?"

"It's sad that you think we're the same size, you fat fuck. But I'll still fight you. Anywhere but here."

"With your friends to protect you? I don't think so, pussy." A small crowd gathered to watch. "Look at the little chicken." Richie made clucking sounds.

"What are you, in second grade? That's why you're not in Phi. Because you're a burnout and an asshole, and everyone here knows it. I don't have time for your crap right now, so I suggest you walk away while you have the chance."

John marched the pledges through the doors, and they all surrounded Richie. "What would you like us to do, sir?" Quentin asked.

"Even for you, Alex, this is a new low. Using niggers to fight your battles," Richie said.

Quentin took a step toward Richie, but John yelled, "Stop!"

Quentin stopped immediately.

"That's right, nigger. You better get used to listening to your masters," Richie said with a nasty laugh.

Quentin looked at Alex for permission to proceed, but Alex shook his head. "This isn't your fight. Richie is an asshole, and that is the reason he got kicked out of Phi. Now, he's jealous of you."

"Jealous of a nigger?" Richie spat. "That'll be the day."

"Mike warned you about what would happen if you used that word." Alex looked at the sophomore when he finished speaking.

Richie took two steps forward and threw a wild right that Alex easily ducked under. Alex connected with two quick left jabs to Richie's ribs. Richie grunted in pain and stepped back to catch his breath.

"I thought you weren't fighting," Richie said, accusingly.

"He's not fighting, asshole, he's defending himself," John said. "If he was fighting, you'd be swallowing your teeth. But trying to punch someone because you don't think they'll fight back makes you a real pussy, Richie."

Richie charged at Alex just as Coach Parisi pushed open the gym's double doors and stepped into the lobby. In addition to being the head coach of the varsity football team, Parisi was also the school's athletic director. He was a solidly built man with salt and pepper hair and a mustache that matched. When he stepped into the lobby everyone moved out of his way.

"What's going on?" he yelled.

Richie turned his head slightly and tried unsuccessfully to stop. Alex used Richie's momentum to flip him on his back and into the wall as first a collective groan and then laughter came from the crowd.

"When you're able to get up, go to the main office, Mr. Dillon," Coach Parisi said sternly. "And wait for me there."

"Me?" Richie asked angrily, his eyes casting daggers at the coach. "You saw what Alex just did. What about him?"

Coach Parisi squeezed his bottom lip between his left thumb and index finger. "Nice takedown, Moran. You used Dillon's unbalanced and uncoordinated attack against him to expend as little of your own energy as possible. What's even more impressive is that you tossed Dillon aside like yesterday's trash when he's probably twice your weight. It looks like you're all ready for wrestling season. Now, let's talk about it in my office?"

Coach Parisi held the gym door open for Alex. Alex kept an eye on Richie in case he thought he had nothing to lose but some extra detention, or possibly an in-school suspension in one of the "rubber rooms" in the school's basement. Each of the five rooms was equipped with only one desk.

Rubber rooms were considered the worst form of punishment. There were no clocks on the walls of the windowless and nearly soundproof rooms, and the only item students were permitted to bring was lunch in a clear plastic bag. Lunch was limited to one sandwich, one piece of fruit, one bag of chips, and two drinks. No watch. No books. No pens or pencils. Not even a sheet of paper to make an airplane. Students staged a walkout every year to protest the use of rubber rooms as punishment, but nothing had changed.

"What would you like to talk about?" Coach Parisi asked as they walked.

"I was hoping you could tell me how Mike is doing," Alex said. "John and I went to the hospital, but they wouldn't allow us above the first floor."

"I spoke to his father last night and he said Mike is taking it hard. Jason is his idol."

"Do you know when he'll be back at school?" Alex asked as the coach unlocked his office door and directed Alex to a seat across from his desk.

The walls of his office were covered with copies of schedules for each of the school's sports teams for the fall and winter. His desk was covered with football stats from the previous Saturday along with stats from every team in their conference. Alex wondered if Coach Parisi sent scouts to every conference game, though that seemed unlikely for a high school football coach.

"He'll be back in school on Wednesday," the coach replied. "They're hoping he'll get to see Jason tomorrow. I think it would be good for him, even with Jason being heavily sedated."

"How is Jason doing?"

"He's been upgraded to stable condition, but he's got a lot of skin grafting ahead of him, which won't be easy."

Alex shook his head sadly as he stood to leave. "Thanks, Coach."

"Thanks for coming in, Alex."

Alex was about to pull the door closed behind him when he turned back to the coach. "Don't go too hard on Richie. I mean, he's an idiot and deserves it, but sometimes I think stupidity is its own punishment."

"I was thinking of making him the ball boy for football practice today," Coach Parisi said. "Maybe it will remind him of what he missed out on."

"That's perfect," Alex said, and laughed.

*　　　　　*　　　　　*

Detectives Henderson and Tallerico stopped at the address Ted Holmes had supplied. It was a cool, breezy afternoon and neither minded being outside. Henderson checked what was visible in the yard before knocking twice.

There were no cars in the driveway and the blinds on the first floor were drawn. If not for the freshly cut lawn and a bag of grass clippings by the curb, the house would have looked abandoned. A blue swing set was visible in the side yard. The front right leg was bent and tilted toward the house, but someone had dug small holes for the other legs to compensate for the bent one.

When no one answered on the first two knocks, Tallerico looked at a small hole in the white trim between the door and the yellow siding where two wires that had once been attached to a doorbell stuck out. "What do you think will happen if I connect those two wires?"

"My best guess is nothing," Henderson said. "But for all I know the house will blow up."

"Maybe I'll try knocking again," Tallerico said.

"Wise choice."

The heavier inside door swung slowly inward and caught on a doormat. "Shit," Frank said softly. He closed the door slightly and used his right heel to pull the mat free. He gave the detectives a once over. "Can I help you?"

The odor emanating from the house caught Tallerico by surprise and he almost gagged. Any interview would have to take place somewhere else.

"Does Marco Scotti live here?" Henderson asked and held up his badge.

"He's my stepson. He's still at school," Frank said.

"Actually, he's absent today," Henderson said.

"Really? Either he's cutting or his mother called the school before I woke up. If you have a minute, I'll see if he's in his room."

"We would appreciate that," Henderson said.

"You can come in if you like," Frank offered.

"Thanks, but I'm allergic to cats," Tallerico said.

"Okay. I'll just be a minute. Why are you looking for him? Did he do something?"

Frank had no intention of getting Marco even if he was home. He might not like Marco, but even that paled in comparison to how much he did not trust the police.

"Nothing, actually," Henderson said. "You might have heard about the kid who got beat up Saturday night. It was Jimmy Kessler, who is one of Marco's friends. According to Kessler, Marco was assaulted, too."

"Dumb ass kids probably mouthed off to the wrong people. I keep telling that kid to watch himself because that little gang he runs around with won't always be there to have his back, but he's sixteen so he does what he wants."

Frank closed the door slightly and went halfway down the basement steps and waited a few minutes to make it seemed like he checked before he rejoined the detectives. He told the detectives Marco wasn't home.

Henderson handed Frank a business card. "Can you call us, or have him call us when he gets home? We want to make sure he's okay and see if he can give us any information."

"Sure thing," Frank said, and closed the door. He tossed the card on the coffee table. He knew bullshit when he heard it. He went down to talk to Marco.

*   *   *

There were no messages when they got back to the precinct, but Officer Gary Cole from NYPD's 143rd Precinct called a short time after regarding an inquiry from Detective Tallerico. Cole sounded like the disgruntled desk-jockey he'd become after more than thirty years on the force. He had been passed over for too many promotions to count and eventually accepted the reality that he would never be the homicide detective he had envisioned upon entering the academy. Cole's patronizing tone as he relayed the information reminded Tallerico how bitter some NYPD officers had become since Newsday revealed that the average salaries of police officers from Nassau and Suffolk counties were well above their New York City counterparts.

"Thank you very much," Tallerico said and hung up. Despite his annoyance with Cole's tone, Tallerico wasn't the type to burn bridges over pettiness.

Tallerico dialed the number he had gotten from Cole. When a woman on the other end answered, he said, "Is Isaiah available?"

"He's working until six," Layla Fisher said. "Can I take a message?"

"Thank you, but I'll try back later if that's okay," Tallerico said.

"Of course."

"Well, what did we learn?" Henderson asked.

"Not much, but it certainly won't hurt to talk to the kid." Tallerico looked at his watch. "He gets out of work at six, so if we give him until seven, we should be okay."

"Let's go get a couple of slices of Pizza at Gino's. My treat."

        *   *   *

The detectives rang Isaiah's doorbell just after seven. It had been a long day, but this house was more inviting than the one they had been to earlier in the day, with open shades and the soft lighting of a green living room. A blue Camaro that matched the description Jimmy had given was parked on the street two houses away.

A quick peek out the front window told Isaiah the men standing on the stoop were cops. They weren't completely unexpected but seeing them at the front door during the evening hours was slightly unnerving. If they were here to arrest him, they had come with the intention of making him sleep in a cell since it was too late to go before a judge. More likely, they just had questions. Isaiah opened the door.

"Who is it?" Layla called from the living room.

"I'm pretty sure it's the police, Mom," Isaiah said.

Henderson and Tallerico each held up their badges to confirm Isaiah's assumption, though he was surprised by the Nassau County badges.

Layla rushed in from the living room in a semi-panic. She nudged Isaiah out of the way and said, "How can I help you?"

Henderson introduced Tallerico and then himself and held his badge closer for Layla to inspect. "If it's okay, we'd like to ask Isaiah some questions about Saturday night."

"Not without his lawyer present," Layla said.

Isaiah laughed and held the screen door open. "Relax, Mom, I didn't do anything," Isaiah assured her. "Besides, I don't have a lawyer because I've never needed one," he added. "Please come in. This is my mother, Layla, and obviously you know I'm Isaiah."

They followed Isaiah and Layla through the living room where Isaiah stopped just long enough to turn off the large console television that faced directly towards the far corner of the room between two large couches. Layla showed the detectives to the dining room table.

"Can I get you gentlemen something to drink?" Layla offered, still wary.

"No, thank you," the detectives answered.

Isaiah sat beside his mother on one side of the large oval dining room table while the detectives sat opposite them. Tallerico took out a notepad.

"We'd like to ask you some questions about this past Saturday night, if that's okay," Henderson said.

"Of course. Anything I can do to help."

"You don't seem surprised to see us," Henderson said.

"Should I be?" Isaiah asked. "I'm friends with Jevonte Jenkins and his cousin Daryl. I drive a blue Camaro, which is obviously a sports car, and according to the Daily News, you're looking for a blue sports car in a series of crimes allegedly committed by black men in Malbrook Saturday night."

"Are you that well versed in all the news, or just this case?" Henderson asked, impressed, and laughed softly.

"I'd like to say all news, but it's just this case and sports."

"Which sports?" Henderson asked. It wasn't relevant to the case but learning more about a potential suspect never hurt, and the more Isaiah talked the more he would relax.

"Mostly football and basketball," Isaiah said.

"Which teams?"

"Giants and Knicks."

"Same here," Henderson said. "Back to the other news though. Why are you interested in this specific case?"

"I wasn't interested until Daryl called me yesterday morning. I was supposed to drive him home from Jevonte's house, but he called and canceled because he didn't want me to get hassled for no reason."

"Does Daryl read the paper every day?" Henderson asked. "I mean as far as you know."

"Daryl's like me, but Jevonte reads the paper cover to cover because he likes to know everything that's going on in the world. If you met him, you'd understand. Jevonte knows what's going on better than most of his teachers."

"We've met both, and that's kind of the impression we got as well," Henderson said. "But how did Daryl know for sure you weren't involved?" Henderson asked. The questions were moving quickly with no hesitation in Isaiah's answers.

"We were at a party Saturday night," Isaiah said. "We weren't side by side the entire night, but we were at the same party."

"Did you leave the party for any period of time?"

"You mean like long enough to drive to Malbrook beat someone up, burn down a temple and paint swastikas all over town? No."

"I don't appreciate the—" Henderson began before Isaiah cut him off.

"Detectives, please explain why I, or any other black person, would target Jewish families? And how many blue sports cars would be required to pull this off since according to the newspapers, the houses were miles apart and the vandalism took place around the same time?"

"We're working on several different angles," Henderson said. "Now, will you please answer my question."

"We didn't leave the party until I dropped Daryl off at Jevonte's house a little before three. Then I came right home, which took about two minutes."

Layla nodded and said, "That's right, because I sleep on the couch until he gets home, and I looked at the clock and it was a few minutes after three when I went up to bed."

"Was there any point during the night after you entered the party that you returned to Malbrook?"

"No. I thought I just answered that."

"You did, but we have three eyewitnesses who say they saw your car in Malbrook around the time of the fire."

"I have thirty eyewitnesses who say your so-called witnesses are full of shit," Isaiah countered without hesitation.

"Isaiah, mind your manners," Layla said.

"You should listen to your mother," Henderson said.

"I do," Isaiah said. "But what my mother doesn't realize is that when two detectives come into *her* house and tell lies about *her* son, they are disrespecting her, and as her oldest child it is my duty to protect her from such disrespect."

"Lying?" Henderson asked.

"If you had even one witness we wouldn't be sitting here. You would have arrested me, and there would have been photographers everywhere by the time we got to the precinct." Isaiah looked Henderson in the eye and added, "Everyone knows white justice is more important than black justice."

"That's not true," Tallerico protested. He was about to go on when Henderson stopped him.

"It's easy to deny when you're white," Isaiah said.

"Actually, Detective Tallerico and I work together because we both believe everyone deserves equal justice, regardless of skin color."

"Are you working on Jevonte's case, too?" Layla asked.

"As a matter of fact, we are," Henderson said.

"How is that going? Are you any closer to catching the people who attacked him?" Isaiah asked.

"We're working that case and think we may recently have gotten a break," Henderson said.

"What kind of break?" Isaiah asked.

"Unfortunately, we can't comment on that because it's an ongoing investigation," Henderson said, and nodded to Tallerico. It was time to leave.

"We have to be going, but thank you for your hospitality, ma'am," Tallerico said.

"Don't you ma'am me. I'm too young to be a ma'am. Isaiah told you, my name is Layla."

"Thank you, Layla," Tallerico corrected.

"Much better," she said.

Henderson turned to Isaiah and said, "Have you ever considered a career in law enforcement? If you're serious about equal justice and making a difference, it's a great way to do it."

"I'll keep that in mind," Isaiah said.

"You do that," Henderson said. "Layla, I want to thank you so much for welcoming us into your home."

As they walked back to the car, Tallerico said, "Do you really believe he wasn't in Malbrook Saturday night?"

"Nope," Henderson said. "Thirty witnesses? Way too convenient."

Chapter 18

Alex finally reached Jevonte by phone late Tuesday afternoon. Between hazing after school and trying to catch up with Mike, Monday had been a lost day.

Jevonte almost hyperventilated from laughing when Alex explained what happened when he and John tried to visit on Sunday. "One of the guys told me there were some white guys looking for Daryl and me, but it never occurred to me it might have been you. It makes so much more sense now."

"I tried calling first, but your phone was busy."

"We left it off the hook unless we needed to make a call."

"So, what happened Saturday night?" Alex asked. "It doesn't take a genius to know the papers got it wrong."

Jevonte filled him in on what really happened without using names. Neither understood how the blame for everything was placed on black men, considering swastikas were associated with white supremacists.

"The detectives investigating my case are on this one, too," Jevonte said.

"How do you know that?"

"They stopped by Isaiah's house yesterday and asked him about Saturday night," Jevonte said.

"They didn't arrest him, did they?"

"No. They just asked him some questions."

"What did they ask about?"

"They tried to tell him people had seen his car in Malbrook by the fire, but Isaiah squashed it with thirty witnesses of his own. Interestingly enough though, they told Isaiah they may have gotten a break in my case."

"How?" Alex asked. "The descriptions you gave weren't even close."

"I don't know why, but I trust they're being straight," Jevonte said.

At least part of the reason for Jevonte's trust was their ease with each other despite numerous differences not limited to age and race. They seemed to care about his recovery and apprehending his attackers. One of them had called each day since his release from the hospital for updates, and to see if he could recall anything new. Unlike virtually everyone else, they weren't giving up.

Alex felt the slight unease of butterflies in his stomach as he took a sip of water from the faucet. "I want to tell you something about the third kid who was involved in beating you if that's okay," Alex said. His mouth went dry immediately, so he filled a glass from the faucet.

"I'm all ears."

A sudden memory popped up and Alex remembered his former friend Jeremy saying disparaging remarks about a girl he like when they were in fifth grade. When he told Jeremy he liked Lisa Montez and was going to ask her to go the movies with him, Jeremy, who had since moved to Texas with his family, said, "Trust me, you don't like Lisa. Take a good look at her, she's all ears with greasy spic skin and nigger lips." Alex never asked her out, and seven years later he was still pissed at himself for listening to Jeremy. *Nigger lips.* The term still disgusted him.

"He told me not to make excuses for him, but I want you to know he's not like the other two," Alex said. "I think he went along with it because he was afraid of what would happen if he didn't." Alex took a sip of water. "He's ready to accept his punishment, and he'll come to you, so you don't have to go looking for him. He just wants a chance to apologize."

"He'll come here?" Jevonte asked and laughed.

"What's so funny?"

"It's kind of ironic that he's less afraid to accept punishment from black kids he doesn't know than his white *friends*."

"I hadn't thought of it that way. They're not his friends though, they tried to kick him out of Phi along with my cousin," Alex said.

"Your cousin got kicked out?"

"Nah. They're all a bunch of morons so we told them we transferred them before that so they couldn't kick them out. Then we transferred six others from their shitty chapter."

"Tell him not to worry," Jevonte said. "To be honest, I think I hurt him worse than he hurt me. I just want him to shake my hand so he can see I'm like any other person."

"I wish I could have met you and Daryl under different circumstances," Alex said.

"My mom says everything happens for a reason and it's all part of God's plan. I think I finally understand."

"Your mom sounds a lot like mine," Alex said.

Everything happens for a reason. Alex recalled the night of the attack and everything that could have gone differently. If Dave hadn't been concerned about the flag, Alex wouldn't have gone to the meeting with him. If Marco and Jimmy hadn't unveiled the flag at that meeting, Alex would have gone back to Dave's house immediately after the meeting. If Alex hadn't stopped to call Julie after the meeting, he could have stopped Marco before he threw a single punch. If Jevonte had taken the ride his uncle offered, he would have been spared his beating. There were probably hundreds of other things he wasn't even aware of that could have changed the outcome of the night. If his chapter hadn't accepted the transfers, they might have been able to stop the temple fire. Alex thought he might even still be dating Julie, though he now considered their breakup a positive. *Everything happens for a reason. Sometimes the reasons just plain suck!*

"On the night they beat me up, you mentioned a flag," Jevonte said. "I'm pretty sure I know what you meant, and I was wondering if it's something you could tell me."

Alex finished his water and refilled the glass. He pulled the curtains to the side and looked at the backyard.

Most of the pears on the tree were gone, but for the past few years they had grown large enough to eat, which was in stark contrast to when he was younger, and he and his friends climbed the tree endlessly throughout the summer and pulled off the small pears before they had a chance to ripen. The pears weren't wasted though, they hurled them at each other like rocks, and some days they all ended up with black and blue marks.

"My cousin didn't tell me beforehand that he wanted me at the meeting because he heard a rumor that they were bringing a Nazi flag," Alex said, letting go of the curtain. "He wanted advice if it turned out to be true."

"I'm guessing it was," Jevonte said.

"Unfortunately. After the meeting, Dave and I rode our bikes to a payphone so I could call my girlfriend—well now she's my ex-girlfriend—"

"That sucks," Jevonte said.

"Nah, it's good. Her father was a real prick and didn't like me because I'm not Jewish. Anyway, after I called, we went to the tunnel under Sunset to hang out and drink a few beers because I figured the beer would loosen everyone up and maybe I could see how many of those idiots were into that neo-Nazi crap. If I'd known only three guys would show up, I wouldn't have bothered."

"Well then, I'm glad you didn't know."

"Me, too. We just entered the opposite side of the overpass when they took off after you."

Alex heard a car pull into the driveway and figured it was his mother. He looked out the side window.

"My mom just got home so I've got to get going, but if you guys run into any trouble, give me a call. I've got a few things to take care of, but I'll call you as soon as it's worked out."

"Thanks. And you let me know if you need help."

"Will do," Alex said and hung up.

*   *   *

Tuesday night was the "Battle of the Bands" at East High, and the cafetorium was packed. Most days, the room which served doubled duty as a cafeteria and an auditorium was a plain old cafeteria just like at West. The only difference between the identical schools was their location on opposite sides of town. There were four-foot by eight-foot paintings on the walls that depicted the zeitgeist conceived by each graduating class's best artist or artists. The room also contained the stage for every performance of the school's band, orchestra, and choral concert as well as every drama club production. But for one night every third year it was reserved for the best bands in which all members were students in one of Malbrook's three high schools.

Each school held auditions and chose up to four bands. The bands didn't represent the school as much as the musical taste of the student body who chose them. The competition's venue rotated between schools and the money from admission fees was split between the senior classes after the winning band was awarded their prize money.

Nine bands had been selected for this year's battle, the lowest number since the inaugural year in 1968. West High had chosen four bands as usual, while Darcy High opted for three and East selected the only two bands who auditioned because other East High bands saw no point in competing with Innocence, a band comprised of the four most talented musicians in the school. Any band unfortunate enough to take the stage after them, even if good, often sounded like untrained monkeys banging on out-of-tune musical instruments.

Each member of Innocence played at least three instruments and were in the school's band and orchestra. In the previous year's battle, during a drum solo, the other three band members left the stage. When they came back, the lead guitarist had switched instruments with the bass player. Moments later, during a guitar solo near the right side of the stage, the drummer and keyboard player swapped instruments. The switches were done with the subtlety of a magician using sleight of hand, and almost no one realized what they had done until the end of the first song. By the end of the second song, each member had performed a solo on the drums or lead guitar. It was something no band had ever done during the competition.

The early battles had taken place on a Friday or Saturday night and started at nine o'clock, but back in 1978 several intoxicated students who arrived late started a fight that broke four chairs in Darcy High's auditorium. The following year, the battle was switched to a Tuesday night at seven o'clock as a deterrent to drinking since students had classes the following day.

Word of the battle was spread through the town's local paper, The Malbrook Sentinel where Detective Henderson came across an article promoting it. He and Tallerico decided to attend, figuring with students from all three schools in one place they might catch some loose chatter.

Ten minutes before the first band took the stage, Marco limped through the rear doors followed by Peter and Steven. He used a cane Frank had given him, which was a gesture almost as surprising as Frank asking if he needed to see a doctor.

Every attempt Steven had made to find out what had happened was met with the same, "Niggers jumped us," response from Marco. What Steven really wanted to know—a question Marco had dodged repeatedly—was how Jimmy could have known about Marco's injuries if they never saw each other after they were beaten as Marco claimed. Steven had gotten the answer from Jimmy when he had spoken to him at the hospital a second time when Jimmy was much more lucid, but he wanted to hear Marco trip over his own words.

Marco sat in an aisle seat in the second to last row. It allowed him to stretch his injured leg and be more visible to his brothers to collect sympathy. He was unaware that the two detectives who had been to his house earlier in the day were two rows ahead to his right.

Steven stepped over Marco's leg and sat two seats away to allow Peter to sit between him and Marco. Next to Steven was an empty chair and beyond it were two girls wearing blue and gold Darcy Gymnastics sweatshirts.

A few of the younger Phi brothers stopped by to check on Marco, whose condition worsened with each retelling. Steven did his best not to listen while he stood and scanned the large room for friends. He spotted Tommy and Dave on the opposite side of the room, sitting with a group of brothers from their new chapter. It reminded Steven of something he had heard earlier in the day that might just get Marco talking about something other than his leg.

As the overhead lights went off and the stage lights went on, Steven leaned across Peter to Marco and said, "Dave told Greg that Alex is going to talk to the detectives investigating the attacks."

"He says anything about me and he's a dead man," Marco replied calmly, surprising Steven. "He doesn't know shit, so let him talk all he wants."

Just as the first band from Darcy High, Infinite Wasteland, began a cover of Cheap Trick's "Surrender," Steven said, "Someone told Dave that you and Jimmy started the fire. Alex supposedly has something he's going to give the detectives." Steven didn't realize Marco hadn't heard him.

During the breakdown of each band's instruments and the setup of the next, there was ample time to talk, but it was dominated by Marco and Peter's opinions of the most recent band compared to earlier bands, so Steven took each opportunity to use the restroom or talk with other friends.

The battle officially ended at nine-thirty, but the contest was really over an hour earlier when Innocence finished playing "Roses for Meghan." The song was about a popular girl from East High who had died by suicide the previous year. Lead singer, Cole Pelfrey, had been one of Meghan's closest friends since kindergarten and didn't hold anything back, including tears, as he sang the words the entire band had put together for their heartbroken frontman. When he finished the ballad, there were few dry eyes in the room. Innocence was the only band to play an original song and did so for both of their selections. Their second song, "I'm Still Here" was a hard rock anthem for teens that shook the entire room.

As they stood to leave shortly after the show was over, Steven turned to Marco and said, "What are you going to do about Alex?"

"Why should I worry about him? He doesn't have shit on me."

"You're not worried about him telling the police you and Jimmy started the fire? Or what it is he might have to give them?" Steven asked.

Marco grabbed Steven's shirt and pulled him closer. In a sharp whisper he said, "Don't you ever say bullshit like that. And why would Alex make shit like that up anyway?"

"Someone told Dave that you and Jimmy . . . were responsible, and he told Alex."

Marco sat, looked at Peter, and said, "Go pull the car around to the teacher's lot and we'll meet you there."

"It'll take me like twenty minutes to get out of the student lot. Why don't you just come with me?"

"Because my fuckin' leg hurts. Go get the car."

Peter lingered at the end of the aisle until a gap too large to pass up presented itself. He was content to wait until everyone was gone, but two towering gentlemen let him into the flow of foot traffic. He had no idea they were detectives.

"Tell me what you know," Marco said.

"Someone told Dave what supposedly happened. Naturally, since you tried to vote Dave out, he told Alex because they both hate you. From what I heard Alex is going to Dave's house after school tomorrow to pick something up before he goes to the police."

"Pick what up?" Marco asked.

"The only thing I can think of is one of the envelopes with names and instructions that you guys handed out. I mean, what else is there?"

Marco banged the cane against the chair in front of him. The plan had worked too well to let that slanty-eyed cocksucker from the west side of town fuck it up.

"The assignments were decided by Peter," Marco said. "I helped him find addresses, but that was it because he wanted complete control. He even decided who did what. It's all in his handwriting."

"Peter said you guys did it together," Steven said.

"Just forget it. I'll take care of it, like I do with everything," Marco said.

"Aren't you worried about Alex going to the cops about the fire? Two people died."

"Why should I worry? The fire was Jimmy. I was there, but he went crazy and nearly got us killed."

"But you told us—"

"I've been taking everything I can find to numb this fucking pain. I haven't been thinking clearly since those niggers jumped me." Marco moved his leg and groaned for effect.

"Maybe I misunderstood," Steven lied. He knew Marco would believe him, too, because Marco was used to everyone taking him at his word. Steven couldn't believe how right Chase Baines was about Marco fucking everyone over to save his own ass. He wasted little time starting with his closest friends.

"Don't worry about it," Marco said. "Just don't mention this to anyone until we take care of Alex. Not even Peter."

"Why not Peter?"

"I'll talk to Peter later. I have to let him know how we're going to deal with problems first, otherwise he freaks out."

"What about Alex?"

"Does your dad still have that gun at your house?" Marco asked as casually as if he was asking for a piece of gum.

Steven knew the ramifications of his answer. He considered his answer long and hard because the thought of Marco with a loaded gun was unnerving. Marco always threatened to stab people, but that required getting close enough to feel the knife penetrate the victim's skin. Pulling a trigger was easy, and a gentle squeeze or a nervous flinch could end someone's life. Steven's father had taught him the proper respect for its power and how to handle it in an emergency. It was in a box on the floor of his father's bedroom closet beneath a pair of shoes he no longer wore.

"Yeah, I'm pretty sure he does."

"Can you get it?"

"Probably," Steven said hesitantly.

"Good. We owe it to Peter, Jimmy and everyone else in our chapter to get that envelope back before it ends up with the police."

One question ran through Steven's mind in an endless loop: *Am I doing the right thing?*

"You're not going to shoot him, are you?" Steven asked.

"I'm not gonna shoot anyone. I want to scare Dave and his gook cousin and get whatever he has back, and find out who gave it to him," Marco said. "Then we'll give that person the beating of a lifetime."

"That makes sense," Steven agreed. "But why do you need a gun? Why not just go to Dave's house with Peter and kick both their asses?"

"I don't trust anyone right now, and it's too important to take chances," Marco said. "Can you run in and get it when Peter drops you off? That way we won't have to worry about getting it tomorrow."

Chairs slid across the tiled floor as three custodians began making room for the lunch tables. "Hey, fellas, you have to go," the head custodian said.

"Not tonight. Tomorrow after school," Steven said to Marco as they stood to leave.

"Why *after* school?" Marco asked, as if Steven was being unreasonable.

"By the time we get back to my house, my parents will be in bed, which is where the gun is. And in the morning, I leave before my mother."

"Can you get it right after school?" Marco asked.

"Definitely," Steven said. He pushed open one of the doors leading to the teacher's parking lot and held it for Marco.

"See if you can find out when Alex will be at Dave's house," Marco said. He put his hands together and held them out like he was aiming an imaginary gun at Peter's car as he drove towards them, pulled the imaginary trigger, and simulated the recoil. "This is gonna be great," Marco said. "Don't tell anyone about the gun. Not even Peter."

*　　　　*　　　　*

On Wednesday morning, Steven's mother picked him up after fifth period to take him to the doctor for a physical. Marco made the requisite joke about turning his head and coughing, and then warned Steven about rumors that had been passed down for years that "Happy Hands Harrison" squeezed harder during private exams. Marco agreed to meet at Steven's house after school and from there they would go to Dave's because Alex was supposed to be there by three-thirty. They would conveniently show up a short time later. With everything falling nicely into place, Marco was practically giddy.

*   *   *

The warm sunny September day felt out of place. Alex appreciated the beauty, but during the worst weeks of his short life he felt like every day should be cloudy with a chance of rain. It was like a decade of bad days had been crammed into the first month of his senior year. Lately, every conversation was a struggle as his mind drifted constantly and he was unable to focus long enough to remember what he wanted to say. His parents referred to them as "senior" moments, but that meant senior citizen not high school senior!

Dave had called Alex the previous night and now Alex had to beg off hazing for the day. Alex finally found the opportunity to catch Kyle up on everything that had happened since he attended the crosstown chapter meeting with Dave. Kyle was one of his best friends and because of everything that had been going on in both of their lives Alex hadn't even had a chance to fill him in on the Nazi flag at the meeting or the attack on Jevonte, not to mention all the other chaos caused by their hopefully soon to be ex-brothers. Dave's phone call had set so many things in motion Alex hoped he remembered to tell Kyle everything. Instead of driving Alex home after school, John dropped him off at Dave's house where Dave was in the driveway playing fetch with his papillon puppy, Bandit.

Once Alex arrived, Dave put Bandit in the house and brought out a basketball. Neither was in the mood to play one-on-one, so they opted for H-O-R-S-E.

The hoop above Dave's garage was six inches shy of regulation height, and Alex jokingly blamed each missed shot on the height difference. With a running start, Alex could get his right hand above the rim, but not while holding anything larger than a tennis ball. He resigned himself to the fact that he would never be able to dunk anything on a rim at regulation height, but that was true of all his friends, including the three on the school's basketball team.

Their game lacked its usual enthusiasm, and fifteen minutes in, Alex had H-O-R and Dave had H-O as Alex readied himself to shoot from four feet to the right of what they considered the foul line while Dave drank from the hose behind the house. Dave flicked water in Alex's face as he was about to release the ball, and the shot hit the back of the rim and caromed to the opposite side, hit the house, and rolled down the driveway.

Alex let the ball roll and went to get a drink. He wiped his face on his blue Giants tee shirt and took the hose from Dave. "Let me get some."

Before Alex drank, he pressed his thumb into the end of the hose and soaked Dave's shirtless back with cold water. He laughed at Dave's high-pitched squeal as Dave ran around the side of the house for cover. It was his first real laugh in weeks.

"Damn, that's cold," Dave said.

Laughter from the front of the driveway preceded the sound of the basketball being dribbled. The laugh was more of a joyless cackle, and Alex knew without looking it was Marco.

Marco's lack of dribbling skill made it obvious that he had never played organized basketball. He had played a few pickup games with friends at Westwood Park in sixth grade, but because he wasn't tall enough, strong enough or fast enough to dominate any phase of the game, he abandoned basketball along with his friends who played.

"Look who has the balls to show his face at my house," Dave said, louder than necessary.

"I thought I smelled gook," Marco cracked when he saw Alex.

"Nah, it's probably just your underwear. Piss yourself lately?" Alex asked, and he and Dave laughed.

"What the fuck are you talking about?" Marco asked, then looked at Peter and shrugged.

"Give me about ten minutes and I'll remind you," Alex said.

"You think I'm scared of you?" Marco asked. He looked from Peter to Steven, laughed, then said, "Fuckin' gook thinks I'm scared."

John's car pulled in front of Dave's driveway. He took a quick look, beeped twice, and pulled ahead to the first open space on the right. Eight cars followed, some parking farther up the block while others pulled into the first available spot before Dave's house. Marco turned as the cars passed.

"Is it my imagination, Dave, or did your street just get really busy?" Alex asked.

"I think Marco's about to get really scared," Dave said.

"Shut the fuck up, dickless!" Marco said. "I'll show you who's scared." He reached behind his back into the waistband of his jeans and pulled out a black handgun. Alex and Dave both took a step back.

Out of Marco's view, the sliding glass door in the back opened. From behind the house, Jevonte emerged, followed by Daryl, Isaiah, Tyrone, and Gerald.

"Nice group there, Dave. What's the matter, don't have any white friends?" Marco asked. He swept the gun in a large semicircle to keep everyone at a distance as he backed down the driveway.

In the street behind Marco, car doors opened and closed in succession as they emptied. Kyle was leading a group of twenty Phi brothers and all thirteen pledges.

"Hey Alex, does this remind you of anything that happened to us recently?" John asked, and he, Alex and Jevonte laughed at the inside joke.

The driveway filled with teenage boys who spread across it to block any attempt to exit. Kyle stepped forward. "You must be Peter and Marco," Kyle said. "I've heard a lot about you two. None of it good."

"Fuck you, pussy," Marco said.

"You're calling me a pussy?" Kyle asked. "That's funny coming from a guy who pissed himself twice Saturday night."

"Two times," Tyrone said with a wide smile as he held up two fingers.

"That's fuckin' bullshit!" Marco yelled.

Kyle ignored the denial and looked at Peter. "I warned you about messing with anyone from our chapter. I told you there would be consequences."

Marco sneered at Kyle and said, "I'm the one with the gun here, asshole, so save your threats!"

"I made myself perfectly clear," Kyle said as he stepped toward Marco. "Gun or no gun, I'm obligated to keep my word. That's how loyalty and honor work in Phi Gamma Alpha, though I've heard it's not the case in your chapter."

"Fuck you!" Peter said. "If you got a problem, let's you and me settle it."

"Oh, we will," Kyle said. "Because you're not leaving. Not now anyway, and not in *your* car." Kyle could see from Peter's unchanged expression that the threat had gone over his head, though the flicker in Marco's eyes meant he had caught it.

"Shut up!" Marco yelled with a frantic edginess to his voice. He motioned with his head to Steven and Peter and said, "Get behind me, and I'll get us out of here. We'll take care of this another time."

"Weren't you listening, Marco?" Jevonte asked. "You're not leaving."

"Fuck you! I could shoot every one of you niggers right now and I'd never see the inside of a cell," Marco said.

"If that's the case, we should probably just kill him right now," Tyrone joked.

"Yeah, let's kill him. He's got a gun, so we'll say it was self-defense," John said, and he and Tyrone howled with laughter.

Alex looked over at John and Tyrone standing side by side and smiled as he realized how much alike they were. If Tyrone had grown up in Malbrook he probably would have been one of his best friends.

Marco stepped sideways along the fence just as Mike's car screeched to a stop in the middle of the street. He unintentionally left it blocking Peter's Nova. He and Declan stepped out. Both were wearing football practice pants with pads but had replaced their cleats with sneakers.

Declan moved in front to clear a path for Mike, though his assistance was unnecessary as every brother stepped aside to let them pass. As soon as Mike passed, the brothers closed ranks and blocked the exit.

The intermittent rising and falling wails of police sirens filled the air in the distance.

"Mike, you shouldn't be here, it's under control," Alex said.

Marco recognized Mike from the few times he'd seen him at the mall. He never paid much attention to

Mike but hated his Lacoste shirts with the stupid alligator, and his Sergio Valente or Jordache jeans. And everything else about Mike, too.

"You got a problem with me, you preppy motherfucker?" Marco yelled, "I got ten rounds in this gun. It's not enough to shoot everyone, but I'd be happy to start with you!"

Mike took two quick steps toward Marco, and to everyone's surprise—including Marco's—he pulled the trigger. To the surprise of only Marco and Peter, the only sound was a soft click.

"That is exactly why I took the firing pin out," Steven said, and backed away from Marco and Peter.

"You are so fuckin' dead!" Marco yelled at Steven.

"You wanna kill me?" Mike asked as he shoved Marco against the fence. "My brother is in the hospital with burns over half his body. I should be the one to kill you!" Mike leveled Marco with a punch to his face. Marco went down and Mike pounced on him, yanking him forward by his shirt and slamming his left fist into Marco's face before he shoved him back to the blacktop and stood over him. Mike lifted the back of his practice jersey and pulled out a gun tucked inside his practice pants. He pressed the gun to Marco's forehead.

"I didn't start the fire! It was Jimmy! You gotta believe me! I tried to stop him!" Marco pleaded.

"Open your fucking mouth!" Mike commanded and Marco did as he was told.

Mike put the barrel of the gun in Marco's mouth.

"Jimmy told the police everything," Steven said. "They suspected you though, because when Jimmy told them what happened, they thought it was strange that you didn't go to the hospital or the police station. Aside from your little followers, pretty much everyone in Phi knows you left Jimmy on the curb and thinks you're a piece of shit. And just like Chase told everyone Saturday night, if you got caught, you'd fuck everyone else over to save your ass."

"Not this time, bro," Daryl said.

"Word," Tyrone said.

"You don't know how bad I want to pull this fucking trigger!" Mike said.

"Hey, hey, what time is it?" Tyrone asked as he nudged Daryl's ribs.

Daryl looked at his watch and said, "Ten to four. You got a date?"

"Nah, I just wanted to see how long it took that little bitch to piss himself," Tyrone said, and pointed to the wet spot on Marco's crotch. "Fourteen minutes."

Mike pulled the gun from Marco's mouth and stood over him with the gun still trained on his face.

"What's the matter pussy? Don't have the balls to shoot me?"

Kyle put a hand on one of Mike's shoulders while Alex knelt beside him.

"You'll be doing him a favor if you shoot him," Alex said. "He's got no friends *and* he's going to jail."

"The police will be here any minute," Kyle said in a reassuring, yet urgent voice. "Jason needs you to be strong for when he gets out of the hospital. If you shoot him, you'll make life twice as hard on your parents."

"He has to pay," Mike said. Tears trickled from his eyes and the veins in his neck bulged as he used every ounce of restraint not to squeeze the trigger.

"He'll pay, but you have to do it the right way," Alex counseled.

Kyle eased Mike's arm down and took the gun from his hand. He carefully handed it to Dave and whispered, "Take this in the house and hide it someplace safe. It was never here." Kyle turned to John, and whispered, "Make sure everyone knows that the only gun here was the one Marco brought."

John made sure each person in the driveway heard it directly from him so there would be no mistakes. *Marco had been the only person with a gun.*

The sirens were getting closer, and everyone was focused on Marco, letting Peter think he might have a chance to plow his way through everyone and down the driveway. He only made it four steps before Declan stepped in front of him, lowered his left shoulder, and planted it in Peter's upper chest. It took Peter's feet out from under him and sent him to the ground on his back. Quentin was on Peter before he could gather his wits to comprehend what had happened. Quentin grabbed Peter's shirt with his left hand, yanked his face up and drove his right elbow into it three times in succession. When he finished, Peter's face looked two-dimensional. He flipped Peter on his stomach and put a knee on his back.

Quentin looked up at Declan and said, "Sir, can you please hold him down?"

"It looks like you have things under control."

Isaiah stepped closer to Declan and said, "I'm pretty sure what he's trying to say is he doesn't want to be on top of that bloody white kid when the police get here."

Quentin looked at Declan and nodded and Declan took his hand and pulled him up. Declan nudged Peter's arm with his foot but Peter's eyes didn't open.

The flashing lights of an unmarked police car reflected off the side of the house and everyone turned. Marco rolled over, pulled himself up and grabbed the fence. He got one leg over the side before Tommy pulled him back and connected with a punch to Marco's left eye. Mike added three more before Marco curled into a ball to protect himself.

"You have no idea how long I've wanted to do that," Tommy said.

"Everybody stay put! Nobody leave!" Detective Henderson yelled.

Henderson and Tallerico walked up the driveway with their badges held above their heads and the group parted to let them through. They were first on the scene because Jevonte had called them immediately after Dave's signal. He was supposed to call the sixteenth precinct, too, but everything happened so quickly he never got the chance.

Three police cars pulled up moments after the detectives, so at least one neighbor had called the precinct.

Marco was cuffed and put in the back of a police cruiser as curious neighbors watched. He would be booked at the precinct and spend the night in a holding cell in Mineola.

Peter was lifted onto a gurney and then handcuffed to it before being loaded into the back of an ambulance. Later in the evening he would have his broken nose reset, and he would spend the night handcuffed to the hospital bed before being arraigned the following morning.

Detectives Henderson and Tallerico went into the dining room with Dave and Alex. They hadn't even asked the first question when Dave's mother, Erin, rushed in through the front door, out of breath from having to park her car on the next block and running home.

"What's going on here?" Erin asked, alarmed as she looked at the six boys in her living room. She fired off four more questions in rapid succession before anyone had a chance to answer.

Detective Tallerico held up his badge and assured her everything was okay. He took her back out to the enclosed porch and filled her in. She was too antsy to stay in the porch because she wanted to see Dave and know he was okay. She had practically been in tears as she ran past the police cars and through the front door of her house.

"Are they in trouble?" Erin asked as she looked and saw not only Dave, but Alex, too.

"No. Your son helped us put two cases to bed today," Henderson said.

"It wasn't really me," Dave said.

Alex nudged Dave's arm and said, "Just once I want to hear you accept credit when it's given to you."

"Everyone here helped us," Henderson said.

"I . . . I'm so confused. What's going on? Why are all those boys in the driveway with police officers?" She had absorbed little of the information Detective Tallerico explained.

"Dave, why don't you get your mom some water and let her sit down?" Henderson suggested.

Henderson caught Dave's mother up once again. Her eyes shifted back and forth between Dave and Alex as Henderson spoke, partly with pride and partly with shock that they would keep something so important from both sets of parents.

"It would be really helpful if we could speak to the boys here while everything is still fresh in their minds," Henderson said.

"By all means. Can I get you detectives some coffee?"

"We're fine," Tallerico said.

"Who are the boys in the living room?"

Dave stood and went to the living room with his mother. "You know Tommy and Steven," he said. Before he could introduce the other four, they walked over and introduced themselves.

"We don't want to put Dave on the spot," Tyrone said. "We know you white folks think we all look alike."

"That's not—" Dave started.

"He's joking," Daryl said. He nudged Tyrone aside and said, "Go sit down, idiot, these people don't know your sense of humor." He turned to Dave's mother and said, "Sorry, Ma'am."

"It's fine," she said with a dainty laugh. "A sense of humor is important."

"Ha!" Tyrone said as he was about to sit.

Mrs. Kane sat at the dining room table and listened to the boys deliver a much more detailed version of the story she had just heard from both detectives. The boys from the living room were invited in at various points, starting with Jevonte.

The teens explained how everything came together, starting with Dave's decision to invite Alex to the meeting, and then to Jevonte's memories from the night he was beaten. Jevonte told how Alex had saved him and left enough clues for him to enlist his cousin Daryl—who was the next one called in—to track him down. Henderson asked questions when he needed clarification.

Tommy bridged the gap between the stories and confirmed both versions. When Tommy began to explain his involvement of the beating portion, Jevonte stopped him before he could incriminate himself. Steven filled in details of what happened within the fraternity following the beating, and Tyrone and Isaiah confirmed the details from the night they had first met Alex.

Steven had been to the precinct earlier in the day with his parents and his lawyer—when he was supposedly going to the doctor—and after a promise of immunity for his cooperation, readily admitted his crime and gave details of the others and who had committed which crimes. He explained that he had been present for the meeting on Saturday night prior to the destruction without alerting authorities but at that point had been given no details about the contents of the envelopes other than that they were anti-Semitic and in line with neo-Nazi beliefs.

*　　　　　*　　　　　*

On Thursday morning, Marco, Peter, Jimmy and fourteen others from East's chapter of Phi who had been arrested the previous night were arraigned on charges related to the previous Saturday night. All but Marco—

whose bail had been set at one hundred thousand dollars—
were released late Thursday afternoon.

Chapter 19

At Alex's urging, West High's chapter of Phi excused their pledge class from Wednesday night's meeting to give them a break after an eventful afternoon. The pledge class had gone beyond expectations by showing blind loyalty and trust. Several brothers had suggested a motion to forego the final two days of pledging and hell night.

As they were waiting for Kyle to come in from the living room, the other members in the family room were alarmed by what sounded like marching in the driveway.

"Let's go!" Declan yelled, instantly alert and ready for action. He jumped up and hurried to the sliding glass door in the back. Every brother in the room followed and filed out the back, hands already balled into fists.

"Wait," Kyle called out as he flipped the light switch, and the backyard was instantly illuminated. "It's the pledge class."

Quentin, who had become the unofficial leader of the pledges, turned the corner into the backyard and saw his future brothers waiting.

"You guys were excused from tonight's meeting," Declan said.

"With all due respect, sir, we want to be the best brothers possible," Quentin said. "We need to know our strengths and weaknesses, because none of us are perfect."

"I honestly had my doubts about a mixed pledge class before you all began," Guy said. Guy had been the one silent member who opposed blacks joining before Kyle called him out. "Even though we pride ourselves on being the best people we can be, I wasn't sure we could be fair and impartial when hazing pledges of different races, but you have all come together to make this the best pledge class I've ever seen."

"I think today was a perfect example of what can happen when you limit your friends to one group, race or religion. It leads to hate," Kyle said.

"I want to apologize for my skepticism and thank you all for demonstrating unity throughout the hazing process," Guy said. "I believe any further hazing of this pledge class as well as hell night should be waived."

Guy's eyes met Kyle's. Kyle's slight nod showed his approval.

Quentin turned to the pledge class. Each one shook their head.

"We appreciate that, sir," Quentin said. "And we thank you for your honesty, but we want to finish pledging and proceed with hell night."

"Why?" John asked, surprised. "If someone let me skip hell night, I would have been kissing their feet."

"Who are you kidding, you would have blown them," Mike said, and drew laughs from everyone.

Xavier stepped forward with a white freshman. The freshman was Robert Dugan, the quarterback of the junior varsity football team who most thought would be starting for varsity the following year.

"Sir, as the first interracial pledge class, we need everyone to know that we received no special treatment," Robert said.

"We don't want you to set a precedent, sir, because we will have no basis to judge pledge classes of the future," Xavier said.

"We did nothing special, sir," Quentin said before he choked up and took a moment to clear his throat. "Sir, on my second day of pledging, a Phi brother I barely knew invited me into his home and listened to what it was like for me to live in Malbrook. Sir, that Phi brother told me to forget how I've been treated in the past because even while pledging I could count on every Phi brother to have my back." He walked to Alex and offered his hand. "Sir, it is our opinion that any pledge not willing to do the same would not be worthy of wearing Phi's colors."

Alex smiled as he shook Quentin's hand.

"That is admirable, and I see no reason not to respect your wishes," Kyle said.

The meeting went on as scheduled and each pledge was apprised of their strengths and weaknesses before being sent home to prepare for their final two days. Thursday was a day of silence which was perfectly timed for this pledge class, and Friday was their last day of pledging. Then hell night.

* * *

The final two days of hazing were tense and filled with drama that kept everyone on their toes. After their former brothers of East High had been arrested and released, they were expelled from school. Rumors of attacks against Phi members from West High were running rampant by Friday morning, and despite being warned not to, every brother wore their colors in a show of solidarity. Multiple bomb threats emptied all three Malbrook high schools on Thursday and Friday. A strong police presence throughout the area around West was comforting to residents, but every Phi brother knew any attacks, however unlikely, would come in secluded areas.

When the final bell rang Friday afternoon, students at West High were not immediately dismissed. Hundreds of Phi brothers—both current and alumni—ranging in age from fifteen to sixty-seven, had gathered on the soccer field wearing their fraternity colors. Their intentions were unclear until police arrived and spoke to the president of the Alpha Beta Chapter, Oliver Reynolds, who assured them that every brother on the field had come to support their brothers and maintain peace. Police cordoned off the student and teacher's parking lots to allow students who didn't feel safe to exit, though most chose to walk along the soccer field anyway.

When word of the brothers on the soccer field spread, every brother and pledge in school were directed to a classroom on the third floor that overlooked the field. As brothers lined the windows of the classroom, the group on the field began to chant, "Thank you West High, Phi brothers till we die!" It went on until every brother and pledge marched down to the field to be greeted by Oliver Reynolds and four other officers. When Kyle saw his father standing beside Oliver with teary eyes, he threw his arms around him and sobbed.

$$* \qquad * \qquad *$$

To ensure hell night would not have to be moved from the bridge behind West where it had always been held, their brothers from Darcy High volunteered to stand guard. Before the pledges lined up one at a time to take shots with paddles and shaved down baseball bats, Kyle reminded the twenty-eight brothers who were present not to hold back with their swings because the pledge class wanted no special treatment.

Each pledge wore jeans with a belt. The belt was removed and placed in their mouth before they bent over to be paddled. Hell night proceeded as planned.

$$* \qquad * \qquad *$$

On Saturday night, Malbrook West's football team played their second road game of the season under the lights at Bethpage Memorial. Mike led the team to a 40 – 8 victory with 368 passing yards and five touchdowns. Two of the five touchdown passes were to Guy, who rotated between tight end and wide receiver. They were the first two touchdowns of his high school career. When asked about his performance by a reporter from the Malbrook Sentinel, Guy credited Mike for well-thrown passes, and Vincent Powell and Omar Clayton, both of whom were black, for requiring double coverage, which left only a linebacker who wasn't quick enough, to cover Guy.

Mike praised his coaches and teammates, but gave most of the credit to his brother, Jason, for showing him what it meant to fight. He accepted the game ball, signed by each team member and coach, and presented it to his brother, though he could only show him the ball through a window.

*   *   *

On Sunday morning, after Julie heard things from friends that hadn't been mentioned in the newspaper, she called Alex. She didn't want to call him, but she needed to know he was okay.

Alex assured her he was fine and tried to get off the phone quickly, but talking with Julie was effortless, even though he didn't want it to be. Conversation flowed, and they filled each other in on things that had happened since their breakup, and for a few minutes it felt like old times.

"Maybe everything that happened is for the best," Julie said.

"I agree, but why would you think that?"

"I didn't want you to hear this from anyone else," Julie said. "But we're moving to Hewlett."

"Hewlett?" Alex choked out as he laughed and spit root beer all over the kitchen floor.

"Hewlett. We haven't found a house yet, but my parents took me for a drive around the village and it looks like a really nice town. And it's not too far, so we can still go out."

Alex wasn't sure what she meant by "go out" but as far as he was concerned, dating was not an option.

"I've heard it's a beautiful town," he said diplomatically.

Alex didn't know much about Hewlett, but he had heard people jokingly—which was apparently the best way for Malbrook residents to teach prejudice—refer to it as "Jewlett" because most of the residents of the high-priced village were Jewish. Alex's only personal memory of the town, aside from wrestling, was during hazing when he and John had been dropped off near Hewlett Harbor and told to find their way home. It took them nearly five hours, but they eventually made it. Hewlett had no streetlights and Alex remembered worrying that if anyone spotted them, they would be picked up by police. It didn't happen, but their hitchhiking attempt also yielded no ride offers until they found their way to East Rockaway and a man in his thirties finally picked them up.

"That's it?" Julie asked, a bit indignantly. "What about going out?"

"Jules, your family is moving to Hewlett. Don't you see what your father is doing? You're his prisoner and you don't even know it. You will never date a non-Jewish boy again."

Alex heard the phone slam down on Julie's end. Friendship over. He took a breath and realized he finally felt better about their breakup.

*   *   *

Two hours later, thirteen new brothers were sworn into Phi Gamma Alpha. Most were still too sore to sit, but the kegs were full, and once everyone had completed their oath and toasted with their brothers, the party was opened to friends from school who were willing to pay the five-dollar admission charge.

Alex sat alone at a table in the back corner of Kyle's yard trying to comprehend the chain of events that had claimed nearly his entire first month of school. At times it seemed like he had really been nothing more than a spectator watching closely. There were moments of which he couldn't forget a single detail and others which seemed like a blur.

"You look like you could use some company," Alyssa said and pulled out a folding chair and settled in beside him.

Alex looked to see where John was, and sure enough he was standing by the keg with a beer in his hand watching. He raised his cup to Alex and Alex did the same and they toasted silently from across the yard.

"As long as you don't have a jealous boyfriend, because after the past few weeks, I'm in no mood to fight."

"No boyfriend to speak of," Alyssa said. "I heard you and Julie broke up. Are you still friends?"

"We were until this morning," Alex said with a laugh.

"What's so funny? What happened?"

Alex explained the breakup, and his almost comical relief that she was moving. He had looked forward to senior year with the bittersweet feeling that it would be his life's first real turning point. Most of his friends would soon be going away to school and likely to move on and make new friends. Presumably, he would do the same, though he and John were both staying close to home for college.

"How can people decide they don't like a person they don't even know?" Alyssa asked rhetorically. "It's just stupid."

"In the past month I've come to realize just how much racism and prejudice there is around here," Alex said.

Alyssa asked Alex about his schedule, and they compared free periods. Alex had told his parents he was going to drop home economics because he didn't need the credit to graduate, and they gave their blessing to do so. He could easily slip into Alyssa's study hall once he spoke to his guidance counselor. When she finished her beer, he took her empty cup to the keg and refilled it.

The conversation between them flowed as the party went on. John coaxed them into a game of badminton against himself and Sara, a girl he had met at the previous day's football game. They ran back and forth trying to outdo one another, each displaying their competitive nature. Alex and Alyssa ended up spending the rest of the afternoon together, and they even took a walk around the block so they could talk without the loud music. Later, John, Mike and Kyle joined them along with a few of Alyssa's friends.

"I have to get going, my mom is picking me up at six," Alyssa said.

"Six?" Alex asked and looked at his watch. Five hours had passed in a heartbeat.

"You didn't notice it getting a little darker?" she asked.

"Not really," Alex said, and walked her past the kegs and down the driveway. "Your mom is okay with you being at a keg party?"

"She knows I won't drink too much. Usually two or three beers."

"If I'm not mistaken, you had four today."

"Five actually, but that wasn't my fault. Someone kept refilling my cup," she joked.

"I was trying to be a gentleman."

"You were very sweet."

A Buick Regal pulled in front of the driveway. The car was sporty in a way that appealed more to adults than kids. The window rolled down and Alyssa's mother waved for her to get in.

"That's your mom? She's so young and pretty!"

"Watch it, mister."

"No, I mean it makes sense, beautiful mom, beautiful daughter."

"Nice recovery," Alyssa said, and kissed his cheek.

"Would you like to go out with me sometime? Maybe catch a movie?"

"Like on a date?" she asked.

The reaction wasn't what Alex was expecting and he felt slightly embarrassed that perhaps he had read too much into their time together. John told him that when girls ask questions like that it usually led to awkward pauses, excuses, and the dreaded, "Let's talk about it later." According to John, "later" would never come and ultimately meant rejection by neglection. Alex opened the passenger door for Alyssa, hoping if she got in quick, he would avoid further embarrassment.

"Forget I said anything," he said in a voice barely above a whisper.

"No, I'd love to go out with you," Alyssa said. Alyssa's mom heard her reply and smiled as Alyssa gently closed the door without getting in. "I just wanted to make sure that's what you meant. I didn't want to think it's a date and you think it's just hanging out as friends."

"Well, I meant a date if that's okay, but if you want to go out as friends, that's okay, too. I really enjoyed myself today and I would like to get to know you better."

"A date it is then," she said. "I'll give you my number in school tomorrow, and we can figure it out from there." She kissed his cheek again, this time closer to his lips.

Alex opened the door for Alyssa, and she introduced him to her mother before he closed it behind her. He watched the car disappear down the block before allowing himself to smile.

"Somebody's in a good mood," John said, as he clamped his arms around Alex and put him in a bear hug from behind. "I guess this means it's okay to move on."

"It's easier now that Julie's moving to Hewlett."

"Hewlett? When?"

"I don't know. She got pissed and hung up."

"Well, she's in the rearview mirror now because it looks like things went pretty well with Alyssa."

"They did. She is so sweet. And she's beautiful."

"And don't forget catholic," John said.

"I never thought it would be all that important, but I guess it is."

"And," John prompted.

"And she's giving me her number tomorrow so we can make plans to go out."

"See, I was right," John preened.

"That you were. Now let's have a beer and celebrate." Alex looked around the backyard. "Where's Sara?"

"I dropped her off a little while ago. She was getting on my nerves."

"Anything happen?" Alex asked.

"If you mean did she blow me, that's a no. Remember when I told you about girls who get uglier when they drink? She's a classic example."

"That sucks. She goes to Darcy though, right?"

"That's what I thought. It turns out she was wearing her older sister's Darcy jacket and she's only in ninth grade."

"You took a ninth grader to a keg party? Now that's funny."

"Don't tell anyone. I only told you because I trust you," John said.

"I can keep secrets just as good as you can," Alex said and laughed.

"No, really. Don't say anything. I'm begging you, Al."

Alex smiled.

*   *   *

Late Monday afternoon Marco's mother was finally able to post his bail and he was released. When he exited the juvenile detention center, he no longer looked like the angry young man who got what he wanted through intimidation and more like the kids he bullied. He was pale, scared and looked like he hadn't slept since he was arrested. He didn't speak in the car ride home.

The first floor of the house was spotless. Maria hadn't worked since Marco's arrest and had spent much of her time cleaning and straightening up the house to keep her mind occupied with tasks she could complete without much thought. She had cleaned the house from top to bottom. Marco didn't stop long enough to notice; he went straight to his room.

In the comfort of his own room, Marco thought he would sleep for days, or maybe forever if he took enough pills. Each time he closed his eyes they opened immediately. He silently wished when he closed them, they would never reopen.

He heard the soft padding of feet coming down the stairs and was surprised to see Frank carrying his little sister. Frank let her down when they reached the bottom, and she ran over and threw her arms around Marco.

Hannah was too young to understand, but she had seen her mother cry enough to know Marco needed a hug.

"Macko!" she yelled as she covered Marco's cheek with kisses.

"I hope it's okay to bring her down, she really missed you," Frank said.

"Thank you," Marco said, and hugged Hannah tight.

"If you need anything—"

"I'm okay," Marco said.

Frank looked at him doubtfully as Marco held Hannah like he would never see her again. They might not have spent a lot of time together in recent years, but Frank had seen Marco's face at his arraignment and as he was being led away in handcuffs and could tell he was anything but okay. *Who would be?*

"Listen," Frank said hesitantly, "I know you never warmed up to me, and after a while I gave up trying and pushed too far in the opposite direction." Frank ran his hand through his hair as he struggled to come up with the right words. He had practiced the conversation in his head dozens of times during the past two days, but still wasn't sure how Marco would react. "I'm sorry; I never wanted to replace your father. I was only trying to be a good stepfather." All his practicing had been for naught as Frank watched Marco hug Hannah with his eyes closed and wasn't even sure he was listening. He waited a few moments until Marco opened his eyes and said, "Anyway, I was hoping maybe we can start over."

Marco looked at Frank and it finally occurred to him that it was nearly dinner time and Frank was sober. He couldn't remember the last time that had been the case.

"You can think about it as long as you want," Frank said awkwardly.

Hannah climbed onto Marco's stomach. "Plane ride," she demanded excitedly.

Marco obligingly put both of his feet beneath her stomach and lifted her in the air as she giggled. It brought a smile to his face when nothing else could have.

"I don't have to think about it," Marco said, as he continued to play with Hannah. He glanced at Frank tentatively. "It would be good. I'm sure it will make my mother happy."

"Thanks," Frank said.

It was the last thing Marco expected to hear, and as much as he believed Frank was sincere, he didn't know if he could trust him. He had trusted his father and that had gotten him nowhere. But what did Marco have to lose? He was persona-non-grata in Malbrook. He had no friends, no school, and his prospects for the moment included only staying home and then spending time in a juvenile detention center or prison.

Marco lifted Hannah past his head until her head touched the wall before bringing her down to kiss her forehead and softly laying her on his chest. She hugged him with all her strength, and he hugged her back.

"Why don't you go upstairs with Daddy?" Marco suggested. He looked at Frank and said, "Would you mind? I think it just hit me how tired I am."

"Sure," Frank said. He lifted Hannah off Marco's chest and playfully tossed her over his shoulder like a sack of potatoes. He turned around and said, "Hey, where did Hannah go?"

"Behind you," Hannah said with a laugh.

"Where?" Frank asked as he turned around.

"Here," Hannah said through her laughter.

He played the silly game with Hannah for another minute and then swung her around in front of him.

"What were you doing back there?" Frank asked, and then tickled her belly. He winked at Marco then carried Hannah up the stairs.

It was the first time Marco had seen Frank play with Hannah that way in a long time. Frank looked genuinely happy.

Marco sat back and kicked off his sneakers. He let his head sink into the soft down pillow, and thought he would fall asleep immediately, but as tired as he was, he felt his mind racing a thousand miles an hour. His cellmate had told him that if he was tried as an adult he could get as much as 25 years to life in prison. Marco didn't know if it was true, but he was too afraid to ask.

The initial "Not guilty" plea Marco gave through his court appointed lawyer had been standard. Anyone who pleaded guilty immediately left no room for a plea deal. His lawyer, who was defending more than sixty other clients, told Marco not to speak to anyone about the case and admit nothing.

The plan to keep his mouth shut sat well with Marco until he saw the difference in Frank. Marco no longer had friends, and aside from his sister, who was too young to understand, he had only his mother and Frank to talk to, so it should have been easy. But it wasn't. He didn't know how or when the awareness had settled in on him, but he was beginning to realize the pain he had caused. The more he reviewed the past several weeks the more self-loathing he felt and wished the kid in the driveway would have just pulled the trigger and put him out of his misery. While he had been in his cell he had struggled with constant thoughts of suicide. He had said, "I'm sorry," hundreds of times since his arrest, but never to an actual person. The widow of one of the firemen who had been killed called him "a hateful monster" at his arraignment and as he stared at the ceiling, he realized she was right. That is what he had become, and no amount of remorse could fix what he had done.

He had been on a path to hell for so long he couldn't remember exactly when or how it had started. It was the only person he ever remembered being. If he considered it long enough, he probably would have traced it back to fifth grade. Up until then, he had been the one who was bullied. A chance encounter with two older boys from Valley Stream at the mall changed everything. They were looking to make some money and he was looking for someone to take care of the bullies. He paid the two boys to come to his school and give the two kids who were bullying a very public beating during recess in front of the entire school. The two from Valley Stream warned that they would be back with the rest of their gang if anyone messed with Marco. That was the day Marco went from bullied to bully.

After a few long minutes of contemplation, Marco reached to the floor beside his bed and picked up a spiral notebook. It was supposed to be his English notebook, but it was empty except for some doodles in the back and song lyrics in the front. Having been expelled from school, the notebook was no longer necessary. He flipped past the first few pages and came to a blank sheet. He stared at the page unsure of what he was going to write until the pen touched the paper. At the center of the top line, he wrote SORRY and below he began to list people to whom he owed apologies at the very least. Names came faster than his ability to write them, and when he was finished, the list contained nine names plus the families of the injured and dead firemen. For most on the list forgiveness would not come easily, if ever. In some cases, he doubted it would come at all. For his own peace of mind, he needed to try. He started with the first name on the list: Frank.

It took Marco more than an hour to write the letter to Frank, and when he finished, he had five pages of the neatest cursive writing he had produced in years. He wasn't even sure it made sense or if he had even scratched the surface of his feelings. At one point when his hand cramped, he banged it on the wall and forced himself to work through the pain.

He took the five pages upstairs, intending to give it to Frank, but when he saw his mother sitting at the kitchen table, decided he wanted her to read it first. He explained to her that while he had wanted to start with a letter to her, there were far too many emotions to capture in a single day, so he would write a little each day until he finished.

His mother, Maria, sat at the kitchen table across from Marco and read the letter. Tears were already trickling down her cheeks before she finished the first page. She had hidden the constant physical and psychological abuse that his biological father had inflicted on her—which hadn't been difficult since he was too young to understand—and while reading the letter, it was obvious she had done it well.

When she finished the third page, which explained the reasons Marco idolized his father, she put the letter down and sobbed into her hands. "That's not who your father really was," she said.

"Mom, I know. Keep reading."

The tone of the letter changed on the fourth page as Marco explained what became clear to him when he had nothing to do but think. His mother had never spoken ill of his father not because there had been nothing to say, but for fear he would return. When it was clear he was gone for good, she continued to withhold the truth because she thought it was better for Marco to idolize what he believed his father to be and hopefully strive to be the same himself someday. She chose to accept the blame for Marco's father's abandonment of them for Marco's sake.

"When did you figure out what your father really was?" she asked while wiping her tears after finishing the final page.

"I think I always knew," Marco admitted. "I just didn't want to believe it because it was easier to blame you than believe he didn't really love me either. And later I took it out on Frank. I hope I explained it okay."

Maria walked around the table and hugged her son from behind. "You explained perfectly." He stood and turned to her as tears welled in her eyes again. It had been a long time since they had hugged. Marco had always stood with his hands stiffly, unwilling to return his mother's hug or give her affection in any way.

"I'm sorry, Mom," Marco said, hugging her tighter and trying to hold back his own tears. "I'm sorry for all the pain I've caused," he whispered.

They held each other and cried for a long time, unaware that Frank had come in and was watching in silence. He finally cleared his throat to let them know he was there. The look on Marco's face was one he had never seen before.

"I was just coming in to get a glass of milk for Hannah," Frank said.

"I'll get her the milk," Maria said. "Marco has something for you."

*   *   *

"You don't have to read this now," Marco said, and handed Frank the letter. "It's just some stuff I wanted to tell you."

"Thank you," Frank said. He took the letter and sat down to read it, not knowing what to expect.

Frank had never been a crier. In his entire adult life, he had cried only once. Not when his mother died of cancer, or when his father died a year later after suffering a massive stroke. The only time he had cried was on a Sunday morning in the middle of summer weeks after he turned twenty-two. The knock on the door was too early to be any of his friends, but he hadn't expected a Nassau County police officer either. Frank had never been in trouble with the police other than a few speeding tickets so he was confused as to why they would be at his door showing their badges. When the officer asked if he was related to Shari Cohen, he thought she must have been arrested for driving while intoxicated since his older sister lately had been pushing her luck in that area and police had begun to set up checkpoints on weekends.

"She's my sister," Frank had said. She was so much more than his sister though. She had watched over him since their father died three years earlier and was more like a mother than a sister.

"I'm sorry, but she was in a car accident early this morning. She expired," the officer said.

"What does that mean? Expired? Where is she?"

"I'm sorry, she's dead."

"No, no, no," Frank said as he dropped to his knees and sobbed uncontrollably.

Maria watched her husband from the doorway. She couldn't see his face since the letter was on the table and he was leaning his head on his interlocked hands as he read. She wasn't sure if he was concentrating intensely or having trouble reading Marco's handwriting, but he was taking considerably longer than she had. When he finished the last page, he unclasped his hands and rubbed them over his eyes. Through wet, glassy eyes, he looked at his wife for a pregnant moment, motioned for her to come to him and then he cried softly into her shoulder as she stroked the hair just above his neck.

*   *   *

After the arrests, Steven's parents sent him to live with his grandparents in a small town on the south fork of Long Island's east end. He began attending Sag Harbor High School the following Monday. He wanted nothing more than to do his work, study and keep to himself but found that difficult to do with a student body a quarter of the size of his previous high school.

On his first day back in Malbrook since the arrests, Steven spent his Saturday afternoon watching college football with his father, which was something he hadn't done since he reached double digits. He still had a few friends in town, but he didn't want to venture out alone for fear of retaliation from Marco or any of his other former brothers who had been arrested and expelled. A few brothers who had transferred, along with Kyle, Alex and Dave offered supportive comments about doing the right thing, but it was the ones he hadn't heard from who worried him.

On Sunday morning, he decided to try to make peace with Peter. He invited him to an early lunch at a Roy Roger's restaurant. He wasn't sure Peter would even take his call and was surprised when he agreed to meet for lunch at noon. There was only one Roy Rogers in Malbrook, and it was on the corner of Sunset and Kennedy, which was the busiest intersections in town.

Had he told his parents, they would have opposed the idea, so instead he slipped out quietly and cut through a neighbor's side yard. It seemed silly to think anyone was watching his house, but he wore a baseball cap and one of his father's jackets to avoid being noticed. He was already taking a risk meeting Peter and didn't want to take any other risks, even if it made him feel he was being paranoid.

As he reached for the handle of the restaurant's door, he regretted his decision not to tell anyone. If Peter hadn't figured out what Marco had done and they were somehow still friends, Marco was likely to show up during lunch. Peter was early and sitting alone in a booth watching cars pass.

Lunch was even more awkward than Steven had anticipated. Although they had spent more time together this past year than they had with their respective families, there was no connection, just a string of awkward silences interrupted by meaningless conversation. The thing that surprised Steven most was how calm Peter was throughout, though later in the conversation he learned that Peter had been taking Klonepin to calm his nerves. Peter's nose was still bandaged, and his voice was nasal, but even with the tranquilizer in his system, he didn't display the slightest bit of anger. At least not with Steven.

"I'm sorry about everything that happened," Steven finally said after thirty minutes of uncomfortable chit chat.

"Why didn't you tell me?" Peter asked. Peter sounded lost without Marco.

"If I told you, you would have told Marco, and neither one of you would have shown up."

"No, I mean before that," Peter said. "You always had your shit together. Why didn't you stop us before things got out of hand?" Peter took a sip from his large Coke. "I may not have been the smartest person in the group, but I tried to be a good friend."

"You really did try to be a good friend, but when it came to Marco, you never questioned anything," Steven said. "Did you really believe Dave was talking about what happened outside of our fraternity? He was never like that. In fact, Dave is probably one of the most loyal people you will ever meet. Marco wanted Dave out because Alex made him look weak."

Peter remained quiet. He had given no indication of whether he still talked to Marco, but Steven was done tip toeing around the bullshit.

"If Alex was such a pussy, why did Marco and Jimmy need bats when we chased him?"

"Just in case, I guess," Peter said.

"Alex called Marco out, and Marco walked away so he could come back with bats. Marco's a pussy and everyone knew it except you and the younger guys."

It was difficult for Steven to read Peter's facial expressions when they changed because his eyes were constantly drawn to the bandage. There might have been an almost imperceptible drop in his eyebrows, or his lips may have curled slightly downward, but Steven saw something change.

"If I had told you what we were doing was wrong and Marco was going to destroy our chapter, I would have been gone before Tommy and Dave."

"I was that stupid?"

"You trusted Marco more than anyone," Steven said. "Even when logic should have told you not to." Steven put the last of his fries in his mouth.

Peter excused himself momentarily and went to the counter and ordered two roast beef sandwiches to take home with him.

"There are things you should know that I found out the day before you were arrested," Steven said when Peter returned.

"I'm sure I've heard most of it by now," Peter said. "I honestly thought Marco would never turn against me or Jimmy. I was wrong."

"What did the police tell you?"

Peter uttered a sardonic laugh. "They told me Marco blamed everyone but himself." Peter put napkins from a black dispenser in the bag with his sandwiches. "Chase was right."

"Have you talked to Marco?"

"You're the only one I've talked to from school," Peter said. "This is actually the first time I've been out. What's it like at school?"

"I don't know. I'm living with relatives and changed to a smaller school where no one knows me. I'm only in for the weekend to visit my parents."

"That's good. Things around here are fucked up."

"I've got to get going," Steven said, then walked to the trash can and dumped what remained on his tray in the garbage and placed the tray on top.

"Want me to drop you off?"

"I'm gonna walk; I need the exercise," Steven said. "I've been spending so much time indoors I got winded walking here and that's pretty sad." He didn't know why he added the lie, but it made him feel worse. Peter had dropped him off dozens of times, but Steven doubted he would ever feel safe in Peter's car again.

"Are we good?" Peter asked. "You and me?"

"We've always been good," Steven lied. "Good luck with everything."

"Thanks."

They shook with the secret Phi grip one last time. Peter walked out to the parking lot and didn't look back. They never spoke to one another again.

*   *   *

In the aftermath of the arrests in Malbrook, the Nassau County District Attorney's office worked quickly to pressure the eleven defendants to accept plea deals and hasten the recovery process not only in Malbrook, but throughout Nassau County. Malbrook had still been reeling from the attack on Jevonte Jenkins when the defendants executed their plan to rid their town of Jews. Danny Woodside was a new assistant district attorney who had been assigned to prosecute the cases. He had one meeting with his boss and his directive to dispose of the cases as quickly as possible became clear: *Handle the cases expediently and satisfy the public outcry for justice.* He had no worries about the younger defendants because they were all being offered the same deal, which entailed paying restitution for the vandalism, two hundred hours of community service and a year of probation. Failure to complete the community service or meet with their probation officer was punishable by up to a year in the juvenile detention center. Most in the community who had been polled by the Malbrook Sentinel said the penalty wasn't harsh enough.

Peter and Marco were granted youthful offender status before they agreed to plead guilty. They were the only two sentenced to time in prison for their crimes and many people in Malbrook thought that in itself was a crime.

Ari Hirsch was the most vocal among the Jewish people who had been forced to go elsewhere for religious services after their temple had been ravaged by fire. He made an impassioned plea to the judge before the first sentence was handed down, and along with supporters at the courthouse was moderately pleased when Peter was given a two-year sentence. When Jimmy, who had been implicated in the temple fire and the beating of Jevonte Jenkins pleaded no contest and was given a suspended sentence of two years, it sparked an angry rally outside the District Attorney's office.

"Surely, this young man deserves more than the slap on the wrist he received!" Reverend Ralph yelled into the microphone while Ari Hirsch stood by his side. "Eleven people were part of this hate spree, and only two received jail time? How can they let this happen? They destroyed a house of worship! We need to send a clear message that if they are not going to punish criminals, we are going to elect new officials who will! We need to hold everyone here accountable, and when it is time to vote we must not forget!"

The crowd was comprised of blacks, whites, Hispanics, and Asians, and together they marched from Roosevelt Field to the District Attorney's office and blocked all six lanes of Stewart Avenue for a quarter of a mile in each direction.

Reverend Ralph's words hit home with everyone in attendance. The District Attorney was besieged with letters demanding that the ringleader of the group, Marco Scotti, face the maximum sentence or there would be dramatic changes in the next voting cycle.

Marco entered a guilty plea and was sentenced to the maximum of forty-six months. With time off for good behavior, he served two years and two months. The first eight months were served at the Ettinger Juvenile Detention

Center in Mineola, and the last eighteen were served on Riker's Island.

Everyone else arrested in the Malbrook hate spree was given youthful offender status and had their records sealed.

*   *   *

Throughout Marco's incarceration, Frank and Maria visited him at least once each week, and twice each month they brought Hannah. Marco's letter had a profound effect on Frank, as he once again resembled the man Maria fell in love with. After Marco's sentencing, Maria showed the remaining letters to Marco's lawyer, and he gave her the okay to mail them.

Alex and Dave each received their letters from Marco on the same day and decided to visit him at the Ettinger JDC after speaking with their parents and Marco's mother. Though he wouldn't admit it, Marco was an easy target for other prisoners, and with fresh bruises each visit, the abuse was obvious.

As they sat in the visiting area and watched a guard escort Marco, clothed in an orange jumpsuit, it brought neither of them joy. They had wanted Marco punished, but this wasn't what either one had pictured. It was *too* real.

Marco sat across from them at a table. His left eye was black and there was a large bandage just above his right elbow.

"How are things on the outside?" Marco asked, hoping to get a smile from the two shocked faces.

"Judging from your eye, a lot better than in here," Dave said.

"This?" Marco said and touched his eye. "This ain't so bad. You should see some of the other guys."

"How are you holding up?" Alex asked.

"I've been better. My mom told me you called after you got the letters. She didn't tell me you were coming though."

"We can't speak for anyone else you sent letters to, but as far as we're concerned, this is behind us," Alex said. In another situation they would have shaken Marco's hand, but physical contact was not permitted.

"Forgive, forget, and move on," Dave added.

Marco leaned back in his chair with a half-smile. He put his cuffed hands together as if praying and put his thumbs at the bridge of his nose between his closed eyes before moving them beneath his chin. When he opened his eyes there were tears.

"You okay?" Alex asked.

Marco nodded and wiped his eyes with his palms.

"Do you need a tissue?" Dave asked and reached into his pocket.

A guard quickly stepped over to the table to see what Dave was taking from his pocket. Dave held up a tissue for the guard to see.

"No passing anything to prisoners," the tall guard said.

"I'm sorry, I didn't know."

"Well, now you know," the guard said pointedly.

"I didn't think I'd hear anything when I wrote the letters. I wrote most of them in the weeks after I was released on bail, and then rewrote some like five or six times with my therapist."

"How many letters did you send?" Alex asked.

"Thirteen, but some went to more than one person," Marco said. "To be honest, I wasn't sure my mom actually sent them. I sent one to Jevonte Jenkins and another to your friend Mike and his brother, but I don't expect to hear from them."

"Sometimes people surprise you," Alex said. "Jevonte had Tommy over to his house."

"That's good, but I think Jevonte hates me on a whole 'nother level, and I can't say I blame him."

The forty-five-minute visit went by quickly. Dave and Alex filled Marco in on what was happening in the schools and around town. For his part, Marco kept up the brave facade and minimized how difficult it was, as he did when his family visited.

Dave and Alex watched the guard escort Marco through two sets of doors that led back to his cell. Marco looked back and nodded just before the second set of doors, and it wasn't until much later that Dave realized the constant scowl Marco had worn prior to his arrest had been replaced by a look of . . . fear? Sorrow? Pain? It was something else entirely, but he didn't mention it to anyone until Marco's mother called a week later to thank them for visiting. She told Dave she hadn't seen the look he was referring to until after their visit, but now she believed the look Dave was referring to was hope. She thanked them for the compassion they had shown her son.

*   *   *

Within the first few months of his incarceration, Marco decided he wouldn't return to Malbrook after his release. He didn't tell anyone—and wasn't sure he would have been allowed since he was a convicted felon—but he considered changing his last name to distance himself from his biological father and his own crimes. He ultimately decided that keeping it was a better way to remember his mistakes. He moved up to Westchester and lived with Frank's cousin Eric, who owned an autobody shop and was willing to train Marco and let him live rent free until he saved enough for a place of his own.

To leave at least some of his past behind, Marco decided that once he arrived in Westchester, he would simply be Marc. The only person who continued to call him Marco after that was his little sister. He was sad that Hannah no longer called him "Macko," as she had before he was arrested.

Chapter 20

The East versus West football game in the third week of football season was stopped three separate times while police broke up fights in the stands. Despite the interruptions, West built a 38-0 halftime lead before Coach Parisi removed his starters, much to their disappointment. With fights going on in the stands and East reeling after winning their first two games handily, Coach Parisi didn't want it to look like he was trying to run up the score to embarrass them, which sometimes led to fights on the field, cheap shots that resulted in injuries and suspensions. East scored twenty-four points against the second string, but West—which didn't throw one pass in the second half— won 47-24 in a game that wasn't nearly as close as the final score.

West ended the regular season with seven wins and one loss, which was good enough for the top seed in their conference playoffs. They avenged their one loss in the first round and then beat Bethpage Memorial 30-7 for the second time to win their first county championship.

The Malbrook Sentinel reported that more than thirty homes in Malbrook were sold between Labor Day and Christmas, and two-thirds had been bought by minorities. The change in Malbrook had begun in earnest.

*　　　　　*　　　　　*

Kyle's speech as valedictorian of the graduating class of 1981 focused on embracing the difference in people of other cultures and not prejudging those of other races or religions. He encouraged his fellow seniors to make a difference and be the change they wished to see in the world. He received a standing ovation.

On the first Friday morning after graduation, the members of West High's Phi Gamma Alpha chapter met at the bridge by the school. It was ten a.m. by the time Mike and John pulled into the teachers' parking lot. They each carried a case of Molson Golden, which was the most expensive beer at Poppi's Beverage Mart, and therefore, according to John, the best.

The meeting on the bridge was always bittersweet. In nearly every case it was the last time all the brothers from that year would be together. They discussed their plans for college and in some cases, it was much different than where their plans had started at the beginning of the year. Kyle, John, and Declan were sticking with their original choices, while Mike decided on pre-med at Penn State, and Alex finally decided to forego wrestling in college to attend the criminal justice program at John Jay College in Manhattan.

*   *   *

The Phi Gamma Alpha photo that appeared in the 1981 yearbook was their last as the schools in Malbrook no longer recognized fraternities. It was the first step towards the eventual ban of high school fraternities on Long Island that came ten years later.

Over the course of the next forty years, Malbrook, along with neighboring towns became among the most diverse on Long Island. Until 2017, Phi Gamma Alpha held a yearly weekend retreat in the Hampton's so brothers could catch up with each other and talk about their glory days of high school. With attendance waning, it was decided to cancel all future outings, though brothers continue to get together in small groups and keep in touch through social media.

Made in the USA
Middletown, DE
05 December 2021